EDWARD MARSTON was born and brought up in South Wales. A full-time writer for over forty years, he has worked in radio, film, television and theatre and is a former chairman of the Crime Writers' Association. Prolific and highly successful, he is equally at home writing children's books or literary criticism, plays or biographies.

edwardmarston.com

By Edward Marston

THE BOW STREET RIVALS SERIES

Shadow of the Hangman • Steps to the Gallows • Date with the Executioner

THE RAILWAY DETECTIVE SERIES

The Railway Detective • The Excursion Train • The Railway Viaduct

The Iron Horse • Murder on the Brighton Express

The Silver Locomotive Mystery • Railway to the Grave • Blood on the Line

The Stationmaster's Farewell • Peril on the Royal Train

A Ticket to Oblivion • Timetable of Death

Signal for Vengeance • The Circus Train Conspiracy

Inspector Colbeck's Casebook:

Thirteen Tales from the Railway Detective

The Railway Detective Omnibus:

The Railway Detective, The Excursion Train, The Railway Viaduct

THE RESTORATION SERIES

The King's Evil • The Amorous Nightingale • The Repentant Rake

The Frost Fair • The Parliament House • The Painted Lady

THE CAPTAIN RAWSON SERIES

Soldier of Fortune • Drums of War • Fire and Sword

Under Siege • A Very Murdering Battle

THE BRACEWELL MYSTERIES

The Queen's Head • The Merry Devils • The Trip to Jerusalem

The Nine Giants • The Mad Courtesan • The Silent Woman

The Roaring Boy • The Laughing Hangman • The Fair Maid of Bohemia

The Wanton Angel • The Devil's Apprentice • The Bawdy Basket

The Vagabond Clown • The Counterfeit Crank

The Malevolent Comedy • The Princess of Denmark

THE HOME FRONT DETECTIVE SERIES

A Bespoke Murder • Instrument of Slaughter • Five Dead Canaries

Deeds of Darkness • Dance of Death • The Enemy Within

Steps to the Gallows

EDWARD MARSTON

Allison & Busby Limited
12 Fitzroy Mews
London W1T 6DW
allisonandbusby.com

First published in Great Britain by Allison & Busby in 2016.
This paperback edition published by Allison & Busby in 2017.

A CIP catalogue record for this book is available from
the British Library.

10 9 8 7 6 5 4 3 2 1

ISBN 978-0-7490-1602-9

Typeset in 11/16 pt Adobe Garamond Pro by
Allison & Busby Ltd.

The paper used for this Allison & Busby publication
has been produced from trees that have been legally sourced
from well-managed and credibly certified forests.

Printed and bound by
CPI Group (UK) Ltd, Croydon, CR0 4YY

CHAPTER ONE

1816

Gully Ackford had forgotten how small, in girth and height, his friend was. When Leonidas Paige walked into the shooting gallery that morning, therefore, Ackford reacted with a delight tempered by disbelief. Could this short, stooping, grey-haired old man really be the same person who'd taught him all he knew about fighting when they were comrades in the 17th Regiment of Foot during the ill-fated War of American Independence? Paige hardly looked strong enough to lift a Brown Bess musket, let alone fire one with the lethal accuracy for which he was renowned. In his dark, sober attire and battered hat, the newcomer looked much more like an impecunious clergyman than a soldier. The only things that remained to identify him were the broad grin and the defiant glint in his eye.

'Don't look so shocked, Gully,' said Paige with a laugh. 'It *is* me.'

'Then you're very welcome, Leo,' said the other, embracing him warmly before standing back to appraise him. 'Yes, I'm sure it's you now. I know that voice well. What on earth has brought you here? No man alive is less in need of instruction in shooting, fencing and boxing. You taught me all three disciplines.'

'I did so for a good reason. I wanted to keep you alive and, by the same token, rely on you to keep *me* alive. And that's what we did at Yorktown. We saved each other. The pity of it was that we couldn't save America as well.' Paige looked his friend up and down. 'You've weathered well. You're in your prime.'

'I don't know about that, Leo, but I have kept myself fit. It's a necessary part of my stock-in-trade. What brings you here?'

'I'm tempted to say that it was for the joy of seeing you again but the truth is that I had no idea this gallery was owned by my old comrade. What I came for was help, Gully. I was told that I might hire a bodyguard here.'

'And so you might. Protection is part of the service we offer.'

'Does that mean I'd have *you* dancing attendance on me?'

'No, I'm needed here to run the gallery,' said Ackford, shaking his head, 'but fear not. I'll provide you with someone as alert and well trained as myself.' He indicated a chair. 'Take a seat and tell me the nature of the problem.'

They were in the room used as an office and place of storage. Large and cluttered, it was essentially functional. A collection of pistols was on display in a glass-fronted cabinet. An array of swords was stacked against another wall. A thick ledger lay on the table. The bookcase was packed with a selection of well-thumbed volumes about shooting, swordsmanship, archery and the noble art of self-defence. Paige didn't even notice the spartan lack of comfort. He sat down opposite his friend and took a deep breath.

'I don't want you to think I can't look after myself,' he said, defensively. 'I go armed and possess all my old skills with gun or dagger.'

'So why do you require a bodyguard?'

'It's because Nature inadvertently forgot to provide me with eyes in the back of my head and I'm in need of them. I'm being stalked, Gully, and I want to know who's taken on the role of my uninvited shadow. A bodyguard can help me catch the rogue who's been trailing me.'

'Do you have no idea who the fellow is?'

'I've made too many enemies. It could be any one of a hundred.'

Ackford was puzzled. 'How did you manage to upset so many people?'

'I can see that you've never read *Paige's Chronicle*.'

'I never have time to read *any* newspapers, Leo,' said his friend with an apologetic shrug. 'But, now I think of it, you were always scribbling away when we were in the army together. And you did have ambitions to make a living with your pen one day.'

'That day eventually came, Gully, and the *Chronicle* was the result. It gained an immediate notoriety and that was its downfall.'

'Oh?'

'I exposed the follies of our so-called masters and I did so in scathing terms. When they are the victims of it, the great and the good regard satire as anathema. Every edition I published brought forth fresh howls of rage,' said Paige, chuckling merrily. 'Each one also produced a flurry of threats and abuse. When they couldn't frighten me into silence, our leading politicians found a way to put me, and those like me, out of business. Last year they passed the iniquitous Stamp Act.'

'I've heard tell of that.'

'Fourpence a copy was levied on my *Chronicle*. When I charged twopence, I had plenty of readers. Most of them baulked at paying three times that amount.'

'Did you abandon the project?'

'I tried to ignore the Act and publish at the old price. That cost me twelve months in prison and a hefty fine. My newspaper had gone but my pen was still itching to write. I therefore harnessed it to a new endeavour, producing a series of sly character assassinations to accompany satirical drawings.'

He was about to describe his work when the door opened and the tall, handsome figure of Peter Skillen glided into the room. Seeing that Ackford had company, he immediately went into retreat.

'I do beg your pardon, Gully – and yours, dear sir.'

Ackford indicated his visitor. 'This is an old friend of mine, Peter.'

'Then I'll leave you to share your reminiscences in peace.'

Peter made a graceful exit and Paige was able to pick up his narrative. He talked of the cartoons being a frontal assault on power, privilege, pomposity and corruption in high places. As he listened to the names of those who'd been satirised, Ackford could understand why Paige had made so many enemies. He was fearless. Regardless of their position, he'd attacked everyone he'd deemed guilty of vice, hypocrisy or gross malpractice. Even the Archbishop of Canterbury had not been immune from censure.

'You can see why I need someone to watch my back,' he concluded.

'I'm surprised you've not already had a dagger between your shoulder blades.'

'It's only a matter of time – unless I have a protector.'

'I have the very man for you,' said Ackford. 'He's quick-witted, sharp-eyed and as reliable a bodyguard as you could wish. His name is Jem Huckvale and he'll not let you down. If someone is following you, Jem will soon find him out. He's done this kind of work before.'

'Then he sounds like the ideal person.'

'Jem is giving a fencing lesson at the moment. As soon as he's finished, I'll introduce you to him and he's yours to command.'

'Thank you, Gully.'

'Fortune guided your footsteps well when they brought you to my gallery.'

'I feel blessed. We must find a time to talk about the old days.'

'Nothing would please me more, Leo.'

'It will give me a chance to remind you of the money you still owe me.'

Ackford grinned. 'As I recall it, *you* are indebted to *me*.'

'I dispute that.'

'I won that card game, Leo. There were witnesses.'

Paige flicked a hand. 'Come, come, let's not quibble over details.'

'Then let's have no more talk of me owing money to you. And be warned. My services come at a price.'

'There's nobody in the world to whom I'd entrust my life

more willingly than you. Name your terms and I'll meet them.'

'It's a bargain.'

They sealed it with a firm handshake.

The door opened and Paul Skillen walked familiarly into the room. Paige gaped in wonder. In every way, Paul looked identical to the person who'd interrupted them earlier. The only difference was that he was dressed with markedly more flamboyance. Paige could not understand how he could have changed his apparel with such speed. Aware that he was intruding, Paul signalled an apology with both palms and backed swiftly out of the room. The visitor was on his feet at once.

'Why on earth did Peter need a change of clothing?' he asked.

'Peter is still dressed as you first saw him, Leo.'

'Then there is something curiously awry with my old eyes. I dare swear that I just saw the same man in different attire.'

'But he was *not* the same man,' explained Ackford. 'The person you just saw was Paul Skillen, brother of Peter Skillen who interrupted us earlier. Your confusion is understandable. After all these years, *I* still have difficulty telling them apart.'

'They are *brothers*?'

'Like two halves of an apple, cleft in twain.'

'By all, that's wonderful!' said Paige, slapping his thigh.

And he went off into peals of laughter that filled the room and penetrated to every part of the gallery. It was the deep, rich, uninhibited laughter of a man in a state of unashamed ecstasy and it went on for minutes.

Gully Ackford was mystified.

* * *

The laughter of Micah Yeomans was of a different order. It was loud and coarse. Standing beside him, Alfred Hale contributed a series of sniggers. The Bow Street Runners were outside a print shop in Holborn, feasting their eyes on the wares in the bow-fronted window. Now in his forties, Yeomans was a big, hulking man of almost unsurpassable ugliness. Shorter, younger and less muscular, Hale was almost invisible beside him. Returning from their duties at a bank, they'd been diverted by the sight of the caricatures in the shop window. Some were subtle and superbly drawn but they preferred the cruder prints with overt sexual overtones. The one that excited their sneers and snorts the most was a cartoon showing a grotesquely fat man, seated beside a table loaded with rich food and strong drink, yet unable to reach it because he had already overeaten and, as the glassy eyes showed, drunk far too much. The caption was *A Voluptuary Enjoys a Light Repast.* The obese figure was easily identifiable.

'Where would the artists be without the Prince Regent to mock?' asked Yeomans, smirking. 'He features in quite a few of these prints.'

'This is the best of them, Micah. Who is the artist?'

'Virgo.'

'That's more than you can say of His Royal Highness,' suggested Hale, nudging his companion.

'He lost his virgo a long time ago – if he ever had it!'

Yeomans guffawed then scanned the other prints in the window. He, too, had a preference for Virgo, an artist who specialised in biting satire of the upper classes, ridiculing them in words as well as cartoons. His prints were part of a series called the *Parliament of Foibles* and he'd pilloried politicians in both Houses quite mercilessly.

'By rights,' said Yeomans, becoming serious, 'we ought not to be joining in the derision. We should be finding out who Virgo is and hauling him before the chief magistrate.'

'The law does not ban drawings, Micah. That's why so many print shops have opened up in London. Virgo and his kind thrive and I'm glad of it.'

'You'd be less glad if you saw yourself in one of these prints.'

'I'm not important enough to be caricatured,' said Hale, 'but *you* are.'

'What are you talking about?'

Hale pointed a finger. 'Look at the print in the corner. Unless I'm very much mistaken, the artist has put *you* in it.'

'It's nothing like me, you dolt,' snarled Yeomans, glaring at the print in question. 'That's not me.'

'I'd say it was a good portrait.'

'Then you must be going blind, Alfred.'

'No other Runner is as big and fearsome as you, Micah. The print has caught you to perfection.' He grunted in pain as an elbow struck him hard in the chest. 'Wait,' he gasped, doubling up in pain, 'I was wrong, I confess it. On reflection, I can see that there's not the slightest resemblance to you. Besides, nobody would dare to mock Micah Yeomans.'

But that was exactly what someone had done. The main target in the cartoon was Sir Humphrey Coote, a prominent Member of Parliament, celebrated for his great wealth and for his readiness to lavish it upon ladies of easy virtue. The print showed him dancing around a bedchamber with a naked female

12

companion. Outside the door was a long queue of prostitutes, held back by officers led by the imposing figure of the most famous Bow Street Runner in the capital. Though he pretended to deny it, Yeomans knew that he was being lampooned. His face was unmistakable. He saw those luxuriant black eyebrows and that twisted nose in the mirror every time he shaved. The print made him seethe with fury.

'That's Sir Humphrey Coote,' said Hale, studying the central figure. 'I'd wager any amount on it.'

'Yes, that's him, to be sure.'

'We caught him once in a brothel in Covent Garden.'

'I remember it well. He was being pleasured by two birds of paradise.'

'It's an excellent likeness of him and that monstrous bulge in his breeches gives him away as the rake that he is.' Hale squinted through the glass. 'Who is the cunning artist?'

Yeomans spat the name out with utter contempt.

'Virgo!'

Jem Huckvale was a slight individual with a boyish appearance. Nobody would have guessed that he was in his mid-twenties or that his diminutive frame contained so much power. Adept at fencing and shooting, he was equally skilled in the boxing ring and many customers had suffered because they'd underestimated his speed and strength. Gully Ackford treated him as the son he'd never had, entrusting all sorts of assignments to him. When he was given his latest orders, Huckvale was thrilled. He'd liked Leonidas Paige on sight and his admiration increased when he heard that the visitor had served in the same regiment as Ackford.

'It was the 17th Foot,' said Paige. 'The Leicestershire Regiment.'

'Gully has told me about his time in America.'

'It was the making of him, Jem.'

'It was certainly an education,' said Ackford, wryly. 'I went as a callow youth and came back as a battle-scarred soldier. But I'm holding you up, Leo. Your request has been met. When you leave here, your back will be well protected. Jem will soon unmask the villain who's been following you.'

'I want him unmasked and brought before me,' said Paige, sternly. 'He and I must have a little conversation.'

Huckvale tapped himself on the chest. 'Leave it to me, sir.'

'Then let's set off.'

'Do you travel by horse or on foot, Mr Paige?'

'I'm an infantryman, lad. I always walk if I can.'

He shook hands with Ackford by way of farewell then left the gallery. Watching through the window, Huckvale saw the direction in which he'd gone and waited. Within a few seconds, a man stepped out of a doorway and went after Paige. It was the signal for Huckvale to leave as well. Once in the street, he threaded his way expertly through the crowd and kept one eye on his target, biding his time until he could find a quiet spot where the man could be intercepted. Huckvale knew little about him beyond the fact that he was obviously lithe and practised in his trade. Moving with furtive ease, the man stayed well behind Paige. Had the latter turned round suddenly, he'd have seen nobody on his tail because his shadow simply melted out of sight.

Huckvale kept him under surveillance for the best part of ten minutes then his view was obscured by a coach that rumbled across his path. When the vehicle disappeared, so had the person Huckvale was following. To his chagrin, he realised that he'd been tricked. Huckvale broke into a run until he reached a junction from which three roads branched off. Which one had the man taken? Paige had given him the address where he lodged so Huckvale knew which route was leading him to his home. Yet he had a strange feeling that the man was no longer on Paige's heels. For some reason, the narrowest of the three roads was the one that beckoned. Acting on instinct, therefore, Huckvale trotted along it in the hope of catching him up but he did not get far. As he passed an alleyway, he was suddenly grabbed from behind, dragged into the alleyway and clubbed to the ground with the butt of a pistol. Instead of being able to offer protection, Huckvale was in dire need of help himself.

For the first time in weeks, Leonidas Paige was able to walk through the streets of London with complete assurance. There was no need to keep one hand on his dagger or to look over his shoulder every so often. His back was now being protected and he could concentrate his thoughts on his work. He'd already singled out his next victim in the *Parliament of Foibles* and he chuckled as he envisaged the expression on the man's face when he eventually saw the print. Paige would be creating a new and dangerous enemy but he was prepared to take that risk. Exposing a cruel and corrupt Member of Parliament was, in his opinion, a public duty. Thanks to Jem Huckvale, he no longer had to worry about his safety. Paige was free to let his mind wander as it devised some doggerel about his latest victim.

Buoyed up by a false confidence, he continued on his way

with a spring in his step. Eventually, he turned down a winding street and walked the thirty yards or so to his lodging. Using a key to let himself into the house, he went up the rickety staircase and into his room. On the table under the window were his writing materials and he couldn't wait to put them to use. The moment he sat down, however, he discovered that he had company. Someone put a rope around his neck and pulled it tight. The garrotte was so sudden and unexpected that it was seconds before Paige realised what was happening. Twisting and turning, he tried to pull the rope away from his throat but could not budge it. Intense pressure was being applied and the pain was agonising. He tried to call out for help but his voice was strangled into silence. When he reached for his dagger, he hardly had enough strength left to pull it from its sheath and all the time the rope was biting deep into his neck and constricting his windpipe.

He squirmed impotently in his chair until he lost consciousness and offered no more resistance as the life was comprehensively squeezed out of him. When he was finally released, Paige lay slumped face down on the table. His killer was not finished yet. On a chest in the corner were several editions of the now defunct *Paige's Chronicle*. They were quickly piled around the dead man's head and set alight. By the time the killer slipped out of the property, all the papers were ablaze.

CHAPTER TWO

'Murdered!' exclaimed Huckvale. 'Mr Paige was *murdered*?'

'He was garrotted,' said Peter Skillen.

'But I was hired to protect him. I let him down badly.'

'You had your own attacker to contend with, Jem.'

'Gully will never forgive me,' wailed Huckvale. 'Mr Paige was a dear friend of his and I failed to guard him properly. I must go back to the gallery at once and apologise to Gully.'

As he tried to get out of bed, however, he felt as if he'd been struck on the head once again, causing him to cry out in pain and fall back on the pillow. He was in a bedchamber at Peter's house, having been carried there when he was discovered in the alleyway. Still groggy and covered in blood, Huckvale had been able to give those who'd come to his aid the address of his friend. Peter and his wife, Charlotte, had been shocked to see the state he was in. They'd summoned a surgeon who'd cleaned the scalp wound and inserted stitches. Huckvale's skull was now encircled by heavy bandaging. As he tried to work out what must have happened, his brain was racing.

'I was completely fooled,' he admitted. 'I thought I was following that man unseen when, all the time, he knew that I was behind him. The moment he had the chance, he vanished from sight then lurked in ambush. He *guessed*, Peter. When he saw Mr Paige going into the gallery, he must have guessed that he went in search of a bodyguard.'

'At his age,' said Peter, 'Mr Paige certainly wouldn't come for instruction of any kind. He was there to seek our help.'

'I'll never be able to face Gully again.'

'A moment ago, you wanted to run back to make your peace with him.'

'I doubt if he'll let me through the door, Peter.'

'That's nonsense,' said Charlotte, softly, 'and you know it. Gully will be very upset that you were injured so badly. A lesser man might have died from the wounds inflicted on you. You need a long rest.'

Huckvale was embarrassed. 'I can't impose on you.'

'It's no imposition, Jem.'

'Charlotte is right,' said Peter with a considerate smile. 'We're glad to look after you and I'm happy to lend you that nightshirt you're wearing. In some sense, you're one of the family, so let's have no more protest. If there's anything you need, ring that little bell on the bedside table and Meg will come running.'

At any other time, Huckvale might have blushed. Meg Rooke was one of the servants and he'd long ago conceived a fondness for the pretty young woman with the dimpled cheeks. Too shy to make his feelings known, he'd worshipped her in silence. The thought that she might now wait on him introduced a whole range of conflicting emotions. Huckvale's mind momentarily wandered from the plight he was in. The pounding inside his skull seemed to ease slightly.

Peter and his wife exchanged an understanding smile. Their house had space and comfort that Huckvale could never enjoy elsewhere and they were pleased to be able to offer hospitality during his short convalescence. Sensing his affection for Meg Rooke, they felt that she might play an important part in his recovery. In the large bed, Huckvale looked impossibly small and vulnerable. The sight of his pinched face and bandaged crown steeled Peter's resolve to find the man who'd assaulted him.

Dismissing his own predicament, Huckvale thought only of Paige.

'He was a soldier,' he said, 'able to defend himself.'

'I fancy that he was caught unawares,' said Peter.

'And he was garrotted, you say?'

'A final indignity awaited him, I fear. His room was set alight. Luckily, the neighbours rallied around and got the fire under control.'

'Who could *do* such a dreadful thing?' demanded Huckvale.

'We mean to determine that, Jem.'

'How did his killer get into the house? Was it not securely locked? Who else was there? Why did nobody come to the assistance of Mr Paige?'

'Those are the very questions that Paul will be putting to the landlord. Even as we speak, he's beginning his investigation. Put your faith in my brother. When Paul is involved in a murder case, he has an uncanny knack of solving the crime.'

* * *

19

Before he could even begin to question the couple, Paul Skillen had to calm them down. The landlord and his wife were astounded to return home and find their house on fire with a murder victim inside. Gregory Lomas was a middle-aged man with a kind face distorted by the tragedy and a voice reduced to a croak. His wife, Eleanor, remained on the verge of hysteria.

'Was nobody else in the house?' asked Paul.

'No, sir,' replied Lomas. 'Our servants had gone shopping and we were visiting relatives. Mr Paige was alone in the house.'

'Apparently not, Mr Lomas – the killer was also in there.'

'How on earth could he have got in? The front door was locked.'

'Yes,' said Paul, 'I took the trouble to examine it. Granted, it's a stout enough lock but it could easily be picked by someone with skill in his fingers.'

'Does that mean anyone can let himself into our home?' asked the wife in alarm. 'Do you hear that, Gregory? We could be murdered in our beds.'

'The door is always well bolted when we're inside, my love.'

'I'll never feel safe inside that place again.'

They were part of a small crowd standing outside the house. The fire had been doused but some stray wisps of smoke still emerged from the room once occupied by Leonidas Paige. Though the corpse of their lodger had been removed, the landlord and his wife were still too nervous to step inside the building. Paul sought to still their mounting apprehension.

'The intruder will not come back, Mrs Lomas,' he assured her. 'He gained entry into your house because he had a mission. Once that was completed, he'd have no reason to return.'

'How did he know that the house was empty?'

'In all probability, he kept watch on it.'

She gave an involuntary shiver. 'Are you saying that somebody was out here, keeping an eye on us?'

Paul gave a nod. 'Do you and your husband go out at regular times?'

'Yes, we do, sir.'

'And our servants do the shopping on the same market days,' added Lomas.

'Then your routine will have been duly noted. It's also likely that today was not the first occasion when the killer went inside the house. He'd want to find out which was Mr Paige's room and look for a place of concealment inside it. This was no random attack, you see,' explained Paul. 'It was carefully planned.'

'But Mr Paige was such a harmless old fellow. Why murder him?'

'That will only become clear in time.'

'We can never put a lodger in that room again,' complained Lomas, bitterly. 'Who wants to sleep in a place where such villainy occurred?'

'I'll not set foot in there,' vowed his wife. 'My nerves wouldn't let me.'

'The passage of time may soothe those nerves,' said Paul, gently. 'But let me ask you a few pertinent questions. Without knowing it, you may have information that will lead us to the killer.' Husband and wife looked startled at the suggestion. 'If the killer didn't break into your house, he might first have got inside it by another means altogether.'

'I don't understand you, sir,' said Lomas.

'He may have been *invited* in. What if the man was a friend of your lodger – a false friend, as it turned out – and called on him here?'

'Mr Paige had very few visitors, sir. He kept himself to himself.'

'He must have had *some* friends.'

'I'm sure that he did because he was such a pleasant gentleman. He must have met his friends elsewhere. No more than a handful came to the house.'

'Can you recall their names?'

'We were never introduced to them. As you can see,' Lomas went on, glancing upwards, 'Mr Paige had the front bedchamber. If he looked out of the window, he'd have seen any guests coming before we did. He always let them in.'

'Are you able to describe any of them?' asked Paul.

'There was an old woman, sir, and another who was somewhat younger. The only man I remember was a tall, upright fellow with the look of a soldier about him. He'd a scar on one cheek and would've been around my age.'

'They've a terrible shock coming,' moaned the wife. 'What are those friends of his going to say when they hear that he's been murdered?'

Paul sighed. 'I feel sorry for them.'

Gully Ackford was in a quandary. Desperate to find out how Jem Huckvale was faring, he was unable to leave the gallery because of his commitments there. It was a source of the utmost frustration. Ordinarily, he'd have responded to a crisis by saddling his horse and riding off, leaving one or both of the Skillen brothers to hold the fort. As it was, neither was available. One of Peter's servants had brought a letter describing the respective fates of Leonidas Paige and of Jem Huckvale. The former was now beyond help but the latter needed the love and support of his friends. Instead of being able to offer it to him, Ackford was forced to spend an hour with an irritating pupil in the shooting gallery. When the lesson was over, he repaired to the office and was overjoyed to see Peter waiting for him. He grasped him by his shoulders.

'How is he, Peter? What did the surgeon say? Is he in any danger?'

'If you'll stop trying to shake me to death,' said Peter, tolerantly, 'I'll tell you.' Ackford let go of him. 'That's better. Jem will be fine. His head has been cracked open and he's still jangled but, in time, I've no doubt that he'll make a full recovery.'

'Thank heaven for that!'

'His main problem concerns you.'

'Why me?' asked Ackford. 'I yearn to offer my sympathy.'

'He's expecting the sharp edge of your tongue, Gully. In fact, he's terrified that his place here is in jeopardy and that he'll lose both his home and occupation.'

'Jem will always be welcome here.'

'Then it's important for you to tell him that in person. Coming from both of you, kind words will aid his recovery more than anything else.'

'What do you mean by *both* of us?'

'Jem's eye has alighted on one of our servants.'

Ackford grinned. 'Then it has to be Meg, the sweet young

23

thing with the dimples, and I don't blame him for a second. Has he declared himself?'

'He's far too timid for that, Gully. Now that Meg will be helping to look after him, the situation may change. However, you'll want to see him yourself. What lessons are booked?'

'Only one, Peter – it's an hour improving someone's swordsmanship.'

'Then I'll take on the instruction.'

'I'll be off immediately,' said Ackford, grateful for the offer and heading towards the door. 'Thank you, Peter.'

'Tarry a while because I have to give *you* instruction as well. Mr Paige was your friend, Gully. On the ride to my house, I want you to dredge up *everything* that you can remember about him. In particular,' added Peter, 'I'll need to know exactly what he told you when he came here. Piece the conversation together word for word, if you can. It may contain something that will ultimately lead us to the killer.'

'I'll do my best.'

'Be quick about it. We'll not be alone in the hunt.'

'I know. A reward notice will prompt others to join in the search.'

'I'm not thinking about greedy individuals with the smell of money in their nostrils. I'm talking about the Runners.'

'They'll *have* to be involved, Peter.'

'We'll be up against Micah Yeomans and his men once again. That's why we must use what little advantage we hold.'

'I concur.'

'Paige turned to you because he trusted you. That places an obligation on us. We failed him,' said Peter, solemnly. 'The only way to atone for that failure is to catch the brutal killer who dispatched him to his grave. And, above all else, we must do so before Yeomans and his crew.'

People who walked past Eldon Kirkwood in the street rarely gave him a second glance. He was a skinny, bearded man in his fifties with a dainty step and an aura of insignificance. Those who faced him in court, however, saw him in a very different light. In his wig and robe of office, the Chief Magistrate at Bow Street took on remarkable substance in every way. When he peered at offenders over the top of his spectacles, he could make even the most hardened criminals quake in their boots. His tongue had a caustic bite, his compassion was almost non-existent and his judgements invariably resulted in the maximum punishment for any convicted malefactors. A dominating figure in court, he was even more intimidating in the confines of his office. Yeomans and Hale, Principal Officers at Bow Street, had faced the most desperate villains in London without quailing but their legs always trembled slightly when they were summoned before Kirkwood.

'You have work for us, sir?' asked Yeomans, tentatively.

'Of course I do,' snapped the other. 'I didn't send for you so that we could discuss the phases of the moon. Use what little intelligence the Lord gave you, man.'

'Yes, sir.'

'And the same goes for you, Hale.'

'Indeed, sir,' said Hale, meekly.

Standing side by side in front of the desk, the Runners felt like two wayward pupils about to face the wrath of their headmaster. They could almost hear the swish of the cane. In all the times they'd been inside the room, they had never once been offered a seat. Kirkwood, by contrast, always occupied the high-backed, elaborately carved oak chair. Perched on three cushions, he looked far bigger and more menacing than ever. In front of him lay a series of papers. He snatched one up, gave it a cursory glance then tossed it back on the table.

'A foul murder has been committed,' he declared.

'What are the details, sir?' asked Yeomans.

'If you will close that uneducated orifice known as your mouth, I will tell you. Before you became a Runner, I seem to recall, you were a blacksmith, were you not?'

Yeomans nodded in assent. 'Then you – more than anyone else – will appreciate the virtue of that old adage about striking while the iron is hot.'

'Yes, sir.'

'In short, take immediate action. The facts are these. A gentleman residing in Bloomsbury was strangled to death then the property was set alight. The name of the murder victim was Leonidas Paige.' He saw the blank expressions on their faces. 'I see that neither of you recognises the name.'

'No, sir,' admitted Yeomans.

'I've never heard of him,' said Hale.

'Were neither of your aware of *Paige's Chronicle*?'

'So many newspapers are printed,' said Yeomans, 'that it's impossible to keep track of all of them. They come and go all the time.'

'This one existed long enough to cause considerable offence to some of the most distinguished men of the realm, myself among them. In essence,' Kirkwood went on, plucking at his goatee beard, 'the *Chronicle* was little more than a disgraceful example of indiscriminate mud-slinging at figures of authority.'

'There's far too much of that, sir.'

'I hoped that the Stamp Act would terminate the vile publication but Paige continued to issue it without paying the duty. His boldness was expensive. His newspaper was closed down, a punitive fine was imposed and the wretch was thrown into prison. If it had been up to me, I'd have sent him there in perpetuity but the case, alas, didn't come before me.'

'Did you say that you were mentioned in the *Chronicle*?' asked Hale.

'I was more than mentioned, Hale.'

'Oh?'

'I was roundly traduced,' said the other, curling his lip. 'My name was changed, of course, but everyone who read the article would have realised that Eldon Kirkwood had been rechristened "Well-done Churchwood".' Yeomans spluttered. 'I'm glad that you find it so amusing. Wait until *you* are the target of some malicious satirist, Yeomans. You feel as if you are being flayed in public.'

'I'm astonished that anyone should dare to mock you, sir,' said Yeomans, trying to win favour by being obsequious. 'If anyone in public life is above reproach, it must be the Chief Magistrate.'

'Paige thought otherwise.'

'It could have been worse,' ventured Hale.

'Keep your idiotic opinion to yourself, man.'

'But it could, sir. Being attacked in a newspaper must be

27

very hurtful but imagine what it must be like to be sneered at in a caricature. Micah and I were passing a print shop only today. The cartoons on show poured scorn on everyone – even on the Prince Regent. The artists who draw them have no respect for anyone. There was the most vicious attack of Sir Humphrey Coote.'

'Then it's not impossible that Paige was party to it.'

'I don't understand.'

'The print, I believe, is part of a series under the collective nomenclature of the *Parliament of Foibles*. Rumour has it that the hand of Leonidas Paige is involved in its production. It's one of the mysteries you need to solve. First, however,' said Kirkwood, picking up the sheet of paper, 'you must set an investigation in motion.' He handed the paper to Yeomans. 'Here is the address and what little we know of the crime. Report back to me when you've made your preliminary enquiries.'

'Yes, sir.'

'Yes, sir,' echoed Hale.

The chief magistrate dismissed them with a lordly flick of his wrist. Once outside the room, Yeomans looked at the details he'd been given.

'We can walk there easily.'

'Wasn't that a strange coincidence, Micah?' said Hale. 'The dead man might have been behind that caricature we saw of Sir Humphrey Coote – when he was alive, that is. Paige, I mean, not Sir Humphrey.'

'Stop blabbering.'

'But the cartoon was part of that series about Parliament.'

Yeomans was rueful. 'I don't need reminding of that, Alfred.'

While his colleague was thinking about the promiscuous politician, all that Yeomans could remember was his own appearance in the caricature. Everyone who saw it would laugh heartily at his expense. The Runner was vengeful. If Paige was indeed responsible for it, he deserved to die.

'Come on, Alfred,' he said, setting off. 'We've a murder to solve.'

Hale fell in beside him. 'I'm with you, Micah.'

'Before we catch the killer and make him face justice, there's something I must do to him first.'

'What's that?'

'I mean to shake his hand in gratitude. He's done me a great favour.'

CHAPTER THREE

Shuttling between guilt and self-pity, Jem Huckvale was close to tears. He blamed himself for Paige's death and he shuddered when he looked into a future without a place at the gallery. What would he do and who would look after him? Where else could he find such friendship and fulfilment? He'd be an outcast, carrying his abject failure like an irremovable brand upon his forehead. He wallowed in anxiety until fatigue finally closed his eyes and made him doze off. Waking after a few minutes, he took time to realise where he was, then saw that Gully Ackford was looming over him. Huckvale put up both arms protectively and cowered before his erstwhile employer.

'Don't hit me,' he pleaded. 'I've already punished myself enough.'

'Why the devil should I hurt you?' asked Ackford, mildly.

'You must be disgusted with me.'

'I'm nothing of the kind. I'm just glad that you're still alive, Jem. If you were outwitted, you'll incur no blame from me. We all make mistakes. Mine was to give you an assignment far more hazardous than I'd ever imagined.' He sat on the bed and put a gentle hand on Huckvale's arm. 'How do you feel?'

'I'm frightened, Gully.'

'Why? You're perfectly safe now.'

'I'm frightened of *you*.'

Ackford's smile was paternal. 'There's no need,' he said. 'I applaud your bravery in taking on the task I set you. Only something very serious could have forced Leo Paige to come looking for a bodyguard. I picked you out at once. You're quicker on your feet than Peter and far less ostentatious than Paul. Unlike either of them, you can merge into nothingness.'

'What I merged into today was a dark alley. All at once, it got even darker.'

'Peter has told me what the surgeon said. You were lucky to survive.'

'I don't *feel* lucky.'

'When he had the chance to kill you, your assailant didn't take it. Leo Paige was the destined target. You just happened to get in the way.'

'Are we still friends, then?' asked Huckvale, hopefully.

'We always will be, Jem.' He squeezed the other's arm then looked around. 'This is a palace compared to the room you have at the gallery. Make the most of it while you can. I'm told you even have a maid to fetch and carry.'

'I hate putting Peter and his wife to any trouble.'

'They're only too glad to take you in. Charlotte tells me that you can stay as long as you wish. Now, then,' said Ackford, standing up, 'let's go back to the attack. You followed that man

31

for some time, I gather. What can you remember about him?'

Huckvale indicated his head. 'He can strike a fearsome blow, Gully.'

'How tall was he?'

'I'd say he was about your height.'

'What age would he be?'

'From the sprightly way he carried himself, he had to be a young man.'

'How was he dressed?'

'Like a costermonger. He wore a large hat that covered his face. I could see nothing of it when he turned his head sideways.'

'So there's nothing that would help you pick him out again?'

'I'm afraid not.'

'That's disappointing. A strong young man of my height is a description that could apply to thousands in this teeming city.'

'I didn't wish to get closer unless he caught sight of me.'

'But he did so, anyway.'

'I've been thinking about that,' said Huckvale, frowning. 'How could he have seen me when he never once turned round? There's another explanation, I fancy.'

'He had an accomplice?'

'That's right. The first man set off in pursuit of Mr Paige while the other waited to see if anybody from the gallery would follow. When I did, he dogged my footsteps. It never even crossed my mind to look over my shoulder.'

'How did the accomplice get ahead of you and hide in that alley?'

'It wouldn't have been difficult to run past me. A number of other people did, most of them children. My eyes were unwisely fixed on one person.'

'You did what you were bidden, Jem. There's nothing wrong in that.'

'I'm so upset about Mr Paige.'

'So am I,' said Ackford, sadly. 'That man was a hero at the battle of Yorktown. He fought like a demon. It makes me sick to think that he was murdered simply because he dared to lampoon someone. I used to believe that there was such a thing as free speech in this country. I learnt otherwise – and so did Leo Paige.'

There was a polite tap on the door and it opened to admit Meg Rooke, who looked as bright and attractive as ever. When she bobbed to the two men, Huckvale sank back shyly under the sheets.

'I've been sent to ask if there's anything you need, sir,' she said.

'No, no,' replied Huckvale, jolted by her excessive deference.

'When you do, sir, you only have to ring that little bell.'

'Thank you.'

She smiled sweetly. 'I'm very sorry that you were injured, Mr Huckvale.'

'Thank you.'

She took her leave and closed the door behind her. Ackford burst out laughing.

'You've ended up in paradise, Jem.'

'She called me "Mr Huckvale". Nobody does that.'

'It shows how much she respects you.'

'Yet I've done nothing to earn it.'

'How long do you expect to stay here, lad?'

'Oh, it will be a few days at most.'

'In your position,' said the other with a sly wink, 'I'd make it at least a few weeks. And that bell of yours wouldn't stop ringing. The very thought of having Meg at my beck and call is dizzying. You could see how willing the girl is. Employ her to the hilt. My guess is that she's going to be the best possible tonic for you.'

Though neither of them dared to go anywhere near the murder scene itself, Gregory and Eleanor Lomas had at last plucked up the courage to step inside their house. The Runners arrived and were told substantially the same story that Paul Skillen had heard from the couple earlier. With the landlord's permission, they went up to examine the victim's lodging. A scene of chaos confronted them. The fire had eaten its way hungrily through the newspapers, clothing and bed linen before starting on the timber. Thanks to help from neighbours, terrified that the flames would extend to their dwellings, an endless succession of wooden buckets of water had eventually managed to douse the blaze. The place was full of charred timbers, shallow pools of water and general debris. A stench of damp hovered. Gaps in the floorboards allowed continuous dripping into the room below. There was an air of devastation.

'Garrotted then set alight,' said Hale with gruff sympathy. 'That's no fit way for any human being to meet his Maker.'

'Don't ask me to feel sorry for the man,' warned Yeomans.

'He was *murdered*, Micah. Show some respect for the dead.'

'I'd rather dance a jig on his grave.'

'You didn't even know Paige.'

'I know his type, Alfred. He's another of those nasty, hateful, conniving scribblers who use words to blacken the reputation of others and cartoons to turn them into scapegoats. I detest the whole breed of cunning back-stabbers.'

'They've never troubled *you*, have they?'

It was a pointed question. They both knew that Yeomans had been derided in one of the caricatures they'd seen earlier. Hale was too scared to say it aloud and Yeomans refuse to concede that – along with a lecherous politician – he'd been the butt of a satirist's joke. He stared so aggressively at the other Runner that Hale was forced to avert his gaze and step quickly backwards. His feet landed in the soggy remains of a blanket and he almost fell over.

Having seen all they needed to, they went back downstairs and questioned the landlord and his wife about their lodger's source of income. Lomas had no idea how Paige had made his money. All that concerned him was that the rent was paid regularly and that they had an unusually quiet tenant.

'We hardly knew he was up there, sirs,' said Lomas. 'Most of those we've taken in as lodgers have given us trouble of some kind or another but not Mr Paige. He's a great loss to us.'

'Who could want to kill him?' asked the wife, wringing her hands.

'It couldn't have been for his money because I don't think he had a great deal. We felt sorry for him, spending his old age in a single room among strangers.'

'We're not strangers, Gregory. We treated him like a friend.'

'Yet he wouldn't let us get close to him, Ellie.'

'Why was that?' asked Yeomans. 'Did he have something to hide?'

Lomas hunched his shoulders. 'Who can say?'

'I'm sorry you had to come back and find your house in this state,' said Hale.

'The damage can be repaired but nobody can bring Mr Paige back to life.'

'Good riddance to him!' muttered Yeomans under his breath. He raised his voice. 'We'll need to speak to your neighbours,' he went on. 'They may have seen the killer coming or going. No man is invisible. He must have been spotted by *someone*.'

'Will you catch him, Mr Yeomans?'

'We'll not sleep a wink until you do,' added the wife.

'It won't take us long,' boasted Yeomans. 'We always catch up with the culprit in the end. It's a matter of pride with us.'

'It is,' said Hale. 'When a murder is committed, they always send for us.'

It was true. They had become a formidable team. Having made their names as efficient thief-takers, Yeomans and Hale had been assigned to the more difficult and dangerous work of hunting killers. As a result, they'd sent a number of people – male and female – to the scaffold. One of the reasons for their success was that they'd built up a wide network of informers in the criminal underworld. The Runners either kept them on small retainers or offered them immunity from arrest for the petty crimes in which they were routinely involved.

'As soon as word spreads,' said Yeomans, confidently, 'information will start to trickle in. We have eyes and ears everywhere in the city.'

'London is a cesspit of crime,' said Lomas, resentfully. 'There's theft and violence everywhere you turn. Because of that, we take care to avoid trouble. What we never expected was that our own home would be invaded by disaster. Can you offer law-abiding citizens no protection at all?'

'No,' replied Hale, bluntly. 'There are far too few of us. We can't police a huge city with a mere handful of men. But we have our successes.'

'The gaols are full of them,' asserted Yeomans. 'We'll never catch every light-fingered rogue who steals for a living or every accursed footpad who knocks his victims senseless before robbing them. What we can do is to put enough of them behind bars to send out a stern warning to the others. And our reputations have made some villains think twice about committing murder because they know we will come after them.'

'That didn't stop it happening right here,' moaned Lomas. 'The killer didn't care two hoots about the Bow Street Runners.'

'He'll die regretting that.'

'You'll have to catch him first.'

'I guarantee it.'

Eleanor Lomas bit her lip. 'I think we should sleep at our son's house.'

'Nobody is going to drive me out of here,' said her husband, stoutly. 'This is our home and we'll stay.'

'But water is still coming through the ceiling!'

'The servants will clear up the mess, Ellie.'

'There are just a few more things we'd like to know,' said Yeomans.

Lomas became tetchy. 'Do you have to pester us like this?'

he demanded. 'Why do you keep asking questions we've already answered? The other man was even more thorough than you've been.'

Yeomans bridled. 'What other man?'

'We thought he was a Runner like you.'

'Is that what he told you?'

'Well, no,' said Lomas, 'but he had the same air of authority.'

'Describe him.'

'He was tall, well dressed and ten years or more younger than either of you.'

'And he was very handsome,' his wife put in, wistfully. 'Even in my distress, I noticed that. The gentleman was kind and reassuring. We trusted him.'

Yeomans turned to Hale. 'It sounds like Peter Skillen.'

'It could equally well be Paul Skillen,' said the other, worriedly. 'We don't want him solving this crime instead of us, Micah. That's happened before.'

'Well, it won't happen again.'

'I hope not. We were made to look like buffoons.'

'Whichever of those infernal brothers it is,' said Yeomans through gritted teeth, 'he is *not* going to interfere in our investigation. I'll make sure that the Skillens understand that.'

When he'd discharged his duty as a fencing instructor at the gallery, Peter Skillen went back to the office to find his brother there. Seated at the table, Paul was making notes of his visit to Paige's lodging. After a last flourish with the quill pen, he put it in the inkwell and sat back in his chair.

'Everything I learnt at the murder scene is down here,' he said.

'It was Charlotte's idea that we should keep written records while memories were still fresh in our minds.'

'Charlotte is brimming with good ideas.'

'That's why she married me instead of you,' teased Peter.

Paul smiled. 'I've recovered from that setback a long time ago.'

'Are there any clues as to the identity of the killer?' asked his brother, picking up the paper and reading the elegant hand.

'None whatsoever, I fear.'

'Then we'll have to rely on Gully. I asked him to rack his brains.'

'I've been doing the self-same thing, Peter.' He got to his feet. 'Why did the killer choose to strike today of all days?' he wondered. 'If it was so important to silence Mr Paige, it should have happened long before now, surely?'

'I hate to say it, Paul, but *we* might be responsible for his death.'

'That's arrant nonsense. We never even knew the fellow.'

'The salient point is that he knew *us* – or, at least, he was aware of the services we offer.' Peter put the paper back on the table. 'Everyone knows that this is no mere shooting gallery. People turn to us to protect them, hunt down stolen property, find missing members of the family or solve a hundred and one other problems they encounter. Our escapades last year were lauded in all the newspapers. The gallery became rightly famous and that fame brought Mr Paige here.'

'I follow your reasoning now.'

'It was Jem's logic I just imparted. When he came here for

help, Paige was followed. Jem feels that a second man was hiding nearby to see if Paige left with a bodyguard. As Jem came out – clearly trailing Paige's stalker – the second man followed and seized his chance to knock Jem unconscious.'

'It's a sound theory,' said Paul, 'but it may turn out to be a misleading one.'

'Oh, I agree. We must take nothing for granted.'

'Jem, poor lad, is not easily tricked. Only a crafty rogue could lure him into a trap. On the other hand, I'm glad that we have another murder to solve. It will test us to the full. I need something like this to sink my teeth into, Peter.'

His brother could understand his sentiments. Paul was not driven solely by the desire to apprehend a killer. He wanted a distraction. Peter was happily married and had a stable existence whereas his brother's private life had been wildly erratic. Over the years, there had been a series of dalliances, all of them conducted with great passion until they inevitably burnt themselves out. The previous year, however, Paul had at last found someone with whom he was ready to share his life, whatever compromises were involved. Hannah Granville was a brilliant actress who'd become the toast of London. Paul marvelled at her. However, she was in demand elsewhere and had to take her talents to Bath, Norwich, York and other cities where avid theatregoers were eager to see her. Paul accepted her need to travel and they kept in touch by letter.

That had become more difficult now. Such was her eminence, Hannah had attracted international attention and been invited to perform in Paris. Sad to see her go, Paul acknowledged that it was an important stage of her career. He waved her off with his best wishes then felt her loss immediately. Only by keeping himself occupied could he fend off the urge to mope. Because the murder investigation would need all of his concentration, he welcomed it.

'Have you heard from Hannah?' asked Peter.

'I had one letter and it took an age to reach me.'

'How is she faring?'

'She loves Paris. I just hope that she misses me as much as I miss her.'

'Can you doubt that?'

'I just wish she wasn't so far away and surrounded by foreigners.'

'Now that it's possible to visit Paris again,' said Peter, 'there are lots of English people there. She'll not lack for people who speak the same language. I'd love to go to the city myself.'

'Yes,' said Paul, 'you'd actually have time to see its sights now. When you worked as a spy during the war, your trips there were fraught with danger. Charlotte was beside herself while you were away.'

'I'm just grateful that she didn't know what I had to endure.'

'She knew that many British agents were captured and killed.'

'I was one of the lucky ones, Paul.'

The door opened and Gully Ackford came in, whisking off his hat. There was an exchange of greetings, then Ackford told them about his visit to Jem Huckvale. When he described how the reluctant patient reacted to the appearance of the maidservant, all three of them shared a laugh.

'I did what you asked of me,' said Ackford, turning to Peter.

'I remembered as much as I could of the conversation I had with Leo. He was full of surprises.'

'Tell us about them, Gully.'

After clearing his throat, Ackford launched into a long, albeit repetitive, account of Paige's earlier visit. The brothers listened attentively, taking it in turns to ask for clarification of some points in the narrative. When their friend had finished, they felt that the investigation had been given impetus and direction.

'We need to get hold of old copies of *Paige's Chronicle*,' said Paul. 'They'll provide us with a list of possible suspects. Those who were denounced in print are unlikely to have dirtied their own hands but one of them might well have hired thugs to do the deed.'

'Yes,' agreed Peter. 'What happened to Jem proves that we're dealing with villains who are proficient in their trade. But where do we get these newspapers, Gully? If your friend had his own collection, they'll have gone up in smoke.'

'We must start in Holborn,' said Ackford. 'That's where a shop sells the prints that Leo told me about. One glance in the window, I daresay, will give us even more potential suspects.'

'Who owns the shop?'

'Leo said that her name was Mrs Mandrake and he spoke very well of her. The premises are in Middle Row.'

'I'll get over there at once,' said Peter. 'Thank you, Gully. What you've told us has been very enlightening. You might care to read what happened when Paul went to your friend's lodging. Like you, my brother has been dredging his memory.'

After bidding them farewell, Peter left the room at speed.

Paul, meanwhile, passed his notes to Ackford who read them with mingled interest and sadness.

'What an appalling way to take leave of the world,' he said, forlornly.

'It was not by choice,' Paul pointed out. 'He lodged in a pleasant enough house but it was much smaller than I'd expected. If he could afford to publish a newspaper and earned money from his satires, I assumed he'd be a man of means.'

Ackford chuckled. 'Then you didn't know Leo Paige,' he said. 'Money ran through his hands like water. He had many virtues but he had one glaring weakness.'

'What was that?'

'Gambling.'

'Ah, I see.'

'It was like a disease with Leo.'

'You don't need to explain, Gully. I've suffered from the affliction myself.'

It was Paul's abiding vice. When he had money in his purse – and was at a loose end for company – he'd often gone off to one of his favourite gambling hells, despite the fact that he usually had a run of bad luck there.

'It's one of the many gifts Hannah bestowed upon me,' said Paul. 'She cured me of that particular malady.'

'You've been healthier and happier as a result.'

'Tell me a little more about this Mrs Mandrake.'

'All I know is that she's owned that print shop for ten years or more.'

'How did your friend describe her?'

'He couldn't praise her enough,' said Ackford. 'She was his guardian angel. Leo described her as the most remarkable woman in London.'

There was a small cluster of people gazing through the window when Peter arrived at the print shop. He could hear their laughs and titters. A few of them drifted away, leaving him space to take a look for himself at the caricatures on display. All were well drawn but those in the *Parliament of Foibles* series had a quiet savagery that set them apart. The text beneath the drawings was clever, amusing and incisive. Leonidas Paige clearly had a way with words. Peter's eye fell on the print that featured Sir Humphrey Coote. Having been employed by the government during the war, and having spent much time in the company of the Home Secretary, Peter knew most of the leading politicians by sight. He recognised Coote at once and grinned at the satirical treatment he'd received. His grin became a laugh of delight when he saw the burly figure of Micah Yeomans in the cartoon. The Runner was belittled in a way that was bound to arouse his desire for revenge but Peter didn't for a second consider him to be a murder suspect. Yeomans might not have seen the drawing and, even if he had, he would – instead of breaking the law – endeavour to use it to punish the artist severely.

Still smiling, Peter let himself into the shop and was met by a short, wiry, white-haired individual dressed in black from head to toe and rubbing his hands together as if washing them with invisible soap. Benjamin Tite appraised his visitor shrewdly then waved an arm to take in the whole shop.

'Welcome to our humble emporium, sir,' he said. 'I can see

that you're a man of fashion with a discriminating eye. Feel free to examine our collection. You're under no obligation to purchase anything, though I sense that something in our window has brought you in here.' Hand on his chest, he bowed slightly. 'I am Benjamin Tite and I'm at your service.'

'One particular print did whet my appetite,' confessed Peter, 'but I came here for another reason. I need to speak to Mrs Mandrake on a matter of urgency.'

'May I know what it is, sir?'

'Mrs Mandrake must be the judge of that. In the first instance, I'll only speak to her. Is the lady available?'

Irritated by the rebuff, Tite signified his disapproval with a loud sniff.

'I'll see if Mrs Mandrake is willing to receive you,' he said. 'May I know who is calling on her?'

'My name is Peter Skillen.'

'Have you come to buy or sell?'

'I've come to tell Mrs Mandrake something of great importance,' said Peter, sharply, 'and I'll thank you to stop delaying my conversation with her. Your employer, I do assure you, will be as displeased as I am.'

After mumbling an excuse, Tite withdrew into the back room and closed the door after him. When it opened again, the commanding figure of Diane Mandrake came into view, filling the doorway and giving off the odour of an expensive perfume. Wearing a striking, high-waisted blue dress, she was a big, handsome woman with a surging bosom. She wore a diamond necklace, a gold brooch in the shape of a horse and a gold bangle studded with gemstones. Rings adorned most fingers on

45

each hand. It was impossible to guess her age with any accuracy. Hands on her hips, she looked Peter up and down.

'You wish to speak with me, sir?' she asked, warily.

'Yes, Mrs Mandrake, but it must be in private.'

'There's a distressing whiff of the law about you, Mr Skillen. I hope that you've not come to initiate a prosecution against me.'

'Far from it,' said Peter, indicating the window display. 'Even on a short acquaintance with them, your prints have given me immense pleasure. I would cheerfully support your right to sell such excellent work'.

She relaxed at once. 'Come with me, sir.'

As she stepped backwards and moved aside, Tite scurried back into the shop. Peter went through into the adjoining room. It was large, high-ceilinged and well proportioned. The furniture was tasteful and there was an abiding sense of comfort. A gilt-framed mirror stood over the marble fireplace. Almost every other inch of wall space was taken up by framed prints. After closing the door, she lowered herself into a chair and invited Peter to do likewise. He sat down opposite her.

'Now, sir,' she said, 'why such a need for privacy?'

'I've brought some news about Leonidas Paige.'

She smiled wearily. 'What kind of a mess has Leo got himself into *this* time? Does he need me to pay off a debt or has he been arrested yet again?'

'It's more serious than that, Mrs Mandrake.'

'He's not ill, I trust?'

'Mr Paige is beyond the help of any physician, alas.'

She rose to her feet in alarm. 'Leo is *dead*?'

46

'My tidings are even more distressing,' he cautioned. 'Since he spoke so fondly of you, I felt that you should hear them as soon as possible. Earlier today,' he went on, lowering his voice, 'Mr Paige was murdered.'

Diane Mandrake looked as if she'd been hit hard in the face by a mallet. Her cheeks reddened, her eyes bulged, her jaw dropped open and she emitted a gasp of sheer horror. Her legs turned to jelly and she swooned.

Leaping out of his chair, Peter was just in time to catch her.

CHAPTER FOUR

They were about to lock up the gallery when there was a thunderous knocking on the door. Gully Ackford opened it to find two glowering visitors outside. Micah Yeomans and Alfred Hale were standing there with stomachs pulled in and chests thrust out.

'Have you come for instruction?' teased Ackford.

'They could certainly do with it,' said Paul, sizing them up. 'The least you should expect of Runners is that they can actually run. This pair can barely waddle. No wonder they catch so few villains.'

'We'd like a word with you two,' said Yeomans, ominously.

'Then say your piece and be off with you.'

'Don't give us orders, Mr Skillen. You've no status in this city. We, on the other hand, certainly have and our territory is well marked. You and that interfering brother, Paul, must not dare to trespass on it.'

'This *is* Paul,' said Ackford with a chuckle. 'Your eyesight is getting worse, Micah. Perhaps it's time you considered retirement.'

Hale snapped his fingers. 'I *knew* it was Paul.' Yeomans glared at him. 'I could have told you if you'd asked.'

'I didn't ask,' snapped his companion, 'so hold your tongue.'

'But I guessed right for once.'

'One of you – Paul or Peter, I know not which – went to the home of a Mr Paige without any writ to do so. Do you confess it?'

'No,' said Paul, tartly.

'Then it must have been your brother.'

'Nobody from here went without a writ,' said Ackford, seriously. 'Leo Paige was a good friend and regimental comrade of mine. He came to us in search of a bodyguard. The person who took on that duty was clubbed to the ground for his pains and might well have died as a result. *That's* our writ, Micah,' he emphasised. 'We have a personal stake in this case. I want to catch the loathsome creature responsible for my friend's death.'

'And I want the man who battered Jem Huckvale,' said Paul, vengefully. 'If you contrive to arrest the culprits before us, we'll be the first to congratulate you. But there's little chance of that happening.'

'When you and your brother get out of the way,' said Yeomans, wagging a finger, 'there's *every* chance. We have a licence to pursue felons.'

'Yes – and you do so with one eye on the reward money.'

'That's not true.'

'We know you too well, Micah.'

'And we've taken *your* measure,' retorted Yeomans. 'You are meddling fools who commit blunder after blunder. And you impede us – damn you!'

'What you mean is that we always outshine you.'

'Ask yourselves this,' said Ackford, 'if a man's life is in danger – as Leo Paige's undoubtedly was – why did he turn to us instead of seeking the protection of the Bow Street Runners?'

'You explained that yourself,' said Hale. 'He sought out a friend.'

'But he hadn't even realised that I own this gallery.'

'He came here,' said Paul, 'because we can offer a service that you do not.'

'And what kind of service was it?' asked Yeomans with a sneer. 'The man you were supposed to protect was murdered and your floundering bodyguard was so inept that he got himself knocked unconscious. What sort of a bill are you going to send to the deceased? Don't be surprised if he refuses to pay it.'

Exposing a row of ugly teeth, he brayed aloud.

Ackford had to rein in his temper and master the urge to throw a punch. Striking a Runner would inevitably lead to a fine, if not a spell in prison, and he didn't want to give Yeomans the pleasure of arresting him. Besides, he had the restraining hand of Paul on his shoulder. There was a better way of getting back at their rivals and that was to solve the crimes ahead of them.

'What have you learnt so far?' demanded Yeomans.

'We've learnt that you're an uncouth oaf unworthy of the office you hold,' said Paul. 'When I went to Mr Paige's house, I spoke to the hapless owner and his wife. You were at liberty to do exactly the same thing.'

'And so we did.'

'Then you don't need me to offer guidance.'

'You may have gleaned something that we didn't.'

'That's always the case, Micah.'

'I won't warn you again,' declared Yeomans. 'If you and your brother dare to get under our feet in this investigation, you'll be in deep trouble. The last thing we need is to have the pair of you treading on our toes.'

Paul grinned. 'How can we tread on your toes if we're under your feet?'

'You know what I mean.'

'We know only too well,' said Ackford. 'You're afraid that we'll expose your weaknesses by competing with you. We've done it time and again in the past. Brace yourselves for further humiliation.'

Yeomans simmered for a full minute. Unable to find a crushing rejoinder, he turned on his heel and strode away. Hale had to break into a trot to keep up with him. Paul could not resist a Parthian shot.

'I lied to you, Micah,' he called out, cupping his hands. 'You were right first time. I *am* Peter Skillen.'

Diane Mandrake slowly recovered consciousness. When her eyelids finally stopped fluttering like a trapped butterfly, she realised that she was stretched out on the sofa with Peter Skillen standing solicitously over her. As she struggled to remember what had happened, he prompted her gently.

'I had to pass on troubling news,' he said. 'You were overwhelmed by it.'

'Of course – poor, dear Leo is dead. When did it happen?'

'We can discuss that when you feel well enough.'

'I'm fine now, Mr Skillen,' she said, adjusting her position, 'but wait a moment. If I fainted, why am I not still stretched out on the floor?'

'Luckily, I was able to catch you.'

'Thank heavens there was a pair of strong manly arms waiting!'

At any other time, Peter would have found the remark flirtatious and her eyes did ignite for a second. In the circumstances, he decided, she was too flustered by the loss of a friend and business associate to know what she was saying. Easing her back onto the sofa had taken some effort. Peter could still feel the weight of her body pressed up against him.

'I owe you a debt, kind sir,' she said.

'I only did what anyone would have done.'

'That's patently not true. You've met little Ben Tite, who looks after the shop. Had *he* tried to catch me when I went down, he'd still be flat on his back beneath me, unable to move a muscle.' She let out a ripe cackle then chided herself immediately. 'I shouldn't laugh. It's a terrible thing to do in the wake of this calamity.' She shook her head in disbelief. 'Leo was *murdered*? Where, when and how did it take place? I thought he was going to engage a bodyguard. I was the one who bullied him into doing so, Mr Skillen. He showed me some of the letters he received. They were vicious. Leo was threatened with torture, disfigurement and a miserable death.'

'What about you, Mrs Mandrake?'

'I don't follow you, sir.'

'His work is on sale in your shop. Did *you* not receive threats?'

'Oh, I have them all the time,' she said, airily, 'and they usually come from people who've been featured in our prints. Prosecution is their weapon. They try to frighten me with the threat of it but, as you can see, I'm still here and my shop is still thriving.' She leant forward. 'But that's enough about me. Stop hovering like that and sit down again. I want to hear about Leo.'

'Some of the details are upsetting,' he warned, resuming his seat.

'I'm past the shock. I have the strength to hear them now.'

'Then I must first tell you how I became involved with Mr Paige . . .'

Peter gave her a brief account of how Paige had come to the shooting gallery, discovered that it was run by his old friend, hired a bodyguard and set off with Jem Huckvale trailing behind him. Diane was saddened to hear how the bodyguard had been assaulted and she attached no blame to Huckvale. When she heard about the murder itself, there was a sharp intake of breath and she brought a hand to her neck.

'Why did he have to be garrotted?' she murmured.

'It was a quick and simple way to overpower him,' replied Peter. 'He'd been a soldier, remember. Unless he'd been caught off guard, he'd have put up a good fight. The killer made sure that he had no chance to do so.'

'And then he set fire to the place?'

'He obviously wanted to destroy Mr Paige's papers. Among

them, I suspect, were early designs for his next drawings.'

'Leo was no artist, Mr Skillen. He just provided the words.'

'Then who drew those exquisite caricatures?'

'I wish I knew. Leo refused to tell me.'

'Didn't you find that odd?'

'I'm used to oddities and eccentricities in this business,' she explained. 'If an artist wishes to remain anonymous, I accept that. All that concerned me was that the cartoons were drawn, engraved and embellished with Leo's venomous pen. I sold the prints on Leo's behalf. The *Parliament of Foibles* was very popular.'

'The prints were signed by Virgo,' he observed. 'I thought that the name had been devised by Mr Paige. Virgo is the sign of the zodiac that comes after Leo. You must have noticed that.'

'I taxed him with it once, Mr Skillen, but he brushed my questions aside. The mystery remains. To this day, I have no idea who Virgo is.'

'You may do so very soon, Mrs Mandrake.'

'Why is that?'

'He's bound to become aware of his partner's death. If he wishes to continue selling prints to you, he will have to reveal his identity.'

'I never thought of that.'

'When he does, I'd be grateful if you'd send word to me at once. Someone who worked hand in glove with Mr Paige will know a great deal about him. He might be able to point us in the direction of his partner's enemies.'

'I can do that,' she said, confidently. 'You simply have to visit the Houses of Parliament. I dare swear that several of its self-seeking denizens had a good reason to see Leo silenced.'

'How many of them would condone murder?'

'That depends on how thin their skins are. Some people can brush off ridicule like specks of dust on their sleeve, but it cuts deeper with others and pushes them to extremes. Study the prints that Leo worked on. Somewhere among them is the man who ordered his death.'

'What about his newspaper? That, too, outraged many people.'

'*Paige's Chronicle* was a masterpiece,' she said, chortling. 'Its principal targets were scheming politicians and corrupt clergy. Leo held their feet to the fire good and proper. The Stamp Act was created to kill off newspapers like his.'

'How often was it published?'

'Once a week, as a rule.'

'I don't suppose that you have a copy, by any chance.'

'I have *every* copy, Mr Skillen,' she said, proudly. 'I sometimes take one to bed with me. Leo's prose is a joy. I never tire of reading it.'

'May I see the collection?' asked Peter.

'I'll insist upon it. I'll also insist on paying for Leo's funeral. He caused me endless trouble over the years, especially when he lodged above the shop for a while, but I loved him nevertheless. Everything I have is at your disposal,' she continued, looking deep into his eyes. 'I intend to be involved directly in the hunt for the killer. Don't consider me to be the mere owner of a print shop. I am made of sterner stuff than that. What you see before you, Mr Skillen,' she announced, arms spread wide, 'is your willing confederate.'

Peter wondered why the offer made him feel distinctly uneasy.

* * *

Though he had a wife and six children, Eldon Kirkwood had little time for family life. Since his appointment as chief magistrate, he was rarely at home during a long day. Dedicated to his work, he was prepared to labour all hours and he expected others to do the same. When the Runners stood before him, therefore, they didn't dare to yawn or show any sign of fatigue. If they did so, they knew that they'd be subjected to his scorn.

Yeomans delivered his report and Hale contributed the occasional remark. Standing before him, they were anxious to get out of Kirkwood's office as soon as possible so that they could repair to the Peacock Inn, their favourite establishment. After a session with the chief magistrate, they always felt in need of a reviving pint of ale. Kirkwood, by contrast, never touched alcoholic liquor and was always preaching the virtues of temperance. It only served to increase their respective thirst for a drink.

Delivered ponderously, the report was short and halting. When Yeomans had finished, he gave a sigh of relief. Kirkwood raised a reproachful eyebrow.

'Your report is woefully deficient in evidence,' he said.

'We've not really had time to gather it yet, sir,' argued Yeomans. 'It was not for want of trying. We spoke to all of the neighbours.'

'Nobody saw anything untoward,' added Hale.

Kirkwood was sarcastic. 'Murder and arson are committed under their noses yet they were completely unaware of the perpetrator? Are they all blind and deaf?'

'They were frightened.'

'Alfred is right, sir,' said Yeomans. 'If they did see or hear anything, they're too scared to admit it in case it brings the wrath of the killer down on their head. It's a common problem in the wake of a felony. People, in the main, don't come forward as witnesses. They're afraid that they'll have to appear in court.'

'But the villains will have been apprehended at that stage,' said Kirkwood.

'Villains always have villainous friends, sir. They seek retribution. Naked fear keeps the mouths of many witnesses firmly shut.'

'There must be a way to open them.'

'We could only do that by offering them protection, sir. That's why some witnesses are struck dumb.'

'How do you break through this conspiracy of silence?'

'It takes time and patience.'

'We don't have unlimited quantities of either, Yeomans. I want results *now*. Some very important people live in Bloomsbury and they take offence at what happened in their midst. Intense pressure has already been put on me. Early arrests are demanded.'

'We'll be as quick as we can, sir.'

'There is another avenue to explore,' suggested Hale. 'We happened upon the shop where Mr Paige's prints were sold. It may be that the owner will be able to help us by disclosing the names of Mr Paige's known enemies.'

'I'd already intended to do that,' said Yeomans, shooting him a hostile glance. 'We will take every step needed to solve this murder.'

Kirkwood stroked his beard. 'What manner of man was Paige?'

'The landlord said that he was secretive, sir.'

'He might have been secretive about his private life but his excursions into the public domain were the very opposite. He did all he could to get attention and always at the expense of his latest victim.'

'That may explain why he tried to cover his tracks,' opined Yeomans. 'Having raised a hullaballoo, Paige felt the need to sneak off and hide. Somebody eventually tracked him to his lair.'

'Your task is to find that somebody,' said Kirkwood. 'Many eyes are upon you. Bear that in mind at all times.'

'Yes, sir.'

'Of course, sir,' said Hale.

'Will that be all, sir?'

'No, it is not. You might care to know that a substantial reward has been offered. You both know what that means.'

'Others will be tempted to join in the search,' said Yeomans.

'People like the Skillen brothers,' said Kirkwood. 'I don't want them putting you in the shade yet again. This is an investigation for the Bow Street Runners and not for bold but misguided amateurs like Peter and Paul Skillen. Their one desire is to get their hands on that reward money.'

'To be fair, sir,' said Hale, 'they have another reason to take an interest in this case. Paige's death was not the only crime committed. Jem Huckvale, who works with the two brothers, was badly injured in a violent attack linked to the murder.'

'That's immaterial,' scoffed Yeomans.

'I don't think so, Micah.'

'Keep your opinions to yourself.'

'Hale makes an important point,' conceded Kirkwood. 'I knew nothing of this secondary crime. How can we be certain that it has a bearing on the murder?'

'Huckvale was acting as Mr Paige's bodyguard at the time,' said Hale. 'That's what we were told by Peter Skillen.' He scratched his head. 'Or was it Paul?'

'You've interviewed the brothers, then?'

'We visited the shooting gallery earlier, sir.'

'It was not a social call, sir,' Yeomans stressed. 'We went to find out what they actually knew of the crimes and to warn them that it was not their place to try to solve them.' He inhaled deeply through his nose. 'By asserting my authority, I've frightened them off from any involvement whatsoever in this case. I think it's safe to say – and Alfred will support this judgement – that there will be no more trouble from the Skillen family.'

Kirkwood's eyes shifted to Hale. 'Do you agree?'

'Yes, sir,' said the other. 'They have been well and truly muzzled.'

It was not often that Charlotte had the two brothers at the house. She was delighted, therefore, to share a meal with them. Though Peter and Paul worked in harness, they rarely spent any leisure time in each other's company. Their inclinations took them in opposite directions. Even when Paul's friendship with Hannah Granville developed into a real commitment on both sides, Charlotte saw little of her brother-in-law. As the three of them sat over the remains of the meal, she reflected on what an appealing man he was. It was not because she had any regrets about marrying Peter. Life with him was far happier and steadier than it would have been with Paul. Both of them had courted her simultaneously and it had inevitably caused difficulties. To the naked eye, they were indistinguishable. In terms of their character, however, she'd very quickly learnt to tell them apart and it had helped her to make the crucial choice between them.

'Tell us more about Mrs Mandrake,' urged Paul.

'I've told you everything,' said Peter.

'That's not true. All we've heard is what she recalled about Paige. You said nothing about the lady herself. What sort of woman is she – young, old, serene, combative, rich, poor?'

'Mrs Mandrake is clearly very resourceful, Paul. She's run a profitable business in Middle Row for a decade and – while not wealthy, perhaps – she is very far from being poor.'

'Paul asked about her age,' said Charlotte.

'He'll have to meet her to determine that, my love. I take her to be older than any of us but younger than Gully. As for serenity, it's not a characteristic that could ever be associated with her. I sensed a combative streak.'

'Is there a Mr Mandrake?'

'There must have been at some stage, Charlotte, but there's no sign of him now. What happened to him, I know not. I didn't go to the shop to enquire into her personal circumstances.'

'I'd like to meet her,' said Paul.

'You won't be able to avoid doing so.'

'Why is that?'

'She's appointed herself as our assistant in the hunt.'

Paul was sceptical. 'Can a woman be of any use in an investigation?'

'I beg your pardon,' said Charlotte with mock indignation. 'In addition to working at the gallery and keeping the records, I like to think that I've helped to solve more than one crime.'

'Indeed, you have, Charlotte,' he agreed, readily. 'Your contribution has been invaluable and I apologise for not acknowledging it. The fact is that you are an extraordinary woman.'

'So is Mrs Mandrake in her own way,' said Peter. 'In lending me those copies of *Paige's Chronicle*, she's already given us an advantage over the Runners. They could be a veritable gold mine.' There was a tap on the door, then Meg Rooke popped her head in to see if she should clear the table. Peter gave her a nod then addressed the others. 'Why don't we adjourn to the other room and start reading through them?'

'That's a splendid idea,' said his wife, rising from the table.

The three of them went into the drawing room where a pile of newspapers stood on a small table. Printed on perilously thin paper, most of them consisted of a single page that was filled on both sides. Handing one each to his wife and brother, Peter picked up a copy of his own and settled into a chair. He was soon laughing.

'The fellow had a wickedly entertaining pen,' he said with approval. 'He's using it to hilarious effect on a certain Well-done Churchwood.'

'Who is that?' asked Charlotte.

'It can be none other than Eldon Kirkwood, my love.'

'Then he's a brave man,' said Paul, looking up. 'Many people will make fun of the chief magistrate at Bow Street behind his back but few would dare do it in print like Paige. That's a case of skating on very thin ice.'

'The ice eventually cracked, Paul, and he ended up in prison.'

'I refuse to believe that Kirkwood is a suspect.'

'Oh, it's quite unthinkable. For all his faults, he's a Christian gentleman who abides by the Ten Commandments as if they were designed specifically for him. He wants the killer apprehended and brought to book. That's why he's authorised Yeomans and his crony to go in pursuit of him.'

'How do we keep ahead of them?' asked Charlotte.

'By doing things that they would never think of,' replied Peter, 'such as doing what we're doing right now – looking for evidence in *Paige's Chronicle*.'

'There's something else they might overlook,' said Paul. 'The landlord told me that only three people ever visited Paige at the house. Each one of them will get a shock when they call again. I asked the landlord to be sure to get their names and, if possible, to find out their addresses. Those close to Paige are the ones most likely to be of any real help to us.'

'Will you call at the house again?'

'I'll do so every day, Peter.'

'Gully told us that Paige was a very amiable and gregarious man. Did he not have more than three friends he'd invite to his lodging?'

'If he did, he deliberately kept them away from there.'

'It sounds to me as if he was in hiding,' remarked Charlotte.

'Can you blame him, my love? He knew that he was a marked man – and he may not be the only one, of course.'

'Yes,' said Paul, 'there's the artist who drew those cartoons.

They'll draw even more blood than Paige's pen portraits. Who *is* this Virgo?'

'Nobody seems to know.'

'He needs to be warned, Peter.'

'We'll have to find him before we do that. I'm hoping that, sooner or later, he'll turn up outside Mrs Mandrake's shop.'

'I'm still worried about her,' confided Paul. 'Having worked with us so often, Charlotte is a proven asset but I can't imagine any other woman having her special qualities. Mrs Mandrake could be more of a hindrance than a help. She's inexperienced and unable to defend herself in situations she may well stray into.'

'We'll have to give her the benefit of the doubt, Paul,' said his brother. 'To some extent, I share your reservations. Yet consider what she's done. Any other woman would simply want to mourn the death of a friend. She, however, is set on hunting his killer. That shows resilience.' His brow furrowed. 'I have this strange feeling that Mrs Mandrake may turn out to surprise the whole lot of us.'

When he first heard of the murder, Benjamin Tite didn't faint nor did he express any deep sorrow. He accepted the fact of Paige's death as if it had been a predictable event. His main concern was for the immediate consequences for the shop.

'What do we do with our stock of prints?' he asked.

'We keep them and sell them, of course.'

'But that will surely endanger us.'

'It's a danger I'm prepared to live with, Ben. Leo Paige and his partner made a lot of money for us. The *Parliament of Foibles* is always in demand. We'll promote it until every print is sold.'

'If they can kill Leo Paige, they can kill us.'

'Forewarned is forearmed,' she said, opening her reticule and taking out a small pistol. 'I will have this weapon beside me night and day. I suggest that you take the same precaution.'

Title quivered. 'I've never fired a gun in my life.'

'Well, I have and – to tell you the truth – I rather enjoyed it.'

CHAPTER FIVE

Still bruised from their meeting with the chief magistrate, the Runners were quaffing their third pint of ale at the Peacock Inn. They traded complaints about Kirkwood until they found a new target for their bile. Chevy Ruddock walked into the room and saw them seated in a corner. He was a tall, gawky young man with an unappealing face redeemed by a willing smile. Proud to become a member of one of the foot patrols, he'd been mocked for his wide-eyed innocence at first but he'd learnt quickly. Ruddock had turned into a plucky and resourceful officer. For that reason, he'd been given an important task.

'Good evening,' he said, sharing a smile between them. 'I did what you asked of me, Mr Yeomans. I've spoken to a dozen of them.'

'And?'

'I'll go back in the morning to sound out even more.'

'*And?*' repeated Yeomans. 'And – and – and?'

Ruddock was bemused. 'And what, sir?'

'Did you bring back any evidence? Has anyone reported a sighting?'

'One man did see someone lurking in the vicinity of the house,' said Ruddock, 'but thought him too old to be capable of strangling anybody.'

'He could have been keeping an eye on the property,' said Hale, thoughtfully. 'Paige's lodging must have been watched – no doubt about that. Who gave you this information?'

'It was Mokey Venables, sir.'

'That little weasel!' said Yeomans with a snort. 'I've lost count of the number of times I arrested him for picking pockets. In the end, he learnt that the best way to keep out of prison was to *report* crimes rather than commit them. Respect where it's due, though. He's got sharp eyes and he knows Bloomsbury as well as he knows the body of that scrawny hag he calls his wife.'

'What else did you learn, Ruddock?' asked Hale.

'Very little,' admitted the other. 'I had the feeling that some of them were holding things back.'

'You should have leant hard on them, lad.'

'I tried to, sir, but it was no use.' He brightened. 'They all asked me the same thing, however. Every one of them told me to pass on their regards to Mr Yeomans and Mr Hale. They hold you in high esteem.'

'And so they should,' said Yeomans, darkly, 'but we want more than their regards. We want names and addresses. We want the evidence to set us on the trail of a killer. One of them must have seen or heard something.'

'I'll try again tomorrow,' volunteered Ruddock.

'Alfred will go with you.'

'Will I?' asked Hale, offended to be given the lowly task of rounding up their informers. 'What will you be doing, Micah?'

'I intend to go to that print shop.'

'That was *my* suggestion. Why don't I come with you?'

'You'll be too busy working with Ruddock.'

'It will be an honour to be at your side, Mr Hale,' said Ruddock, beaming. 'I learn so much when I'm with someone of your standing.' He looked at Yeomans. 'What's this about a print shop, sir?'

'It needn't concern you,' replied Yeomans.

'Does it have any bearing on the murder?'

'Indirectly, it may have.'

'Then it must be the shop where Mr Paige sold his prints.'

Instead of impressing him, the glimmer of intelligence shown by Ruddock only annoyed Yeomans. Downing his drink with a loud gulp, he handed the empty tankard meaningfully to the younger man and Hale followed suit. With a smile of resignation, Ruddock went off to buy another pint for each of them.

'Don't be too hard on him,' advised Hale. 'He's eager to help.'

'Then why did he come back empty-handed?'

'You heard him, Micah. People were holding something back. That means they're hanging on to information in the hope that they can squeeze more money out of us. I'll shake the truth out of them, be assured of it. As for that print shop,' he went on, 'are you certain that you wouldn't prefer *me* to go instead of you?'

'Why, in hell's name, should you do that?'

'I'm only trying to save you the embarrassment.'

'What embarrassment?'

'I had the feeling that one of the prints in that window upset you.'

'They *all* upset me,' roared Yeomans, 'because they're an affront to decent people. What appals me most is that the shop is owned by a woman. It's shameful that she should brazenly sell those prints in the knowledge that they'll spread their poison far and wide. It's iniquitous.'

'What do we know of Mrs Mandrake?'

'I know all I need to know. She's no better than a whoremonger.'

'I'd be interested to meet her.'

'Leave that task to me,' said Yeomans. 'I have a way with women.'

'Are you going to arrest her or simply put the fear of God into her?'

'I'm going to make her tell me everything there is to tell about Paige. She's been his accomplice all this while. Mrs Mandrake should be able to give me vital intelligence.'

They chatted for a few minutes then broke off as Ruddock arrived with a full tankard of ale in each hand. As he set them down on the table, he got no thanks.

'I've been thinking,' he said. 'How do we beat off our rivals?'

'What are you mumbling about?' asked Hale.

'Peter and Paul Skillen have caught wind of this murder.

What's to stop them solving the crime before we do?'

'We have an army of informers who usually catch the first whiff of any serious crime,' said Yeomans. 'That means we'll have access to evidence that the Skillen brothers will never even see.'

'Yet they always seem to have success,' argued Ruddock. 'How do they manage that?'

'It's Peter Skillen's doing,' said Hale, glumly. 'He has the most amazing luck.' A thought struck him. 'Or maybe it's Paul Skillen who's blessed with good fortune. After all, he was lucky enough to ensnare that beautiful actress whose name was always in the newspapers. Only a man with the luck of the devil could manage to do that. Then again,' he added, 'Paul rarely had much success at the card table so maybe it was Peter Skillen, after all, who brings in the good luck.'

'It's not a question of luck,' growled Yeomans. 'Solving crimes is a question of skill and experience and we have more of both than the Skillens. That's why *we* are charged with solving this murder. They are mere interlopers. Forget about them, Ruddock. In a case like this, we know how to identify the right people and ask the right questions. Peter and Paul Skillen, meanwhile, will be running around in circles. When we've put the killer behind bars, they'll still be groping in the dark.'

It was a paradox. Jem Huckvale had prayed that he'd one day be able to spend time alone with Meg Rooke yet, now that it had actually happened, he was tongue-tied and unable to enjoy her company. She, by contrast, showed no embarrassment at all, treating him like any other guest and doing her best to put him at his ease. The most agonising moment for Huckvale was when she lifted the bed sheets to peer under the bed in order to find if the chamber pot had been used. Seeing that it was empty, she gave him a smile and left the room. Huckvale's cheeks were on fire. Proximity to someone he cared for had strict limits for him. Much as he adored the servant, he was not prepared to share the secrets of his bodily functions with her. He resolved instead to pay an occasional visit to the privy in the yard, no matter how painful the journey there and back. The suffering involved would pale beside what he'd already endured in terms of shame.

When there was a knock on the door, he braced himself against Meg's return but, in fact, it was Charlotte who sailed into the room.

'How are you, Jem?' she asked, crossing to the bed.

'I think that I'm on the mend now.'

'You certainly have more colour than when you first arrived. Is Meg looking after you properly?'

'Oh, yes, she's in and out all the time.'

'She said that you ate most of the meal we sent up. Had you been able, we'd have invited you to join us in the dining room.'

'Thank you, Mrs Skillen.'

'But you need to stay up here and rest.'

'I thought I heard the front door opening a while ago.'

'Paul was just leaving,' she explained. 'He was going back to the gallery to see if Gully had anything to report.'

'Why – what has he been doing?'

'He's been trying to turn the tables on your attacker, Jem.

We know that *he* must have kept watch for a bodyguard to come out. According to Gully, he'd have been out there for some time because Mr Paige had a long story to tell. The chances are, therefore, that someone noticed the man lying in wait for you.'

'But there were *two* men – the one who followed Mr Paige and the one who tried to knock my brains out.'

'Then someone may have noticed *both* of them,' she said, hopefully. 'If they loitered together, they'd be more likely to arouse curiosity.'

Huckvale was pleased. 'We have good friends who live or work near the gallery,' he said. 'If anyone behaved suspiciously, they'd be seen. Thank you so much for telling me. It's really lifted my spirits.'

He made the mistake of sitting up quickly in bed, only to set off the pounding of a sledgehammer inside his head. Holding him gently by the shoulders, Charlotte eased him against the pillows. She could see the anguish and frustration in his eyes.

'I know you want to be involved, Jem,' she said, 'but you're simply not well enough.'

'But I may be well enough to get up tomorrow.'

'I won't hear of it. You must listen to medical advice. Peter, Paul and Gully will find the killer somehow. All you have to do is to enjoy a life of leisure.' Huckvale grimaced. 'Yes, I know it's against your nature to lie there and do nothing but Meg is only a tinkle on that bell away from you.' Charlotte smiled. 'She'll help you to stave off boredom.'

* * *

Though it was late evening, the streets were full of people and horse-drawn traffic. As he walked along, Paul Skillen heard the familiar tumult and inhaled the familiar stink of London. Neither had existed when Hannah Granville had been there. Her presence in the city seemed to banish both its abiding clamour and its cloying stench. Now that she was on the other side of the Channel, he was made brutally aware once more of the capital's shortcomings. With a supreme effort, he put Hannah out of his mind and thought about the task in hand. He was soon entering the shooting gallery.

'Did you have any luck, Gully?' he asked.

'I hope so,' replied the other. 'It was a costly business.'

'What do you mean?'

'Well, as you know, it was market day. The traders were outside in the street. When their work was done, some of them went straight to the White Hart to slake their thirst. That's where I found Quint.'

'Is he that fishmonger?'

'You'd be left in no doubt about that, Paul. Get within a yard of him and the smell is enough to make your toes curl. However, he keeps his wits about him and was far more use than any of the others.'

'What did he tell you?'

'When I'd bought his ale,' said Ackford, 'he remembered two men lurking outside the gallery around the time when Leo Paige was in here. They pretended to look at items in the market but their real interest was in this place.'

'And did Quint remember what these men looked like?'

'Yes, he did – but only after I'd jogged his memory with a second pint. Once he'd taken a first mouthful of that, he described both of them. One was a young man dressed like a costermonger and wearing a wide-brimmed hat pulled down over his face. He sounds very much like the person that Jem followed.'

'What about the other, Gully?'

'Quint had a better look at him. He was somewhat older and had the air of the sailor about him. The fishmonger spends all his time among sailors so I'd rely on his judgement. The man had a flat face, a broken nose and a rough beard. He was wearing an old coat, dark breeches and a battered hat.'

'At least, we know *something* about the two rogues.'

'We may know enough to put a name to one of them,' claimed Ackford. 'When you came in, I was just about to go through Charlotte's record book.'

'Don't let me stop you,' said Paul with rising interest. 'When she first suggested keeping it, I wasn't at all sure of the value of that book, but Charlotte's rogues' gallery has proved its worth time and again.'

The record book contained a description of every criminal with whom they came into contact. In some cases – where Charlotte had seen them in court – she'd even been able to draw a sketch of them. Her portraits of some villains adorned the book. When they were hunting for particular characters, Gully and the Skillen brothers frequently made use of the record book. As well as a physical description of someone, it often contained a list of his favourite haunts and criminal associates. Had the man served a prison sentence, it was duly noted. While the book was predominantly a male preserve, there were some female malefactors as well.

'Let's have a look,' said Ackford, sitting to the table and opening the book.

Paul watched over his shoulder. 'We must have dozens of sailors in there. When they come ashore after a long voyage, they always get drunk and search for women or start an affray.'

'I know. One crew wrecked the Hope and Anchor in Thames Street. The landlord turned to us for help. We rounded up the ringleaders next day and hauled them before a magistrate.'

'Charlotte made a sketch of them somewhere.'

Ackford turned over a page and ran his eye down the list of names. Charlotte might be no artist but she had enough talent to catch the salient features of a person.

'Ah,' said Ackford, jabbing a finger down, 'here's our first broken nose.'

'You'll find plenty of those among sailors, Gully. Who is this fellow?'

'It doesn't matter. We can discount him straight away. He died years ago. We even know where his funeral was held.' He looked up. 'That raises the question of Leo's funeral.'

'Someone has already volunteered to pay for that, Gully. It's the lady who runs the print shop where Mr Paige sold his wares. She told Peter that she would meet all the expenses.'

'That's uncommonly kind of her.'

'Evidently, she was very fond of him.'

Ackford grinned. 'A lot of women were, Paul. In his younger days, Leo had great charm and, like any soldier, he took his pleasure where he found it. If he'd ever written his life story, most readers, I fancy, would have been scandalised.'

'From what Peter said about her, the lady who sold his prints is far more likely to cause a scandal than to be upset by one. He described her as a woman of the world,' said Paul. 'Well, you can make up your own mind about her. Mrs Mandrake has put herself forward as our assistant.'

Ackford was startled. 'Our *assistant*, did you say? Would she willingly place herself in jeopardy?'

'Nothing would deter her, by all accounts.'

'I don't like the notion. I have grave doubts about relying on a woman.'

'Yet you're doing so at this very moment,' Paul pointed out. 'When you picked up that record book, you were relying on Charlotte. Without it, we'd have gone from case to case without building up an archive. In listing all the villains who've crossed our paths, Charlotte has given us a useful weapon. Let's use it to the full. As for Mrs Mandrake,' he continued, 'we can leave her to her own devices.'

Diane Mandrake had just finished adjusting her hair in a mirror when she heard the rapping on the door. Since it was well before opening time, she was irritated by the disturbance. Cocking an ear from which a diamond earring dangled, she listened to the sound of the door being unlocked and to a muffled conversation. The voice of Benjamin Tite eventually came up the stairs.

'You have a visitor, Mrs Mandrake,' he called.

'Who is it?'

'His name is Mr Yeomans and he's a Bow Street Runner.'

'Has he brought a warrant with him?'

'He merely wishes to ask you some questions.'

'Show him into the back room and stay with him. I don't want a Runner poking about among my treasures.'

Diane deliberately kept her visitor waiting before she deigned to descend the stairs. She entered the room in a regal manner. Tite introduced Yeomans then, in response to a nod from his employer, he scuttled off into the shop. She peered at the Runner.

'I've seen you before somewhere,' she said.

Yeomans was firm. 'I think not.'

'How can you be so sure?'

'I'd never forget meeting a lady of distinction such as you,' he said with a doomed attempt at gallantry. When she ignored the compliment, he surged on. 'I've come to talk about Mr Paige. You'll be aware of his death, I daresay.'

'I am indeed, sir,' she replied, plucking a handkerchief from her sleeve and dabbing at her eyes. 'It was a profound shock and I may never recover from it.'

'I want you to help me find the killer.'

'How can I do that, Mr Yeomans?'

'Just answer my questions and all will become clear.'

She studied him. 'I *do* think I've seen your face before, you know.'

'It must have been someone else, Mrs Mandrake.'

Having arrived with the intention of grilling her, Yeomans was taken aback by her striking appearance and by the bewitching odour of her perfume. He'd raided many brothels in his time and arrested many a procuress. Although he'd used

76

the word of her, Diane Mandrake could never be described as a whoremonger. Clearly, she was a gracious woman with a quality he found instantly alluring. Instead of berating her for selling satirical prints, he found himself apologetic and deferential.

For her part, she'd taken an instant dislike to him. Peter Skillen had been kind, considerate and gentlemanly. Yeomans could not compare with him. While she was prepared to help Peter in every way, therefore, she saw no reason to give any practical assistance to a Runner. She had clashed with too many representatives of law and order in the past to have any respect for them. With her visitor, therefore, she decided that her best plan was to act more like a grieving widow.

'How well did you know Mr Paige?' asked Yeomans.

'I knew him very well, sir, and loved him dearly.'

'You must have realised that his prints would upset certain people.'

'They upset some and delighted others. I was one of the latter.'

'The *Parliament of Foibles* caused untold dismay in certain quarters. To a man, politicians condemned the series for its cruelty.'

'Nobody likes to have their faults pointed out, Mr Yeomans.'

The handkerchief came into play again and she pretended to weep into it. When she'd dabbed at her eyes, she indicated that he should continue. He began his tentative interrogation. Yeomans asked many of the questions that Peter Skillen had first put to her. While she'd given straightforward replies to him, she was far more evasive with her visitor, either misleading him on purpose or simply pleading ignorance. Enthralled by her at the start, Yeomans became disconcerted that he was getting so little help. At the same time, however, he didn't wish to upset someone who – to his eyes, at least – was so obviously in mourning. Having gathered all the information he felt he could, he glanced towards the shop.

'Turning to another matter,' he said, casually, 'I couldn't help noticing one of the prints in your window when I happened to pass by yesterday. It was the work of Mr Paige, as it happens, and he'd drawn a good likeness of Sir Humphrey Coote.'

'I remember the print well, Mr Yeomans.'

'It's no longer in the window, I see.'

'No, that's true. It's not for sale.'

'There were other copies, surely?'

'They were all sold. It was one of Virgo's most successful prints.'

Yeomans goggled. Having hoped to buy up her entire stock of the drawing that lampooned him, he had the discomfort of knowing that several people had already purchased copies and would be sniggering happily at both Coote and him. He was shaken to the core. Yet he could not bring himself to blame Diane Mandrake because she still held a strange fascination for him. She was merely a conduit between Paige and his admirers. One hope remained for him.

'You say that the last print is not for sale, Mrs Mandrake.'

'It will be given as a gift to someone.'

'You'll get no payment for it, then?'

'I wish for none, sir.'

'What if someone offered you double the price?'

'My answer would be the same. I would not sell.'

'Even you would part for it if I was prepared to give you *three* times its original value,' said Yeomans, squirming inwardly at his financial recklessness. 'Nobody who runs a business could refuse such a bargain.'

'It smacks of desperation to me,' she said, crisply. 'Why are you impelled to spend so much on a single print?'

'It . . . aroused my interest, that's all.'

What he didn't tell her was that, in buying it, he would at least take one print out of circulation. Had he been able to buy every copy, he felt, he could silence the crude jeers that would come his way. Another possibility nudged him.

'Might the person who receives it from you be tempted to part with it on very favourable terms?'

She was shocked. 'That's a monstrous idea, Mr Yeomans.'

'Why is that?'

'Are you married, sir?' He nodded dolefully. 'Imagine how you would feel if you bestowed a gift on your wife and she sold it for three times the cost? I can't think that that would be conducive to marital harmony. Do you agree?'

'I do,' he confessed.

She fixed her gaze on him. 'Ah, of course,' she went on as realisation dawned. 'I have it now. *That's* where I must have seen you before. In that self-same print, Sir Humphrey Coote occupies the foreground but someone looking remarkably like you is in the background.'

'I never noticed that,' he lied.

'Then why show such an interest in the print?'

He smiled weakly. 'It . . . caught my imagination, that's all.'

'It did the same to someone else,' she told him. 'When he

was here yesterday, he rhapsodised about the *Parliament of Foibles*. That's why I'm presenting him with the last copy of that print. He loved it for its wit and ruthlessness.'

'Those were not the qualities that I detected.'

'Yet you are two of a kind, Mr Yeomans.'

'In what way, may I ask?'

'Like you, he came in search of information about Leo Paige.'

'Really,' he said, stiffening. 'What would his name be?'

'Peter Skillen.'

His mortification was complete.

On the previous evening, they'd gone to the White Hart in search of him but – though he'd left strong aromatic memories of his visit – the fishmonger was no longer there. Since they had no idea where he lived, they had to bide their time until the following morning. Gully Ackford had to stay at the gallery so Paul Skillen walked down to the river alone. The early morning catch was being unloaded and Simon Quint was haggling over prices with some fishermen. He was a short, bustling, round-shouldered man in his fifties. Paul knew him by sight and had often eaten fish bought from him. With the record book under his arm, he approached the man.

'I'd like a minute of your time,' he began.

'My time is money, sir,' said Quint, eyeing him carefully. 'I *know* you, I think. You work at the shooting gallery.'

'That's correct. Mr Ackford spoke to you last night, I'm told.'

'He did, sir, and he was kind enough to buy my ale.'

'You'll have money to buy even more if you help me,' said

Paul, securing his attention instantly. 'You described two men who were standing outside our gallery yesterday.'

'I never forget a face,' boasted the other.

'Then let me show you a few sketches. When I do so, mark you, I want an honest answer. If you try to fob me off with a lie in order to get your reward, I'll knock the daylights out of you and throw you in the river. One of the men you saw was involved in a vicious assault and a foul murder.' He squeezed the man's shoulder hard enough to make him wince. 'Do you understand what I'm saying?'

Quint yelped. 'Yes, sir, I do.'

'Then say nothing until you're absolutely sure.'

Paul opened the record book and flipped through the pages, stopping at one with three of Charlotte's drawings on it. After staring at each one, Quint shook his head. Paul turned over the page and got the same result. He went patiently through some other examples of his sister-in-law's art until he came to one showing a man with a misshapen nose in the middle of a flat face fringed with a ragged beard.

Quint stared at it for a long time then shook his head. As Paul was about to turn the page, the fishmonger stopped him and took a second protracted look at the latest sketch. Paul could sense him hovering.

'Don't give me a wild guess,' he warned. 'I want certainty. Is that the man you saw lurking at the market yesterday?'

'Yes,' said Quint after a pause. 'It's those eyes of his that give him away. They're too far apart. There's room for a third between that pair. He was *definitely* one of the men I saw yesterday.'

'Thank you.'

Paul was elated. After pressing a few coins into the fishmonger's hand, he walked back to the gallery with a spring in his step. They'd made progress.

They had a name.

CHAPTER SIX

Peter Skillen studied the five names on the list and wondered
if the person they were after was not among them at all. The
list was the fruit of the collective trawl that he, his wife and his
brother had made through copies of *Paige's Chronicle*. It had been
a lengthy process because they kept breaking off to read out to
each other passages that had made them laugh uncontrollably.
The five people they'd isolated were those most regularly under
attack in the newspaper and therefore the people most likely
to want retribution. Peter had been the final arbiter since his
knowledge of the political scene was comprehensive. He and
Charlotte went through the list once more.

'Sir Humphrey Coote must be the leading contender,' he
decided. 'He was reviled in the *Chronicle* and in the *Parliament
of Foibles*.'

'Can he really be the rake that he's portrayed?'

'It's common knowledge.'

'Is there no Lady Coote to keep him under control?'

'It's difficult to subdue a goatish husband when you live in the depths of the Yorkshire countryside, my love, and Lady Coote rarely comes to London.'

'His behaviour is outlandish.'

'Sir Humphrey is a master of indiscretion, Charlotte. While most men try to hide their peccadilloes, he glories in them.'

'Yet he takes offence when they're voiced abroad in a newspaper.'

'I suspect that the depiction of him hurt the most. He's rather vain about his appearance but his physical shortcomings were exposed brilliantly by Virgo.'

Charlotte was puzzled. 'Who *is* the man, Peter?'

'Perhaps you are asking the wrong question, my love.'

'Oh? Please explain.'

'What if the artist is a *woman*?'

'That's impossible.'

'I don't think so. There *are* female artists. I married one, did I not?'

'I could never draw anything as lewd as that,' she said. 'I lack both the skill and the desire.' She heard the noise of movement above her head. 'It sounds as if Meg has taken up Jem's breakfast.'

'Has he found the courage to speak to her yet?'

'No, he just gazes at her in wonderment.'

'I used to do the same to you, Charlotte.'

'Do you mean that you've *stopped*?' she scolded. 'At what point in our marriage did my charm start to fade?'

'It shines as bright as ever,' he said, kissing her softly on the cheek. 'Now that we have five prime suspects, we must discuss ways to tackle each one of them. You, meanwhile, can nurse Jem back to health.'

'He's already improved a little, Peter. I heard him get up in the night.'

'Are you sure? He could hardly move yesterday.'

'I couldn't sleep for some reason. There was no mistaking the sound of his door opening or of footsteps dragging past our bedchamber. I'd half a mind to get up and see where he was going.'

'Well, it wasn't to Meg's room,' he said, jocularly, 'because he has neither the strength nor the boldness. Besides, Meg shares a bed with Sarah and no man would dare to climb in beside *her*.' He stepped back to avoid a dig in the ribs. 'That was unkind. I take it back.' He looked upwards. 'So where *was* Jem going?'

'Take the trouble to ask him before you leave.'

'I will – and I'll also tell him about the five names we've picked out. One of those grand gentlemen might well have ordered the murder of Mr Paige and, as a result, turned Jem into an incidental casualty. He'll be cheered by our diligence.'

'Have you told him about your visit to the print shop?'

'I haven't dared.'

'Why ever not?'

'I don't think he's ready for Mrs Mandrake yet,' said Peter. 'She's a potent lady. Because he's helpless in the company of the fairer sex, Jem has trouble coping with a pretty little servant like Meg. Frankly, someone like Mrs Mandrake would terrify him.'

'What's his name, Paul?' asked Ackford.

'Abel Fearon.'

'How certain was the fishmonger?'

'It took him time,' recalled Paul, 'but he was convinced in the end. Fearon was one of the sailors involved in that brawl at the Hope and Anchor. They caused so much damage that the inn was closed for repairs for almost a week.'

'I remember it well.'

In a break between lessons, Ackford had joined Paul in the office and was looking at the sketch of the man singled out by Quint. Since the fishmonger would be back with his cart on the next market day, his word could be trusted. If it was deliberately false, Paul simply had to cross the road to remonstrate with him in public and Quint would not wish that to happen. Ackford looked at the notes Charlotte had made beneath the drawing. There was a brief description of the sailor and of his crime. Arrested by them as one of the ringleaders in the affray, Abel Fearon had been convicted and sent to prison with his shipmates. Ackford noted the length of his sentence.

'By rights, he should still be languishing under lock and key,' he said. 'I can't believe that he escaped from Newgate.'

'There are other means of getting out of prison, Gully.'

'He'd hardly have enough money to buy his freedom.'

'Someone with influence might have intervened.'

'Why?'

'Because Fearon might be useful to him,' suggested Paul. 'If you wanted to hire an assassin, Newgate would be a good place to start looking for one. Prisoners will do anything to get out of that hellhole. All that we have to do is to track Fearon down and discover whose creature he is.'

Ackford grinned. 'If only it was as easy as that!'

'I've just had another thought. Fearon may have seized the chance to kill two birds with one stone, so to speak. He knew that we were responsible for his arrest and conviction and was aware that we operated from the gallery. When he stood outside, he must have been burning with resentment at what we'd done to him.'

'I see what you mean, Paul. In that brutal attack on Jem, he was getting revenge on us. If you or I had acted as Leo's bodyguard yesterday, we'd have been the victims instead. Fearon had a score to settle.'

'*We* have one of those now, Gully.'

There was a sharp tap on the door and it opened wide for the ample figure of Diane Mandrake to step into the room. When she saw Paul, her face lit up at once.

'There you are, Mr Skillen,' she said, crossing over to him and thrusting a package into his hands. 'I've brought you a gift.'

Paul blinked. 'What have I done to deserve this?'

'Open the present and you will understand.'

'You must be confusing me with someone else.'

She nudged him. 'Stop teasing me, Mr Skillen. How could I ever forget someone as handsome and debonair as your good self? Were you not in my shop only yesterday?' Both men laughed. 'I'm not aware that I made a jest,' she protested.

'Let me explain,' said Ackford. 'You, I take it, are Mrs Mandrake?'

'I am, indeed, but Peter here should have recognised me at once.'

'Peter would assuredly do so but this is his twin brother, Paul.'

She was amazed. 'There are *two* of you?' she exclaimed, looking at Paul. 'You are the image of him in every particular. That being the case,' she continued, taking the package from him, 'I'll wait until I meet your brother.'

'He's probably on his way here even now, Mrs Mandrake,' said Paul. He indicated his friend. 'Let me introduce you to Gully Ackford, who owns the shooting gallery.' She greeted Ackford warmly. 'And I apologise for the lack of comfort here. This is not the sort of place you'd ever be likely to visit.'

'On the contrary,' she said, whipping the pistol out of her reticule, 'it is the ideal establishment in which to practice. I am, as you see, prepared for trouble.'

As she pointed the weapon at each of them in turn, they stepped back warily.

'Is it loaded?' asked Paul.

'Why else should I carry it?' She put it away in the reticule. 'I came to offer what help I can. Employ me as you think fit. I'll not shrink from danger.'

Impressed by her vigour and determination, they nonetheless had doubts about her abilities in a murder investigation. Selling satirical prints was hardly the ideal preparation for a possible confrontation with a killer. If they were concerned for her safety, Paul and Ackford feared that they'd be distracted. Charlotte was an important member of the team, and her record book alone justified her place among them, but she never ventured into a hazardous situation. She worked quietly and effectively in the background and that was something Diane Mandrake was manifestly unready to contemplate. She intended to be at the heart of the action.

As the two men sighed inwardly, she proved that she did, after all, have something useful to contribute. Holding up the package, she cackled with joy.

'The gift is a print that Peter admired in my window,' she explained. 'It's a drawing that features Sir Humphrey Coote, a Member of Parliament with a roving eye. Imagine my surprise, then, when someone comes into my shop this morning, fires endless questions at me, then tries to buy this print off me for three times its price. I wouldn't sell it for ten times its value,' she insisted. 'It has Peter Skillen's name writ indelibly upon it.'

Paul was interested. 'You say that someone came to question you?'

'Did he ask about Leo Paige?' said Ackford.

'What did you tell him, Mrs Mandrake?'

'I told him nothing of any use to him,' she said, 'but, then, I've no time for Bow Street Runners. This one was especially objectionable. I discovered the perfect way to get rid of him,' she added, gleefully. 'I simply mentioned Peter's name.'

The ale went down so quickly and smoothly that Yeomans did not even taste it. Slumped over a table at the Peacock Inn, he was in a state of depression that bordered on despair. He had never met anyone like Diane Mandrake. Her effect on him had been extraordinary. Feelings that had lain dormant for many years had suddenly been rekindled. He had long since looked for any happiness in his marriage. The endless hours he spent on duty meant that he saw little of his wife and children. They were very much in the hinterland of his life. Out of the blue, he'd now met a woman who reminded him of long-forgotten pleasures and aroused a desire that caused a nagging unease. Since she sold satirical prints, Mrs Mandrake was, by definition, a person he should detest and harass. Yet he was moved to protect her. Even though she'd stuck a knife in his heart when she told him that the print he sought would go to Peter Skillen, he couldn't condemn her. When he'd stepped into her shop, he'd been a conscientious Runner about to demand answers to important enquiries. At a stroke, she'd robbed him of his bristling self-confidence and made him unnervingly vulnerable. The irony of it all was that, in her brusque treatment of him, she'd made herself even more irresistible.

Confused, dispirited and tormented by a vision of Diane Mandrake, he could do nothing but sit there and suffer in silence. When he was joined by Hale and Ruddock, he was so locked into his reverie that he had to be forcibly shaken out of it.

'What are you doing?' he shouted, brushing Hale's hand off his shoulder. 'Don't you dare to touch me like that again, Alfred.'

'You were miles away,' said Hale.

'Then you should have waited patiently.'

'Did you learn anything at the print shop, sir?' asked Ruddock, recoiling slightly when Yeomans turned a murderous glare upon him. 'You thought that it would provide you with some important evidence.'

'Shut your gob, Ruddock!'

'Well . . . if you say so, sir.'

'Speak only when you're spoken to.'

'Yes, Mr Yeomans.'

'Chevy asked a reasonable question,' said Hale, coming

to the younger man's rescue. 'You told us you expected to get crucial intelligence from Mrs Mandrake.'

Mention of her name made Yeomans leap a few inches out of his chair as if he'd suddenly realised that it was covered in sprigs of holly. When he sat down again, he made an effort to master his emotions.

'I gathered some useful information,' he explained, 'but I may have to return to the shop again at some point.'

'It's a pity we can't close the place down altogether. Mrs Mandrake and her kind are nothing but excrescences.'

Yeomans bunched a fist. 'Don't you dare call her that, Alfred!'

'I've heard you use the same word of dealers such as her.'

'Mrs Mandrake is a lady. Treat her with respect.'

'Only yesterday, you called her a whoremonger.' Seeing the look in Yeomans's eye, Hale held up apologetic palms. 'I'll never describe her as such again, I promise. You have met the woman – the lady, I should say – whereas we have not.'

'If you have changed your mind about Mrs Mandrake,' said Ruddock, 'does that mean you think more kindly of the murder victim? Must we treat Mr Paige with respect as well?'

'No,' barked Yeomans, 'we must not. I don't give a trooper's turd for Paige. I'm very glad that he was killed and I wish the same fate on those like him. But the murder must be solved and it falls to us to solve it.'

'We've not been idle this morning,' said Hale.

'How many heads have you knocked together?'

'More than I can remember, Micah. The first person we tackled again was Mokey Venables. I was much harsher on him than Chevy.'

'You boxed his ears,' said Ruddock.

'It helps to clear the brain. Mokey gave us names of people we'd never heard of before, obnoxious maggots who infest Bloomsbury and know its darkest corners. We paid several of them a visit. One of them was very helpful.'

'His name is Dirk Poyesdon,' said Ruddock.

Yeomans glowered. 'I told you to shut your gob.'

'Then I'll let Mr Hale do the talking,' whispered the other.

'Who is this Poyesdon?'

'He works as a doorman at Doll Fortune's house,' said Hale, 'and he's used to seeing a stream of gentlemen going in and out there every night. Doll's ladies are not common trulls. They are expensive company.'

'I'm well aware of that.'

'Last night, two unlikely visitors rolled up, drunken sailors with an urge to dip their wicks into quality for a change. Poyesdon was minded to turn them away but the bribe they gave him was generous enough to get them through the door. Once inside,' Hale went on, 'they paid for the two most exclusive rooms in the house.'

'Where is this tale leading, Alfred?' asked Yeomans, impatiently.

'Hear me out. Poyesdon spoke to the two Cyprians afterwards. They'd each endured rough company. Each man had said the same. It was a day of celebration for them. They'd performed a service for someone and been handsomely rewarded. Instead of patronising the riverside brothels,' said Hales, 'they could at last afford the finest bawdy house in Covent Garden.'

'What possible use is this tittle-tattle?'

'One of them let slip *why* he was in such high spirits. He said that he was on fire because he'd enjoyed the rare thrill of actually killing someone.'

'Men always make the most stupid boasts between the sheets.'

'He frightened her, Micah, and the woman he'd bought for the night is not easily scared. She took him at his word. He left her covered in bites and bruises. She told Doll Fortune she'd never share a bed with him again at any price.'

Yeomans was suddenly interested. 'This fellow is coming back?'

'He vowed that he'd return one day this week. His friend did the same.'

'How trustworthy is this Poyesdon?'

'I think we can rely on what he told us.'

'Then we have the place watched until these two sailors roll up again.' He rounded on Ruddock. 'That's work for you.'

'I can't stand outside a brothel all night,' complained the other. 'I'm a married man. What will my wife say?'

'She'll think you were stupid to tell her in the first place – and so do we.'

'Micah and I are both married,' said Hale, 'and we've done more than our share of standing guard outside houses of ill repute.'

'Then you're much more experienced,' urged Ruddock.

'It's your turn now, lad. It will be an education for you.'

'Will I be on my own?'

'Dirk Poyesdon will be there to point the rogues out.'

Ruddock was anxious. 'What can I do against two killers?'

Yeomans laughed crudely. 'I can see that you've never been inside a place like that, Ruddock. When they've drunk their fill and taken their pleasure, this pair will barely have the strength to stagger off to their lodging. You don't need to apprehend them at all. You simply follow them and bring us word of their whereabouts. We'll storm the place in numbers and haul them off in chains.'

'This is a big chance for you, Chevy,' said Hale, patting him on the back. 'Serve us well and you'll get a feather in your cap. As for your wife, tell her that you're being paid to stand guard over someone's valuables. There's a degree of truth in that. The ladies that Doll employs are like the Crown Jewels to her.'

'I don't believe it!' cried Diane Mandrake, clapping her hands. 'It's remarkable. You are like two peas in a pod.'

When he arrived at the gallery, Peter Skillen stood beside his brother and she was unable to tell them apart until she scrutinised them more carefully. There was a contented quality about Peter that spoke of a happily married man. Paul, on the other hand, seemed more lonely and unsettled. With no more ado, she handed the package to Peter and waved away his protests. When he opened it, he saw that he was holding the print that featured Sir Humphrey Coote. Peter burst out laughing and showed it to his brother and to Ackford, pointing out the figure of the Runner in the background. Both men shook with mirth.

'You obviously recognised Micah Yeomans?' said Peter.

'I did so instantly,' said Ackford.

'And so did I,' added Paul. 'I can see why he wanted to buy

this print from the shop. It portrays him as the bloated fool he is.'

'I couldn't wait to get him out of my shop,' said Diane. 'He thinks that Leo Paige was the artist and I didn't disillusion him. Why should I? Let him think that Virgo is lying on a slab at the morgue.'

'Your reminder is timely, Mrs Mandrake,' said Ackford. 'I must find a moment to pay my respects to my old friend.' A bell rang outside. 'That will be Mr Cordery ready to test my mettle in the boxing ring again.'

After excusing himself, he went out of the office and left her to marvel again at the brothers. Peter offered to pay for the drawing but she refused to take any money. The fact that he and the others had sworn to hunt down Paige's killer was reward enough to her.

'Thank you so much for this,' said Peter. 'This will be treasured. Thanks, also, for those copies of *Paige's Chronicle*. It afforded us endless amusement.'

'More to the point,' said Paul, 'they gave us names to ponder.'

'I have the list here.' Peter produced a sheet of paper from inside his coat and showed it Diane. 'You'll know these august gentlemen because they've all been portrayed in your prints.' She looked at the five suspects. 'Well? Which of these men is most likely to engage an assassin?'

'All five of them, I'd say,' she replied. 'Wait, I'd draw the line at Lord Elphinstone. I know that he's a grasping landlord but he's also a man of delicate sensibilities. He'd never be party to a murder.'

'That reduces the number to four, then.'

'One moment,' said Paul, 'there's something that neither of

you know as yet. It may well make you look at those names somewhat differently.'

He told them about Ackford's conversation with the fishmonger and how the man had been shown the record book that morning. Thanks to Charlotte's deft skills, Quint had been able to pick out one of the men waiting outside the gallery while Paige was inside. They now had both a name and a description of him.

'That's a wonderful discovery,' said Diane with delight. 'All that we have to do is to link this man, Fearon, with one of the people on this list.'

'That won't be easy,' warned Paul. 'There are over a million people in this city. Trying to find one man among a population like that could take a long time. And don't forget,' he continued, 'that we need to look for Fearon's accomplice as well, and we have no idea who he is.'

'What can I do, Mr Skillen?'

'There's not much that I can suggest, to be honest.'

'But I want to be *used*.'

'Then there's something that would be helpful,' said Peter. 'You've told me a great deal about Mr Paige, I know, but there are probably small details that have been overlooked so far. The more we learn about his life and habits, the better we'll be able to understand why he was the target of an assassin. His landlord told Paul that only three people ever visited the house,' he remembered. 'There was an older woman, a younger one and a tall, straight-backed man with the look of a soldier.'

'I can identify two of them, Peter. The old lady was the widow of a friend of Leo's. Whenever she needed money, he gave her a little. He was kind-hearted to a fault. As for the younger woman,' she said, striking pose, 'you are looking at her. I may not be in the full flush of youth but, apparently, I seemed so beside the widow.'

'That leaves the soldier,' said Paul. 'Who is he?'

'The likelihood is that he's an old comrade of Paige's,' said Peter. 'Did he ever mention this friend to you, Mrs Mandrake?'

'No,' she replied. 'All I can tell you is that Leo only let three of us know where he was living. I've accounted for two of us. The third is a mystery.'

Tall, gaunt and upright, the man had a long, urgent stride that belied his age. When he came to a corner, he took the precaution of stopping to look in every direction. Reassured that nobody was watching him, he marched on briskly until he came to the house. There was a disturbing amount of debris on the ground and, when he looked up, he saw that the pane of glass was missing from the bedchamber at the front of the house. He used the knocker to rouse the occupants. Gregory Lomas opened the door. Recognising the visitor, he gave a gesture of despair.

'Is he at home?' asked the man.

'No, sir, and he's never likely to be here again.'

'Why not – has he moved his lodging?'

'He no longer has need of one, sir.'

'Stop talking in riddles, man.'

'Mr Paige is dead,' explained the landlord, 'and not of natural causes, alas. He was murdered here only yesterday and his room was set alight.'

The newcomer was shocked. 'Who killed him?'

'Some villain strangled him to death.'

'But he was going to employ a bodyguard. He swore that he would.'

'There was nobody protecting him yesterday, sir.'

'And you say that there was a fire?'

'It was a bad one,' replied the other. 'If it hadn't been for my neighbours, the whole place could have burnt to the ground.' Shoving him aside, the man rushed into the house and up the staircase. 'You can't do that, sir. Come back!'

Lomas went after him but he was far too slow to stop him reaching the room and flinging open the door. The visitor stood there in horror. Fire had blackened everything and ash lay everywhere. The place was uninhabitable. When the landlord came up behind him and put a hand on his shoulder, the man shrugged him off and rushed across to an old oak chest in the corner. Flinging open the lid, he looked in and saw that it was empty. He spun round to challenge Lomas.

'How did you let this happen?'

'We were not at home, sir.'

'What about the servants?'

'They'd gone to the market. Mr Paige was alone in here.'

'There was something in this chest,' said the man, pointing at it. 'Did you take it out?' Lomas shook his head. 'I want the truth, man. If you try to deceive me in any way, I'll beat you black and blue.'

'Don't hurt me, sir,' said Lomas, shrinking back. 'As God's my witness, I never touched anything of Mr Paige's. He wanted privacy and that's what we gave him. I've no idea what he kept in that chest because I never once looked in it. Who knows?' he went on, gibbering. 'Perhaps the villain who killed him took whatever was hidden in there. What was it?'

'Never you mind,' snapped the other. 'Where's the body?'

'They took it away, sir. It was in a terrible state.'

'Has anyone been here to investigate the crime?'

'Yes,' said Lomas, 'the Runners came yesterday. Before them, a stranger was here, asking all sorts of questions about Mr Paige. He never gave me his name but the Runners seemed to know who he was.'

'Go on.'

'They called him Peter Skillen.'

After a last look at the oak chest, the man brushed Lomas aside, clattered down the stairs, left the house and strode purposefully away. As he joined the main street, he was soon swallowed up in the crowd.

Drawn back to the print shop by some ineluctable force, Yeomans walked up and down Middle Row like a nervous suitor. Every time he passed it, he kept looking through Mrs Mandrake's bay window in the hope that he might catch a glimpse of her. But she never appeared. He was still debating whether to go into the shop or to walk away altogether when Benjamin Tite emerged into the street.

'Did you want something, Mr Yeomans?' he asked.

'No, no, I was on my way back to Bow Street.'

'If you came to see Mrs Mandrake, you'll be disappointed. She's not here.'

'Oh,' said Yeomans, head sinking to his chest. It jerked

back up again. 'Then perhaps I could speak to *Mr* Mandrake.'

'There's no such person any longer,' said Tite, sadly.

The Runner's hopes stirred. The woman he'd come to admire so fervently had no husband. Palpably, she was free and unencumbered. His long perambulation in Holborn had been more than justified. Yeomans smiled for the first time that day.

CHAPTER SEVEN

Accustomed to living solely with men, Jem Huckvale was disconcerted to be left alone in the house with nobody for company but women. The fact that they were all concerned for his health made it even more uncomfortable. Meg Rooke was the real problem. His affection for her was stronger than ever but it was replaced by diffidence and hesitation whenever she was actually close to him. What irked him most, of course, was that he was trapped in bed when there was a murder to solve and when the person who'd attacked him was still on the loose. Instead of staying as a guest at the home of Peter and Charlotte Skillen, he wanted to be involved in the hunt for the culprits. Such was his eagerness to join the others that he elected to ignore the dull ache in his head and manoeuvred himself slowly out of bed. Unsteady on his feet at first, he soon regained his balance and crossed to the chair over which his clothing had been draped. Huckvale was just about to dress himself when he heard footsteps ascending the stairs. Panic-stricken in case Meg caught him with bare feet exposed, he tried to clamber into bed again.

Instead of the usual timid knock, however, there was a resounding thud before the door swung open. Gully Ackford stepped into the room in time to see his friend pulling the bedclothes protectively up to his chest.

'You're in no danger from me, Jem,' he said, amused. 'How are you?'

'I'm bored to death.'

'What – with a comely girl like Meg at your command?'

'I want to be with you and the others.'

'There's time enough for that.'

'What's happened, Gully?'

'A great deal – some of it is bad and some of it good.' He perched on the edge of the bed. 'Let me tell you the worst news first. I've just come back from viewing Leo's body. If I hadn't been told it was him, I'd never have recognised my old friend. Fire ravages the human body in cruel ways.'

'When is the inquest?'

'It will be very soon and very short. There are no witnesses to offer evidence. The verdict is thus obvious. Leo was killed by person or persons unknown. Except,' he added with a smile, 'one of them, we believe, *is* known now.'

Huckvale was excited. 'You've put a name to him?'

'Strictly, speaking, it was Charlotte who did that. Her record book helped to unmask the rogue. It was someone we once arrested for starting an affray and causing damage to the Hope and Anchor.'

He went on to tell the full story of their discovery. It only served to make Huckvale even more eager to return to the gallery and take part in the investigation. Convinced that Abel Fearon must have been his attacker, he was desperate for a second encounter with the man. On the next occasion, however, he vowed to wreak his revenge on the former sailor. Thrilled by most of what he heard, he was jolted by the news that they had a self-appointed assistant.

'This is no work for a woman, Gully,' he said.

'Mrs Mandrake insists.'

'What can she possibly do?'

'To begin with, she can fire a gun. I let her have use of our targets and she hit them every time without any difficulty. Her real value, however, is that she knew Leo very well and is able to tell us a lot about him. When she heard that he was being stalked, it was Mrs Mandrake who badgered him into finding a bodyguard.'

'Do you mean that this lady sent him to us?'

'She didn't exactly recommend the gallery because she'd never heard of it. When he made enquiries, Leo learnt of our reputation and that's what brought him back into my life.' Ackford heaved a sigh. 'It was an all too brief reunion.'

'I've heard enough,' said Huckvale, throwing back the sheets.

'Hey, you must stay in bed, Jem.'

'Not while there's work to do. *That's* the best remedy for me.'

Ackford stood up. 'Are you sure you feel well enough?'

'I feel as if I'm at death's door, Gully, but that won't stop me doing my share.' Pulling off his nightshirt, he began to dress himself. 'I'm coming with you.'

'We certainly need more help. I have people coming for

instruction in the shooting gallery this evening. If you could handle them, it would set Peter free. He's looking after the clients at the moment.'

'What about Paul?'

'He's on the trail of Abel Fearon.'

'Where will he start?'

'In the obvious place,' replied Ackford. 'Fearon was a sailor at one time. There may be old shipmates of his who remember him. If Paul can track some of them down, he might pick up useful information about Fearon's whereabouts.'

Paul Skillen took the necessary precautions. Ordinarily, he dressed well and – since he'd befriended Hannah Granville – had taken even more notice of current fashion. His tailored elegance would be quite out of place along the wharves and in the riverside taverns. He'd be viewed with suspicion and shunned as a result. Putting on nondescript attire, he also changed his voice so that his educated vowels gave way to a rougher mode of speech. With a hat obscuring much of his face, he adopted a bold strut and headed for the Thames. In putting on a costume to play a part, he was irresistibly reminded of Hannah Granville and felt her absence keenly. She'd often complimented him on his histrionic skills and told him that he could make a living on the stage if he put his mind to it. Paul, however, was a born thief-catcher who loved the thrill of the chase. In his mind, it was a worthier profession than any other.

The river was the city's lifeline and thousands earned their living along its serpentine reaches. In the general pandemonium, languages from all over the world rang out. Wharves were teeming, cargo was loaded or unloaded, carts were trundled to and fro and crews prepared to set sail. Paul's casual enquiries along the bank were fruitless. Nobody had heard of Abel Fearon and, consequently, had no idea of his whereabouts. When he ventured into the various taverns, he had no success either. He spoke to dozens of men, all to no avail. Undeterred, he pressed on until he eventually came to the Jolly Sailor. His first impression was that jollity was in very short supply among the seafarers there. Those sitting at tables or slouched against the bar seemed more interested in rehearsing their woes than in celebrating a leisure moment with their shipmates. Paul drifted across to a stocky, bearded man with a peg leg. An unlit pipe between his teeth, the sailor sat alone in a corner. He had a solid, reliable air. In response to his greeting, Paul got no more than a nod.

'I'm looking for a friend of mine,' he began. 'I always used to find him somewhere like this if he was ashore but there's no sign of him this time. I've tried five or six taverns so far.'

'What's his name?' asked the man, watchfully.

'Fearon – Abel Fearon. Have you ever come across him?'

'Yes.'

The man glanced down at his empty tankard and Paul took the hint. He ordered two pints of ale and took a long sip of his own drink before resuming the conversation. He hoped that he'd at last found someone who could help him. He wiped his mouth with the back of his hand.

'Abel's not long out of prison,' Paul said.

'That's a pity.'

'Pity?'

'It's the best place for him.'

'Why d'you say that?'

'If he's your friend, you should already know. I sailed with him once on the *Albatross*. Every time we put into port, Fearon got into a fight. When he'd ale inside him, he was like a mad dog.'

'He's not so bad when you get to know him,' said Paul, tolerantly.

'I don't *want* to get to know him.'

'Newgate may have calmed him down. When I went there this morning, they told me they'd let him out. I thought he'd head for one of his old haunts.'

'Thanks for the warning,' said the man, removing his pipe so that he could gulp down some ale. 'If I see him coming, I'll duck out of the way.' He narrowed his lids to appraise Paul. 'You're no sailor, are you?'

'No, I'm a friend from Abel's younger days. We grew up together. When he went off to sea, I stayed working as a bricklayer. It's an honest trade and it keeps you out of trouble.'

'Why are you after that wild bastard?'

'He wrote to me,' said Paul. 'At least, he got someone else to scribble a note. Abel never learnt his letters properly.'

'He never learnt to control that foul temper either.'

'I'm in London for a few days visiting family. But I'd like to get in touch with Abel as well.' He looked around. 'Are you always in here?'

'I'm here or somewhere like it. Some taverns are like bear pits. I avoid those. I prefer a little peace while I enjoy a drink. As you can see,' he went on, indicating his wooden leg. 'My sailing

106

days are over. I like to sit and talk about old times with beached vessels like me.'

'You must pick up a lot of gossip, then.'

'There's nothing wrong with my ears.'

'Could you ask around if anyone's seen Abel Fearon?'

'I'd need talking into it,' said the man, removing the pipe to spit on the floor.

'You'd get money to buy yourself some baccy,' said Paul, 'and there'd be enough to keep yourself in ale for a while as well. All I need to know is where I might find Abel.'

'If he's that keen to see you, why doesn't he come looking for you?'

'That's what I want to ask him.'

'He doesn't sound much like a friend to me.'

'I agree but . . . well, the truth is I owe him a favour. Could you find out if anyone's seen him in the area?'

The man was reluctant. 'Maybe I could.'

'Take this,' said Paul, pressing some coins into his hand. 'There'll be more to come. I'll call in here tomorrow to see if you've had any luck. But be warned, old man,' he added, fixing him with a stare. 'I'll not be tricked. I paid for the truth. If you try to palm me off with anything else, I'll know it straight away.'

'You'll get what you asked.'

'Find him – it means a lot to me.'

'I won't make any promises.' He glanced at the money. 'Bricklaying must be a good trade if you can spare this much.' He slipped the coins into his pocket. 'Who shall I say is after him?'

'Don't give him my name. I'd like to surprise him.'

* * *

Micah Yeomans was bubbling with optimism. It was not often that he called on the chief magistrate with such feeling of elation. He had good news to report for once and was entitled to expect congratulations. But he was not merely thinking of Eldon Kirkwood. The person he really wanted to impress was Diane Mandrake and the one way that he could do that was to catch the man who'd killed her friend. If he did so, he hoped, he might overcome her patent dislike of him. The news that she was a widow had pleased him. It also explained her air of independence. In solving a murder, Yeomans felt that he would be able to win her friendship and, in time, even to begin a sly courtship. It could not be rushed. Patience was needed.

Kirkwood was about to leave his office when his visitor arrived.

'I hope that you've brought glad tidings, Yeomans,' he said.

'I believe that I have, sir.'

'You've made an arrest?'

'No,' said the Runner, 'but we may be soon in a position to do so.'

'Then you've shown commendable speed.'

'Thank you, sir.'

'Enlighten me, I pray.'

Yeomans was far too excited to be succinct. Making no mention of the work done by Hale and Ruddock, he gave a long-winded account of how he'd cornered one of his informers, heard the story about a doorman at a Covent Garden brothel and deduced that the killer was almost certainly one of the clients that night. All that they had to do, he said grandiloquently, was to bide their time until the villain and his accomplice returned.

'And is that all?' asked Kirkwood, stony-faced.

'We have, in effect, solved the murder, sir.'

'You've done nothing of the kind, you imbecile.'

'Venables is a man whose word can be trusted.'

'It's not him that worries me. It's this other fellow. How much reliance can you place on the testimony of a doorman at a bawdy house? We both know the kind of individuals who do such work – they're big and strong but blessed with few other qualities. They draw pleasure from listening to the sordid tales of the misbegotten whores who inhabit the place.'

'Doll Fortune's house is a class above any other, sir.'

Kirkwood screwed up an eye. 'How do you know that?'

'Word travels. These men had money to spend and they wanted the best.'

'If one of them was as rough and ready as you claim, I'm surprised that he was allowed through the door. As for this nonsense about committing a murder, I think it was an idle boast made by someone who wanted to shock the prostitute in whose lascivious arms he was lying at the time.'

'The evidence is inescapable, sir,' insisted Yeomans. 'Killers do behave strangely in the wake of their crimes. We've seen it happen before. They're in the grip of some frenzy. They seek excitement through drink and loose women. Such monsters have no boundaries. They get carried away. *That's* why the whore was terrified.'

'Have you spoken to her?'

'No, not yet.'

'Have you verified the doorman's story?'

'I was intending to speak to Doll herself when I leave here,' claimed Yeomans, inventing the lie in the hope of convincing

Kirkwood that he'd been thorough. 'I've no doubt that she will confirm the details.'

'You speak as if you know this disgusting abbess.'

'Our paths have crossed before, sir.'

'Are you telling me you've been *inside* this disorderly house?'

'I had to threaten her – Doll, that is – with arrest on one occasion. I'll do the same again if she refuses to help.'

'Why didn't you do that before you came here?'

'I was anxious to get the evidence to you as soon as possible.'

'But it's not evidence,' said Kirkwood, waspishly. 'It's mere hearsay, concocted by a fanciful whore who wanted to get the attention of the doorman. Enough of these unsubstantiated tales – give me *facts*, man, hard, cold, irrefutable facts that will stand up in court and secure a conviction.'

'I sense that we have the killer within our grasp,' argued Yeomans.

'What you have is a cock-and-bull story. It may not have a single grain of truth inside it. Don't bother me again until you have credible evidence.'

The Runner crumpled inwardly. In calling on the chief magistrate, he'd hoped to set in motion a train of events that would end in the capture of the killer, earn him a handsome reward, gain the unstinting approbation of Kirkwood, bolster his reputation in the criminal fraternity and, most telling of all, melt Diane Mandrake's icy disregard of him and bring her within his reach. None of that seemed likely now. As he left the room in despair, he felt that the woman on whom he'd set his heart was slipping irretrievably through his fingers.

* * *

The first thing he heard when he reached the gallery was the familiar sound of gunfire. Huckvale was delighted to be back in the safety of his home and place of work. He was finally at ease. The feeling, however, did not last long. When he went to relieve Peter Skillen of his duties, he came upon an extraordinary sight. The person firing at the target with such accuracy was not a man, as he'd expected, but Diane Mandrake. Huckvale was open-mouthed as he was introduced to her. Realising that he'd been injured while acting as Paige's bodyguard, she gushed with sympathy.

'Oh, you poor, dear fellow,' she said with maternal concern, 'you shouldn't be abroad in that state. By rights, you should be in bed with someone at hand to nurse you back to full health.'

'I'm bound to agree, Jem,' said Peter.

'I wanted to come back,' explained Huckvale. 'I can't offer instruction in fencing or boxing – still less in archery – but I can teach people how to fire a pistol properly. That will set you free.'

'Thank you. I appreciate that.'

'There's nothing you can teach *me* about using a pistol,' said Diane. 'My father was a gunsmith and I grew up helping him to test the weapons he made. Mother always thought it too unladylike a pastime but I loved it. Well, now,' she continued, 'if you spurned the attentions of Peter's servants, you won't be without someone to take care of you. I'll make it my task to act as your physician. Gully Ackford will have told you that I am to work alongside you all. Leo Paige was a very special friend of mine and I'll commit every hour of the day to the search for his killer.'

'Let's leave him for now,' said Peter, seeing that Huckvale

was positively dazed by her attention. 'Jem will soon have to deal with a client in here.'

Before she could object, he guided her out of the shooting gallery, collecting a look of gratitude from Huckvale on the way. Diane Mandrake had made a deep impression on him and it had been a blistering experience. The thought that he'd rejected the gentle care of Meg Rooke only to be enfolded in the capacious bosom of an overpowering woman made Huckvale's head throb violently. He saw trouble ahead for himself and for the investigation. While he would be under her thumb as an unwilling patient, the work of the others would be imperilled by someone with no experience of what was involved in the pursuit of dangerous criminals. On balance, he wished that he'd stayed in the comfort of a bed at Peter's house. At least he hadn't felt so threatened by female tenderness there. In returning to the gallery, he'd been too impulsive. A sense of loss welled up inside him. He missed Meg Rooke. She seemed a hundred miles away now.

The aspect of his work that Chevy Ruddock least enjoyed was the necessity of lying to his wife. She was a good, kind, loving person and he hated having to deceive her. It was necessary, however, to conceal from her the hazards of his life on foot patrol. London had a large, volatile, highly active criminal community and he moved among it every day. His latest assignment was of a slightly different order. He had to keep watch that night outside a fashionable brothel and couldn't bring himself to be honest with his wife about his unwanted duty. He therefore fell back on the kind of blatant lie that was second nature to people like Yeomans and Hale but which still had the power to disturb Ruddock. When he arrived at the appointed place in Covent Garden, he took his misgivings with him.

His vigil got off to a bad start. Rain began to fall, obliging him to move into a doorway from which he could keep the house under surveillance. From the vulgar remarks he'd heard passing between Yeomans and Hale, he believed that it was the most sinful establishment in a city that had a vast number of places serving the perverted desires of lecherous men. Coaches and carriages came at regular intervals to deposit clients at the door, where they were met, with great deference, by a big, burly man who seemed to know most of them. Ruddock could only begin to imagine what was happening inside the house. Even being so close to the place was enough to make his cheeks burn.

His attention was soon diverted by the sight of a shadowy figure, making his way along the street by dodging from doorway to doorway to keep out of the rain. Ruddock was alerted. The sailors who, reportedly, had visited the house on the previous night had done so on foot, whereas the majority of clients arrived there by private transport. Could this be the very man they were after? Was he returning for another night of bestial abandon? Ruddock had been warned simply to follow the man back to his lodging before calling on reinforcements but that was because he'd been with an accomplice before. He was now alone. If he could be arrested outside the house, it would not only spare one of its occupants a revolting ordeal, it would put more than a single feather in Ruddock's cap. Thrilled by the prospect, he drew back in the doorway and got ready to pounce.

The closer the man got, the more convinced was Ruddock that the killer was hurrying towards him. Since he had the advantage of surprise, he felt that he could overpower the man without difficulty. He could hear the footsteps getting closer and closer. Arms at the ready, he waited for the moment to strike. When the stranger finally ducked into the doorway occupied by Ruddock, he was grabbed by his shoulders and pushed hard against the pillar supporting the portico.

'You're under arrest!' declared Ruddock, stoutly.

'What, in the bowels of Christ, are you doing?' roared Yeomans.

He was released at once. The younger man gabbled his apologies.

'I thought you were going to the house, sir.'

'That's where I *am* going.'

Ruddock was shocked. 'Do you mean that you're a . . . ?' The word died on his tongue. 'Have you no respect for your marriage vows, Mr Yeomans?'

'I'm not here as a client, you fool!' snarled the other. 'I came in search of evidence. I need to speak to the doorman and converse with Doll Fortune.'

'But she's the lady who—'

'I know full well who and what she is, Ruddock. Obey your orders, man. Keep your eyes peeled for the two people who came here last night. And whatever you do,' he cautioned, 'don't try to arrest them – watch, wait and follow.'

'Watch, wait and follow,' echoed Ruddock.

'I want no more heroics from you. It will ruin my plan.'

Ruddock nodded respectfully. Without warning, Yeomans

hurried across the road to the house under observation and spoke to the doorman. Moments later, he was ushered inside. Secure in his hiding place, Ruddock was left to wonder if Yeomans was really there to seek evidence or to sample the exotic fare on offer. His cheeks began to burn with more intensity.

Peter and Paul Skillen, meanwhile, were poring over copies of the newspaper once more. Even on a second reading, they could produce a lot of smiles and chuckles. They were at Peter's house and his brother was still dressed as the bricklayer he'd claimed to be. As she came into the room, Charlotte was startled.

'Good heavens!' she exclaimed. 'Is that *you*, Paul?'

'No,' he replied, 'I'm an itinerant beggar who popped in for a meal.'

'I don't think you'd let Hannah see you looking like that.'

'She prefers you in full fig,' said Peter. 'You were at your best last year when posing as the Duke of Wellington. You've been reduced to the ranks now.'

Paul nodded. 'I'll wear any costume if it helps us to get close to Abel Fearon.' He put down his newspaper and turned to Charlotte. 'We've been taking another look at *Paige's Chronicle*.'

'I couldn't resist doing that myself,' she admitted.

'The same names keep popping up all the time.'

'I know them off by heart, Paul. Our list comprises Sir Humphrey Coote, Gerard Brunt, Julian Harvester, Dr Guy Penhallurick and Lord Elphinstone.'

'We've eliminated one of the suspects, Charlotte.'

'Oh – who is that?'

'It's the last name on your list – Lord Elphinstone.'

'It was Mrs Mandrake's doing,' explained Peter. 'She knows the fellow. For all his faults, she attests, he would never condone violence. We're able to concentrate our fire on the other four gentlemen, and now that Jem is back at the gallery, we have the freedom to do so.'

'He should have stayed here,' said Charlotte with concern.

'He's where he prefers to be, my love. At least, he was until he met Mrs Mandrake. He was horrified when she offered to mother him.'

'Meg was equally horrified when she saw Jem leave.'

'There's one advantage. You won't be woken up by the sound of him sneaking off on tiptoe to the privy in the middle of the night.'

'Let's go back to that list of suspects,' said Paul. 'I've heard of Sir Humphrey Coote and his antics before. The other names were new to me but not to Mr Paige. He had great fun lampooning them.'

'Gerard Brunt, as you've seen, is another politician,' said Peter, 'and he's best described as a man on the rise. I've met him when I've been with the Home Secretary and he struck me as the kind of oily, ingratiating parasite who's dedicated himself to the search for power. While some achieve it on merit, Brunt will only acquire it by sycophancy.'

'Dr Penhallurick is the man who intrigues me,' remarked Charlotte. 'As a medical man, he's sworn to save lives. Could he really be party to a murder plot?'

'He could if you believe the *Chronicle*. Penhallurick is physician to the high and mighty and has even been consulted by His Majesty, the Prince Regent.'

'And yet Mr Paige denounces him as a quack.'

'He must have had good cause to do so.'

'Somehow I don't see him hiring an assassin, Peter.'

'Why not?'

'Well,' she said, pensively, 'if he was minded to kill someone – and that's very much open to question – he wouldn't need to get someone else to do it. With his knowledge of poisons, he could have contrived a way to dispatch Mr Paige with a lethal concoction.'

'Poison is usually a female prerogative,' said Paul with a teasing smile. 'It all depends on how offended Dr Penhallurick was by the attack on him. If he was enraged by it, he might have wanted the victim to suffer a brutal death followed by the destruction of his papers.'

'Yes,' agreed Peter, 'we must bear the fire in mind. Someone was bent on burning anything else intended for the *Parliament of Foibles*. That's why there has to be a political connection to the murder. Penhallurick qualifies there, I suspect. He's the physician to a third of the cabinet.'

'So far we have two politicians and a highly regarded medical man. That leaves Julian Harvester. He was portrayed as a real ogre in the *Chronicle*.'

'That's rightly so, in my opinion, Paul. Harvester exemplifies the random capriciousness of the rich. When one of his tenants had the courage to defy him, Harvester not only had the man and his family driven from the estate. Out of spite, he had everyone else evicted from their tied cottages. According to the *Chronicle*,' added Peter, 'he was guilty of far worse than that. He once had a whole village moved three miles to a less desirable location because, he claimed, it spoilt his view. Think of the immense upheaval that must have caused to all those families.'

'What's the political connection this time, Peter?' asked Charlotte.

'It comes from vast inherited wealth, my love. Harvester doesn't need to sit in the House of Commons because he has a whole bevy of Members in his pocket. When he barks an order, they jump to attention.'

'Our prime suspect must remain Sir Humphrey,' asserted Paul. 'While I'm trying to find Abel Fearon, someone must go after the politician.'

'I'll take a closer look at all of them,' said Peter.'

'Isn't there something you should do first?' asked Charlotte.

'What's that?'

'Well, I can see that you're desperate to track down the killer and link him to his paymaster but there's someone you seem to have forgotten. He's a person who might be able to help you the most.'

'To whom do you refer?' asked Paul.

'I'm thinking about the man who was Mr Paige's partner – Virgo.'

Gully Ackford flopped into a chair in his office and offered up a silent word of thanks to his Maker. After hours in her company, he'd finally got rid of Diane Mandrake. While she had sterling qualities, she was oddly reminiscent of an army of occupation. In the case of Jem Huckvale, she inspired a sense of lasting panic. Her one-woman invasion of the gallery was over for one day. Ackford could relax and reflect on events. He was soon joined by Huckvale who had just seen their last client off the premises. In his hand, he was carrying a letter.

'As I was locking up,' he explained, 'I found this. There's no name on it.'

'Then I'll assume that it's for me,' said Ackford, taking the missive from him. It took only seconds to read it. 'Peter and Paul must see this immediately.'

'Why?'

'It's from Virgo.'

CHAPTER EIGHT

Micah Yeomans made a swift assessment of Dirk Poyesdon, the doorman. The latter was slow of speech and possessed of minimal intelligence but, when he told his story, it had the ring of truth to it. Yeomans was convinced that the man had almost certainly met with the murder suspect and his confederate. Bearing in mind what the chief magistrate had decreed, he went in search of additional evidence and that meant questioning Doll Fortune, the owner of the house and its alluring occupants. Though displeased to see him, she conducted him into her private domain, a large room with a beautiful Turkish carpet in it and a prevailing opulence. Half-hidden by a decorated silk screen was a daybed on which she entertained favoured clients from time to time.

Doll Fortune was the opposite in every way to Diane Mandrake. She was short, slim, sinuous and, even in her forties, had a youthful bloom that disguised her innate ruthlessness. A lover of ostentation, she wore a full-length dress of red velvet with puffed sleeves and a low décolletage that exposed enough of her perfumed breasts to command curiosity. They certainly gained the attention of Yeomans but only fleetingly. Now that he'd met Diane, all women were found wanting beside her.

'Why are you bothering me, Micah?' asked Doll, truculently.

'I need some help.'

'You know my charges. Pay up or get out.'

'Don't be so churlish, Doll.'

'If it's *my* services you seek, then you can take yourself off. I'm in a position to pick and choose and – with the greatest respect – I'd never pick and choose you.'

He smirked. 'Compliments pass sweetly among friends.'

'What are you after?'

He looked around the room. 'You've done well for yourself,' he said. 'I remember a time when you were to be seen on street corners, hawking your wares for all and sundry to buy. Then you began to haunt theatre foyers and tempt more moneyed clients. Now you have your own stable of thoroughbred mares and a growing notoriety.'

'Say what you're here for, Micah.'

'I was just remarking on how much work you had to put in on your back to fulfil your ambitions. Having built up this little empire, it would be such a shame if you had to lose it.'

'Are you threatening me?'

'I'm just reminding you of the wisdom of cooperating with the law.'

'I'm cooperating with it of my own free will. At this very moment, one of my girls is probably milking the epididymis of a senior member of the judiciary. That's how I would define

121

cooperation. It's not *my* position that's at risk – it's yours. I have access to loyal friends in high places who could have a Runner dismissed at the snap of his finger. Now be on your way, Micah. You can't afford to slake your lust here.'

'There's no need to be so harsh,' he said, adopting a conciliatory tone. 'I came for the pleasure of seeing you again and because I'm on the trail of a killer. Your doorman tells me you had some unwelcome clients last night.'

'Then he'll be lucky to keep his job. Nobody tells tales here.'

'One of your ladies did – a certain Kate Castle. I'd like to talk to her.'

'That's out of the question.'

'You're welcome to be present, Doll.'

'Kate is not even here tonight.'

'Why is that?' For the first time, she looked uneasy. 'Ah, so that's the explanation, is it? Because she was so badly mauled last night, she's not fit to work here today. That partly confirms the doorman's story. Why don't you tell me the rest of it? We want to put this man and his vile friend on the scaffold. Wouldn't you enjoy seeing the pair of them swinging in the wind?'

'I'd sit there and throw rotten fruit at them.'

'There we are, then. You and I are on the same side, Doll.'

She turned her back on him and walked around the room as she reviewed the situation. Biting her lip, she waved him to a chair and sat opposite him.

'The first thing you must know,' she began, 'is that I was not here last night. I was . . . entertaining elsewhere. Had I been on duty, those horrible men would never have crossed the threshold. They treated two of my finest girls like pieces of meat. I've seen the injuries inflicted on Kate. She won't be fit to work again for weeks.'

'Who were they?'

'All I know is what I've been told.'

Doll gave him an abbreviated account of what had taken place. It tallied very much with what the doorman had heard but included some new, disturbing details. Of their occupation, there was no doubt. The clients admitted that they were sailors, abroad after a long voyage and desperate to lie between the thighs of a warm woman again. It was only because they had full purses that they were allowed in.

'We've been regretting it ever since, Micah.'

'What if they should return?'

'The doorman has orders to turn them away – as he should have done the first time. He's in disgrace for admitting them last night and his wage will be docked. I'll not have thugs mistreating my girls.'

'Did you get a description of them, Doll?'

'All I know is that they were black-hearted bastards with no respect for the beauty of the female body. That's as much as I can tell you – except that one of them gave his name.'

'Really?' said Yeomans, excitably. 'What was it?'

'Leonidas Paige.'

It was late for someone to call. When she heard the doorbell ring, Meg Rooke was curious to see who it was. She was surprised and pleased to find Jem Huckvale standing self-consciously on the threshold.

'Oh,' she said, 'I'm so glad that you came back to us, Mr Huckvale.'

'I'm not here to stay.'

Her smile congealed. 'That's a pity.'

'May I come in?'

'Yes, yes, of course – Mr and Mrs Skillen are still up, and Mr Paul Skillen is here.' She stood back. 'You'll know where to find them.'

Huckvale removed his hat and stepped into the house. As he brushed against Meg's arm, he felt a frisson of pleasure. For her part, she was saddened to see once again the heavy bandaging around his head. According to medical advice, the injury should have kept him in bed for several days.

After tapping on the door, Huckvale opened it and went in to join the others. Charlotte rose to her feet and made the same mistaken assumption as the servant. She was disappointed to hear that he would not be staying the night.

'I only came to deliver a message,' he said.

'Then it must be an important one.'

'Gully said that it was very important. He wanted to bring it himself but I insisted on coming so that I can be part of the investigation instead of being on the outside of it.' He took the letter from his pocket. 'I don't know if I should give this to Peter or Paul. There's no name on it so Gully opened it. He said that both of you should see it at once.'

The brothers reached out their hands simultaneously. Everyone laughed. Peter withdrew his hand and nodded at his brother.

'You read it, Paul.'

'Thank you.'

Taking the letter, Paul opened it and glanced at the brief contents.

'It's from Virgo,' he revealed.

'What does he say?' asked Peter.

'He wants one of us to meet him tomorrow.'

'Then we must oblige him.'

'Gully would rather not take on the office,' Huckvale put in. 'We've a busy day at the gallery tomorrow and all I can do is to instruct people in shooting. It will have to be one or both of you.'

'We must divide our time,' said Peter. 'I'd planned to visit Sir Humphrey Coote to see what I could learn about him. After that, there are three other suspects who deserve close study.'

'It looks as if I should go, then,' said Paul. 'I'm glad to do so. Ever since we learnt that Mr Paige was not Virgo, I've wondered who the artist really was.'

'So has Mrs Mandrake.'

Paul was adamant. 'If you're suggesting that I take her with me, then I refuse point-blank. Virgo has hidden his identity very well for a long time. There's a reason for that. If he sees me arriving with someone else, he'll probably turn tail at once. It's a situation that needs careful handling.'

'Say no more, Paul. You must go alone and win his trust.'

'His or *her* trust,' Charlotte interjected.

Peter smiled indulgently. 'My wife has this weird idea that Virgo is a woman.'

'It's not that weird, Peter. In many ways, given the opportunity, we can compete on equal terms with men. It might explain why Virgo is so secretive. She prefers to hide her light under a bushel.'

'One thing is certain. He or she knows that Mr Paige has been murdered. That's why Virgo has reached out to us.' Peter turned to his brother. 'Where will the meeting take place, Paul?'

'I'm to stand outside the King's Bench Prison.'

The rain had stopped in Covent Garden but Yeomans was not even aware of it. He came out of the house in a state of heightened satisfaction. What he'd been told had, in his view, confirmed the fact that the killer had been an unwelcome client on the previous night. Only someone as evil as the man obviously was would use the name of the person he'd murdered. It was all the evidence that the Runner needed. Crossing the road, he went over to Chevy Ruddock.

'The men we're after *were* here last night,' said Yeomans.

Ruddock was suspicious. 'You were in there a long time, sir.'

'I had to speak to Doll Fortune.'

'Is that all that happened?'

'What do you mean?'

'You seem to be . . . very happy, sir.'

'I'm extremely happy, Ruddock. I got exactly what I wanted.'

The younger man said nothing but his censure was unmistakable. He was both appalled and disappointed. Thinking that Yeomans had taken advantage of what the house offered, he could not even look the older man in the eye. It was a moment of disillusion for him because he'd always admired the Runner.

Yeomans was quick to correct the younger man's misapprehension.

'You don't seriously think that . . . ? Clearly, you *do* and that's insulting to me. I would no more pay for my pleasure than I would sell my grandmother to a slave-trader. I went in there to gather evidence and – thanks to Doll Fortune – I have it. One of the men who inflicted themselves on the house last night was indeed the killer. He even had the gall to use the name of the victim as his own.'

'That's outrageous, sir.'

'It shows you the kind of person he is, Ruddock. We must catch him.'

'Yes, sir.'

'There's no guarantee that he'll return, of course,' said Yeomans, 'but we must be ready for that eventuality. You'll stay on duty until first light.'

Ruddock blanched. 'What about my wife?'

'This is no place for her. Remain here on your own.'

'I wasn't asking if she could join me, sir. I'm just wondering how I can explain why I was away all night.'

'Tell her that you were helping to rid the city of two arch-criminals.'

'She'll be expecting me back sooner than first light.'

'A wife must learn to expect you when she sees you. Mine did years ago.'

'Will you tell her that you went into a brothel tonight?' Hearing an angry growl, Ruddock spluttered an apology. 'No, no, of course not – and, in any case, it's none of my business.' Yeomans was about to turn away. 'One moment, sir,' he said. 'If

127

the suspects do turn up tonight, and if I follow them when they come out again, where can I reach you and Mr Hale?'

'The first thing you must know is that they'll be refused entry. When they're turned away, they'll be angry and disappointed so you must be careful. They may go on to another brothel, of course, in which case you'll wait and watch outside that.'

'Where will you be all this time?'

'Mr Hale and I will be at the Peacock.'

'Surely, it will be closed by then?'

Yeomans grinned. 'It's always open for us.'

Before he rode back to his own house, Paul Skillen changed back into his normal attire. He was pleased that Virgo had been in touch with them and intrigued by Charlotte's suggestion that the cartoonist might, in fact, be female. Short and explicit, the letter had been written by a graceful hand that might support the notion. It was difficult for women to make their way into certain professions and some resorted to male names in order to do so. Had a lady chosen the ambiguous name of Virgo in order to disguise her gender? Paul was anxious to find out.

Having stabled his horse, he was admitted by Timothy Crabbe, his wiry, old, manservant. Paul handed him his hat, gloves and riding crop and went into the drawing room. Holding it near the candle, he read the letter once more.

Crabbe appeared at his shoulder. 'You had a visitor earlier on, sir.'

'Who was that, pray?'

'He gave his name as Gregory Lomas.'

'Did he have a message for me?' asked Paul.

'Yes, sir, and it was an urgent one. Mr Lomas was breathless when he got here and distressed that you were not at home.'

'What did he have to report?'

'A man turned up at the house earlier to speak to Mr Paige, unaware that the gentleman had departed this life. When he was told the grim news, the caller pushed Mr Lomas aside, rushed upstairs to Mr Paige's room and searched in an oak chest. He was furious when he saw that it was empty.'

'Did Mr Lomas know the intruder?'

'Oh, yes, sir – he's been to the house before.'

'Then he must be the tall man with the aspect of a soldier.'

'That's correct, Mr Skillen. Unfortunately, he has never given his name to the landlord and nor did Mr Paige.'

'This is interesting news,' said Paul. 'I must remember to thank Mr Lomas for passing it on. Am I the only recipient of it?'

'I believe so, sir. Mr Lomas said that he came to you at once.'

'Why was that?'

'He trusted you, Mr Skillen.'

Paul was touched. He'd felt very sorry for Lomas and his wife. They were decent people with contented lives that had been shattered by the events in an upstairs room at their house. It had left them in a state of heightened anxiety.

'The Runners must also have been there.'

'Mr Lomas didn't take to them at all, sir.'

'Why was that?'

'He didn't say,' replied Crabbe, 'but he explained why he relied on you. He said that you seemed to be on his side. Mr Lomas didn't get that feeling from the Bow Street Runners.'

* * *

The rain had stopped but cramp was attacking both of Chevy Ruddock's legs. He tried stamping his feet but the pain only grew worse. The one way to relieve it was to walk up and down the street. As he strolled along, he began to rehearse the excuse he'd have to give his wife, Agnes, for being out all night without warning her. If he told her that he was stalking two men involved in murder and arson, she would fear for his safety and beg him to return to his former occupation as a cooper. Making barrels was hard work but at least he didn't have to court an early death in the process.

Every so often, he stopped to look across at Doll Fortune's. Visitors continued to arrive throughout the night, replacing those who'd departed once their needs and fantasies had been satisfied. Since he couldn't understand what impelled men to desert their wives in order to consort with prostitutes, Ruddock oozed disapproval. It was well past midnight when two more clients arrived. What distinguished them was that they came on foot and were so inebriated that they had to hold each other up as they staggered along the pavement. Though he was on the opposite side of the road, Ruddock heard their coarse language clearly as they walked past. Young, sturdy, roughly dressed and uncouth, they stood out from the wealthy patrons who arrived in style.

Having made one mistake, Ruddock didn't wish to make a second. He therefore suppressed his hopes at first and simply kept watch. The two men went up to the house and were accosted by the doorman. He gestured that they should leave but they refused and a scuffle broke out. Since they were unsteady on their feet, they were unable to overpower the doorman. Howling abuse at him, they gave up and retreated. It was them. Ruddock was certain of it now. As Yeomans had predicted, they were turned away and bristling with anger. When they rolled past him again, expletives poured out of their mouths in a torrent. Luckily for him, they were too drunk and too preoccupied to notice that Ruddock was following them. Keeping well back, he trailed them through a labyrinth of streets, urged on by the conviction that he was doing something of great importance. It would not only lead to the arrest of a killer, it would earn him enough kudos to be considered for promotion. If that happened, his wife would be intensely proud of him.

A problem then occurred. The two men split up. Though they seemed barely able to stand, they came to a fork and parted company. Ruddock had no idea which of them to follow. When he walked tentatively down one street, he heard the telltale trickle of urination. It persuaded him to go off in the other direction instead. He had to lengthen his stride to catch up with the other man. It was too dark for him to see his quarry so he simply listened for the sound of dragging feet. After a few minutes, to his dismay, the noise stopped altogether. Had the man collapsed or stepped into a house? Ruddock was baffled. He walked on until he came to a lane on the right. Something told him that he'd find the man down there, possibly in a heap on the ground. He edged his way down the lane until he came eventually to a blank wall and realised that he was in a cul-de-sac.

He did hear the noise of feet now and there were two pairs of them. Out of the gloom came two swaying figures, getting close enough for him to smell the ale on their breath. Ruddock was the quarry now.

'Why were you following us?' demanded one of them.

One of the qualities that Benjamin Tite admired in his employer was that she had indefatigable energy. If she was engaged in a project, Diane Mandrake was ready to work from dawn until long after dusk. With light blazing from the candelabra, she was seated at a table littered with correspondence, searching through it methodically. Tite came into the room wearing a dressing gown and a nightcap.

'You need your sleep,' he said.

'Leave me be, Ben.'

'Can't you do whatever you're doing in the morning?'

'It *is* morning,' she replied, 'and I don't care if I never get to bed. This takes precedence. Over the years, I've had scores of letters from Leo Paige. Somewhere amongst them, there must be a hint as to the identity of Virgo.'

'If there is, you'd have spotted it at the time.'

'Not necessarily – even I am prone to make mistakes.'

'You're making one at the moment.'

'Go back to bed, Ben.'

'I'll have to,' he said before stifling a yawn. About to turn away, he remembered something. 'An odd thing happened while you were away.'

'What was that?'

'Mr Yeomans turned up again.'

'Did that dreadful man pester you with questions?'

'He didn't even come in the shop.'

'So what did he do?'

'He simply walked up and down the street and glanced in this direction every time he passed. In the end, I went out and asked him what he wanted. He asked if you were here and I told him you were not.'

'How did he react to that?'

'To tell you the truth,' said Tite, fighting off another yawn, 'he reacted very strangely. He asked if *Mr* Mandrake was here and, on receipt of the news that there was no Mr Mandrake, he seemed unusually pleased.'

'*Pleased?*' she repeated, 'That big, black-eyed, beetle-browed oaf of a Runner is pleased that I have no husband? This intelligence has made me feel quite sick. If he *ever* comes near the shop again and asks after me, tell him that I am not here even though I may well be. Pleased, is he? Then here's something to curdle his pleasure. You may add that I am indisposed because I have gone to my seamstress to try on a bridal dress for my forthcoming wedding.'

'That should spike his guns,' said Tite, chortling.

'I'll do more than that if he comes sniffing after me, Ben,' she vowed. 'Here we are, trying to catch the man who murdered dear Leo, and all that Yeomans can do is to eye me up like a bull in a field with a prize cow. He's an abomination. I'd no more marry him than I'd couple with a giant hedgehog.'

Left alone in an ill-lit room, Yeomans and Hale sipped their beer and speculated on the possibility that they were wasting their time. It might well be that the two men who'd scandalised Doll Fortune's house would not return again that night. They might seek their pleasures elsewhere. There was also the possibility that, if they did appear, Ruddock would be found unequal to the task of trailing them to their lodging and bringing back details of its location.

'You ask too much of the lad, Micah,' said Hale. 'There's a real downpour out there now. He'll be soaked to the skin.'

'He has to take responsibility.'

'I'd have given him company at his vigil.'

'Two people are more likely to be seen, Alfred. One is always better. In any case, he's not there to tackle these villains, merely to observe where they go. That involves no great skill or effort. Besides,' said Yeomans, 'he's earned the right to the assignment. Ruddock is a good man. When he learns to handle his wife as cunningly as we handle ours, he'll be a real asset to us. We simply have to cure him of being too honest with the woman.'

'Chevy is still in thrall to her. I've seen the wife so I can understand why.'

Yeomans went off into a reverie about Diane Mandrake, wondering how he could best approach his beloved and what gifts would endear him to her. A woman of striking beauty and patent appetite needed a man to bring real fulfilment. He was ready to put himself forward. His meditations were rudely interrupted by a knock on the door of the tavern. Holding a lantern, Hale got up and went to see who it was. When he opened the door, he was amazed to see Ruddock there, sodden, bent double and clearly exhausted. As he held the lantern close to the newcomer's face, he saw that it was bruised and that there was a river of dried blood coming from his nose.

'What happened, Chevy?' he asked.

'I got them, Mr Hale,' said the other, triumphantly. 'I got them both.'

He stood back to reveal the bodies of the two men he'd dragged all the way from the lane. Though they'd tried to give him a beating, he'd proved far too strong for them. Weakened by drink, they spent most of the fight flailing impotently away. Ruddock had taken some punishment but had retaliated by knocking both of them senseless. Gulping for air, he recounted the whole episode. Torn between scepticism and disbelief, Yeomans came out to hear it. When the narrative tailed off, he grabbed the lantern from Hale and held it to the face of each of the captives in turn.

Ruddock smiled bravely. 'Did I do well, sir?'

'You did very well, lad,' complimented Hale.

'When I saw the chance to arrest them, I took it.'

'There's only one problem,' said Yeomans, kicking one of the prone figures and eliciting a deep moan. 'You followed the wrong prey. They deserve arrest for being drunk and disorderly and that's the condition in which they're usually found. Do you see who we've got here, Alfred?'

Hale took a close look. 'It's Cullen and Roach.'

'You *know* them?' asked Ruddock in astonishment.

'We ought to, lad. We arrested them often enough.'

'Jabez Roach is the worst one,' said Yeomans, pointing to one of the bodies. 'I once caught him pissing over the flowers in the chief magistrate's garden. It wasn't a wise thing to do. These rascals are petty criminals. While they steal anything they can, they don't kill and ravage women. In other words,' he concluded, 'the men we want are still at liberty. Get back to Covent Garden and wait for the real villains to appear.'

A shudder ran through Chevy Ruddock. He had to start all over again.

'What shall I tell my wife when she sees I've been in a fight?' he bleated.

The Runners gave a mirthless laugh.

Paul Skillen had always been an early riser but he was up soon after dawn that morning. The thought of meeting Paige's partner was an enticing one. Whether male or female, the person who drew the brilliant caricatures in the *Parliament of Foibles* was self-evidently an artist of rare talent. Paul longed to meet Virgo. As well as solving a mystery, he would be keeping his mind off Hannah Granville and grieving because he'd not heard from her for well over a week. Doubts began to trouble him. No time for the meeting had been suggested in the letter nor had a specific location been given. Crowds flocked past King's Bench Prison every day. Caught up in the bustle, Paul might stand in the wrong place and be completely missed by the person he was supposed to meet. Something else worried him. How would Virgo recognise him? As far as he knew, Paul had never met the artist.

As he set off, therefore, his excitement was tempered by niggling anxieties. Why had Virgo chosen a Southwark prison as the venue? Would it not have been easier for the artist to present himself, or herself, at the gallery? Paige had apparently confided to his friend that he was going there in search of a bodyguard. What prevented Virgo from turning up on the doorstep? Was he only prepared to share his secret with one person? Once they'd met, would Paul be sworn to silence about Virgo's identity? And why did he choose that pseudonym in the first place?

Paul had a great deal on which to reflect as he rode over the bridge towards the south bank and picked his way through the multitudes coming in the opposite direction. In earlier days, Southwark had been the centre of crime and dissipation, a place of refuge for outlaws and immigrants. Theatres and bear-baiting arenas had flourished there, bringing in crowds that were liberally sprinkled with prostitutes and pickpockets. The area was a little more civilised now but there was still a whiff of corruption in the air. It was a place where Paul remained alert and kept a hand on his dagger. He was glad to be travelling in bright sunlight.

King's Bench Prison had been demolished in the middle of the last century and rebuilt on a new site. Much of it was destroyed by fire during the Gordon Riots so more rebuilding had been needed. Its high perimeter stone walls were forbidding in their solidity. All sight of the cheerless accommodation inside was blocked out and, by the same token, prisoners were unable to enjoy any view of London during their incarceration. Paul rode to and fro past the main gate in the hope that he'd be seen and stopped but nobody stepped out of the throng to hail him. He therefore dismounted and led his horse slowly along the same route and back. Still there was no sign of Virgo. Paul decided that the meeting might not even take place that morning and steeled himself for a lengthy wait. The first hour sped by but the second one seemed to limp past. Patience waning and nerves frayed, he considered for the first time that he was the victim of a hoax. Someone posing as Virgo was having fun at his expense.

He was about to leave when a small boy came running across to him. He wore tattered clothes and had straggly fair hair poking out from beneath his hat. Protruding front teeth gave him the appearance of a baby rabbit. His voice was high-pitched.

'Ya from the gall'ry, sir?'

'That's right,' replied Paul.

'I'm to arsk ya nime.'

'It's Skillen – Paul Skillen.'

'Why d'ya come?'

'A letter was delivered to us. It said that I could meet someone here.'

'I knows, sir,' said the boy, grinning. 'I brort it. When I puts it under ya door, I arsked a shopkipper nearby who works in the gall'ry. Your name was one he give me – Paul Skill'n.'

'And what's *your* name, lad?'

'Me, sir? I'm Samuel Snape but they calls me Snapper.'

Paul was impressed by the boy. He had bright eyes and spoke with a confidence beyond his years. Having been told to confirm that someone from the gallery had turned up, he did so. Paul surmised that Virgo was afraid that an impostor might appear. Through the boy, he was checking up on the visitor. Paul found that reassuring.

'Well, now, Snapper,' he said, 'is there anything else you want to know?'

The boy eyed the horse. 'Can I 'ave a ride, please?'

'Why – where are we going?'

'Iss nor far.'

'You can have a ride if you tell me Virgo's real name.'

'Doan know it, sir.'

'Where do I meet him?'

'Inside there,' said Snapper, jerking his thumb.

Paul was taken aback. 'He's a *prisoner*?'

'Yes, sir – so am I.'

CHAPTER NINE

Peter Skillen accompanied his wife to the gallery before going off to make enquiries about the four suspects they'd identified from a study of *Paige's Chronicle*. He was certain that Paige's murder had been ordered either by a vengeful politician enraged by the unflattering portrait of him in the *Parliament of Foibles*, or by someone with connections to the government. That raised the question of where the journalist and his partner, Virgo, got their intelligence. Paige seemed to be remarkably well informed about the private lives of the people he satirised yet he had no practical experience of the political scene. He was only a former soldier with the gift of writing scabrous prose. When the Stamp Act had silenced his newspaper, he'd found another way to strike at some of the men who'd helped to put it on the statute book.

Whoever had ordered Paige's assassination would be unaware that he had a partner in the enterprise. Peter was bound to wonder what would happen if and when they did so. The likelihood was that Virgo would also become a target. When he actually met the artist that morning, therefore, Paul Skillen would do his best to ensure his continued safety. There was a whole raft of unanswered questions to consider, yet Peter nevertheless felt a degree of confidence. They'd discovered the name of one of the assassins and an old sailor had been employed to seek the man's whereabouts. Notwithstanding her tendency to interfere, Diane Mandrake had given them priceless help when she handed over her copies of the *Chronicle*. The newspapers had not only provided huge entertainment, they'd given Peter and the others an insight into the quirky mind of Leonidas Paige and into the mission he'd apparently set himself.

Peter drew comfort from something else. Having learnt so much in such a short time, they must have made more progress than the Runners. Yet he was not complacent. Yeomans and his men would be working hard to solve the case. In order to trounce their rivals, Peter and the others needed to push themselves to the limit.

His first port of call was the Home Office. Though Parliament was not in session, he knew that Viscount Sidmouth, the Home Secretary, would be at his desk, grappling with the many problems that landed on it at random. They were old friends who shared a mutual respect. Working as an agent in France during the war, Peter had reported directly to Sidmouth. The previous year he'd been engaged to find the Home Office cleaner when she mysteriously disappeared. In tracking the woman down, Peter had exposed a plot to strike at the very heart of government as the nation celebrated its victory at the Battle of Waterloo. Given his run of success, therefore, Peter felt that he'd earned the right to have privileged access to Sidmouth.

It was the ideal place to start.

'How long have you been here?' asked Paul.

'I've lost count.'

'Don't you have enough money to buy your way out?'

'As it happens, Mr Skillen, I do.'

'Then why stay here?'

'It's my home.'

'Do you actually *enjoy* rotting in a debtors' prison?'

'I don't rot, my friend. I thrive.'

'Life would be far better in more comfortable surroundings.'

'I'd have too many distractions.'

'It's so unhealthy in here. The place stinks.'

'You get used to things like that.'

Virgo was quite unlike the man Paul had envisaged. Tall, sinewy and with a livid scar on his cheek, he was obviously the person who'd called at Paige's lodging and heard of his death. There were well over two hundred rooms in the prison and Virgo had secured one of the best of them, enjoying the luxury of being its sole occupant. Yet the room was cold, bare, featureless and short of natural light. The only thing that brightened it was the selection of his prints on the walls. On the table was a box of candles. Evidently, he needed extra illumination when he was at work. As well as paper, paint and writing materials, he had some engraver's tools.

Conscious that he was still being weighed in the balance,

Paul tried to win him over by telling him about the investigation. Virgo was grateful.

'You're doing all this for Leo?' he asked.

'He came to us for help. Since we couldn't provide it *before* he died, we're doing it after his death. That help, of course, extends to you.'

'Why do I need help?'

'We're assuming that you'd like to stay alive.'

'Nobody knows who I am.'

'What if someone finds out?'

'I know how to defend myself, Mr Skillen.'

'I daresay that Mr Paige felt the same.'

When Paul had asked him for his real name, the man had declined to give it. Evidently, there was no point in trying to force it out of him. There was a tough, decisive, unrelenting quality about Virgo. If he wanted to confide in anyone, he'd do so at a time of his choosing.

'If you're locked in here,' said Paul, 'how could you visit Mr Paige?'

'Fortunately, I can afford to buy Freedom of the Rules,' explained Virgo. 'That means I can venture out into the three square miles surrounding the prison. Were I to wish it – and, frankly, I do not – I could visit any tavern or place of entertainment I chose. My work absorbs me. Here at the King's Bench things are very lax. As you know, it's largely a place for debtors and for people convicted of defamation. That's why it's my spiritual home. I'm the prince of vilification.'

'I've seen and admired your work. The wonder is that you and Mr Paige managed to escape being arraigned for libel.'

'Leo and I came within inches of that fate many times. Nearly fifty years ago,' he went on, reflectively, 'John Wilkes was put in here for writing an article in the *North Briton* that dared to criticise the king. A mob assembled outside with the object of escorting Wilkes to the House of Commons where they felt their hero belonged. When they refused to disperse, the crowd was fired on by soldiers.'

'I've heard tell of the massacre.'

'It was an example of the common people rising up to defend a man they believed had simply told the truth. Leo and I have followed in Wilkes's footsteps. We show no respect to people in authority. We strip them of their finery and display them naked to the public.'

'You are both artist and engraver, I see.'

'My task was to turn Leo's wonderful words into memorable pictures.'

'What was kept in the oak chest at his lodging?'

Virgo was surprised. 'You heard about my visit?'

'The landlord reported that someone had forced his way into his lodger's room. What were you looking for?'

'That's my business.'

'Why do you have to be so secretive?'

The man smiled. 'For the same reason that you have to be so inquisitive, Mr Skillen,' he said. 'It's in our natures.' He glanced towards the door. 'What did you think of my young messenger?'

'Snappy? I liked him.'

'He's a clever boy. Snappy runs errands for me.'

'He's looking after my horse at the moment.'

'If I know him, he'll be riding it around the courtyard

to the envy of all the other children. We've whole families in here. Snappy's family has been here for years. In fact, his youngest sister was born here. Poverty is a crime – that's what the law tells us. So they put people in the one place where they have little chance of paying off their debts. What money they *do* have goes on food and accommodation. The system has been skilfully devised to keep poor people even poorer.' He ran his eye over Paul. 'If you work at the shooting gallery, you must be proficient in all forms of fighting. Leo and I were the same at one time, but I traded my sword for an artist's tools.'

'Art can be a very powerful weapon. You've proved that.'

'Thank you.'

'Why won't you tell me your name?'

'I'm biding my time.'

'What made you pick the name of "Virgo" as your sobriquet?'

'When I feel I can trust you,' said the other, 'I might explain.'

'Who are your sources of intelligence about leading politicians?'

Virgo sat back in his chair and subjected him to close scrutiny.

'Tell me a little about yourself, Mr Skillen. You interest me.'

Having heard so much about her, Charlotte Skillen had some idea what to expect when she met the owner of the print shop. In the event, Diane Mandrake exceeded those expectations. When she came into the gallery, she seemed to fill it with her presence and with the bewitching odour of her perfume. What Charlotte saw was a woman of substance, authority and independent spirit. Neither Peter nor Paul had told her how extremely handsome Diane was. It took Charlotte a few moments to adjust her opinion of the woman. For her part, the newcomer was delighted to meet her, embracing Charlotte as if they were old friends, then standing back to appraise her.

'We are two of a kind, Charlotte,' she said, dispensing with formalities. 'We are purposeful women, making our way in a man's world. I have my print shop and you, I see, have a small kingdom here.'

'I'd hardly call it that, Mrs Mandrake.'

'Diane, please,' corrected the other.

'I simply work in here behind the scenes while the others deal with our clients and take on dangerous assignments.'

'You're an important member of the team. Gully Ackford said as much.'

'That was kind of him.'

'And so did Jem Huckvale. Not that he stayed long enough to explain why,' added Diane with a laugh. 'For some reason, he seemed frightened of me. I never thought of myself as intimidating.'

'Jem is very shy.'

'He's also very courageous. In taking on the task of guarding Leo, he was putting himself in jeopardy.'

'He's done that sort of thing many times, Diane. So, of course, have Peter, Paul and Gully. We live in a violent city, alas. One has to be on guard all the time. Whenever he took on hazardous assignments,' she confessed, 'I used to fear for Peter's life. But I've learnt to trust in his abilities now.'

'And so you should.'

'He and Paul have remarkable talents.'

'I know. Incidentally, how on earth do you tell them apart?'

Charlotte smiled. 'It's a question of instinct.'

'My instinct would be to favour the wilder of the two.'

'Then you'd have to pick Paul.'

'Yet I couldn't think of turning Peter down,' said Diane, chortling. 'If I was not constrained by the laws of decency, I'd marry the pair of them and have the best of both worlds. Paul's madcap tendency would then be counterbalanced by Peter's steadiness.'

'Paul is less of a madcap since he fell in love.'

'Really – who is the lady?'

Charlotte told her about her brother-in-law's romance with Hannah Granville and how he'd pined for her ever since she went off to Paris. Diane listened with great interest. Feeling that she could confide in Charlotte, she broached a topic that had been on her mind all night.

'Are you able to keep a secret?' she asked.

'I like to think so, Diane.'

'This is not something I wish to be common property. Men would only snigger whereas a woman like you, I suspect, would understand.'

'I'm all ears.'

'You are, I take it, familiar with Mr Yeomans.'

'It's in the nature of our work to meet the Bow Street Runners all the time, Micah Yeomans, in particular.'

'What do you think of him, Charlotte?'

'I think he does his job to the best of his limited abilities.'

'I was talking about his appearance and character. Be candid, please.'

'Then I have to admit that I find him ugly, unpleasant and overbearing.'

'How would you cope if he took an interest in you?'

'That would *never* happen.'

'It's happened to me.'

Charlotte gaped. 'Are you saying that . . . ?'

'So it appears,' said Diane, grimacing. 'When he came to the shop, he was far less hostile than Runners often are. He kept staring at me as if I were a celestial being. Ben Tite, who works for me, said that Yeomans came back later on and walked up and down the street so that he could peer into the shop. Tiring of the fellow, Ben went out and asked him if he wanted anything.'

'What was his answer?'

'Hearing that I was not there, he asked if *Mr* Mandrake was at home. When he was told that I no longer had a husband, Yeomans was plainly delighted. Can you think of anything worse than attracting an insufferable boor like that?'

'No,' said Charlotte, amazed at the news. 'You may no longer be married but he certainly is. What would his wife think of his behaviour?'

'If he bothers me too much, she may get to hear about it.'

'What are you going to do?'

'I'm not entirely sure, Charlotte,' admitted the other. 'How would you deal with unwanted advances from a man you despised?'

'Oddly enough, I've been in a parallel situation. Not that the advances were exactly unwanted and I couldn't possibly have despised the man. But,' Charlotte went on, 'I was in something of a dilemma.'

'How did you resolve the situation?'

'I married his brother, Peter.'

The visit to the Home Office had been productive. Sidmouth had been glad to see Peter Skillen and given freely of his time. A degree of tact and diplomacy was involved. Peter took care to say nothing about the *Parliament of Foibles* because he knew that Sidmouth was rather sensitive on the subject of satire. When he'd been a rather undistinguished prime minister years earlier, he'd been the target of vicious caricatures. Peter recalled seeing one that showed Britannia in a sickbed – the country's economy being in a parlous state at the time – with the prime minister being kicked unceremoniously out of office through the door. After over a decade, he felt it must still rankle with Sidmouth.

While admitting that he'd been drawn into a murder investigation, therefore, Peter gave few details but turned the conversation around to a discussion of what politicians did when Parliament was not in session. Sidmouth was happy to regale him with anecdotes about his colleagues and about his political opponents. Peter had been able to slip the names of Sir Humphrey Coote and Gerard Brunt into the conversation, discovering that the former had a passion for cricket and that the latter was always trying to present his latest Private Members Bill in the Commons. Sidmouth made mention of Dr Penhallurick of his own volition, revealing that he had parliamentary ambitions and that he would be standing at the next election. The one person about whom Peter learnt nothing new was Julian Harvester.

When talk turned to other matters, the conversation became slightly strained. Sidmouth insisted on the necessity of suppressing Luddite activity with maximum force. While he didn't condone destruction of property, Peter had sympathy for those thrown out of work by the introduction of new machines into factories and wondered how such an essentially kind, tolerant, fair-minded man as Sidmouth could employ such brutal methods. Having gathered as much information as he'd hoped for, Peter excused himself and left. On the ride back to the gallery, he hoped that Paul was having an equally profitable visit.

Paul Skillen had always preferred to look to the future rather than dwell on the past. In order to win Virgo's trust, however, he was compelled to talk about the various escapades in his career, recalling how many times he and his brother had taken enormous risks in the pursuit of criminals. Virgo eventually raised a hand.

'That's enough, Mr Skillen, that's enough. Your life story would fill a dozen novels of adventure. The miracle is that you've survived it all unscathed.'

'Not entirely,' confessed Paul. 'I have scars all over my body and some of the worst are in my mind. Memories can be more painful than wounds.'

'You speak to one who is all too aware of that.'

'Is it *my* turn to ask questions now?'

Virgo spread his arms. 'Be my guest.'

'How did you come to know so much about Parliament?'

'What did you see when you first came through the prison gates?'

'I saw that the courtyard was thronging with life,' replied Paul. 'There was no real sense of it being a place of detention. I saw tailors, hatters, barbers, chandlers, grocers, oyster sellers and twenty or thirty gin shops. It was a boisterous market.'

'Take a closer look on your way out.'

'Why should I do that?'

'Because you will observe what a rich variety of people have ended up here. They're not all impecunious souls who scratch a pathetic living. Some of them have enjoyed wealth or power or both. Last year, for instance, Lord Cochrane was in here for alleged complicity in fraud on the Stock Exchange. He was a peer of the realm and a naval hero yet he ended up in prison. So did a bookseller found guilty of selling prints and books likely to inflame the passions of the young and tender mind. In short,' said Virgo, 'he offered erotica to his customers, almost none of whom, by the way, had young and tender minds. Some of those who bought obscene material from him were ageing politicians with dull wives. They needed stimulus.'

'I begin to see what happened,' said Paul. 'Your sources are actually in here.'

'Exactly,' replied the other. 'I befriended Lord Cochrane and had long conversations with him. The bookseller and I were instant comrades. From them and from the dozens of others in here who've brushed shoulders with the government, Leo and I amassed enough scandal to go on producing the *Parliament of Foibles* for years. Ignorant and unwitting electors have no idea how many monsters they send to the House of Commons. It was our duty to point that out to them.'

'What will happen now Mr Paige is no longer with us?'

'I don't know, Mr Skillen. I'm no wordsmith.'

'You could still go on creating those wonderful prints.'

'But I can't haggle over their selling price with Mrs Mandrake.'

'Why not? She seems an amenable lady.'

Virgo laughed. 'Leo found that out. She was very amenable.'

'I believe that Mr Paige lodged with her for a time.'

'He did rather more than that. Where women were concerned, Leo had a craggy charm. It obviously worked on Mrs Mandrake. Until she tired of his faults, she . . . indulged him.'

Paul was interested to hear of the intimacy. It explained why Diane Mandrake was so eager to be involved in the hunt for the killer. Paige was both a source of prints that were always in demand, and her former lover. The information cast the print shop owner in a new light. Behind the carapace of respectability was a woman of strong emotions and impulsive action, aspects of character that she shared with Hannah Granville. Both women, Paul noted, were ready to defy convention and follow their heart.

The visit to the King's Bench Prison had been a revelation in many ways. Virgo had turned out to be a man who'd found peace of mind in the least likely place. He was happy with his lot and – until Paige's murder – had been happy in his work. That happiness had come to an abrupt halt and thrown his future into doubt.

'What were you looking for in that oak chest?' asked Paul.

'I was hoping to find Leo's latest instructions for me but all his papers had been consumed by the fire and the chest itself was charred.'

'Why did you choose a nom de plume for your work?'

'I sought anonymity.'

'But why choose that particular name?'

'There's no mystery about it,' said the other. 'I was born under that sign. Though I can't claim to be a virgin holding an ear of corn, I do acknowledge my place in the zodiac. Leo was born under Leo and I under Virgo.'

'And what is your *real* name?'

'If I tell you, I don't want it spread far and wide. And I certainly don't want it whispered into Mrs Mandrake's ear.'

'You can trust me, I do assure you. I'll not vouchsafe it to anyone, except perhaps to the few of us searching for the killer. You have my word on that.'

Virgo explored Paul's eyes for a long time before speaking.

'I believe you, Mr Skillen,' he said at length.

'Thank you.'

'My name is Virgil Paige.'

Paul was startled. 'Paige? Then you must be . . .'

'That is correct. Leo was my brother.'

During a break between a boxing lesson and a fencing bout, Gully Ackford was able to spend some time with Peter Skillen.

The latter recounted what he'd heard at the Home Office about three of the suspects on their list. Ackford was pleased.

'And they both have homes in London, you say?'

'Yes, Gully, they represent far-flung constituencies that they rarely visit. This is where they spend their time. In other words, they were here when Fearon and his accomplice were hired to kill Mr Paige.'

'What about this doctor?'

'He, too, is based here in London. Opinions are evenly divided about him, it seems. Some people acclaim him as a genius whereas others think him a charlatan.'

'Virgo belongs to the second camp.'

'Yes,' said Peter. 'Judging by the drawings that feature Dr Penhallurick, he is a particular target of Mr Paige and his partner.'

'So which of the three suspects engaged an assassin?'

'It might be none of them, Gully.'

'You think that Mr Harvester is our man?'

'Like the others, he remains under suspicion until we can eliminate him.'

'It may be someone else altogether,' said Ackford, ruefully. 'Leo did tell me that he'd made a lot of enemies.'

'All that we can do is to concentrate our attention on the four we've selected and,' said Peter, 'hope that my brother may be able to shed more light for us.' He glanced towards the office. 'Is Mrs Mandrake here?'

'Yes, she and Charlotte have become bosom friends.'

'I had a feeling that they might do so.'

'Jem, however, is avoiding her like the plague.'

'She is a rather overwhelming example of womanhood.'

Ackford grinned. 'Your pretty maidservant is more to his taste.'

'How much have you divulged to Mrs Mandrake?'

'I followed your advice and told her as little as possible. She knew that you went in search of intelligence about our suspects but is quite unaware that Paul went on our behalf to King's Bench Prison.'

'It's better to keep Mrs Mandrake ignorant of that. Apart from anything else, we need to protect her. Fearon and his accomplice wouldn't scruple to attack a woman. In fact,' Peter went on, 'I'm surprised that she hasn't suffered some sort of retribution already. After all, she sells the prints that have caused so much fury and offence.'

In charge of the shop, Benjamin Tite was showing off a new print when it happened. He heard the sound of a galloping horse but never for a moment connected it with danger. Luckily, his back and that of the customer were turned to the bow window. The next moment, there was a loud crash as a large stone smashed the glass and sent a blizzard of shards in every direction. The rider galloped on down the street and the pummelling hooves soon died away. Tite, meanwhile, was shaking all over and apologising profusely to the customer. The one consolation, in his opinion, was that Mrs Mandrake had not been in the shop at the time of the attack. Had she been facing the window, she could easily have been blinded. It was an alarming development. Now that Paige was dead, someone was targeting her.

* * *

Chevy Ruddock had had to drag himself out of bed that morning. When he finally presented himself to Yeomans and Hale at the Peacock Inn, he looked as if he'd climbed off a slab at the morgue. No sympathy awaited him.

'Where've you been?' complained Yeomans.

'I didn't get to bed until after dawn, sir.'

'Then you shouldn't have gone to bed at all. Being a Runner means that you sometimes have to sacrifice sleep altogether.'

'My wife was very worried when I didn't get home last night.'

'Didn't you tell her that you made two arrests?'

'Agnes was more worried about my injuries. When she saw the state of my face, she screamed.'

'We feel like doing that whenever we see you,' joked Hale.

'I stood outside Doll Fortune's house until I was fit to drop,' wailed Ruddock. 'I hope I don't have to do the same thing again.'

'But you must, lad, because you do it so well.'

'It's true,' said Yeomans. 'You've made the job your own.'

'The people we wanted never turned up, sir.'

'They probably went somewhere else and will be back again tonight.'

'Why can't someone else do my duty?' asked Ruddock.

'The other members of the foot patrol have been deployed elsewhere. Every one of the infamous brothels in Covent Garden will have one of our men standing outside it tonight. If these sailors show their faces,' said Hale, 'we'll have them.'

'But we don't even know what they look like.'

'We know how they *behave*, lad. That's what will give them

away. They're like animals. Recognise them by their coarseness.'

'And when you do,' added Yeomans, 'bring word to us at once. It will advantage you, I promise. If you're the man who spots these savages tonight, your name will be mentioned to the chief magistrate.'

Ruddock rallied. 'You'll speak to Mr Kirkwood about me?'

'I will, but only if you bring us certain news that you've seen the men.'

'I told my wife that I stood guard outside a church all night.'

'In a sense, that was the truth.'

'Yes,' said Hale with a guffaw, 'men worship at the shrine of Doll Fortune. Like the Virgin Mary, she's been known to answer the prayers of many sinners.'

'How do we know that these men will come back?' asked Ruddock.

'They're bound to,' said Hale.

'They're still celebrating,' argued Yeomans. 'They have money in their purses and an urge to spend it on nights of madness. Well, *you'd* do the same, surely?'

'That's not true,' said the younger man, indignantly. 'When I have money, I give it all to my wife. That's what a loyal husband should do.'

'These men have baser tastes. Two of Doll Fortune's ladies were victims of it. Mark my words, Ruddock. When swine like that get a taste for blood, they always want more of it.'

They were sharing a room above a tavern. When he returned, Abel Fearon saw that his friend was still dozing in the chair. He gave him a nudge to wake him up. The other man blinked and sat up.

'What's happened?'

'You had too much to drink last night,' said Fearon. 'That's what happened. It makes you drowsy. If you drank less, you'd be able to fuck more.'

The other man smirked. 'I had my fair share last night.'

'That was before you fell asleep in her arms. I had to haul you off the woman then drag you back here.'

'Thanks, Abel.' He rubbed his eyes. 'Where've you been?'

'You already know.'

'Ah, yes, you went to that print shop.'

'I had to deliver a message through the window.'

'Will you get paid well?'

'Very well,' said Fearon. 'If we obey orders, he's very generous.'

He was a thickset man in his late twenties with eyes set unusually far apart. His friend was of the same age but more angular and with a pockmarked face. Both were former sailors. Imprisoned in Newgate for quite different crimes, they'd formed a bond. Fearon's leadership was never questioned.

'What happens next, Abel?'

'We have to see if the warning works.'

'It's bound to work,' said the other. 'She's only a woman. She'll be too frightened to keep the shop open now.'

'Don't be so sure. I'm told she's very stubborn.'

'What do we do if she carries on as before?'

'What else?' replied Fearon. 'We do what we did to Paige.'

158

The other man was jolted. 'We *kill* her?'

'If that's what we're told to do, we'll do it. I've never murdered a woman before,' he went on, smiling at the thought. 'I've got a feeling I'd enjoy it.'

CHAPTER TEN

Henry Legge, the old sailor hired by Paul Skillen, hobbled into the tavern and lowered himself gratefully on to a seat. By a cruel twist of fate, Legge had lost one of his lower limbs and been forced to wear a wooden substitute. At the time when his right leg had been amputated by a cannonball during a sea battle, his shipmates were amused rather than sympathetic. There were so many jests about his name that he even thought about changing it. The promise of a reward had sent him wandering from one place to another, asking questions of everyone he met and listening out for a mention of Abel Fearon's name. Moving about so much was tiring work and he had to endure some foul language from sailors who didn't like him hounding them. He did find two people who'd actually sailed with Fearon but, like Legge, they had no wish to do so again.

When he'd fortified himself with another pint of ale, Legge felt able to continue his search. He drifted around the bar and got into conversation with several people in turn. Once again, he drew a blank. Nobody had a clue as to the whereabouts of the man he'd named. Legge was just about to finish his drink and move on to another tavern when he finally heard someone mention Fearon. He went across to the man at once and grabbed him by the arm.

'Take your hand off me,' protested the other.

'I'm sorry, my friend,' said Legge, letting go of him, 'but I couldn't help hearing you name someone I know – Abel Fearon.'

'What of it?'

'I sailed with him once.'

'That's not something *I'd* care to do.'

'I hated the man.'

'Then we've something in common,' said the other, warming to him. 'Fearon is a fiend in human form. He should be kept in a cage and fed off scraps.'

'How do you know him?'

'We were in Newgate together. For some reason, he was let out before he'd served his sentence. We were glad to see him go.'

'Do you know where he is now?'

'I'd like to think he was at the bottom of the sea with a knife in his back.'

'So would a lot of us.'

'Wherever he is,' said the man, vehemently, 'he'll be causing trouble. That's what they did all the time in Newgate. I was tempted to tackle Fearon many times but I couldn't take on both of them.'

'What do you mean?'

'He had this friend, a grinning hyena of a man. They used to

161

bully people for money, tobacco and whatever else they could get. I did my best to keep clear of the pair of them.'

'What was this friend's name?'

'Higlett,' replied the other. 'It was Sim Higlett. You don't want to run into either of them,' he warned. 'He's just as bad as Fearon.'

When the messenger arrived at the gallery, he handed the letter to Diane Mandrake. On reading it, she let out a shriek of anger.

'What's happened?' asked Charlotte.

'Some devil has smashed the window of my shop.'

'That's dreadful!'

'Was anyone seriously hurt?' asked Peter.

'No,' said Diane. 'By the grace of God, both Ben Tite and a customer had their backs to the window. They had slight cuts from the pieces of flying glass but no real wounds.' She handed the letter to him. 'Read it for yourself, Peter.'

He took it from her and noticed how shaky the handwriting was.

'Mr Tite was frightened when he wrote this,' he observed, 'and with good cause. Had he been putting a new print in the window, he could have had his face and hands cut to pieces.'

'I must get back there.'

'Be careful, Diane. It may not be safe.'

'A fig for safety,' said the other. 'I'm far too angry to fear anything. I bought that property years ago and built it up into one of the best print shops in London. I'm not having it ruined by a man on a galloping horse.'

'I'll come with you,' volunteered Peter.

'You don't have to.'

'I want to see the damage for myself.' Taking the letter back from him, she headed for the door. 'You'll have to excuse me, Charlotte.'

'And the same goes for me,' said Peter, kissing his wife on the cheek. 'Tell Gully and Jem what happened. I'll be back in due course.'

He followed Diane out and offered to drive her in her curricle. Refusing even to hear of it, she clambered into the vehicle, snatched up the whip and let the horse feel it on his rump. The curricle set off immediately. Riding behind her, Peter had great difficulty keeping pace with it. Diane Mandrake seemed to work on the principle that the streets of London had been designed solely for her purpose and that anyone who got in her way was deliberately obstructing her.

When she arrived in Middle Row, Diane brought the curricle to a skidding halt then leapt out of it as fast as her dress would allow. Tite was still clearing up the mess on the floor. She let herself into the shop then embraced him like a mother finding a long-lost child. Peter dismounted and went in to join them. He assessed the damage, then saw the large stone that had caused it. He picked it up from the counter.

'You were lucky, Mr Tite,' he said. 'Had this struck you in the head, you might no longer be with us.'

'I've been haunted by that thought ever since it happened, Mr Skillen.' Tite brushed a tiny sliver of glass off his shoulder. 'Luckily, none of the prints was damaged. I've moved them all into the back room.'

'That was very sensible, Ben,' said Diane.

'I have no idea who threw that stone. I remember hearing a horse coming at a gallop and then . . .' He waved a nervous hand. 'You see the result.'

'It's appalling.'

'The shop will have to close,' said Tite.

'We'll do nothing of the kind.'

'But we have no place to display our wares.'

'Our reputation will do that for us,' she insisted. 'If the shop closes, the villain who did this will think he's achieved his aim. No, Ben, we'll have the window boarded up with a large sign that says we're open for business as usual.'

'That could be tempting Providence,' cautioned Peter.

'I live to sell prints. Nobody will stop me doing that.'

'I'm afraid that they might well try.'

'Then they'll have to deal with me,' she said, pulling herself up to her full height. 'And I won't have my back to the window. When it's been restored, I'll be looking through it with a pistol in my hand.' She stared with dismay at the debris. 'You shouldn't be clearing up, Ben. It's a job for the servants.'

'They're cowering in their room,' said Tite.

'I'll soon get them out of there.'

'While you're doing that,' suggested Peter, 'I'll speak to your neighbours. Some of them may have seen the horseman galloping past and be able to give me a description of him and his mount.'

But he set off with little hope in his heart. The sight of a horse ridden hell for leather was not an unusual one in London. If people were in a hurry, they, like Diane, showed little regard for anyone in their path. In this case, the

164

horseman had a clear objective. It was to smash the window of the shop and spread panic. The stone was a message in itself. It was a warning to stop selling prints or to suffer the consequences. Peter recalled with a shudder how Paige had been silenced. He vowed that Diane Mandrake would not meet the same grisly fate.

Eldon Kirkwood had been in court all morning, sentencing malefactors with the full rigour of the law. It was not until afternoon that he was able to see the Runners. Hats in their hands, Yeomans and Hale walked into his office with customary trepidation.

'What have you brought me this time?' asked the chief magistrate. 'Is it news of an arrest or is it the usual paltry excuses?'

'We are making progress, sir,' said Yeomans.

'I hope it's not based on the tittle-tattle of a whorehouse doorman.'

'That story has been verified now, sir, because I spoke to the doorman and to the lady who runs the house. Both told the same tale. Two men did descend on the establishment and treat two of its prostitutes in the most reprehensible way. One of them even gave his name.'

'What was it?'

'Leonidas Paige.'

Kirkwood blinked. 'Isn't that the name of the murder victim?'

'Yes, it is, sir.'

'I think he was playing a joke on them, sir,' said Hale, 'but it worked against him. In giving that name, he was confessing to the crime.'

'That *proves* we're on the right track,' emphasised Yeomans.

Kirkwood rose to his feet in silence and walked to the window as he took in the information. Though he realised that he'd been unduly sceptical during the earlier visit from Yeomans, he never for a moment considered an apology. All that the Runners had done was what the chief magistrate had ordered. Dubious facts had been properly checked.

He faced them again. 'Did these two men return there last night?'

'No, sir,' replied Yeomans.

'You say that with confidence.'

'One of my best officers had the property under surveillance.'

'In the process,' Hale put in, 'he managed to arrest two thieves.'

'A brace of thieves is a poor exchange for a brutal killer,' said Kirkwood, acidly. 'Thieves are ten a penny in London. Those who stoop to a deplorable act of homicide are, thankfully, in shorter supply.'

'And they are usually more difficult to catch, sir.'

'However,' said Yeomans, eager for approval, 'we have hopes of catching this one tonight. Information came to us this morning that the men we're after did venture out last night. But instead of going to Doll Fortune's house, they sought pleasure elsewhere.'

'How do you know that it was the same men?' asked Kirkwood.

'It's because they behaved in the same crude way, sir.'

'Crudity is surely standard practice in such places.'

'Violence is not,' said Yeomans. 'These men treated their whores so badly that the women had to be rescued.'

'That sort of thing must happen on a nightly basis, Yeomans.'

'There's a telling detail in this instance.'

'What is it?'

'One of the men called himself Leonidas Paige again.'

'Who else would do that but the killer?' asked Hale.

The Runners had the pleasure of seeing a smile of congratulation flit across Kirkwood's face. It was not translated into words. The chief magistrate resumed his seat and made a few notes in a ledger. He looked up again.

'What's your plan, Yeomans?'

'I'm having every brothel in Covent Garden watched tonight, sir.'

'Will they come back again?'

'I'd bet my gold watch on it.'

'You don't *have* a gold watch, Micah,' said Hale.

'It was simply my way of saying that I'd place a large wager on it.'

'I take your point,' said Kirkwood. 'Over the years, you've developed your instincts. In this case, I believe them to be sound.' Yeomans winked at Hale. 'That's not to say you can't be hopelessly mistaken, of course. Very well,' he went on with a dismissive gesture. 'Off you go. I don't wish to see either of you until you can report the arrest of these two men. And if the Skillen brothers apprehend them before you do, I'd advise you not to come back to me at all.'

* * *

Returning to the gallery, Paul Skillen heard the latest news from Charlotte. The damage inflicted on the print shop upset and annoyed him. He felt that it was a prelude to even more serious attacks.

'How far do you think they'll go?' asked Charlotte.

'They'll go as far as they judge necessary.'

'Are you saying that they'd commit murder?'

'One of them has already done so.'

'In that case, Mrs Mandrake is in mortal danger.'

'I don't think she'd lose any sleep over that, somehow,' he said.

'I admire her bravado,' she declared, 'but I think it's misplaced. Peter will think the same. I'm hoping that he can persuade her to move in with us until the case is solved.'

'Your hopes may be dashed. Moving out of her own home would be in the nature of a defeat for her and Mrs Mandrake would never give ground.'

'Then perhaps you or Peter should move in with her?'

Paul laughed. 'Do you mean that one of us should share a bed with the lady?' he said. 'Neither of us would be equal to that test. Beside, Peter is married to you and I'm already spoken for.'

'She needs protection, Paul. We failed Mr Paige. I'd hate to see us fail Mrs Mandrake as well. What can one woman do against a murderous villain and his accomplice?'

'She can shoot straight, Charlotte.'

The door opened and Ackford came into the office. He asked for a report on the visit to the prison. As Paul described his visit to the King's Bench, they were spellbound. One detail made Ackford slap the table hard.

'So *that's* the explanation,' he said. 'When I told Leo that you and Peter were brothers, he burst into laughter. I couldn't understand why. What tickled him was the coincidence that, just as you and Peter work in harness, he and *his* brother were also yoked together. They were another family enterprise.'

'Both began as soldiers,' said Paul, 'then decided to fight another war by very different means. As brothers, they'd have a sort of understanding.'

'It could never be like the understanding that you and Peter share.'

'That's different, Gully. We're twins.'

'Should we tell Mrs Mandrake what you've discovered?' asked Charlotte.

'No,' said Ackford, firmly, 'we shouldn't. Peter advised against it and I agree.'

'We say nothing at all about Virgo,' decreed Paul. 'Mrs Mandrake has enough to worry about at the moment. She must be thinking the same thing as us. If someone is prepared to smash the shop window in broad daylight, what would he be prepared to do under the cover of darkness?'

Hauling himself up from the bed, Abel Fearon grabbed his hat from the hook on the back of the door. Sim Higlett looked up from the game of patience he was playing on the table.

'Where are you going?' he asked.

'I'm going to collect my money.'

'*Our* money,' corrected Higlett. 'You promised to split everything in two.'

'I was the one who rode the horse and threw the stone.'

'Who told you where you could hire the horse?'

'You did, Sim.'

'Then I deserve my share.'

'I'll think about it,' grumbled Fearon.

'How much will you get paid?'

'Enough.'

'Maybe I should come with you.'

'Why – don't you trust me?'

'We're partners, Abel. We're in this together.'

'Then you ought to be able to trust me. Have I ever let you down before?' Higlett shook his head. 'No, I haven't – and I'm not going to start now.'

'I know.'

'Then why are you bleating about equal shares? I never stint you. Take what you get and be glad.'

'How long will you be?'

'That depends on how long he keeps me.'

'Where are you seeing him?'

'It will be in the usual place, Sim. He's a man for taking precautions.'

'I still wonder what his name is,' said Higlett. 'I like to know the person I'm working for. This man is a complete stranger.'

'He got us out of Newgate. That's all that matters.'

'Yes, but why did he pick *us*?'

'I'm a handsome man.' Fearon grinned. 'He liked the look of me.'

* * *

Peter Skillen's search was futile. Several of the neighbours remembered seeing the man on the galloping horse but nobody could give a description of him because he'd flashed past them at such speed. Other shopkeepers in Middle Row were simply grateful that it had not been their windows that had been smashed in. Apart from expressing sympathy for Diane Mandrake, they had little to say about the incident. When he returned to the print shop, Peter found that the terrified servants had been flushed out of their room by Diane and ordered to get rid of the remaining debris. On their knees in the shop, they kept looking anxiously into the street as if expecting a second visit from the horseman.

Since the entire stock was now in the back room, Peter was able to look through all of the folders. They contained prints he'd never seen before. He hadn't realised there were so many. It was an education for him. Virgo was well represented but there were many other excellent drawings, all with a sharp bite and many with grotesque obscenities. It was interesting to compare Virgo's caricatures of certain politicians with others who chose the same targets. All had seized on a significant feature of each individual and magnified it to the point of absurdity. Peter noticed that Viscount Sidmouth still got some critical attention but it was the more flamboyant characters who tended to dominate the collection. Nothing he saw persuaded him to change his opinion of who the prime suspects should be. On the evidence of the prints, nobody's name could either be added or taken away.

Sir Humphrey Coote was popular among all satirists, as was Gerard Brunt. Whenever Dr Penhallurick was introduced, he was always depicted offering bogus remedies to Lord Liverpool or to members of his Cabinet. Julian Harvester was also shown in the company of the prime minister, shovelling handfuls of money into Liverpool's pockets by way of a bribe. Peter laughed out loud at some of the wicked comments and lewd innuendoes. When he looked at all of Virgo's cartoons ridiculing Harvester, he saw something he hadn't noticed before. Most of them had a sumptuous mansion in the background. Sketchily drawn, it nevertheless had a symbolic value.

Having calmed down Tite at long last, Diane peered over Peter's shoulder.

'What have you found?' she asked.

'It's this mansion – at a glance, it tells you that Mr Harvester has immense wealth.'

'I realise that every time I go past it.'

He looked up at her. 'This place is *real*?'

'It's his London residence, Peter. He may be a commoner but Harvester lords it when he comes to town. Leo was enraged whenever he saw houses of that size. He thought it was disgraceful that a privileged few enjoyed such luxury while the masses lived in squalor and degradation. It's what drove him on to pillory the idle rich.'

'In fairness, some of them are far from idle.'

'Yes, that's true,' she conceded, 'they're too busy making more money and seeking power over the rest of us. Leo wanted to call the series the *Parliament of Fools* but thought that it was too close to that poem by Chaucer, 'Parliament of Fowls'. We scratched our heads for a long time before coming up with the title on which we settled. After all, the series is about the idiosyncrasies of politicians. Leo and Virgo mock their foibles.'

'It's an appropriate title for such astringent cartoons.' Peter took a closer look at the print he was holding. 'Do you happen to know how often Mr Harvester is in London?'

'He spends most of his time here, by all accounts,' she said, 'and retires to the country for the winter. Virgo has drawn a good likeness of the mansion. He must obviously have seen it.'

'I'd like to do so myself,' he said. 'Where exactly is it?'

'I'll take you there, Peter. It's not far away. When you see the house, you'll be overwhelmed by envy. Mr Harvester lives in a different world to us mere mortals.'

Abel Fearon was kept waiting for a long time. He began to wonder if he was in the wrong street. Yet it was where the previous meeting had taken place because it was a haven from the busier thoroughfares. He idled his time away by walking up and down and whistling tunelessly as he did so. The coach eventually veered into sight, drawn by four horses. Seeing Fearon, the driver hauled on the reins. When it came to a halt beside him, he removed his hat out of respect and opened the door of the vehicle. Beckoned inside, he sat opposite the sole passenger and pulled the door shut.

His companion was a middle-aged man in an impeccable suit and a hat with a tall, gleaming crown. Before he spoke, he removed a glove, plucked an enamelled box from his waistcoat pocket, flicked open the lid, took a pinch of snuff and inhaled it. While he was waiting, Fearon played with his hat and kept his head down. Putting the snuff box away, the man eventually deigned to look at him.

'Well?' he said.

'I did as I was told, sir. I rode past the shop and threw a stone through the window. The glass was shattered.'

'Was the woman there?'

'I didn't see her.'

'What did you do next?'

'I took the horse back to the stables I hired it from.' He took out a stub of paper. 'I have the receipt here.'

'Throw it away.'

'You told me to give it to you, sir. You said you'd give me fifty times the value of it for work well done.'

'But your work was *not* well done, Fearon.'

'Go to Holborn,' urged the other. 'See for yourself.'

'There's no need. I know you can be trusted to throw a stone through a window. My concern is with an area in which you *can't* be trusted.'

Fearon was perplexed. 'We've followed your orders to the letter, sir.'

'Did you?'

'Yes, we did.'

'Then why will the Bow Street Runners be lying in wait for you this evening in Covent Garden?' Fearon was startled. 'I'll tell you. It's because you were stupid enough to draw attention to yourselves. My orders were to stay out of sight and wait until you were needed again. Instead of that, you and your greasy friend cause mayhem in a brothel run by Doll Fortune.'

174

'We did no harm, sir.'

'You did a lot of harm. You injured two of the women and got yourselves talked about. By extension, you've also wounded me and I take exception to that. I chose you and Higlett on the advice of someone at Newgate. They said that you were fearless and would do anything I ordered.'

'We will, sir, I promise you.'

'Then you must keep your breeches on and control your lust.'

'Sim and I were only—'

'I know what you were doing,' said the other with asperity. 'The money was burning a hole in your purses so you decided to spend it on pleasure. You couldn't be discreet about it, though, could you? That would have been out of character. So you choose the most exclusive brothel in the city and behave like a pair of rutting stags.'

Fearon was cowed. 'How do you know about it, sir?'

'You admit it, then?'

'We'd not had a woman for a long time.'

'If you disobey orders again, I'll make sure that you and Higlett will never be able to have a woman again.' Fearon put a swift hand over his crotch. 'How do I know about your disgusting antics? By chance, I'm a member of the same club as Mr Kirkwood. Does that name ring a bell?'

Fearon scowled. 'He's the chief magistrate. He sentenced me to prison.'

'You'll be sentenced to death if the Runners catch you. They were out watching Doll Fortune's clients last night. Had you gone there a second time, you'd be in chains by now.'

'Is this what Mr Kirkwood told you?'

'It's what I overheard him telling someone else. You can see why I took such an interest. I could guess who he was talking about – you and Higlett, two drunken idiots led astray by the twitching of their pricks.'

'We wanted to celebrate, sir.'

'Well, you won't do it again,' said the other, harshly. 'You'll lie low until I have further use for you. Disobey me again and you'll wish you stayed in Newgate. Do you understand?'

'Yes, sir, I do. I'm sorry, sir – we both are.'

'Get out of the carriage.'

Fearon held up the stub. 'What about this receipt?'

'It's worthless.'

'But you promised to pay me, sir.'

'*You* promised to do what you're told.'

'Don't I get any reward?'

'You've had it.'

'Have I?'

'Yes,' snarled the other. 'You and that halfwit are still alive.'

Fearon was shaken. 'Are you telling me that . . . ?'

'That's exactly what I'm telling you, man.'

'We won't let you down again, sir. I swear it. And Sim will swear it as well. Give us a chance to prove our worth, sir. That's all we ask.'

'Get out of the coach.'

'I promise you that—'

'Get out!' roared the other. 'And leave the door open when you do. I need some fresh air in here to get rid of the stink.'

* * *

Paul Skillen was too impatient to wait until evening. Keen to find out if his trust in a one-legged old sailor had been misplaced, he set off for the tavern where they'd first met. Because he was not posing as a riverside habitué this time, there was no need for any disguise. He wore a light-blue coat with brass buttons and long tails, pantaloons strapped under the shoe, a dark-blue waistcoat, a frilled shirt and a large muslin cravat. On his previous search, he'd ended up at the Jolly Sailor. This time it was the first place he visited. To his delight, he saw the old man nursing a tankard in a corner. Paul went across at once and sat at the same table. The man was astonished to see such a debonair gentleman choosing to sit beside him.

'What have you found out?' asked Paul.

Legge was confused. 'Who are you, sir?'

'I asked you to make enquiries about Abel Fearon.'

'Oh, I see . . . Bricklaying pays better than I thought.'

'What did you discover?'

'I asked lots and lots of people about Fearon.'

'Did you find out where he is?'

'No, sir,' replied the other, 'but I did learn something. I met a man who'd been in Newgate with the two of them.'

'*Two* of them?'

'They were devils, he said. Everyone was glad when they were let out.'

'Are you talking about a friend of Fearon's?'

'Yes, sir.'

'What's his name?'

'It was Higlett, sir. Sim Higlett is just as bad as Fearon. That's

177

what I was told.' He moved his pipe from one side of his mouth to the other. 'I'm sorry, that's all I can tell you.'

'It's a help,' said Paul, slapping some coins on the table. 'Thank you, my friend. We know who both of them are now.'

It was a mistake to let Diane Mandrake drive him there in her curricle. Peter would have been far safer in the saddle of his horse and he would have heard far fewer expletives on his journey. She drove as if she was trying to outrun a pack of highwaymen. He was grateful when they swung round a corner and she pulled on the reins. On the opposite side of the road was the mansion he'd seen in some of the prints. In reality, it was much bigger and more luxurious than he'd been led to believe. Set well back from the road, it had a semicircular drive. Julian Harvester owned one of the finest dwellings in London.

'What do you think of it?' she asked.

'I hadn't realised the scale.'

'Can you see why it made Leo's blood boil?'

'I can see why Virgo included it in all of his caricatures.'

'He loathed it.'

'The place speaks volumes about the man who lives there.'

'It's disgusting for one man to have so much wealth.'

The clatter of hooves made them turn their heads. A gig was heading in their direction. It was being driven at a much more sedate pace than Diane's curricle had been. When it drew level with them, it turned into the drive but not before Peter had been able to take a close look at the driver.

'Did you see who that was?' he asked.

'His face is familiar but I can't really place it.'

'Go back to the shop and study Virgo's prints again,' he advised.

'Why?'

'That face appears in many of them.'

It slowly dawned on her. 'Now that you mention it . . .'

'Yes, Mrs Mandrake. We've just had our first sighting of Dr Penhallurick.'

CHAPTER ELEVEN

Higlett was still hunched over the table, trying to remember the rules of the particular game of patience that he was playing. From time to time, he added variations of his own, turning over a second card if the first one he picked up was unsatisfactory and changing that as well if it was not what he'd hoped for. By a combination of cheating, swearing and ignorance of the game, he slowly manoeuvred himself into a winning position. When he turned over the last card, he let out a whoop of joy and banged the table with a fist. It would be something he could boast about to Fearon.

When his friend appeared soon after, however, he was in no mood to hear about Higlett's card game. He was simmering with anger at the way he'd been treated in the carriage. It had been humiliating.

'Did you see him, Abel?' asked Higlett.

'Yes, I did.'

'How much did he give you?'

'Nothing at all.'

'But he promised you a reward.'

'I didn't get it, Sim.'

'Why not?'

'We disobeyed his orders.'

'Who cares about his frigging orders?'

'He does. From now on, we stay in all night.'

'That's ridiculous. We're entitled to—'

Fearon cut him short by grabbing his collar and lifting him to his feet.

'We were too hasty,' he explained. 'When we went to Covent Garden the first night, we got ourselves noticed.'

'That was your fault. You shouldn't have bitten her like that.'

'Shut up!'

'I could hear her screams from the next room.'

'Shut up, I said. Shut up and *listen*.'

He reinforced the command by pushing his friend roughly away. Though he protested loudly, Higlett could see that Fearon was talking in earnest. He was far too dangerous a man to cross. Without interrupting, he listened to what had happened when his friend had climbed into the carriage. By the end of the recitation, he was thoroughly chastened.

'We'd have been walking into a trap tonight,' he said, fearfully. 'That's why we must stay here.'

'But there are women all over London. Forget about Covent Garden. We'll find juicier fruit somewhere else.'

'Haven't you heard what I said?' demanded Fearon.

'Yes – we keep away from those two places we went before.'

'We follow orders. If we don't . . .'

181

He ran a hand quickly across his throat in a dramatic gesture. Higlett gulped.

'He'd have us *killed*?'

'Yes,' said the other, 'he would.'

'But we've done him a lot of favours.'

'They don't count.'

'He can't have us murdered.'

'He can do what he likes, Sim. He *bought* us. We're his slaves.'

'I'm nobody's slave,' said Higlett with token defiance.

'I dare you to tell him that.'

Higlett thought better of it. On the one occasion he'd met the man who'd arranged their early release from prison, he'd been struck by his peremptory manner and by the ruthless glint in his eye. Confrontation with him would be a form of suicide. He sought another way out.

'Let's cut and run, Abel,' he advised. 'We've got plenty of money left. I say that we disappear from here and enjoy spending it.'

'And what happens when he finds us?'

'We make sure that he doesn't.'

'How do we do that?'

'There are hundreds of places to hide in London.'

'He'd track us down somehow, however long it took. Men like him never give up. We'd always be looking over our shoulders. Is that the kind of life you want?'

'It's better than being treated as a slave.'

'We're slaves who get *well paid*,' Fearon reminded him.

'You didn't get a penny today.'

'That was a punishment because we sailed too close to the wind.'

'We needed women,' complained the other. 'It's only natural.'

'We can have as many as we like when things die down, Sim. Right now the Runners are looking for us. There's a price on our heads so we need to be careful. Also,' he continued, 'there'll be further work for us. That means another full purse. Until then, we do as we're told.'

'Can't we get a doxy or two up here?'

'No, we can't.'

Higlett pulled a face. 'So what do we do while we wait for a call?'

'We play cards,' replied Fearon, grabbing a flagon of ale and taking a long swig from it before handing it to his friend, 'and we drink until we keel over.'

Peter Skillen returned to the gallery and told his wife and his brother what had happened. Charlotte was alarmed on Diane Mandrake's behalf.

'She *spurned* your offer of help?'

'She turned me down flat, my love. Mrs Mandrake said that there was no need for me to stay the night there. They can manage on their own.'

'Who else will be there with her?' asked Paul.

'Mr Tite, who works in the shop, and the servants – that's all. Tite is not what I'd describe as able-bodied and the servants will make poor sentinels. I know that Mrs Mandrake has a weapon but she could be up against the killer.'

'Did you suggest that she might stay with you and Charlotte?'

'I pressed her to do so.'

'What was her answer?'

'She said that she'd never desert her property. If there was going to be a second assault on it, she had to be there to deal with it.'

'Diane is too brave for her own safety,' said Charlotte with a sigh.

'You might say the same of Paul and me.'

She smiled. 'I've said it a hundred times, Peter, but you take no notice.'

'We were born with a sense of adventure,' remarked Paul. 'You can't deny what's in your blood, Charlotte.'

Peter was curious. Having told them about his visit to the print shop, and of his subsequent drive in the curricle to the home of Julian Harvester, he was eager to hear what his brother had learnt. Paul talked about his discoveries at the King's Bench Prison and, even though she'd heard his story before, Charlotte was still fascinated. She simply could not understand why anyone would choose to stay locked up when he had the money to pay off his debts. Peter was glad that they'd finally solved the mystery of who'd actually produced the cartoons. Paul described his second visit to the Jolly Sailor.

'Did anyone know where Fearon might be?' asked Charlotte.

'No,' replied Paul, 'I'm afraid not. But the man I paid did glean one important piece of information – the name of Fearon's accomplice.'

'Who is he?'

'Sim Higlett – he was in Newgate with Fearon, it seems. Someone arranged for them to be let out together.'

'I'll see if we have any mention of him,' said Charlotte, reaching for her record book. 'I don't recall the name but he may be in my collection.'

'What can you tell us about him, Paul?' asked his brother.

'I simply know that he's as bad as his partner,' said Paul. 'They're a gruesome pair, by the sound of it, and made themselves very unpopular in prison. Which one of them killed Paige, I don't know, but it's likely to be the same man who gave Jem such a beating.'

'I'm sure that Jem would love to be there when we catch him.'

'I don't blame him, Peter.'

'Well, at least we know who we're actually looking for. Yeomans and his men are looking for two phantoms. We have names and – in the case of Fearon – a good description of what he looks like.'

'You'll have to be satisfied with that,' said Charlotte, flicking through the pages. 'There's no Higlett in here, so I can't even tell you why he was put in prison. Is there any way to find out?'

'Newgate is nowhere near as lax and obliging as the King's Bench,' said Paul. 'We've tried to get information out of them before and they insist that their records are confidential. That's as it should be, I suppose. Unlike the Runners, we have no warrant to make enquiries like that.' He turned to Peter. 'I was interested to hear that you saw Dr Penhallurick at Harvester's mansion. That puts two of our suspects under the same roof. Are they in league with each other?'

'It's conceivable,' said Peter, 'but it may just be that Penhallurick is his physician and was calling on Harvester today to relieve his gout or whatever affliction he suffers from.'

'His affliction is having far too much money.'

Peter laughed. 'Then it's one I wouldn't mind having myself.'

'What about our other suspects?'

'I found out something interesting about them. Sir Humphrey Coote may be an inveterate lecher but he has his good side as well. It turns out that he's obsessed with the game of cricket. I admire him for that. It's a game I love, but I'm prepared to make the supreme sacrifice. You can go in my stead, Paul.'

'Go *where*?' asked his brother, mystified.

'To Thomas Lord's cricket ground,' said Peter. 'I've seen the handbills advertising a match tomorrow. It's between two Select Elevens of all England. The finest players in the country will be on display. If he's *that* avid a spectator, Sir Humphrey is certain to be at the match. You'll be able to take a close look at him.'

'Don't I get to watch the cricket as well?'

'That's up to you, Paul.'

'Where will you be?'

'I'll be checking up on our other suspect – Gerard Brunt. He was trained as a lawyer and is always trying to get new laws on the statute book or to amend existing legislation.'

'Where are you going to meet him?'

'Oh, I won't see him in person,' said Peter. 'Parliament is in recess at the moment but, according to no less a person than the Home Secretary, Brunt will be working on speeches to deliver in the Commons when it reconvenes.'

'So what do you intend to do, Peter?' asked his wife.

'I plan to find out how his mind works, my love. If he likes pontificating in Parliament, then there'll be a record of exactly what he said. While Paul is watching a cricket match in St John's Wood, I'll be getting acquainted with Mr Gerard Brunt in the pages of Hansard.'

As evening shadows lengthened, Yeomans and his men descended on Covent Garden. Every member of the foot patrols was there. After speaking to them as a group, and stressing the importance of their night's work, he handed them over to Alfred Hale who read out the list of places to which each of them was deployed. They scattered immediately and went off to take up their respective positions. A killer was likely to be abroad and there was a sizeable reward for his capture. Hoping that he would be the one to encounter the villain, each man had his own seductive vision of heroism.

Chevy Ruddock was the exception to the rule. He thought only of his wife.

'Agnes keeps asking why I have to stand guard over a church,' he said, morosely, 'and I can't think of an answer.'

'Tell her that you're the guardian of precious relics,' suggested Hale.

'Or that the archbishop asked for you by name,' added Yeomans. 'When you tell a lie, make sure that it shows you in a good light. It helps a wife to sleep more easily if she feels that her husband has achieved something.'

'But I haven't,' moaned Ruddock.

'Tonight may be your night.'

'What makes you think that, Mr Yeomans?'

'We're dealing with slavering dogs,' said the other. 'When

the sun goes down, Covent Garden is full of gorgeous bitches on heat. Once they get that smell in their nostrils, the dogs find it irresistible. They'll be here.'

'Let someone else watch Mrs Fortune's house.'

'To start with, Ruddock, she is not a married lady. Doll has a ring on every finger but none of them happens to be a wedding ring. The second thing is that Alfred went to great trouble to work out the best use of our resources. Believe it or not,' said Yeomans, 'yours was the first name on the list.'

'You should be pleased about that, Chevy,' said Hale.

'I am,' said the other, 'but I find that watching a brothel is . . . unsavoury.'

'You have an unsavoury occupation in an unsavoury city, lad. The sooner you accept that, the better it will be for you. Besides, it will be an education for you. Doll attracts the cream of society.'

'Yes,' said Yeomans. 'Step in there and you're likely to see members of the peerage romping about. Covent Garden is a version of Eden for some people. Having said that, it's nothing like the den of iniquity it used to be in the old days. Do you know how John Fielding, the Blind Beak, who helped to found the Runners, described it? He said that you would imagine that all the prostitutes in the kingdom had chosen this particular rendezvous. Think of that, Ruddock. Everywhere you went here at night, you were likely to trip over a naked woman open and ready.'

'The place was full of gambling houses and Turkish baths in those days,' said Hale. 'Are you partial to a hot bath with four female hands to soap you, Chevy?'

'No,' exclaimed Ruddock in alarm.

'You should broaden your horizons.'

'I don't want to, Mr Hale.' He moved away. 'I'll get off to my station.'

'If you see anything of interest,' Yeomans called after him, 'you know where to find us. We'll be in the Peacock.' He grinned at Hale. 'We frightened Ruddock away, Alfred. He's still a little raw at times.'

As they set off for the tavern, a clock chimed in the distance.

'In another hour,' said Hale, 'it will be dark and the night people will come out to play. Will our killer be one of them?'

'There's no doubt about it. He and his friend have come here two nights in a row. They'll be back again tonight to revel in the fleshpots. This is our big chance,' said Yeomans, rubbing his hands together. 'It will be a case of third time lucky.'

Higlett was getting progressively more restive. Having drunk ale steadily for hours, he was playing cards with Fearon and losing money at every turn. Frustration eventually got the better of him.

'This is no way to spend an evening,' he said, truculently.

'It's the way it has to be, Sim.'

'Think of all those lonely nights we spent in Newgate.'

'They were hardly lonely,' said Fearon. 'We shared the place with the scum of the earth. If they weren't snoring, they were farting all night like cart horses.'

'But there were no *women*, Abel.'

'There were none that we could get at, anyway.'

'We promised ourselves we'd make up for lost time when we got out.'

'And we did just that. The trouble is that . . . well, I got too excited. It was reported and the Runners came looking for us.'

'They're easy enough to dodge.'

'Not when your breeches are around your ankles. I told you what he said. He heard it from the chief magistrate's own lips. They're after us, Sim. They're keeping watch in Covent Garden.'

'So we go somewhere else.'

'We stay here and play cards.'

'That's boring and, in any case, you keep winning.'

'You keep *letting* me win,' said Fearon with a snigger. 'It's your deal so let's get on with it.'

Higlett picked up the cards and shuffled them clumsily. He was just about to deal them out when he was troubled by a sudden thought.

'Why is he keeping us, Abel?' he asked.

'He has more work for us.'

'We were hired to follow Paige and kill him if he ignored the warnings.'

'So?'

'We did that. What's left for us to do?'

'The woman who owns the print shop needs to be scared.'

'That's what you did earlier on. You smashed her window.'

'We don't know if it worked, Sim. He told me that Mrs Mandrake was as tough as any man. She won't be frightened easy.'

'Then we kill her as well, I suppose.'

'And we get even more money than we did for Paige.'

Higlett's face puckered. 'Then what?'

'We wait for orders.'

'But there may never be any. He wanted a man killed and a shop closed. If we commit a second murder, it's all over. He doesn't need us any more, Abel.'

'In that case,' said the other, shrugging, 'we go our merry way.'

'Are you sure he'll let us do that?' asked Higlett. 'We've seen how he treats people who get in his way. Once we're no longer any use to him, *we'll* be in the way as well. Do you see what I mean?'

Fearon swallowed hard and shifted uneasily in his chair.

'Deal those frigging cards,' he snapped.

Returning home at the end of the evening, Peter and Charlotte were let into the house by Meg Rooke. The hopeful look on her face vanished when she realised that they had come alone.

'Is Mr Huckvale not with you?' she asked.

'No, Meg,' said Charlotte. 'He's staying at the gallery.'

'But he had a bad injury, Mrs Skillen. He needs looking after.'

'We've told him that but he prefers to be back in his own room.'

Her face clouded. 'Oh, I see . . .'

'However,' said Peter, 'it doesn't mean that you can't see him. He'll be working at the gallery. I can even tell you what times he has appointments. If you happened to call in when you've been to market, you could ask him how he is.'

She brightened at once. 'Yes, I could, couldn't I?'

'He'll be delighted to see you,' said Peter.

The maidservant went off happily, allowing them to go into the drawing room. Charlotte sat down with a sigh of relief but Peter hovered near the door.

'What's the matter?' she asked.

'I'm wondering if I should go to Holborn, after all.'

'Diane doesn't want you there, Peter. She made that clear.'

'She need not be even aware of my presence,' he said. 'I can just loiter outside for an hour or two to make sure that there's no further trouble.'

'You heard her. She can look after herself.'

'Mrs Mandrake is a forthright woman, I grant you that, and she wouldn't hesitate to fire that weapon she carries. Gully was amazed by the way she handled it. But, when all is said and done, she's only a woman.'

Charlotte bridled. 'I object to the word "only", Peter.'

'I apologise unreservedly, my love.'

'Sit down and forget all about Diane.'

'Very well,' he said, taking a seat. 'After what happened, she won't venture far from that shop. We'll not have her impeding us at the gallery.'

'She wasn't impeding us – she was helping.'

'Well, now it's time for us to help *her*.'

'I don't want to hear her name mentioned again, Peter.'

'I thought you liked Mrs Mandrake.'

'I do,' she said. 'I'm full of admiration for what she is and what she's done in building up the reputation of her shop. But we have lots of other concerns and its time we turned to them. Diane will be fine. She's probably fast asleep by now, enjoying a well-earned rest after the vagaries of the day.'

'You're wrong, my love,' he argued. 'She'll be wide awake.'

Diane Mandrake was as good as her word. She was determined to protect her property at all costs. Since the shop window

192

had now been boarded up, she could not act as a sentry on the ground floor. Loaded pistol at hand, she therefore took up her position in the window of the front bedroom. There was a timid knock on the door. In answer to her summons, Tite came into the room.

'You can't stay there all night,' he said.

'I'll do whatever is necessary, Ben.'

'What if someone through a stone through *this* window?'

'He'll be shot before he even has a chance to hurl it,' she said, resolutely. '*You're* the one who needs his sleep. Leave me be and go back to your room. It's my property and I'll defend it.'

'You should have let Mr Skillen stay the night.'

'It's a very appetising thought,' she said under her breath.

'He's accustomed to this kind of work.'

'Peter Skillen's offer was kind and well meant but it was asking too much of him. He's already committed himself to finding Leo's killer. That will keep him more than preoccupied.'

Tite adjusted his nightcap. 'I'm sorry to be so inadequate,' he said, meekly.

'You do what you're paid to do, Ben, and I have no complaints. When I asked you to sell prints for me, I didn't expect that you would also be my bodyguard.'

'Heaven forbid!'

'Besides, you're the person who was here when the outrage took place. I feel very guilty about that. You take yourself off and have a good night's sleep.'

'Can't I prevail upon you to do the same?'

'I'm staying here.'

When she heard a horse approaching outside, she grabbed

the pistol and parted the curtains even more, but there was no real threat. The animal was moving at a gentle trot along the street and the rider didn't even look in the direction of her shop. Diane relaxed and set the weapon aside.

'How many times has that happened?' asked Tite.

'Too many,' she admitted. 'Every time I hear a hoof beat or a footstep in the street, I anticipate danger. So far it's never actually come.'

'Mr Skillen felt that an attack would be unlikely tonight. He only offered to stay here in order to calm our nerves. He said that whoever ordered the attack would wait to see what effect their warning had had on you.'

'I'm taking no chances.'

Tite made an effort to sound brave. 'I'll stay in here with you.'

'What a suggestion!' she exclaimed. 'It would be very improper.'

'We could take it in turns to sleep, Mrs Mandrake.'

'This is my battle and I'll fight it on my terms.'

'I was only trying to—'

'Goodnight, Ben,' she said, pointedly. 'I won't discuss it any further.'

Issuing a stream of apologies, he backed away and went out.

Diane, meanwhile, stared through the window in a vain attempt to pierce the darkness. When people did walk or ride past the shop, she could only see them in a blurry outline. It put a strain on her eyes and her neck started to ache. It was well past midnight when she dozed off, willing herself instantly awake and getting up to shake herself all over. She could not keep a yawn at bay, however. Resuming her seat, she looked out into the gloom.

An hour later, she was fast asleep.

Covent Garden remained alive at night. Clients came and went to its tempting array of brothels and gambling dens. Revellers sang their way home. Yapping dogs scavenged. One of them took a keen interest in Chevy Ruddock and he had great difficulty in scaring the animal away. Having taken up a position outside Doll Fortune's house, he was close enough to glimpse the men who arrived there and even heard some of the banter and ribaldry of those departing. Paying for sexual favours was something so far outside his experience or inclination that he couldn't understand the motive behind it. Apart from anything else, the women who sold their bodies were often old, ugly and repellent. He had to contend with more than one example of the breed.

'Can I 'elp ya, sir?' asked the woman in a hoarse whisper.

'No, thank you.'

'Ya looks lonely, sir. A big, strong man like ya needs a bit o' comp'ny at noight. I'll take care of ya.'

'Go away,' he said.

'Gintelmen likes me. I never 'ad no complaints.'

When she rubbed up against him, he went puce with embarrassment. The street prostitute was worlds away from the perfumed princesses of the trade operating in Doll Fortune's house. The woman was old, bedraggled, heavily powdered and had such bad breath that he recoiled from it. Feeling her hand on his thigh, he leapt back as if she'd sunk a dagger into him.

'Come wi' me, sir,' she purred. 'Annie'll look arfter ya.'

'Go away, woman. If you don't leave me alone, I'll arrest you.'

She became combative. 'Doan ya touch me, ya long, tall, nasty turd!'

He tried to push her away but she became even more abusive. Ruddock was still trying to get rid of her when Hale came down the street. He recognised the woman by the sound of her screech.

'Is that you caterwauling again, Annie?'

'Yes, Mr 'ale,' she replied. 'This filthy scab 'ad 'is way wi' me but woan pay up. Iss nor right, sir – 'e left bruises all over my tits.'

'I never touched the woman,' said Ruddock, indignantly.

'Yes, ya did, ya bleedin' liar.'

'As God's my witness, Mr Hale, the woman is lying.'

'She always does, lad,' said the other before rounding on the prostitute. 'If you're still standing here by the time I've counted to ten, I'll have you locked up and fed on stale bread and water. Now disappear, Annie.'

After ridding herself of a string of imprecations, she hobbled swiftly away.

'Thank goodness you came along when you did,' said Ruddock.

'How many times do I have to say it? You'll have to learn to cope with trulls like her, Chevy.'

'She made the most appalling suggestion.'

'Well, she won't be able to make it again tonight,' said Hale, 'and neither will anybody else like her. You're off duty, lad. We've watched all night and there's been no sign of the people we're after. Mr Yeomans is standing everyone down.'

Ruddock was delighted. 'Does that mean I can go home?'

'It does.'

'Thank you, Mr Hale.'

'But you may have to return here tomorrow night.'

'Oh, no!'

'Duty calls, lad.'

'Can't I keep vigil in another part of the area?'

'This is your own special spot,' said Hale. 'You've earned it. I know that it's lonely out here in the dark but don't worry. Annie might well turn up again tomorrow night to keep you company. You'd like that, wouldn't you?'

It was just before dawn when the man strolled along Middle Row. When he reached the print shop, he paused to look at the boarding and the large sign that had been stuck to it. He could just make out the letters of BUSINESS AS USUAL. Using a dagger to slip under the edge of the sign, he tore the whole thing off, scrunched it up and tossed it into the gutter. Then he walked calmly on down the street.

Fearon and Higlett had drunk themselves into oblivion. The clip-clop of horses, the rattle of vehicles and the sound of raised voices began soon after first light. They were not enough to disturb the two men. It would be hours before they finally stirred. The room was small, airless and hopelessly untidy. Empty flagons of ale were all over the floor and the cards were spread wide on the table. There was a musty atmosphere. It was Abel Fearon who was first roused from his slumber. The persistent barking of a dog in the street outside finally penetrated his hearing. He opened an eye then closed it at once when it was dazzled by the sunlight slanting in through the window.

Excess of alcohol had left its legacy. His head ached, his stomach was queasy and his bladder was uncomfortably full. Struggling to his feet, he took a few moments to steady himself, then parted his eyelids enough to see out of them. The first thing he noticed was Higlett, sprawled on the floor because he'd been too drunk to reach the bed. On the bare boards behind him was something that had obviously been pushed under the door. Apart from the landlord of the tavern, only one person knew where they were hiding. If there was a message, it had to have come from him.

He staggered across to the door and bent down to scoop up the letter. It took some time for his eyes to obey him. He was then able to read the short message. Turning round, he kicked Higlett's leg.

'Wake up, Sim!'

'What?' moaned the other. 'Who's that kicking me?'

'It's me,' said the other, giving him a second kick.

'Stop it, Abel. I want to sleep.'

'It's time to get up.'

'What's the point when we can't have women up here?'

'Get up,' said Fearon, shaking him. 'We've got orders.'

'Who from?'

'Who d'you think, you numbskull?'

'Has he been here while I was asleep?'

'Someone delivered a letter from him.'

'What's it say?'

'Wake up and you'll be able to read it.'

'Is he going to pay us this time?'

'Oh, yes,' said the other. 'For this kind of work, he's going to pay us a great deal. I gave them a warning in the print shop yesterday. It didn't work. There won't be a second warning. They signed their death warrant.'

CHAPTER TWELVE

Now that he was feeling better, Jem Huckvale was determined to shoulder as much of the load as possible at the gallery. Fencing and boxing were still beyond him but he was at last capable of giving instruction in archery as well as in shooting. Since Ackford had lingering doubts about his abilities with a bow and arrow, Huckvale gave him a demonstration, hitting the centre of the target time and again with a satisfying thud. Before his young assistant could reach into the quiver again, Ackford stepped forward.

'No more, Jem,' he said. 'You've convinced me.'

'I told you I could do it, Gully.'

'I admire your pluck in even trying. You never were one to give up easily.'

Huckvale put the bow and the quiver of arrows aside. He was pensive.

'I wonder which of them it was?' he said.

'Who are you talking about?'

'Fearon and Higlett – those are their names, aren't they? Which of them did his best to smash my skull in two?'

'Does it matter? We'll catch the pair of them in time.'

'I want to look my attacker in the eyes.'

'You're not equal to that, Jem.'

'Yes, I am. I can handle a dagger or even a cudgel.'

'Leave them to Peter and Paul,' said Ackford, firmly. 'They're experts with every weapon under the sun. I'd like to meet Fearon and Higlett myself so that I can strike a few blows on Leo Paige's behalf but I'm unlikely to get the chance. The one thing I *am* set on, mind you, is attending my old friend's funeral this afternoon. That comes before everything.' He sighed. 'There won't be many of us there, I suspect.'

'What about Mr Paige's brother – Virgo?'

'He may well turn up. I know that Paul sent him word of the arrangements. Virgo will undoubtedly want to pay his last respects. I'll be interested to meet him.'

Huckvale walked up to the target and started to pull the arrows out of it.

'How will we find them, Gully?'

'Peter has the answer to that. The surest way is to identify the man who employed them in the first place. By right, those rogues should still be festering away in Newgate. Somebody needed to hire assassins and they were selected.'

'Where are they now?'

'They'll be in hiding somewhere.'

'One of them must have thrown that stone at the print shop.'

'Agreed,' said Ackford. 'It shows that someone is determined

201

to punish Mrs Mandrake as well. She'll not stand for that, I can tell you.'

Huckvale gave a shiver. 'She frightens me.'

'I suffered a few qualms myself when she was here,' confessed Ackford with a chuckle. 'But she's a brave, honest, hard-working woman and, out of the kindness of her heart, she's paid for Leo's funeral. She didn't deserve that attack on her shop. Who gave the order for it, I wonder?'

After putting the arrows in the quiver, Huckvale felt a twinge of uncertainty.

'We *will* catch them, won't we?'

'Do you even need to ask that question?'

'They mustn't get away with it.'

'Everyone involved will be caught and convicted. Peter and Paul will see to that. You're their inspiration, Jem. One glance at that bandaging around your head always spurs them on. Look how much intelligence they've gathered already,' he went on. 'We know who the culprits are, for a start. That puts us way ahead of the Runners.'

'What are *they* doing?'

'Whatever it is,' said Ackford, 'it won't help them to solve the murder.'

'Mr Yeomans has got more resources than we have.'

'That's never made any difference in the past.'

'I'd *hate* it if he made the arrests in this case.'

'There's no chance of that, Jem. The Runners may have more men at their disposal, and they have a legion of informers, but we have two prize assets.'

'I know – Peter and Paul Skillen.'

'When it comes to fighting crime, they have no peers. Micah Yeomans would love to have men like that at his disposal but he doesn't. They're *ours*.'

She was never far from his thoughts. As he lay in bed for a few hours that morning with his wife, Yeomans was toying with the fantasy that the woman beside him was, in fact, Diane Mandrake. The reality was daunting. He was tied to a wife he now found hideously predictable and largely irrelevant to his life. While acknowledging her loyalty to him and her essential goodness, he could find nothing in her – or in their marriage, for that matter – that provided even an ounce of excitement. Now that he entertained hopes regarding Diane, he pushed his wife to the back of his mind. Creeping out of bed, he left her in a deep sleep.

When he slipped out of the house in due course, he was hit by the realisation that the previous night had been a signal failure. Having managed to impress the chief magistrate by talking about the certainty of arrests, he would now have to avoid him in order to escape the inevitable scorn that would be heaped upon him. Yeomans had arranged to meet Alfred Hale but his feet took him insensibly in a different direction altogether. He was walking instead towards Holborn and the woman who aroused such powerful feelings in him. While not expecting to see her in person, he felt that he had to go past her shop at least once. Simply being in the same street where she lived would be a blessing.

His arrival, in fact, was well timed. Not only did he see her on the pavement outside the shop, he noticed the boarding over the window. His protective instinct made him quicken his step until he was almost running.

'What happened, Mrs Mandrake?' he asked, breathlessly.

'You let me down, sir,' she replied, tartly. 'The Runners are supposed to make the streets of London safe yet this kind of atrocity can happen. Someone galloped past my shop yesterday and hurled a stone through the window.'

'I hope you were not hurt in any way.'

'As luck would have it, I was not even here.'

'Thank God for that!'

'My property was not only damaged, there was a second outrage.'

'What was that, I pray?'

'When the boarding was put up,' she explained, 'there was a poster nailed on it proclaiming that there would be business as usual. Nothing will deter me from offering my prints to the general public.'

He looked at the window. 'Where is the poster now?'

'I found it in the gutter, Mr Yeomans. During the night, would you believe, some vile wretch sneaked past and tore it down. What do you think of that?'

'I think it very disturbing indeed.'

'My assistant and my servants are quaking.'

'You should be alarmed yourself, Mrs Mandrake,' he advised. 'Whoever broke your window expected you to suspend business. The fact that you intend to carry on regardless has evidently angered him. If your poster was torn down, it's a dire warning. I beg you to close the premises for a while.'

'That would suit you, wouldn't it?'

'Not at all, dear lady, not at all.'

'Come now, sir, cease this parade of false concern.'

'But it's *not* false,' he declared. 'Truly, I'm worried on your account.'

'You're only worried that we'll remain open if every window in the property is smashed to smithereens. You despise what I do because you recognised yourself in one of my prints. Have the decency to admit it.'

Yeomans measured his words carefully. 'I did take exception to some of the prints in your window, Mrs Mandrake,' he said, quietly. 'I'll own that. They showed a worrying disrespect for authority. A man in my position must necessarily look askance at that. As for your good self, however,' he added, 'I'm bound to admire your courage and sense of purpose. My worry is that those same qualities will lead you unwittingly into harm's way.'

Diane looked more closely at him. When he first appeared, she'd been tempted to turn on her heel and go back into the shop, but there was a note of sincerity in his voice that held her back. The anxiety he was displaying was palpably real. In a man like Yeomans, it seemed incongruous but it was nevertheless there. It did nothing to change her opinion of the man. She still found him despicable.

'What are you doing here, Mr Yeomans?' she demanded.

'I was on my way to meet someone.'

'So you came down this street by chance, is that it?'

'Yes, I did.'

'It's not the first time you came down here by happenstance, is it? Ben Tite tells me that you've been skulking about before. For what purpose, may I ask?'

'It was out of consideration for your safety, Mrs Mandrake.'

'I'd prefer you to have more consideration for my peace of mind,' she said with emphasis. 'That would involve going about your business by different means than this particular street and leaving me alone. Do I make myself plain?'

'Don't spurn my protection. I offer it in good faith.'

'Good day to you, sir.'

He raised his hat to her. 'Good day to you, Mrs Mandrake.'

Accepting her rebuke, he walked swiftly away. It was only when he reached the end of the street that he dared to turn around. Hoping for a final glimpse of her, however, he was disappointed. She had vanished from sight.

The day got off to a troubling start for Paul Skillen. A letter from France finally arrived to rekindle his hopes that Hannah Granville would soon return. It was full of endearments that reminded him just how much he loved and missed her, and it gave a summary of her activities in Paris. Well received by theatregoers in the city, she had given a number of poetry recitals and, as a result, had steadily widened her circle of admirers. Hannah spoke of several English visitors to the French capital who'd come to support her. Paul read that she was now rehearsing for a production of *Macbeth* to be performed in French. Having seen her in Shakespearean roles at the Haymarket Theatre, he'd witnessed her greatest triumphs. Whether or not she could repeat that triumph abroad was, however, an open question. Hannah did have one advantage. Having been taught by a French governess, she'd achieved a fluency in the language that gave her the confidence to take on the difficult challenge. Paul was proud of her for that.

His early euphoria soon changed into disappointment, then apprehension. On the surface, the letter was all he could have desired but, when he read between the lines, he detected that something was wrong. Was the unhappiness he sensed simply occasioned by absence from her lover or was there another, darker reason? Were her reservations about tackling a Shakespeare play in French the real cause of her unease or was she hinting at problems with the rest of the cast? At all events, Paul was anxious. He read the letter a number of times in search for clues on which to build his theory but they were elusive. What exacerbated the situation was that it had taken ten days for the missive to reach him. Much could have happened in the interval. Was Hannah still struggling to master her role? Did she have to cope with envy and spite from French actresses who might feel they were more suited to play Lady Macbeth than an imported foreigner? Was there tension with the man playing her husband? Worst of all in Paul's mind, had her striking beauty attracted the kind of urgent suitors who always besieged the stage door after one of her performances?

His initial impulse was to take ship to France and rush to her assistance but he had other priorities. A murder investigation kept him in London and required all his attention. At a time when Hannah needed him – he could almost hear the cry for help in her letter – he had to spend the day at a cricket match. It was excruciating.

Peter Skillen hadn't realised how long and tortuous some of the speeches in the House of Commons really were. As he sat at a table with copies of recent Hansard journals in front of him, he read through many examples of Gerard Brunt's rhetoric. Clearly, the man had had a good education. Greek and Latin phrases peppered his speeches and Roman emperors were mentioned on a regular basis. The overwhelming impression was of a Member of Parliament trying to curry favour with those in the senior ranks of his party. Brunt went out of his way to make ingratiating remarks about this or that Cabinet minister, congratulating them on some action taken or pending. Peter had never read anything so full of unashamed fawning.

Yet the man's legal skills were undeniable. He could mount a cogent argument on almost any subject and back it up with an effortless command of precedents. Faithfully recorded in Hansard, his interventions during the speeches of others were also notable. Peter was getting to know Brunt extremely well. The parliamentarian's most recent speech had concerned an amendment to the law of libel. It was patently something close to his heart because he spoke about it with a fiery passion that was lacking in other debates. There was no room for tributes to political colleagues this time and no toadying. All his rhetoric was concentrated on a group of people he described as the caterpillars of the commonwealth, eating remorselessly away at the very foundations of English society.

'I put it you, Mr Speaker, that the law of libel offers insufficient protection from defamation that can lead to the complete destruction of a person's character and reputation.

It is, to me, the most heinous of crimes. Were any of the Honourable Members here present to walk down the Strand and find themselves pelted repeatedly with cattle dung, they would be understandably angry and take immediate steps to avoid the malodorous assault. When exactly the same thing happens in a newspaper or in a caricature, however, it's impossible to duck out of the way. We unfortunate victims have to stand there and put up with the verbal ordure that is gleefully hurled at us. We have to tolerate the indignity of being caricatured in prints that are the most grotesque examples of defamation. It is wrong, Mr Speaker. It is wrong, deplorable and uncivilised. The law of libel should give us stronger protection and more easily accessible retribution. Why should we be exposed to hatred, ridicule and contempt by our enemies? How can we frame the law so that it has wider scope and sharper teeth? Cow dung smells, Mr Speaker. Its reek is abhorrent. It also sticks. I ask this House to support an amendment that will give us the power to strike back at those who seek to deride us as individuals and undermine us as a government.

'Let me, if I may, Mr Speaker, move on to the instance of a pernicious series of caricatures entitled the Parliament of Foibles . . .'

Peter set the journal aside. He'd read enough. Gerard Brunt had the controlled fury of a man who would resort to any means in order to retaliate against those who sought to mock him. All of a sudden, he'd become the chief suspect.

* * *

When they'd reached their destination, they paused on the corner of the street.

'You walk past the print shop and have a good look at it,' said Fearon.

'Why don't you come with me?'

'It may just be that someone saw me galloping past on that horse and can recognise me. We don't want that to happen. Besides, I've got other work to do.'

'What is it, Abel?'

'I need to look at the street that this one backs on to.'

'The shop is *here*,' said Higlett, 'not in the next street.'

'It's got a garden at the rear. I want to see if we can get into it somehow. It will be far safer than going this way.'

'But it will be in the dark. Nobody will see us.'

'Mrs Mandrake might have someone guarding the building. I would.'

'Then we deal with him before we follow our orders.'

'Too dangerous,' said Fearon. 'The garden is the best answer, Sim. I'll poke around until I can find a way into it.'

'Where do we meet?'

'Back at the tavern – don't loiter.'

Higlett was on the point of moving away when a thought made him frown.

'Is this *it*, Abel?'

'What do you mean?'

'Is this the last thing we do for him? Is he going to pay us off and let us go our own sweet way? I'm getting tired of taking orders.'

'Do as you're told and don't ask questions.'

'I'm bound to wonder.'

'All you need to think about is what we have to do tonight,' said Fearon, voice laden with threat. 'Now get on with it.'

A cricket match at Thomas Lord's ground was always going to attract a large number of spectators. When Paul Skillen arrived there that morning, thousands were converging on what was, in fact, the third venue selected by Lord. After three years at Lisson Grove, the enterprising property dealer had moved the ground, turf and all, to the site in St John's Wood. It was the designated home of the Marylebone Cricket Club and, as such, was effectively the guardian of the laws of the game. Members of the aristocracy and the gentry flocked to a match that would last two days and was advertised as For Five Hundred Guineas a Side. Substantially more money than that would change hands because there would be some assiduous gambling throughout the game. It was an aspect of cricket that had always appealed to Paul but his penchant for gambling had been banked down since he met Hannah and he was resolved to resist temptation.

His main worry was how to identify and get close to Sir Humphrey Coote. He'd seen many caricatures of the man but the latter's features were distorted for the comic effect in them. All that he could do was to lurk near the entrance and hope that he singled out the right person. It would be difficult. There was an atmosphere of high excitement as the crowd pushed forward to pay the admission price of sixpence. What he did know was that Sir Humphrey would arrive by coach. He therefore studied each vehicle as it arrived and deposited its passengers.

His mind, however, kept wandering. In his pocket was the letter from Hannah Granville and it seemed to be giving off intense heat. Instead of watching a cricket match, Paul wanted to be sailing to France to be at her side. He envisaged the moment of reunion time and again.

Only a firm slap on the shoulder could bring him out of his reverie.

'Well met, sir!' said a hearty voice. 'Is it Peter or Paul Skillen I see?'

'Good morning, Mr Reddish,' said Paul, recognising him. 'You're speaking to Paul. It's good to see you again, sir.'

'That's no small thanks to you.'

'I simply gave you the instruction you sought, sir.'

'Yes, and it saved my life. What you didn't know at the time was that I came to the shooting gallery because I'd been challenged to a duel. Your advice gave me the courage to go through with it and an unerring accuracy with the duelling pistol that I'd never have achieved otherwise.'

Paul remembered him well. Gilbert Reddish was a corpulent man in his forties with an unquenchable ebullience. His voice, mien and attire suggested considerable prosperity. He'd needed a lot of instruction before he was ready to fight a duel. Paul was glad to see that he'd survived it.

'I shot him in the arm holding the pistol and that was that,' explained Reddish with a triumphant guffaw. 'He'll know better than to take me on again.' He slapped Paul on the shoulder again. 'Are you on your own today?'

'Yes, Mr Reddish.'

'Then you must join our party. Watching cricket is a barren

affair if you're by yourself. Three of my very best friends will soon be here to drink, gamble and enjoy the festivities. You'll make a fifth.' He held up a handbill. 'Have you seen the names in the respective teams?'

'I have, indeed, sir,' replied Paul. 'Lord Frederick Beauclerk will lead one side and the other will have Squire Osbaldeston in its ranks. There are no better players in the whole kingdom.'

Flattered by the attention from Reddish, he was also dismayed. If he was trapped with a group of people, he would not be free to hunt down the man he was after. Paul was about to offer an apology and say that he was unable to accept the kind invitation when Reddish stood on his toes to look over the heads of the crowd.

'Here they are!' he cried. 'I'd recognise his coach anywhere.'

'Mr Reddish . . .'

'They're splendid fellows, each and every one. You'll get on famously with them, especially with Sir Humphrey. He's very knowledgeable about the game.'

Paul's apology died on his lips. 'Sir *Humphrey* . . . ?'

'Yes,' said the other, waving an arm to attract the three people alighting from the coach. 'Sir Humphrey Coote. He's always riotous company.'

It was a quiet funeral. Held in the parish church, it was short but moving. Peter Skillen was there and so was Gully Ackford. Gregory Lomas had also come to see his former lodger laid to rest but, since neither of them had ever met the man, they didn't recognise him. The coffin concealed the ugly injuries inflicted on Leonidas Paige by the murderous assault and by the subsequent fire. Flowers provided by Diane Mandrake were sent with her love and deep regret. Peter and Ackford had been able to identify Virgo the moment he appeared but it was only afterwards that they were able to speak to him. After tossing a handful of earth into the grave, Paige's brother came over to them.

'Thank you, Mr Skillen,' he said, shaking Peter's hand. 'It was good of you to send me details of the funeral. I'd not have missed it for the world.'

'Actually,' Ackford pointed out, 'this is not *Paul* Skillen but his twin brother, Peter. We're pleased to meet you at last, sir. My name is Gully Ackford. Leo and I fought together in America.'

'Then I owe Mr Skillen my apologies and I owe you profound thanks.' He exchanged a handshake with them. 'Paul told me that you and his brother were helping in the search for the killer. I just wish that I could do more myself but I'm too distracted by grief. As he got older, Leo and I grew so much closer.'

'Working together does that,' said Peter. 'It's the same with Paul and me.'

'I'd assumed that he'd be here.'

'He's shadowing one of our suspects, Mr Paige.'

'Then there's no better excuse.'

They chatted for a few minutes, then, after shaking hands in turn with the vicar, they walked away from the grave. Lomas had been loitering self-consciously on the fringe of the little group. After the earlier abrasive meeting with Paige's brother, he took care to keep well away from him. Seeing his chance to speak to the person he mistook as Paul Skillen, he came over to him. Peter had to explain the situation.

'Oh, I'm sorry, sir,' said Lomas. 'I didn't realise there were two of you.'

'We are working together to solve the crime.'

'Is there any chance of an arrest yet?'

'We are getting ever closer to that point, sir.'

'The killer should be made to pay for the damage to my house.'

'I fear that the only compensation you'll get is the pleasure of knowing that he'll be tried for murder with his accomplice.'

Lomas nodded towards Virgo. 'Who's that gentleman over there?'

'A friend of the deceased,' replied Peter, unwilling to disclose the man's identity. 'My brother told me that he called at your house.'

'He did more than that, Mr Skillen. He forced his way in.'

'This may not be the time to press for an apology, Mr Lomas. I'm sure that it would be forthcoming but our thoughts should be with Mr Paige at this moment.'

'You are right, sir. Forgive me. I spoke out of turn.'

'We will keep you informed of any developments.'

'Your brother made the same promise,' said Lomas, 'but it's not one I received from the Bow Street Runners. They gave me no such assurance.'

'They have their methods and we have ours.'

'I know which I prefer, Mr Skillen. You and your brother have shown a sympathy and consideration that I appreciate. As you can imagine, it's been a very trying time for us. Mr Paige was a friend as well as a lodger. We feel his loss sorely. The other Mr Skillen consoled us,' he went on, 'whereas the Runners simply trampled over our feelings. We'll be glad if we never set eyes on Mr Yeomans ever again.'

Alfred Hale's reaction to the news was a dry laugh and a raised eyebrow.

'Are you surprised?' he said.

'I'm very sorry for the lady.'

'It's amazing that nobody has smashed her window before. Let's be honest, Micah. When we looked at those prints the other day, you'd have been tempted to grab a brick and throw it through the glass.'

'That's a lie!' retorted Yeomans. 'I have respect for property. I'd never dream of damaging that shop or any other.'

'Why are you so concerned about Mrs Mandrake all of a sudden?'

'I fear for her safety, Alfred.'

'But she was not on the premises when the stone was thrown.'

'She'll certainly be there in the event of a second attack and I have a feeling that it's likely.'

'I'm not so sure about that,' said Hale. 'Just because someone tears down a poster, it doesn't mean that the shop is in imminent danger. The poster might have blown off in the night or been ripped off the boarding by mischievous children. It may just be that it was never fixed securely to the wood in the first place.'

'It was another warning,' asserted Yeomans.

'Need it concern us?'

'Yes, it should. As Runners, we're charged with the protection of property and with the safety of our citizens. The print shop is under threat and so is its owner. Has it not yet dawned on you that the person who ordered the killing of Mr Paige is the same man who had Mrs Mandrake's property attacked?'

Hale's mouth fell open. 'Is that really the case?'

'Who sold Paige's drawings?'

'*She* did.'

'How do you stop Paige from producing those caricatures?'

'You have him silenced.'

'What if they continue to be on sale in the print shop?'

'You try to scare the owner of the shop.'

'Well done, Alfred,' said Yeomans, sarcastically. 'You are making the right deductions at last. Make one more deduction for me, if you please. What should we be doing tonight?'

'We must keep watch in Covent Garden until those two villains roll up with their tongues out and their pricks throbbing.' He saw the look of contempt on the other's face. 'You tell me, then.'

'If there's to be another attack on the shop, it will be at night. Mrs Mandrake and her assistant are on guard during the day. Forewarned is forearmed. At night, however, she is more vulnerable. When I offered my help, she refused it outright. Now, isn't it logical to suppose that the men hired to dispose of Paige will also be engaged to cause some sort of damage in Middle Row?'

'I never thought of it like that, Micah.'

'You never thought at all.'

'What are we going to do?'

'We'll maintain some surveillance in Covent Garden,' said Yeomans, 'but I'll also deploy men in Holborn. The print shop must be guarded all night.'

'We should take on that task ourselves.'

'No, we shouldn't. It's work for someone with sharper eyes and quicker legs than ours. You can guess who I mean, I think.'

'Oh, I do – Chevy Ruddock.'

The irony was that, in other circumstances, Paul Skillen might have relished the occasion. He loved the game of cricket and he found his companions uniformly amiable. When they heard that he'd helped to prepare Gilbert Reddish for a duel, they accepted him at once and insisted on paying for everything he needed. Swept into the largest of the marquees, Paul was plied with drink and urged to make a wager. He was in a situation that was familiar to him, hobnobbing with the sort of people he'd met dozens of times in a gambling den. What made him even more popular with his new friends were his insights into the game. He knew the worth and potential of every player on both sides and was happy to give advice before anyone placed a bet. It was not long before all four of them were deferring to him.

When the game finally started, Sir Humphrey Coote insisted that Paul sat beside them so that he could savour his observations. He was a tall, lean man of middle years with piggy eyes and an aquiline nose markedly increased in size in all the caricatures of him. His laugh was a high-pitched cackle of pure joy. He was so generous and good-humoured that Paul had to remind himself that he could be talking to a man who'd instigated a murder.

'I'm so glad that we met,' said Sir Humphrey, patting him on the thigh. 'I may have need of your services one day. In the course of my favourite recreation, I have cuckolded an untold number of husbands. Sooner or later, one of them will want his revenge in a duel. You, Mr Skillen, will act as my instructor and as my second. Is it agreed?'

'It's agreed, Sir Humphrey,' said Paul, forcing the words out.

'If you saved Reddish's life, you can do the same for me.'

'I hope that the need never arises.'

There was a loud noise as the batsman hit the ball with fearsome power and sent it hurtling in their direction.

'Look out!' exclaimed Reddish, bending down with his hands over his head.

'Good lord!' said Sir Humphrey. 'What a mighty blow!'

He, too, took evasive action when he saw the ball descending out from the sky. There was general commotion as it sped towards them. Paul was the only one of the group to stand up and keep a careful eye on the missile. When it got within a few yards of them, he shot out a hand, caught the ball with ease and gained a small ovation. Acknowledging the applause, he tossed the ball to the fielder who'd come to retrieve it. His new friends showered him with praise.

'Excellently done, sir!' shouted Sir Humphrey.

'You should be *playing* in the match,' said Reddish.

'I could never do anything like that.'

'Your skills are with balls of a different kind, Sir Humphrey.'

There was general hilarity among his friends and he didn't seem at all perturbed. Next moment, he was applauding another fine shot. His dedication to the game was genuine and he was well informed about its rules. Paul and he spent some of the time discussing new rules that might be introduced to make the game even more exciting. Sir Humphrey gave him a nudge.

'What I'd enjoy seeing most,' he said, licking his lips, 'would be a match between ladies. When I watched Hampshire and Surrey lasses playing each other at Newington Green some years ago, I was transported by the sight of all that grace and energy. It was magnificent, Mr Skillen.'

'So I've heard,' said Paul.

'They played with real heart.'

'And the standard was high, it's said.'

'The only rule I'd insist upon is that they were not wearing those unbecoming dresses and bonnets. The female body is a source of great beauty. I'd have them playing naked for my delectation.' He cackled merrily. 'And I'd engage an artist to paint the scene so that I could hang it in my bedroom as a souvenir.'

'I know the perfect artist for the commission,' announced Reddish.

'Who's that, Gilbert?'

'A man who has portrayed you many times and always with a sense of your virtues – I talk of Virgo.'

It was meant as a joke and the other two men laughed but Sir Humphrey drew no amusement from the remark. His affability vanished in a flash to be replaced by a towering rage. Swinging around to confront Reddish, he jabbed him angrily in the chest.

'You are behind the times, Gilbert,' he said with vehemence. 'Virgo is no longer alive to torment me. I have it on good authority that his candle has been snuffed out. That man was anathema to me and to friends in the House. I rejoice that he was killed. My regret is that I wasn't there at the time. It would have been an absolute pleasure to commit the murder with my own hands.'

Paul shuddered.

CHAPTER THIRTEEN

Charlotte Skillen was waiting for them when they got back to the gallery. She was interested to hear what had happened at the funeral. Peter and Ackford took it in turns to give her an account of it.

'There was one disappointment,' said her husband.

'What was that?' she asked.

'I half-expected that the man who'd ordered Mr Paige's murder might turn up to gloat. It's happened before in cases like this. People derive a ghoulish fascination from seeing their enemies lowered into the ground.'

'In the event,' said Ackford, 'the man we want didn't appear.'

'I think that he did, Gully, but it was not at the funeral.'

'Where else?'

'In the pages of Hansard,' said Peter. 'Gerard Brunt is so incensed at the caricatures of him that he actually wants to change the law of libel. That's the effect that Mr Paige and his brother have had. They've provoked someone into demanding new legislation.'

'They might regard that as an achievement,' said Charlotte.

'One of them does, my love. I told him about Brunt.'

'What sort of man is Virgil Paige?'

'He's very reserved. When it was all over, he was quick to leave.'

'It's unusual in a soldier,' said Ackford. 'We're a friendly breed, as a rule. There's no room for privacy in the army. Perhaps that's why he tired of it.'

'But why seek solitude in a prison?' asked Peter.

'It may be some kind of penance, Gully.'

'He didn't strike me as an overly religious man.'

'The sad thing is that Diane was unable to be there,' observed Charlotte. 'After all, she organised the funeral. Given his situation, that was something Mr Paige's brother was unable to do. But custom decrees that ladies have no place at the graveside. As a sex, it is assumed, we're too frail – though I've yet to meet anyone less frail than Diane Mandrake.'

'That reminds me,' said Peter. 'She asked for a report of the event. I must get over to Holborn to deliver it to her.'

'Persuade her to come and stay with us.'

'Wild horses wouldn't be able to drag her away from that shop.'

'She must consider her safety. Talk to her, Peter.'

'I'll try my best, Charlotte, but I know her response already.' Putting on his hat, he moved away. 'Do please excuse me. I'll ride over to Holborn at once.'

When he opened the door of the office, he was surprised to

see someone standing there. Meg Rooke was carrying a basket laden with food. She looked as if she'd been there for some time but had been too shy to knock. After inviting her in, Peter went off to find his horse.

'I thought that I would call in,' said Meg, nervously.

'You're always welcome here,' Ackford told her.

'Thank you, sir.'

'But there's no need to pretend that you came to see us,' said Charlotte with an understanding smile. 'Jem is alone in the shooting gallery.'

'How is he?'

'Why don't you go and find out? It's upstairs.'

'Is that possible?' she asked, turning to Ackford. 'I don't wish to be in the way, sir.'

'You've come at a perfect time, Meg,' he said. 'He'll be pleased to see you.'

'Try to convince him to come back to us,' suggested Charlotte.

Meg nodded enthusiastically. 'Oh, I will, Mrs Skillen.'

'Off you go, then.'

The maidservant scampered out of the room.

'Don't be too free with your invitations,' said Ackford, chuckling. 'The house will soon fill up if you do. You've already offered accommodation to two people. How many more will you recruit?'

'I haven't recruited any so far, Gully. Diane will spurn our offer and so will Jem. Unless, of course,' she said, glancing towards the door, 'the invitation comes from someone else.'

* * *

Huckvale had just finished the task of whitening the target when he heard the door open behind him. Swinging round, he was amazed to see Meg Rooke. For a whole minute, neither of them was able to say anything. They just stared at each other with a blend of affection and discomfort. Huckvale found his voice first.

'What are you doing here?' he asked.

'I wanted to see how you were, Mr Huckvale.'

'I'm very well, thank you.'

'You don't look very well,' she said, putting her basket on the floor and crossing over to him. 'You've got more colour but you're still not yourself.'

'My head does still ache sometimes,' he conceded.

'There you are, then.'

'The pain disappears when I'm working.'

'You shouldn't be working at all, Mr Huckvale.'

'We have to keep the gallery open, Meg.'

She looked around. 'I've never been here before,' she said. 'I didn't realise that the place was so big. Is this where you teach people how to shoot?'

'It is,' he replied. 'We have other rooms for boxing, fencing and archery.'

Meg was impressed. 'You teach *all* of those things?'

'I will do when I'm fully recovered.' He became uneasy. 'It was very kind of you to pop in but this is no place for a woman.'

'Yes, it is – Mrs Skillen works here.'

'That's different.'

'I don't see why.'

225

'When the gallery is full, there's a lot of noise and danger. People sometimes get hurt in the boxing ring. I'd hate you to hear the language they use. It's the same during a fencing lesson. It's a man's world in here, noisy and violent.'

'Then I won't intrude any longer, Mr Huckvale.'

'You don't need to call me that. Call me what everyone else does – Jem.'

'May I?' She smiled at what she saw was a sign of progress. 'Thank you. Thank you very much . . . Jem.'

'And thank *you* for coming, Meg.'

'I'd prefer it if you were still staying with us.'

'I'm needed here.'

She walked back to the door to pick up the basket but he got there first.

'I'll carry it out for you.'

'That's very kind of you.'

'As for my injury,' he assured her, 'it's not as bad as it looks.'

'I believe you,' she said. 'Nobody else would.'

'Goodbye, Meg.'

'Goodbye, Mr . . . goodbye, Jem.'

After the outburst of anger at the cricket match from Sir Humphrey Coote, the mood had changed abruptly. There was a general awkwardness among them. His friends had done their best to smooth his ruffled feathers and Reddish apologised time and again. What restored the conviviality at once was another massive hit by the imperious Lord Beauclerk, an aristocrat of the game in every way. As the ball came speeding towards him, he timed his stroke perfectly, hooking it with such force that

226

it sailed way over the heads of the spectators and out of the ground. Sir Humphrey laughed and cheered as much as the rest of them.

Paul Skillen had the urge to slip away but that was impossible now that he was a feted member of the group. Besides, there was some exquisite cricket to watch and some delicious refreshments at hand. Betting was brisk throughout the game and it took a real effort for him to hold back. He resigned himself to finding as much about Sir Humphrey as he could. When play finally ended, he thanked his new-found friends for the pleasure of their company. There was genuine affection in their farewells. Gilbert Reddish took him aside.

'You must forgive Sir Humphrey,' he said.

Paul shrugged. 'I see no need to do so.'

'He has a temper and I inadvertently sparked it off.'

'I was not aware of it, Mr Reddish.'

'That's very tactful of you.'

'I was enjoying the game too much,' said Paul, discreetly, 'all the more so because I was in such pleasurable company. I can't thank you enough.'

'Your comments were a source of interest throughout.'

'All I gave you were my humble opinions.'

'They were far more pertinent than any we could muster,' confessed Reddish with a laugh. 'Ah,' he went on as he saw someone approaching through the crowd, 'everyone of consequence is here today. Do you know Mr Harvester?'

'If it's Mr Julian Harvester, then I've certainly heard of him.'

'He's as rich as Croesus and generous with his wealth.'

It was an unexpected bonus and Paul was quick to take

advantage of it. Reddish exchanged greetings with Harvester then introduced him to Paul.

'Without the help and encouragement of Mr Skillen,' he explained, 'I might not be standing here today.'

'Why is that?' asked Harvester.

Reddish went on to boast about his success in the duel and earned Paul a glance of approval from Harvester. The newcomer was an elegant man in his fifties with a benevolent smile. Not without envy, Paul admired his suit, hat and general appearance. Harvester was an ageing dandy with a twinkle in his eye. Since he obviously took great care with his attire, Paul wondered why the man had allowed snuff to drop on to the front of his coat.

'What did you think of the cricket, Mr Skillen?' asked Harvester.

'It was even more exciting than I'd hoped it would be,' said Paul.

'Beauclerk was magnificent.'

'He always is,' interjected Reddish. 'Mr Skillen, here, is quite an expert on the game and, indeed, on all forms of physical exercise.'

Harvester declared himself pleased to hear it and engaged Paul in a long discussion of what they'd seen that day. Evidently, he was a devotee of the game and loved talking about it. He was duly impressed by Paul's knowledge of the finer points of cricket.

'I wish that you'd been sitting next to me, sir,' said Harvester, tetchily. 'Your advice might have saved me from losing a hundred guineas. I bet that Lillywhite wouldn't take a single wicket and the fellow bagged four of them. But at least he bowled in the proper manner.'

'The game is bound to evolve.'

'Then let it do so in the correct way.'

'Cricket has come a long way since it was first played. Look at the bats, for instance. The original ones were curved and heavy. Players were encouraged to slog the ball hard because that was the easiest way to score. Today's bats allow for more subtlety and for a greater range of strokes.'

'By George, that's true!'

'In future, I predict, both the bat and the ball will change radically. In a hundred years, cricket will be a game that would be totally foreign to us.'

Paul went on to explain why and, to his credit, Harvester listened without interrupting him. Though not entirely convinced by Paul's argument, he was struck by its force and reasonableness.

'You make me regret even more that I didn't have you at my side today,' said Harvester. 'As it was, I made the mistake of bringing Dr Penhallurick with me. He's a dear fellow but has no feeling for the sport. When I turned to him at one point, I was horrified to see that he'd gone off to sleep. Sleep!' he exclaimed. 'How can one sleep at such a banquet of excellence? I'll never coax Penhallurick in here again.' He touched his hat. 'I bid you good day, gentleman.'

As he walked towards the exit, Paul was shocked at himself. He had just talked at length with someone who was even more amicable and passionate about cricket than Sir Humphrey Coote. He had taken a liking to the man from the start and relished their exchanges. It was only now that he remembered who Julian Harvester was. Along with Sir Humphrey – and Dr Penhallurick – he was a main suspect in a murder investigation. Paul felt profoundly guilty.

'When did it happen, Mrs Mandrake?'

'It was some time during the night.'

'Why didn't you send for me at once?'

'What could you have done?'

'I'd like to have been told, that's all.'

'Then I apologise,' she said, 'but, as I've made clear before, I'm old enough to fight my own battles.'

'You could be up against impossible odds,' said Peter.

'I'll struggle on until I've no more strength to do so.'

'Charlotte insists that you come to stay with us.'

'Please thank her on my behalf and tell her that it's impossible.'

'At least let me move in here to protect you.'

Wanting to smile at what she felt as an agreeable prospect, she instead shook her head. The debate was over. His offer was declined. They were standing outside the shop. On receipt of the news that her poster had been torn down, Peter had been disturbed, fearing that her action in keeping the shop open would be duly punished.

Diane conducted him inside and took him through to the room at the back. As they sat down, he noticed a tear in the corner of her eye.

'Tell me about Leo's funeral,' she said.

'It was a . . . rather subdued occasion.'

'What did the vicar say about him?'

'He was full of praise for Mr Paige and strong in his condemnation of the way he'd died. It was a very touching service. Mr Paige's landlord was there and a small handful of mourners. I don't know their names.'

Since Diane was unaware of the existence of Paige's brother, Peter felt it wiser to keep her in ignorance. The moment she knew who Virgo was, she'd insist on seeing him and that could have unforeseen consequences. If the shop was being watched, it was likely that Diane, too, was under surveillance. Peter did not want her to be followed to the King's Bench Prison because Virgo's anonymity might be compromised and his life imperilled. If his role in the creation of the prints was discovered, he would follow his brother into an undeserved grave.

Peter described the ceremony in more detail, telling her how beautiful her flowers had been. His one regret was that nobody linked to the murder had turned up.

'That's a source of relief rather than regret,' she argued. 'I hate to think that someone was deriving *pleasure* from Leo's funeral. When this is all over – and I can get back to running my shop without hindrance – I want you to take me there, Peter. Will you do that?'

'Of course, I will.'

'I have to pay my respects in the churchyard.'

'I understand.'

'In time, I'll arrange for a headstone to be erected.'

Getting up from her chair, she crossed to a table on which a decanter and two glasses were set. After pouring the sherry, she offered one glass to Peter then lifted her own in a silent toast. He did likewise.

She resumed her seat. 'I have some more unpleasant news to report.'

'Oh – what is it?'

'That oaf, Yeomans, called on me this morning. When he saw that my window had been smashed, he offered to stay out there all night like a guard dog. I gave him short shrift and sent him on his way.'

'What was he doing in Holborn?'

'He was pretending that he came this way by chance, Peter.'

'In other words . . .'

She laughed harshly. 'Can you think of a more repulsive suitor?'

When his wife had told him about Yeomans's interest in Diane, he'd only half-believed it. The Runner was very much a man's man and so committed to his work that he had no time for dalliances of any kind. The latest news convinced Peter that his rival *had* developed an interest in Diane. He was unsure whether to be stunned or amused. A whole new aspect of the character of Micah Yeomans had come into view. It was a revelation.

'Forget about him,' she said, brusquely. 'What have you and your brother been doing while I've been stuck here?'

'I've been getting acquainted with Mr Gerard Brunt.'

When he told her about the way he'd resorted to the Hansard journals, she was taken aback. It would never have occurred to her to do some research of that kind. Like Peter, she thought that Brunt's virulent attack on the *Parliament of*

Foibles had marked him out as the most likely agent of the murder.

'So my prints were mentioned in the House of Commons, were they?' she said, chortling. 'That's fame, indeed.'

'Fame or infamy?'

'A little of both, I fancy.'

'I must contrive a meeting with Mr Brunt somehow.'

'Tell him that my caricatures of him sell extremely well.'

Peter grinned. 'That news would not be well received.'

'Well,' she said, 'now that I know how *you've* been spending your time, tell me about your brother. What has *he* been doing?'

'Paul has spent the day at a cricket match.'

'At a time like this?' she asked with annoyance. 'What can he possibly learn there?'

Paul Skillen couldn't wait to get back to the gallery to tell the others about his good fortune. By the time he arrived, his horse's neck and flanks were sleek with sweat. Charlotte and Ackford gave him a cordial welcome.

'What was the match like?' asked Ackford, eager for detail.

'Gully!' chided Charlotte. 'Paul was not there to watch cricket. His task was to find Sir Humphrey Coote.'

'I did both,' said Paul. 'I sat next to Sir Humphrey and managed to watch some superb cricket at the same time. What's more, it didn't cost me a penny.'

They were astonished to learn that he'd befriended Sir Humphrey and had a chance encounter with Julian Harvester, another of their suspects. Like Paul, they thought the fact that Harvester and Dr Penhallurick had been there together was significant. Had two of Virgo's prime targets united to strike back at him?

'You said that you actually *liked* Sir Humphrey,' observed Charlotte.

'He had great charm at first, Charlotte. It was only when I saw his eyes blaze that I realised there was another side to him. Harvester was also congenial company. I kept wishing that I could afford his tailor – though he needs to be more careful when he takes his snuff.'

'Which of the two is more likely to plot someone's murder?'

'Both are capable,' said Paul, 'but neither may actually have been involved. That's why I'm not jumping to any hasty conclusions. Each of them has the money and the influence to buy the release of prisoners from Newgate and each of them received a sound whipping in *Paige's Chronicle* – Harvester for his obscene wealth and Sir Humphrey for his rampant promiscuity.'

'Which is Dr Penhallurick?' said Ackford. 'Is he wealthy or promiscuous?'

'I can't speak for his inclinations, Gully, but if he can rub shoulders with Harvester, then he must be a rich man.'

'Birds of a feather?'

'That would be my guess.'

Ackford looked up at the clock on the shelf and realised that he was due to give instruction in fencing in a few minutes. He made his excuse. When he'd left the room, Charlotte pressed her brother-in-law for more information about Sir Humphrey.

'Was he a handsome man?'

'His knighthood makes him extremely handsome to some

women, I daresay. A combination of rank and prosperity is almost irresistible.'

'Not to me, Paul.'

'You have too much self-respect.'

'I also have a loving husband. When you've someone like Peter at your side, you never take an interest in another man.'

'My brother would love to hear you say so, Charlotte. However,' he went on, lowering his voice, 'you've touched on something vexing me at the moment.'

She smiled knowingly. 'Then it must be related to Hannah.'

'It is, Charlotte.'

'Are you worried because you've not heard from her?'

'On the contrary, I had a letter only this morning. I was overjoyed at first. It was wonderful to hear of her performances and her adventures. After the initial joy, I began to have misgivings.'

'Why – what did she say?'

'It's really a question of what was omitted.'

He went on to describe the contents of the letter. Charlotte was the only person in whom he could confide on such a personal matter. In the early days of his romance with Hannah Granville, there'd been misunderstandings that led to a separation between them and he'd sought his sister-in-law's counsel. Her uncritical sympathy and her common sense had been a tonic. It was the reason he turned to her now.

'Well,' she said at length, 'I can see why the letter has given you some food for thought but there's no specific complaint in it. If something had been troubling Hannah, I'm sure that you'd have heard about it.'

'Perhaps she's too embarrassed to tell me about it.'

'I'd never associate her with embarrassment, Paul. She's one of the most self-possessed people I've ever met.' He laughed. 'In a profession like hers, one has to develop an inner toughness, as Hannah has certainly done.'

He was rueful. 'Yes, I know, I've been its victim from time to time.'

'Could it be that you're imagining difficulties that don't actually exist?'

'I'd love to think that, Charlotte, but somehow I can't.'

'Has it preyed on your mind?'

'There were moments when it got between me and the cricket match,' he said, 'but I put it aside most of the time. It's bubbled back to the surface now.'

'Then my advice is simple. Find out the truth.'

'I can only do that by going to Paris.'

'Go – Peter and Gully will understand.'

'They'll also be nettled by my sudden disappearance. And think of Jem – how will *he* feel if I stop hunting the man who almost killed him? It would hurt Jem dreadfully.'

'In that case, you must stay and redouble your efforts,' she said. 'Today has yielded so much in the way of evidence – for Peter as well as for you. We may be closer to identifying the man we're after than we think.'

'You're right,' he said, purposefully. 'Hannah must wait. While she's inciting a murder on stage as Lady Macbeth, I'll be trying to solve one in reality.'

Eldon Kirkwood pored over the document and read it with great care. He and his visitor were in the chief magistrate's office in Bow Street. It was a long time before he raised his head.

'I can't fault it, Mr Brunt.'

'Is the wording precise enough?'

'Oh, yes.'

'Will it make the law easier to enforce?'

'In theory, it should do.'

'Like me, you were trained as a lawyer and have always had a good legal brain. Of more importance, perhaps, is your instinct, honed, as it has been, by sitting in judgement on countless crimes.'

'Am I to be your only counsellor?'

'No,' said Brunt. 'I plan to show it to a couple of colleagues in the House.'

'Both of them lawyers, I take it?'

'Indeed, they are.'

'There'll be discrepancies,' warned Kirkwood. 'If you lock ten lawyers in a room and show them this document, you'll get nine conflicting opinions and one man will reserve his judgement.'

Brunt's laugh was like the rustle of leaves blown about in a high wind. He was a rather fleshy middle-aged man with a habit of hunching his shoulders and keeping his palms together as if in a state of continual prayer. Having met Kirkwood years earlier, he'd cultivated his friendship and flattered him on more than one occasion by asking him for an opinion of legislation he'd drafted. The magistrate handed the document back to him.

'Thank you for coming to me,' he said. 'I feel honoured.'

'I know that you have strong opinions on the laws of libel. It's one of the things we have in common. Both of us have been maligned in print and in caricature. It's time that we struck back hard at these vipers.'

'The law already allows us to do so, Mr Brunt.'

'It's too blunt an instrument as it is. It needs to be more of a rapier and less of an unwieldy battleaxe. Don't you agree?'

Kirkwood rose to his feet. 'Sections of the press are very responsible,' he said, 'but there are those whose sole purpose seems to be to denigrate people in authority. In essence, freedom is a wonderful concept, but too much licence brings out the spirit of recklessness.'

'People have to be kept in check.'

'That's the purpose of the magistracy.'

'Thank you for your time,' said Brunt, folding the document before slipping it into his pocket. 'I needed the scrutiny of someone like you.'

'I'm always at your disposal, sir.'

'Have you never considered framing legislation yourself?'

'Dear me – no,' said Kirkwood. 'I've no wish to enter Parliament.'

'You'd make a worthy contribution, if you did so. I'd sooner welcome another lawyer like you than a doctor like Guy Penhallurick. You've probably heard that *he* has ambitions to join us,' said Brunt with a sneer. 'Who needs a doctor in the House of Commons? It will be a distraction. He'll be besieged by Members asking for prescriptions to cure their sciatica or ease their haemorrhoids.'

'I don't blame them. Dr Penhallurick is reputed to charge exorbitant fees. If one sees an opportunity for a free consultation, one should take it.'

'You're probably right.' Brunt looked as if he was about to leave then he thought better of it. 'Tell me,' he said, casually, 'as a matter of interest, has any progress been made in the search for Mr Paige's killer?'

'Evidence is still being gathered.'

'There was no love lost between Paige and myself but I'll not speak ill of the dead. His murder is a reminder of the danger that's ever present in this city.'

'His killer will be caught and hanged.'

'What steps have been taken?'

'The Runners are out in force.'

'Are they sanguine?'

'They are officers of the law, Mr Brunt,' said the other, 'and they are very experienced. Where they are at the moment, and what they're doing, I can't rightly tell you. Of one thing I can assure you. They'll catch the person or persons who perpetrated this terrible crime. I believe that Mr Paige was buried this afternoon. He will not be fully in peace until his killer has a noose around his neck.'

They waited until the early hours of the morning before they made their move. Armed with a lantern and kindling materials, they walked to the street directly behind Middle Row. On his earlier visit, Fearon had found a side entry beside one house. It led to a garden. If they could get into it, they would have access to all the gardens in the street and those in Middle Row. The side door posed no problems for Higlett. Once a burglar by trade, he was adept. It was the work of seconds to open the lock on the gate to the garden. They crept swiftly to the fence at the back and looked at the houses opposite, silhouetted against the sky.

'How will we find the right one?' whispered Higlett.

'We do it by numbers, Sim. I counted eight in the terrace before I came to the print shop.' He studied the looming properties beyond. 'We're too far to the right of it. Climb over the fence and we'll work our way from garden to garden.'

'What if we pick the wrong house?'

'I don't make mistakes like that,' said Fearon, grimly. 'Our orders are to burn her out. If we go to the wrong house, he'll flay us alive.'

Chevy Ruddock was delighted with the change of plan. Instead of being sent to Covent Garden once again, he was in a more salubrious neighbourhood. There were no brothels and no stray harlots to bother him. Because he was able to walk up and down, there was also no danger of cramp. The print shop was his major interest. Every time he went past, he glanced across, conscious for the first few hours that he was being watched from the front bedroom. Eventually, however, the curtains stopped twitching. The street was silent and unthreatening.

His gentle patrol lulled him into a state of complacence. Convinced that nobody would come and that nothing would happen, he let his mind dwell on the welcome that his wife would give him on his return. He was still luxuriating in his daydream when someone leapt out of the shadows at the corner of the street and clapped a hand over his mouth. Ruddock tried to struggle but he was held too tightly.

Suddenly, he was released. Yeomans was highly critical.

'If I can do that to you,' he said, 'then *anybody* can.'

'But there's nobody about, Mr Yeomans. The street is empty.'

'I was here and you didn't even notice me. Why was that? Were you half-asleep or was your mind elsewhere?'

'I'm sorry, sir.'

'You were chosen, Ruddock. You were selected for this task because Mr Hale and I had faith in you. Keep your eyes open and your ears pricked. Look in every doorway, gaze up at every window.'

'Yes, sir, I will.'

'And don't be caught out again.'

'No, Mr Yeomans. Where will you be, sir?'

'You don't need to know that. Just do as you were told.'

The Runner vanished as quickly as he'd appeared. Ruddock blinked in the gloom and tried to work out where Yeomans had gone but it was impossible. He gave up trying and returned to his perambulation. A rider trotted by on a horse, hoof beats echoing. Two hazy figures came walking unsteadily towards him but, before they reached him, they let themselves into a house and shut the door. He was alone again. There was no sign of Yeomans and no movement of the curtains in the front bedroom of the print shop. After the noise and bustle of Covent Garden, the street was blissfully quiet. He schooled himself not to take it for granted. Bent on proving his worth, he was determined to remain alert.

It was almost an hour before he heard the faint crackle. It slowly grew in volume. Carried on the wind, the first wisps of smoke drifted into his nostrils. They seemed to be coming from behind the print shop. The crackle was now audible and he suddenly realised what had caused it. Ruddock exploded into life, charging across the street and hammering on the door of the shop with all his might.

'FIRE! FIRE! FIRE!'

CHAPTER FOURTEEN

The response was immediate. The curtains in the front bedroom of the shop were pulled back and the window flung open. The head of Diane Mandrake appeared, her nightcap tied in place.

'Who's down there?' she demanded.

'Look to your house, madam! It's on fire!'

'Good gracious!' she exclaimed as she smelt the smoke swirling overhead.

'Save yourselves!' advised Ruddock. 'I'll rouse the neighbours.'

While she ducked out of the window, he ran in turn to the adjoining houses on both sides and raised the alarm. Lights were already appearing in other windows and some were opened. There was no missing the sound of the blaze or the stench of smoke now. Loud screams from the servants above the shop spread news of the danger far and wide and the whole street came out of its slumbers. People were soon rushing out of doors to add to the commotion. The fire had now got sufficient hold to send flames dancing in the air, lightening the sky and giving the shop an eerie glow. Ruddock was still shouting at the top of his voice when Yeomans came hurtling towards him. When he saw what was happening, the Runner went berserk and banged on the shop door as if trying to break it down with his fists.

It finally opened and the terrified servants came running out in their dressing gowns and nightcaps. Yeomans grabbed one of them.

'Where's Mrs Mandrake?' he demanded.

'She's still inside with Mr Tite,' said the woman.

'Come on, Ruddock – follow me.'

Yeomans plunged into the shop with Ruddock at his heels. They ran through to the back of the house and saw that the outhouse was ablaze and that the flames had set the ivy on the back wall alight. Wearing dressing gowns but standing in bare feet, Diane and Tite were bravely throwing buckets of water at the fire but the wind kept whipping it up. Yeomans took control at once, taking the bucket from Diane, easing her across to a position of relative safety, then giving orders to Ruddock and to the other people who came surging through the house with buckets of water to lend their assistance. The noise was ear-splitting.

It was exactly a hundred and fifty years since the Great Fire of London but the tragedy remained fresh in the minds of its citizens. Though thatched roofs and other combustible materials might have vanished, terraced housing always posed a problem. Once a fire got a strong purchase on one property, it could quickly spread and destroy the whole row. That was why almost everyone in the street came to the rescue. Under the supervision of Yeomans, a small army of men and boys fought the blaze with frantic energy. Refusing to be left out of the action, Diane wielded a large wet mop as she tried to beat out the roaring flames threatening her property.

Tite was in despair. 'It's hopeless!' he cried. 'We're done for!'

Fearon and Higlett didn't stop running until they were hundreds of yards away. Having started the fire in the shed attached to the house, they'd hurdled over the fences of a dozen gardens until they reached the side entry in the street at the back of Middle Row. There was no time to enjoy their handiwork. They had to make do with the sound of the blaze and the howls of despair. When they'd sprinted until their lungs were on fire, they allowed themselves a respite.

'We did it,' said Fearon, gasping for air.

'There won't *be* a print shop tomorrow – just a pile of ashes.'

'That will please him.'

'We deserve a big reward for this, Abel.'

'I'll make sure we get it.'

'We took risks,' said Higlett, 'a lot of them.'

'He'll know that.'

'We did what he wanted.'

'We don't know that yet.'

Higlett was indignant. 'Yes, we do. That fire will burn down the shop.'

'But has it killed Mrs Mandrake? That's what he really wants. You saw his orders. He didn't want her coming out alive.'

* * *

Anxious, perspiring, almost dropping with fatigue, Diane was still very much alive. She continued to make her contribution with the others, wetting her mop every time it began to smoulder. Water had now reached the seat of the fire and sapped its resistance. Flames no longer licked away so hungrily at the back of the house. Thanks to the concerted efforts of dozens of people, the blaze was finally brought under control and, ultimately, quelled completely. When it was no more than a hissing pile of wood, a ragged cheer went up.

Nobody had worked harder than Yeomans and Ruddock, strong men who battled the fire with a skill born of experience. They were as relieved as anyone that their efforts had been successful. Yeomans put an arm around his companion.

'Well done, Ruddock.'

'You led the fight, sir.'

'Yes, but you raised the alarm. That probably saved lives.'

'I was only doing my duty, Mr Yeomans.'

'You went beyond that,' said the other. 'Mr Kirkwood will hear of this.'

'Thank you, sir!'

Ruddock was thrilled. For a change, he would have good news to take back to his wife after night duty. Yeomans was treating him like a hero and the chief magistrate would learn of his prompt action. It helped him to ignore the singed patches on his coat and hat, the weariness of his body, the cloying stink of smoke and the trickling of sweat down his face.

Diane, meanwhile, was thanking her neighbours in turn for their help. She was a popular figure in the street and had already received a lot of sympathy for the way that the shop window had been smashed. The fire had been a far greater blow for her.

'How did it start?' asked a man.

'I wish I knew,' she replied.

'Was it some kind of accident?'

'Oh, no – this was deliberate.'

He was aghast. 'You could have been burnt alive.'

'I think that that was the intention.'

When the man staggered away to pass on the news to others, Diane went over to Yeomans who was stamping on the last embers to make sure that the fire was out. By the light of a lantern, she could see how parts of his sleeves had been burnt away and how his eyebrows had caught fire at some point.

'I owe you a huge debt of gratitude, Mr Yeomans,' she said.

'I feared that something like this might happen, Mrs Mandrake.'

'Were you standing out there all night?'

'I had a man on patrol in the street.'

'Yes, I noticed him. He woke me up by yelling.'

'Ruddock woke up half the street,' said Yeomans with a tired smile. 'He showed his true mettle tonight – and so did your neighbours.'

'They wanted to save their own houses as much as mine.'

'Who can blame them?' He looked down. 'You should not be out here in bare feet, Mrs Mandrake.'

'There was no time to find my slippers.'

'You were brave to join in the fight.'

'This is my property, Mr Yeomans. I'll defend it to the death.'

'Do you have *any* idea who started the fire?'

'I wish I did.'

'It's probably the same man who smashed your window. Who is he?'

'Seek him in hell, sir, for that's where the devil resides.'

Overcoming an urge to put a consoling arm around her, Yeomans took off his hat and used the back of his hand to wipe the sweat from his brow. He glanced at the blackened brickwork.

'You can't stay here, Mrs Mandrake.'

'That's my business.'

'I beg you to move elsewhere.'

'If friends took me in, that would only put *them* in danger.'

'This was the most terrible warning yet.'

'I'm fully conscious of that, Mr Yeomans.'

While she could never like a man she found so repellent, she had to admire the way he'd behaved in an emergency. While she was angry that he'd disregarded her refusal to have him near her shop at night, she was also extremely grateful. Tite and the servants were heavy sleepers and they occupied the rooms at the side of the house. But for the intervention of the officer placed outside by Yeomans, they could have been killed and the whole property destroyed.

'I ask one favour of you, Mrs Mandrake,' he said.

'What is it?'

'If you change your mind, please let me know. I can arrange accommodation for you elsewhere. You'll be safe and sound.'

'I thank you for your kind offer but my answer remains the

same. Besides,' she continued, 'if I did consent to move out, it would not to be somewhere of your choosing. It would be to the home of good friends.'

Peter and Charlotte Skillen had just finished breakfast when the messenger arrived. They read the letter with an amalgam of fear and outrage.

'They set fire to the house?' said Charlotte, trembling.

'There was a precedent, my love. Think of Mr Paige's lodging.'

'I do feel for poor Diane. What a hideous experience!'

'By the grace of God,' said Peter, 'she survived and so did the others in the house. Anyone else would have passed on the news with their hand shaking but, as you can see, the calligraphy is firm.'

'I must go to her.'

'You're needed at the gallery. Leave it to me.'

'Do whatever you can to bring her back here, Peter.'

'My efforts will be in vain.'

'We must be able to help *somehow*.'

'I'll find a way.'

'Her servants must be worried out of their minds.'

'And so must Mr Tite,' he said. 'I'm sure that he's an efficient print-seller but that doesn't fit him to protect his employer in a crisis and to put out a fire. It may well be that neither he nor the servants agree to remain there.'

She winced. 'Diane can't be left completely alone.'

'She won't be, my love.'

* * *

Paul Skillen returned to the cricket ground in St John's Wood but it was not to watch the game. He was drawn there by the coincidence that three of the suspects they'd identified had actually been there on the previous day. On reflection, he decided that it was not so much of a coincidence. Cricket had an enthusiastic following among the privileged classes. People who had no trade to keep them occupied on a daily basis found it an ideal way of passing their leisure time. It was a social as much as a sporting event. Members of the lower orders did attend in numbers, and there was an inevitable smattering of pickpockets, but the prevailing tone was set by the aristocracy and the gentry.

Since he had no intention of spending the whole day there again, Paul had gone in disguise, donning the costume he'd first used when scouring the taverns near the riverside. It made him completely invisible to the quartet with whom he'd sat during the first day's play. Conclusive proof of the effectiveness of his disguise came when he walked to within a few yards of Gilbert Reddish. Waiting for his friends, the man didn't even spare Paul a glance.

The crowds descending on the ground were as large and vociferous as on the earlier occasion. Speculation as to the likely winner of the match was rife and Paul heard loyal supporters of both sides engaged in lively argument. He had his own opinion about the likely outcome but it was irrelevant. His task was simply to watch and listen for anything useful he could pick up.

Reddish was getting impatient. The match would soon be resuming but there was no sign of his friends. He looked at each new vehicle rolling up but could not see Sir Humphrey Coote's coach. Eventually, a carriage swept into view and he was hailed by its three occupants. Reddish went across to greet them and there was some cheerful banter. Paul was not close enough to overhear it. As the four friends brushed past him, however, he did pick up one exchange.

'You're devilishly late, Sir Humphrey,' said Reddish.

'It's a privilege of rank.'

'And why come in a carriage? You're so intent on travelling in style that you always prefer your coach.'

'Someone had a greater need of it than me,' explained Sir Humphrey. 'I've loaned it for the day to Guy Penhallurick.'

'Why can't I come with you?' asked Higlett.

'It only needs one of us.'

'But why must it always be you?'

'I was picked out, wasn't I?' said Fearon, tapping his chest. 'When he bought my release from Newgate, he thought it might be work for two of us. I recommended you. Otherwise, you'd still be in there for another year. Be grateful, Sim.'

'I am, honest.'

'Then stop bickering.'

'It's just that I'd . . . like to see him.'

'What's the point?'

'I want to know who he is and what he looks like.'

'I can tell you that.'

'You can't tell me his name,' challenged the other, 'because you don't know it. All you tell me is that he's very rich and

251

dresses well. I want to know more, Abel. I want to know his name and what he's going to do with us.'

'You ask too many questions.'

'What if he double-crosses us?'

'He hasn't done that so far,' Fearon pointed out. 'We killed Paige and we got a lot of money for doing so. I expect even more for last night's work.'

They were in the room above the tavern. It was almost noon and time for Fearon to keep an appointment. Higlett made the mistake of demanding to go with him and was hurled to the floor. He yelled in pain when he was kicked.

'There's no need for that!' he protested.

'It'll teach you to keep your gob shut.'

'Why can't I even get a glimpse of him?'

Fearon raised his foot. 'Do you want another kick?'

'No, no,' cried the other, cowering on the floor.

'I'll see you when I get back – and no more questions.'

He went out and slammed the door behind him. Rubbing his back where the kick had landed, Higlett struggled to his feet and crossed to the window. He waited until he saw his friend come out into the street. Then he put on his hat, tripped down the stairs and followed him at a safe distance.

When Peter got to the shop, it was in turmoil. The servants were crying, Tite was trying to persuade Diane Mandrake to leave the house and she was packing the prints into a series of boxes. At least she was making no attempt to keep the shop open for business. Peter saw that as a wise move. Clearing the others out of the way, she took her visitor into the back room.

'I know what you're going to say,' she warned, 'and you can save your breath. I'm staying here.'

'But this place is obviously a target.'

'That doesn't worry me. I'm concerned about Ben Tite and the servants, of course, and I've said that I won't force them to stay. It's their decision.'

Peter offered all the arguments he'd rehearsed on his way there but she was adamant. He changed tack and asked to see the fire damage. She took him into the garden and showed him the charred remains of the outhouse before indicating the marks on the brickwork.

'Who ever lit that fire did me a favour,' she said with a half-laugh. 'The whole of that wall was covered in ivy and it was starting to penetrate the brickwork. It's pernicious stuff. As you see, it was obligingly burnt off for me.'

'That was not the purpose of the blaze,' he said. 'The ivy was an incidental casualty. You were supposed to have been killed.'

'I realise that. Fortunately, I was roused from my bed.'

'Did you hear the crackle of fire?'

'*I* didn't but, luckily, someone did.'

'Who was it?' asked Peter.

'The man patrolling the street,' she replied. 'He was put there by Mr Yeomans. They're largely responsible for the fact that my house is still standing.'

Peter was astounded. 'What was Micah Yeomans doing here in the night?'

'He was showing a concern for my safety even though I'd spurned his help. He's an insufferable man, Peter, but a courageous one to boot. He and his officer fought the fire as if they were trying to save their own homes. Yeomans even got his eyebrows singed in the process.'

When she gave him a more detailed account, he had to admire what the Runner had done. In the confusion and the pandemonium, Yeomans had asserted his authority and got everyone working systematically. Without him, it was clear, far more than an outhouse and some ivy would have been destroyed.

'You're insane to stay here, Mrs Mandrake.'

'People said that when I first opened the shop.'

'Move in with us for a time.'

'That's a kind offer but I must decline it. On the other hand, I will accept the accommodation for my stock. That worried me even more than the prospect of losing my own life. My prints are my pride and joy. I don't want them destroyed by fire. Is there any way that I can prevail upon you to store them for me?'

'I'll do so with pleasure,' he said.

'And there are some trinkets I'd like you to look after as well.'

'We'll take whatever you wish and be glad to do so.'

'Thank you, Peter.' She peered closely at him. 'It *is* Peter, isn't it? Or are you Paul masquerading as your brother?'

He laughed. 'As it happens,' he said, 'Paul *is* masquerading as someone today but it's not as me. He's turned tradesman and gone to Thomas Lord's cricket ground again. Paul told us that he's hoping his disguise brings rewards.'

He found it surprisingly easy to get close to Sir Humphrey Coote and his entourage. When they went into the marquee to buy drinks and place bets, Paul was able to get within a couple of yards of them. Most of their comments were about the match and, whenever there was a roar of approval from outside, they ran to the exit to see what had caused it. Mindful of the way he'd upset his friend the other day, Reddish made no remarks about caricatures of Sir Humphrey. He went out of his way to keep his friend in good humour. Hoping to hear something of interest, Paul instead listened to a conversation that filled him with rage.

'Did you have your rendezvous last night?' asked Reddish with a smirk.

'I did, Gilbert,' replied Sir Humphrey. 'I came, I saw, I conquered.'

'She was a willing filly, then?'

'They always are. Some of us were born with irresistible charm.'

'You're not *always* irresistible.'

'Yes, I am. The fair sex fall before me like rosebuds strewn in my path.'

'What about that actress who rebuffed you?'

'She was merely postponing the time when we have divine congress. I like that in a woman,' said Sir Humphrey. 'It heightens the pleasure.'

'You'll get no pleasure from Miss Hannah Granville,' warned Reddish. 'I'm told that she already has a beau.'

'Then he'll have to be replaced by a more worthy suitor.'

Sir Humphrey struck a pose and made his friends shake with mirth. Paul fought hard to control his fury. The fact that Hannah's name was being mentioned in a derogatory way by a seasoned lecher made him want to strike out. To regain his composure, he walked away and finished the tankard of beer he was holding. The four men then drifted out of the marquee. Paul hurried after them and was in time to catch a reference to one of the other suspects.

'Why did you lend your coach to Penhallurick?' asked Reddish.

'I owed him a favour.'

'He's wealthy enough to buy his own coach, Sir Humphrey.'

'Guy would prefer to borrow mine. He's done it before, actually. He told me that it was in order to impress someone.'

It was mid-afternoon. Fearon had to wait so long that he wondered if he'd got the time wrong. It was the same spot as before but nobody came for him. As he slouched against a wall, he was quite unaware that Higlett was watching slyly from a hiding place in a porch. The man had kept him waiting the last time they met but the delay was much longer now. A thought stabbed at him. What if their paymaster never showed up? Having got what he'd ordered – the destruction of the print shop – he'd have no more use for Fearon and Higlett. Instead of paying them, he could simply melt away. They had no idea who he was, where he lived and why he hated certain people enough to have them killed. Preoccupied with the notion that he'd been tricked, Fearon didn't hear the clatter of hooves and rasping sound of wheels on the cobbles. When he looked up and saw the coach, he was caught unawares.

The door was opened from inside. He ran across to the vehicle and got in.

'Good day to you, sir,' he said, politely.

'Close the door.'

Fearon obeyed. 'We did what you wanted, sir.'

'I only have your word for it.'

'It's true, sir. The print shop was burnt to the ground.'

'I'll need to see it with my own eyes.'

'I wouldn't dare lie to you, sir.'

'Be quiet until we get there.'

The man used a stick to hit the roof of the coach twice by way of a signal. There was a snap of reins, a curt command and the vehicle drew away.

The dramatic events of the night had given Yeomans the courage to face the chief magistrate again. His heroics, he felt, would exonerate him in the man's eyes. Keeping watch in Covent Garden had not delivered what he'd promised but night duty in Holborn had been far more profitable. He managed to catch Kirkwood during a recess that afternoon and walked into his office with a broad smile. The magistrate studied him.

'What's happened to your eyebrows?' he asked.

'I'll come to that, sir.'

'It changes your appearance completely.'

'My wife told me that.'

'I can't decide if it's for the better or not. What do you want?'

'First,' said Yeomans, 'I must tender an apology.'

'Be quick about it, man. I've sentences to pass.'

'We were disappointed during our surveillance of Covent Garden.'

'I was told to expect arrests.'

'Let me finish, please . . .'

'Then get a move on.'

Yeomans explained what had happened in Holborn, carefully doctoring his narrative to give himself more prominence. It was he who'd been on duty outside the print shop, he claimed, and he who'd first become aware of the fire, saving lives as a result. When he moved on to a description of the fire itself, his role became even more central. The blaze in his version was several times bigger and the number of those helping to douse it had been reduced to a mere handful. He made it sound as if he'd extinguished the inferno more or less single-handed.

'*That's* how my eyebrows came to grief,' he concluded.

Kirkwood was anxious. 'And the lady was uninjured?'

'Thanks to my warning, she was unharmed.'

'Unharmed in body, perhaps, but her mind must be sorely troubled.'

'I didn't leave until I'd calmed her down, sir.'

'Dear me!' said the other, hand to his head. 'This is an unlooked-for turn of events. What does it portend, Yeomans?'

'Mrs Mandrake's life is in danger,' said the Runner, 'yet she won't leave.'

'The lady must be *made* to leave.'

Yeomans grimaced. 'That's a labour even Hercules would not take on.'

'What would you advise?'

'The street must be patrolled again at night, sir. She's up against an enemy who'll persist until he achieves his aim.

258

Because I was on hand to intervene, the attempt on her life failed.' His vestigial eyebrows twitched. 'I regret to say that there'll be another one.'

Abel Fearon was starting to enjoy himself. He'd never been driven through the streets of London in a coach before. When he'd been convicted, he'd travelled to Newgate in chains in a rattling cart, sneered and yelled at by pedestrians. They looked at his mode of transport with awe now. It was a satisfying feeling. The man sitting opposite said nothing. He simply averted his gaze. The coach eventually reached Holborn and turned into Middle Row. Fearon sat up with an anticipatory smile on his face. He was about to receive approval and, he was certain, a large amount of money.

Then the impossible happened. When they passed the print shop, it was still there. Instead of the ruin he'd expected, he saw that, but for the broken window, it was undamaged. To compound his misery, Diane Mandrake was standing on the pavement, talking to Tite. Fearon was petrified. His companion made no comment. After gazing at the shop and its owner for a few seconds, he let the coach roll on until it turned into a quiet, tree-lined avenue. He used his stick to signal to the coachman. The vehicle came to a halt.

'We lit the fire, sir,' insisted Fearon. 'I swear it. When we ran away, it was blazing like hell itself. Nobody could have come out alive from that.'

'You failed me again,' said the man, coldly. 'I abhor failure.'

'But we did everything you asked of us.'

'The print shop is still there. The woman still lives. Explain.'

'I can't, sir. I really can't.'

'You're becoming a liability, Fearon.'

'Don't we get any reward?'

'For *what*, damn you?'

'We took a big risk for you last night, sir. It was hard work.'

'And what has it achieved?' The man snapped his fingers. 'Nothing.'

'I still think we deserve some sort of payment.'

The man thrust his hand inside his coat and pulled out a pistol, clicking back the trigger and holding it against his companion's forehead. Convinced that he was about to be shot, Fearon began to plead and jabber.

The man silenced him with a raised palm. His tone was menacing.

'What am I going to do with you?' he asked.

Paul Skillen didn't stay for the afternoon session. It grieved him that he was walking away from a cricket match of superlative quality but he'd got all he had expected to glean from Sir Humphrey Coote and, when the man left the ground early, Paul followed suit. On the previous day, Julian Harvester had also been in attendance but he had not turned up this time. Paul had looked for him in all parts of the ground. He was bound to wonder why someone so obsessed by the game of cricket had sacrificed an opportunity to watch a match between teams made up of outstanding players.

There was another reason why he forced himself to leave. Sir Humphrey's mention of Hannah Granville still rankled. Deep down, he hoped that it was indeed Sir Humphrey who had hired Paige's assassin because he relished the idea of being able to overpower and arrest him. The man had designs on Hannah Granville. That made him Paul's enemy. If it turned out that he was innocent of any involvement in the crimes, there was another way to defend Hannah's honour.

Paul could challenge him to a duel.

Driving it with more consideration for others than Diane ever showed, Peter used her curricle to transport the prints to the safety of his home. Meg Rooke came out to help him unload them. Once the job was done, he drove to the gallery to tell Charlotte and Ackford what had happened. They were astonished to hear that Yeomans had been her saviour.

'It made me feel ashamed,' said Peter. '*I* should have been on patrol in that street last night. It's galling to think that Yeomans earned plaudits instead of us.'

'Thank heaven he was there!' said Charlotte.

'Yes, I've been to *one* funeral. I don't wish to go to another.'

'What are you going to do?' asked Ackford.

'I'm going to stay the night at the shop.'

'Then you deserve a medal for bravery. I don't think I could spend a night under the same roof as Mrs Mandrake. She'd have to be in charge.'

'What's wrong with that?' said Charlotte, robustly. 'She's been in charge of that shop for ten years now and it's become very successful.'

'I've never doubted it.'

She turned to Peter. 'What about the others in the shop?'

'The servants were refusing to stay the night until I

volunteered. Mr Tite seemed pleased with my offer as well and, eventually, it was accepted.'

'Do you expect another attack?'

'Oh, yes,' said Peter. 'The person who's set on destroying the shop will certainly try again. It symbolises something he detests. Yet he's unlikely to strike again immediately. He'll know that the place will be defended at night from now on. He'll wait until he thinks the danger has gone away.'

'What about Yeomans?' said Ackford.

'He's a worthy rival for once. We must show him more respect.'

'We can't have him doing our job for us.'

Peter grinned. 'You sound just like him, Gully. Anyway,' he went on, 'I must drive the curricle back to Holborn and reclaim my horse. I'll be back directly.'

Before he could move, however, there was a bang on the door. When he opened it, Peter was surprised to be looking at a diminutive figure in tattered clothing and a shabby hat. The boy's smile exposed his rabbit-like teeth.

'Glad I cort ya, Mr Skillen,' he said. 'Gorra message for ya, sir.'

Paul was bewildered. 'Who are you, lad?'

'I'm Snapper, sir. Ya 'members Snapper.'

'I've never seen you before. Wait a minute,' he added as light dawned, 'I *have* heard that name before. My brother mentioned a Snapper.'

'Ya mean ya ain't Mr Skillen?'

'I'm *Peter* Skillen. The person you met was Paul Skillen.'

'They're twins,' explained Charlotte.

Snapper was amazed. 'Ya looks juss like ya brother,' he said, staring at Peter. 'I gorra twin sister bur Lizzie ain't nothin' like me to look at.' He glanced around the room. 'Where's the other Mr Skillen?'

'He'll be back soon,' said Ackford. 'What's the message, Snapper?'

'Virgo wants to see 'im.'

'Do you know why?'

'Yeah – 'e's needed ergent.'

CHAPTER FIFTEEN

It was a tiring walk back to the tavern. On previous occasions, Fearon had been dropped off at the spot where he was picked up in the first place. This time, as a mark of disgrace, he was left a long way away from his destination. When he finally got there, he came into the room in a surly and uncommunicative mood.

'What happened?' asked Higlett.

His friend ignored him and reached for a flagon of ale. After taking a long swig, he slumped into a chair and stared at the window. Seeing the state he was in, Higlett was hesitant.

'What kept you so long?' There was no answer. 'You were gone for ages.'

Fearon had another mouthful of ale. His mind was miles away. It was several minutes before he even noticed that somebody else was in the room with him. Higlett was watching him open-mouthed.

'Don't look at me like that!' snapped Fearon.

'I'm sorry.'

'I've got things to think about.'

Higlett smirked. 'How much did we get?'

'What for?'

'He owes us money for burning down that shop.'

'It's still standing.'

'It can't be,' said Higlett with passion. 'There was a big bonfire when we left. How can you say that it's still standing?'

'We went there.'

'Didn't he take your word, Abel?'

'He refused. We went to Holborn. The shop was still standing and, even worse, the woman who owns it was out in the street. She didn't seem to be injured in any way at all.'

Higlett was baffled. 'How did she escape the fire?'

'They must have put it out somehow.'

'It was blazing when we left.'

'That's what I told him.'

'What did he say?' Fearon remained silent. 'It was hard work getting over those fences. We could have been seen and caught. Didn't he realise that? We want paying for the risks we took.'

'I told him that as well.'

'What was his reply?'

Fearon went off into another trance. His friend quickly wearied of standing there and waiting for answers that never came. He shook his friend's shoulder.

'Tell me what he said.'

'It doesn't matter.'

'Well, it matters to me,' said Higlett, confronting him. 'You went off in that coach and you didn't come back for ages. Why not? What happened? There must be something you can tell me.'

Fearon was roused. 'How do you know about the coach?'

'It was . . . just a guess.'

'You followed me, didn't you? When I left here, you followed me.'

'Yes, I did,' retorted the other, going on the attack. 'I'm fed up with being the one left behind while you get to meet him and handle any reward. It's not fair, Abel. What's the point of being friends if you shut me out all the time?'

Fearon leapt out of the chair and grabbed him by the throat.

'Be quiet, you frigging idiot!' he snarled.

Higlett gasped. 'You're hurting me. I can't breathe.'

'I'll tell you what he said to me. We let him down again. If we ever did that again, he promised – and he really meant it – that he'd have us strung up naked by our feet then skinned alive before being dipped into a vat of acid. Think about that, Sim. Think about someone slicing bits off your carcass and you'll see why I came back in the state I did.' He flung Higlett on to the mattress and stood over him. 'But I warn you,' he said, pulling out a dagger and brandishing it in the other man's face, 'if you *dare* to follow me again, I'll kill you myself and save him the trouble.'

Paul Skillen returned to the gallery to learn about the summons from the prison. He gave Ackford an attenuated account of events at the cricket ground, taking care to make no reference to Hannah Granville. That was a private matter.

'So you didn't see Mr Harvester this time?' said Ackford.

'He wasn't there, Gully. I searched.'

'Yet you told us that he loved watching cricket. What kept him away?'

'I don't know,' said Paul, 'but I can tell you what kept Dr Penhallurick away this time. He's not really interested in the game. It sent him to sleep yesterday. He'd much rather ride around in a coach he borrowed from Sir Humphrey Coote.'

'I thought the doctor was Harvester's friend.'

'He latches on to anyone with power and wealth.'

'That's his reputation,' said Ackford. 'He's a great sponger. But there's something you should know before you charge off.'

'What's that?'

'Last night, there was another attack on the print shop.'

Paul was horrified to hear that someone had tried to burn the place down. He was highly sympathetic. The news about Yeomans' earlier part in saving the house came close to making him froth at the mouth.

'It's our responsibility to look after Mrs Mandrake. We can't have a Runner showing us up like that.'

'Peter vowed that it wouldn't happen again.'

'He's right, Gully. We mustn't give Yeomans a chance to crow over us.'

'Then we have to catch the killer before he does,' said the other. 'You get off to Southwark. Leo's brother wouldn't send for you unless it was urgent.'

'Why didn't he come himself?'

'I can't tell you that.'

'He has licence to leave the prison.'

'I know. I met him at the funeral.'

'Why did Snapper bring the message and not Mr Paige?'

'You'll soon find out.'

* * *

Micah Yeomans enjoyed a celebratory drink at the Peacock. During the night, a fire had been put out, lives had been saved and he had won deserved thanks from the woman he coveted. As he explained to Alfred Hale, there'd been additional gains. The first was his warm reception by the chief magistrate.

'Mr Kirkwood praised me to the skies,' said Yeomans, complacently.

'And so he should. You guessed that the print shop would be in danger.'

'It was no guess, Alfred. It was pure instinct.'

'Chevy Ruddock deserves a kind word as well.'

'Yes, yes, of course.'

'Did you mention his name to Mr Kirkwood?'

'I did so a number of times,' lied Yeomans.

'Good – we have to encourage the lad.'

'He acted well in a crisis.'

'That's what we've taught him to do, Micah.'

'He's modelled himself on us.'

'There's no better training for him,' said Hale. 'What happens tonight?'

'We'll go back on patrol again.'

'Does Mrs Mandrake know we'll be there?'

'Oh, yes.'

'What did she say when you told her?'

'Well, she wasn't as grateful as I expected,' admitted Yeomans. 'I offered to take her to a place of safety but she refused to come. Diane – Mrs Mandrake, that is – is resolved to stay at the shop. If she did leave, she claimed, she'd go to friends.'

'And we know who they'd be – the Skillen brothers.'

'Where were they last night when they were needed?'

'Snoring in their beds, most like.'

'While I protected her.'

'Strictly speaking,' said Hale, 'it was Ruddock who did that. He was outside the shop when he realised it was on fire. He told me so himself.'

'Don't believe everything Ruddock says. *I* was first into the property.'

'And you battled with the fire for a long time. It's left its mark on you, Micah. Half of your eyebrows have disappeared. It makes you look years younger.'

'Does it?' said the other, brightening at the thought that he might now be more appealing to his beloved. 'Perhaps I should keep them trimmed.'

'What does your wife say about them?'

Yeomans was bitter. 'She didn't recognise me at first.'

'I'll wager that Mrs Mandrake did.'

'Yes, Alfred, she did.' A fond smile touched his lips. 'Rescuing her and the house were the major triumphs last night but there's another one to add.'

'I know – the brothers were shown up for the fools they are.'

'Peter and Paul Skillen have no place in law enforcement. When we've caught whoever was behind the murder and the fire,' said Yeomans, lifting the remains of his eyebrows to maximum altitude, 'we can enjoy the pleasure of a visit to the shooting gallery to trumpet our victory.'

Raising his tankard, he swallowed the last of his ale with a thunderous gulp.

* * *

As soon as he reached the King's Bench Prison, Paul realised that something serious had happened. Snapper was waiting for him at the main gate. Instead of wanting to ride Paul's horse, the boy tethered it and led the visitor to the room occupied by Virgil Paige. The door was firmly shut. Snapper knocked four times, waited, then knocked again another three times.

'Thass wor 'e told me to do, sir,' he explained.

'Why?'

'No strangers muss ger in there.'

The chair wedged up against the door was moved so that it could be eased far enough ajar for Paige to look out. Opening the door wide, he ushered Paul inside, thanked Snapper, sent him on his way then closed the door again before putting the chair back in place.

'What's going on?' asked Paul.

'I wish I knew, Mr Skillen.'

'Why couldn't you come to the gallery?'

'I was stopped at the gate.'

'I thought you had special privileges.'

'They've been withdrawn,' said Paige, sourly, 'but that's not the worst of it.'

'Oh?'

'I've been here long enough to earn respect. Nobody bothers me and nobody would dare to come in here while I'm out taking exercise. Earlier today, that all changed. When I tried to venture out of the prison, the gatekeeper refused to let me go. He said that he'd had orders from the marshal himself. So I came back here and was shocked to find that it had all gone.'

'What had?'

'Everything I used to produce my caricatures, Mr Skillen. While I was away, they were kept in a locked cupboard. Someone broke into it.'

'Can't you complain?'

Paige gave a hollow laugh. 'To whom, I ask? As well as debtors and those in here for defamation, we have our share of thieves and footpads. Look through that window and you'll see dozens of possible suspects.'

'I thought you said that you were respected in here.'

'I was. Everyone left me alone and kept away from my room. It was a sort of unwritten law. Somebody broke it.'

Paul was worried. 'Last time I came here, you talked about having peace of mind,' he said. 'That seems to have gone altogether now.'

'It has, Mr Skillen, and it was my own fault.'

'Why do you say that?'

'I went to my brother's funeral.'

'You were fully entitled to do that, Mr Paige.'

'I think I was followed,' said the other. 'I fancy that somebody asked why I had the urge to attend that particular funeral when there was hardly anyone else there. I met your own brother, by the way, and a Mr Ackford. It was kind of them to come.'

'Had I not been busy elsewhere, I'd have attended myself.'

'Grief bestows its own blindness. Like Leo, I usually know if someone is stalking me but I was too caught up in my bereavement. All I wanted to do was to get back here to be alone with my thoughts.'

'I understand.'

'Someone *knows*,' said Paige, solemnly. 'Someone knows that I'm Virgo.'

'That's very disturbing.'

'It's somebody with influence, that's clear.'

'The likelihood is that it's the person we seek,' said Paul. 'He has the power to control access in and out of prison. The men who killed your brother were released from Newgate and you were stopped from leaving here even though you had a legitimate right to do so. Did you question the marshal?'

'I tried to do so, Mr Skillen.'

'What happened?'

'He refused to see me.'

'You deserved an explanation.'

'I got that when I returned here and found that my things had been stolen. That's why I have to exercise great care. Snapper is the only person who knows how to make me open that door. That lad has been a godsend to me.'

'I'll remember to slip him a coin or two when I leave.'

'He saw something that may be significant.'

'What was that?'

'This may be fanciful supposition on my part,' said Paige, 'but I'm reduced to the position of grasping at straws.'

'What did the lad see?'

'Well, we live in mean accommodation here, as you can see, but the marshal does not. He has splendid apartments outside the prison. Snapper was playing with friends at the gate when he saw a fine coach roll up. When it stopped at the marshal's lodging, he came out in person to welcome his guest. He'd only do that for someone of real importance.'

Paige bit his lip. 'An hour later, I was stopped from leaving the prison. Is that what the visitor came to demand?'

Julian Harvester took the bottle from him and held it up to the light to examine the liquid inside. After putting the bottle on the table, he looked at his visitor.

'Are you sure that this will solve the problem?'

'It will ease the discomfort,' replied Penhallurick. 'That's all I can claim.'

'I want a cure, Guy, and not simply a way of subduing the pain.'

'The cure lies in your own hands, Julian. You must look to your diet. If you eat less and cut down on your consumption of wine and brandy, your abdominal woes will eventually disappear. There is, of course, another way we can proceed.'

'What's that?'

'Let me open you up and I may be able to cut out the problem altogether.'

'Oh, no,' protested Harvester, a hand on his stomach. 'That's out of the question. I'd sooner suffer than commit myself to your scalpel.'

'So be it.'

Guy Penhallurick was a tall, solid, good-looking man in his early fifties with a patrician air. His voice had the distinctive burr of the West Country. As well as being a friend of Harvester, he was his physician.

'I'm surprised to find you here this afternoon,' he said. 'I thought that you'd be at the cricket match for the second day.'

'I had pressing business to attend to,' explained Harvester.

'Nothing comes before cricket. That's what you told me.'

'Ordinarily, that's the case. I can see that *you* weren't tempted to return to St John's Wood again.'

Penhallurick gave a mock yawn. 'It was an essay in sustained boredom.'

'How can you say that of some sublime batting?'

'It failed to excite me, Julian. While I'm grateful that you took me there, it's a game that will never be dear to my heart. But then, unlike you, I've never been a natural sportsman.'

'You actually went to sleep. That's sacrilege.'

'I apologise. The truth is that I'd been up most of the night.'

'Were you called out by a patient?'

Penhallurick smiled. 'You could put it like that.'

He tried once again to persuade his friend to moderate his intake of rich food and strong drink. The advice was studiously ignored. Harvester was not a man to change the habits of a lifetime. They were in the library of his London home. Bookshelves covered most of the wall space but a large painting of a cricket match hung above the marble fireplace. Harvester strolled across to it.

'This match was held at Thomas Lord's present ground when it was first opened. I was there at the time,' he went on, pointing to the myriad spectators. 'Somewhere among those delighted onlookers are me and my friends. Nobody in the whole ground, I can assure you, committed the sin of falling asleep.'

'You'll never let me forget that, will you?'

'Sir Humphrey thought it was an appalling thing to do.'

'I know. I had to tender my apologies when I saw him this morning.' He tapped the bottle of medicine. 'Take a spoonful of this every day and it should do the trick.'

'What if it doesn't?'

'I'll keep my knife well sharpened,' said the other, jokingly.

'Your surgical operations have not always been a success,' observed Harvester with implied criticism.

Penhallurick was caught on the raw. 'There are unforeseen hazards sometimes.'

'David Bellmain never recovered from your ministrations.'

'He was the exception to the rule, Julian,' said the other, unhappy at being reminded of a failed operation. 'He came to me too late. Nobody could have saved him. All that I could do was to prolong his life by a few weeks.'

'Is that what your medicine will do for *me* – keep me alive for another few weeks?'

'Oh, I think you'll last a bit longer than that. My medical opinion is that you'll have several years left to watch cricket matches and exert your firm but invisible pressure on the government of the day.' He saw the clock on the mantelpiece. 'I must away, Julian. I have another patient waiting.'

'I'll see you out.'

As they went into the hall, the butler was standing by to open the front door. Harvester was surprised to see a coach standing outside on the drive.

'Isn't that Sir Humphrey's coach?'

'I borrowed it for the day.'

'Why did you do that?'

'I needed to create an impression on someone, Julian.'

'Why didn't you borrow my coach?' asked the other. 'It's even bigger and better than this one. You'd have cut a dash in that.'

'I'm sure that I would have, but your coach has one defect.'

'That's nonsense!'

'It has your coat-of-arms emblazoned on the doors,' said Penhallurick, putting his hat on. 'If I travel in *this* coach, I can look as if I own it. Anybody seeing me in *your* vehicle would assume that I was Julian Harvester, one of the wealthiest men in the realm. That would not be sensible.'

Back at the print shop, Peter Skillen had managed to convince Tite and the servants that they were not actually on the verge of being killed. With the confidence he'd instilled in them, they went into the garden to clear up the debris. With Diane Mandrake at his side, Peter looked through the window at them.

'I think they'll stay the night now,' he said. 'I doubt if they'll sleep, mark you, but they'll be on the premises.'

'How did they start the fire?' asked Diane. 'That's what puzzles me. How did they get into my garden?'

'They must have climbed over the fence.'

'But how did they get into the garden at the rear of mine, Peter?'

'If they were agile – and if there were, indeed, two of them – then hopping over a six-foot fence would have been quite easy. It was also their escape route. Once the fire was well established, they'd have fled, convinced that they'd done exactly what they'd been told to do. They probably don't realise that the blaze was actually put out. It will come as a rude shock to them.'

'Nowhere near as rude as the shock that *I* got last night when I heard someone bellowing outside in the street,' she said. 'It made me leap out of bed as if the fire was directly beneath me.'

'Was it Yeomans who actually called out to you?'

'No, it was a member of the foot patrol. His name was Ruddock, as I recall.'

'Chevy Ruddock,' he told her. 'We've had dealings with him before.'

'He was fearless in the face of that blaze.'

'What about Yeomans?'

'He was a Trojan as well, Peter. I have to give him credit for that. The fire burnt off part of his eyebrows. That must have been painful.'

'His pride will have been badly wounded by that. He's cultivated those eyebrows for years.'

'Let's put him aside,' she said, turning to look at him. 'I've something very important to ask you.'

'Go on,' he invited.

'Do you think that Virgo is aware of what's going on?'

'He must be. Since he kept in touch with Mr Paige all the time, he'll certainly know that his partner was murdered.'

'Then why hasn't he been in touch with *me*?'

'He must have his reasons,' said Peter, guardedly.

She put her face close. 'I think you might know what those reasons are.'

'Why do you say that, Mrs Mandrake?'

'I've been checking up on you and your brother, Peter. Together with Gully Ackford, you have an astonishing record of success. If anyone in London could track down Virgo, it's you or Paul. Am I right?'

It was a moment that Peter had known would come sooner or later. She was a woman of great intuition. Preoccupied with events at the shop, she hadn't been able to ask him about the search for the cartoonist. But she hadn't forgotten it and she wanted an answer. They had deliberately held back the information before but Peter could not lie to her now. Since she'd sold Virgo's prints for so long, she deserved to know who he actually was.

'Yes,' confessed Peter, 'you are right. We did run him to ground.'

'Why didn't you tell me?'

'You had enough on your plate as it was, Mrs Mandrake.'

'I don't accept that.'

'Then I apologise. It was Paul who first met him.'

'And what's his real name?' she demanded.

'It's Virgil Paige.'

'Paige? Then he's—'

'He was Mr Paige's brother.'

'I didn't even know that Leo *had* a brother,' she said, peevishly. 'He lodged with me all that time yet he never once talked about his family.'

'Well, he did have one sibling and they produced the *Parliament of Foibles* between them.'

'That's very enterprising. I just wonder why I wasn't let in on the secret much earlier. Why has this brother been hiding his light under a bushel? In the wake of the murder, I expected him to come forward.'

'That's rather difficult, I fear.'

'Why?'

'He's in prison.'

* * *

278

Virgil Paige walked up and down the room to relieve his anxiety, occasionally going to the window to look out. Though his army service had given him the ability to defend himself, he couldn't do that if he was up against unfair odds. His enemy knew who he was and where he lived. There was no escape. Someone was keeping him there for a purpose. It was only a matter of time before they struck.

Paul Skillen watched him for minutes then offered his advice.

'Go to the marshal and explain the situation,' he suggested.

'I told you. He wouldn't see me.'

'What about the turnkeys? After all your time in here, you must have got to know them fairly well.'

'I have, Mr Skillen.'

'Choose the most reliable of them and explain your dilemma to him.'

'What can a turnkey do?'

'He'd have access to the marshal.'

'It's pointless,' said Paige. 'Nobody would pay heed to my predicament. Someone called at the prison and ruined my character by giving trumped-up evidence against me. That's what the marshal is acting on. Put yourself in his position, Mr Skillen. If you're given contradictory information by a prisoner and a person of considerable standing, which are you going to believe?'

'You don't *have* to be a prisoner.'

'I do now.'

'You said that you had enough money to discharge your debts.'

'That's true.'

'Then you can buy your way out of here immediately.'

'It's not as straightforward as that,' explained Paige. 'First of all, the money is not here. It would have to be obtained from the bank where it's kept. Second, I chose to stay here as a matter of honour.'

Paul was perplexed. 'What honour is there in imprisonment?'

'You don't understand the situation. I only have one outstanding debt but it's a sizeable one. It's claimed that I owe three hundred pounds to someone who's the biggest scoundrel I've ever met. Under the guise of friendship, he loaned me a much smaller amount of money then presented me with a bill that showed exorbitant interest. When he took me to court, his lawyer managed to convince everyone that I was deliberately refusing to pay off my debt as an act of spite. As a result,' he went on, waving a hand to take in the whole room, 'I ended up here. And I'm damned if I'm going to give that bloodsucker three hundred pounds to which he's not entitled.'

'So you're staying in here on a point of principle.'

'And because – believe it or not – I *like* it here.' He looked out of the window again. 'At least, I did until today.'

'We've got to get you out,' decided Paul.

'That's impossible now. Even if I did try to discharge the debt, I'd not be allowed to do so. Someone else has a bigger claim on me. The only way that I can pay him off is with my life.'

'Then the man who visited the marshal must be one of our suspects.'

'If he owns a coach, we have some idea of his position.'

'Which of them is he?' wondered Paul, counting the names off on his fingers. 'Is it Sir Humphrey Coote, Gerard Brunt, Julian Harvester or Dr Penhallurick?'

'It might be all four of them together.'

'No, I don't think that's the case.'

'Why do you say that?'

'I had the good fortune to meet Sir Humphrey. Strangely enough, I sat next to him at a cricket match. He wasn't there with any of the others even though Harvester and Penhallurick were in the ground. If the three of them were engaged in a conspiracy,' Paul continued, 'you'd have expected them to sit cheek by jowl.'

'What about Gerard Brunt?'

'My brother, Peter, claims that Brunt is the main suspect now.'

'That's not much help to me, Mr Skillen. Whichever one of them wants my pelt as a trophy, he's going the right way about it. He's got me penned in here with nobody but Snapper on my side.'

'There's me as well, remember.'

'What can *you* do?'

'I can get you out of here,' said Paul, looking him up and down.

'They'd stop me at the gate.'

'They might stop Virgil Paige but they'd have no cause to refuse to let Paul Skillen out. Dressed like that, you'd be turned away. Dressed like me, however, you'd ride out of the King's Bench like the visitor you are.' A look of hope was kindled in Paige's eye. 'My clothes might be a tight fit on you but does that matter if they're able to get you to safety?'

'Yes, but in saving me, you'll put your own life at risk.'

'I want the men who killed your brother and who assaulted Jem Huckvale,' said Paul, sternly. 'The chances are that they'll be sent here on a mission to murder you.'

'Then you'll be caught like a rat in a trap.'

'I'm the one laying the trap. My brother and I have been searching all over London for these villains. Instead of looking for them, I simply have to stay here and they'll come to me.'

They'd sat in a brooding silence for the best part of an hour. Higlett kept drinking from the flagon of ale but Fearon left it untouched. He was still trying to work out how the print shop had escaped their arson attack. Failure had robbed them of a substantial amount of money and subjected him to an ordeal in the back of a coach. Fearon knew that there'd be terrible repercussions if they let their paymaster down again. He suddenly remembered a detail that he hadn't passed on to his friend.

'There was something else, Sim.'

'What was it?'

'He talked about after.'

'After what?'

'When we've done all that he wants us for.'

'That's what I was asking you about,' said Higlett. 'What happens next?'

'He says that we have to leave London altogether.'

'Where are we supposed to go?'

'He'll arrange that,' explained Fearon. 'We're to go abroad. It may be to America or somewhere else.'

'I was hoping we'd turned our back on the sea.'

'We'd not be going as sailors. We'd be passengers. He's got friends who own vessels that sail the globe. We'd have money in our purses and a chance to start a new life.' His smile froze. 'But only if we obey orders. If we fail . . .'

Higlett blenched. 'I know. We'll be skinned alive.'

'Which country would you prefer to go to?'

'America would be my choice. I've sailed into Boston harbour twice.'

Fearon was about to recount some of his own reminiscences of a voyage across the Atlantic when they heard a rustling sound. Glancing across at the door, they saw that a letter had been slipped under it. Fearon went over to snatch it up and opened it. He read the instructions then looked up.

'We're going to prison.'

Higlett was disturbed. 'Is he sending us back to Newgate?'

'No, Sim. It's the King's Bench this time.'

'Why do we have to go there?'

'We have orders to kill someone.'

CHAPTER SIXTEEN

Though he'd never particularly liked him, Penhallurick knew that he had to befriend Gerard Brunt. The latter was universally spoken of as a coming man in Parliament. In time, when Penhallurick was elected to represent a constituency in the House of Commons, he would need to align himself with people like Brunt. The man would be a definite asset. For that reason, he manufactured a smile of welcome.

'Good evening,' he said, offering his hand.

Brunt shook it. 'Hello, Penhallurick.'

'I haven't seen you at the club for a while.'

'I've been rather preoccupied with parliamentary matters.'

'Is it true that you're devising a means of getting cartoonists off our back?'

'Left to me, they'd be submerged in boiling oil,' said Brunt, malevolently. 'And yes, I've been canvassing support for my latest Amendment.'

'I'd give it my endorsement without even seeing it. I know

that you and I are of the same mind when it comes to the libel laws.' He saw a waiter approaching. 'Let me buy you a drink, Mr Brunt.'

They were soon seated side by side in leather armchairs with a brandy apiece on the table between them. Brunt was pleased by the other man's attention. As a rule, it was he who spent his visits to the club smiling obsequiously at people he needed to cultivate. Being treated with exaggerated respect was a pleasant change for him.

'How is the world of medicine?' he asked.

'It keeps me busy.'

'I'm told that you look after Sir Humphrey Coote. There are lots of fat fees to be earned there, I suspect.'

'I never discuss my patients,' said Penhallurick. 'They're entitled to expect confidentiality.'

'My physician keeps advising me to take more exercise,' said Brunt smirking. 'No need to say that to Sir Humphrey, is there – the one thing he's not short of is vigorous exercise.'

'*Chacun à son goût.*'

'The wonder is that you've not had to treat him for the pox.'

'His treatment is strictly a private affair.'

'His luck must run out in time. The law of averages dictates that, sooner or later, he'll seduce the wrong woman and wake up with a nasty rash and a persistent itch. How does he find the *time* for his nocturnal antics?'

'I'll not be the one to throw the first stone,' said Penhallurick, tolerantly. 'We all find time for things that really obsess us. In your case, it's a mission to repair the glaring faults in the statute book.'

'That's the work of a lifetime.'

'In my case, it's a desire to keep my patients alive and well.'

'It's the way it *looks* that bothers me,' said Brunt.

'I don't follow.'

'Sir Humphrey is a Member of Parliament. He should behave like one.'

'As far as I know, the position doesn't involve a vow of chastity. The House of Commons is an organ of government and not a monastic institution. As for Sir Humphrey,' he went on, 'he's very selective with regard to his conquests.'

'Yes,' said Brunt with a disapproving sniff, 'he was indiscreet enough to boast that his haul included a countess, the wife of a privy counsellor and the daughter of a bishop. One never knows, of course, if he's telling the truth.'

'Oh, he doesn't lie about things like that, Mr Brunt. He's very proud of his tally. He once told me that he'd stalk his target for a year, if need be. That's what he's been doing with one of his latest prospects.'

'And who might that be?'

'Do you ever go to the theatre?'

'I'd never dream of it, sir. It's too full of riff-raff.'

'Yet it's also patronised by the aristocracy.'

'I don't care. It's a complete irrelevance to me.'

'Then you've missed seeing one of the wonders of the age. She's an actress who can even challenge Sarah Siddons as a queen of her profession. The lady I speak of is Miss Hannah Granville and Sir Humphrey is besotted with her.'

'Then she has my sympathy.'

'On the face of it,' said Penhallurick, 'Miss Granville is

way out of his reach. She's repulsed his overtures thus far and is already spoken for but that won't hold him back. He's even prepared to overcome the final hurdle.'

'And what's that?'

'Miss Granville is reported to be in Paris at the moment, way beyond Sir Humphrey's grasping hands. You'd imagine that he'd be deterred by geography, but not a bit of it, Mr Brunt. The last time I met him, he was talking about sailing to France in order to court her there.'

Brunt pursed his lips. 'Is there no limit to the man's debauchery?'

'I fancy that he'd describe it as a romantic impulse.'

'Then Sir Humphrey Coote's capacity for self-delusion is greater than I'd thought.' Brunt rose to his feet. 'Please excuse me a moment. I've just seen Kirkwood come in. I need to have a word with him . . .'

Paul Skillen was also gripped by the urge to go to France in order to be with Hannah Granville but that was out of the question for a time. He was now entombed in the King's Bench with the rest of the prison population. A long, cold, lonely and very uncomfortable night beckoned. He took consolation from the fact that he'd managed to get Virgil Paige out of danger. It had taken some time to transform the artist into a passable likeness of Paul Skillen. To start with, there was the age difference between them. Paige had shaved carefully, concealed his hair underneath the hat and tilted it sharply to hide the scar on his cheek. Mounted on a horse and with Snapper there to distract the gatekeeper, he'd been let out of the establishment. All the gates were locked now and the prisoners had retired to their respective rooms. To all intents and purposes, Paul was now Virgo.

As a result, he had the disagreeable experience of wearing the other man's shabby clothing and putting on ill-fitting shoes that pinched his feet. Thinking about Hannah helped him to escape the multiple shortcomings of his accommodation. His overriding concern was for the undisclosed problems that she was facing in Paris. Before she'd set sail, he'd made her promise that, in the event of a crisis, she'd send for him and he wondered if, in a covert way, she was doing that. Having read her last letter so many times, he knew it by heart and realised that the words could be interpreted in a number of ways. The only sure means of finding out what Hannah was really trying to tell him was to go to her. Since that option was denied him, all that he could do was to worry, speculate feverishly and resolve that they'd never be apart for so long again.

For a man who relished his freedom of action so much, being locked up was a trial for him, but it was a necessary evil. Snapper had schooled him in the prison routine. When the turnkey had come to check on him that evening, therefore, Paul lay face down on the mattress under a blanket as if fast asleep. All that he was spared was a cursory glance before the turnkey moved on. Somebody would come in due course for the purpose of silencing Virgo. He was certain of that. Sleep was therefore out of the question. The killer might come at night or by day so Paul had to be on continuous guard. His only ally was Snapper and he couldn't expect the boy to forfeit his sleep entirely. In essence, he was on his own.

Virgo might have adapted completely to life in a prison but Paul found none of the virtues talked about by the other man. Being in the King's Bench was a twilight existence. In spending a night away from it, he expected, Virgil Paige might come to realise what he was missing.

At the shooting gallery, meanwhile, the former prisoner was facing a volley of questions. Seated in the office, he was surrounded by Gully Ackford, Jem Huckvale and Charlotte. While they were quick to offer him food and shelter, they were also keen to hear details of the person who'd replaced him in the King's Bench.

'Was it Paul's idea to get you out of there?' asked Charlotte.

'Yes, Mrs Skillen,' replied Paige. 'It would never have crossed my mind.'

'He must have thought you were in real danger,' said Ackford. 'Paul is very vain about his appearance. He wouldn't have surrendered his clothes and hat like that unless he thought that danger was imminent.'

'It is.'

'Does he have anyone to help him in there?' said Huckvale.

'Yes, he does – Snapper.'

'But he's only a boy, isn't he?'

'Don't be fooled by the lad's age,' said Paige. 'He's as sharp as a razor and quite fearless. He won't let Mr Skillen down.'

'How certain are you that your life was under threat?' said Charlotte.

'Absolutely certain.'

'Mr Paige served in the army,' remarked Ackford, 'like me

and his brother, Leo. You develop a strong sense of when you're in danger, believe me. It's been my salvation more than once.'

'It didn't save Leo,' Paige reminded him.

'Too true.'

'That was my fault,' confessed Huckvale. 'I was hired as his bodyguard. Because of that, he felt that he didn't have to watch his back.'

'Don't start blaming yourself again, Jem.'

'I'm bound to, Gully.'

'Nobody else blames you.'

'I certainly don't,' said Paige, looking with sympathy at his bandaging. 'You got injured trying to protect my brother. I'm very grateful to you.'

'It's Paul who needs protection now,' said Charlotte, worriedly.

Ackford smiled confidently. 'He'll cope with any situation.'

'But he's completely on his own in there.'

'You're forgetting Snapper,' said Paige. 'He's a good lookout.'

'Did Paul send any message?'

'Yes, Mrs Skillen. He said that you should look after me and stop fretting about him. Also, he promised that Mr Ackford would find me some clothing that actually fitted.'

'I can certainly do that,' said Ackford, sizing him up.

'I still think Paul needs help,' said Huckvale.

'What do you suggest, Jem?'

'At least we can stop the killer getting in during the night. We could go armed and stand outside the gate.'

'Southwark is not a place you want to be doing that,' warned Paige. 'Hazards lurk at every corner after dark.'

'We can't just leave Paul at the mercy of an assassin.'

'I fancy that the assassin will be at Paul's mercy,' said Ackford with a grin. 'Besides, you're assuming that the man will strike at night.'

'That's the most likely time, isn't it?'

'It's much easier to get inside the King's Bench during the day,' said Paige. 'When night falls, it turns into a fortress.'

'But you told us that someone had sufficient influence with the marshal to revoke your licence to walk outside the prison,' recalled Charlotte. 'Couldn't that same person get hold of a pass to gain entry to the King's Bench at night?'

'It's possible.'

'Then we ought to be on sentry duty,' insisted Huckvale.

'You could be too late.'

'Why?'

'You're forgetting something.'

'What's that, Mr Paige?'

'The killer could already be inside.'

Peter Skillen had been politely insistent that he should spend the night at the print shop. His presence, he hoped, would still the fears of everyone there. Diane Mandrake was pleased and dismayed, glad to have a handsome man on the premises at night yet upset because it meant that her much-vaunted independence had to be sacrificed. She'd always lived her life on the principle of being able to cope on her own with any circumstance that fate decreed. The fire had disposed of that illusion. She needed help and – since Tite and the servants were unable to supply it – Peter Skillen was there as a line of defence.

The two of them sat alone together in the back room. While Peter enjoyed the comfort of a high-backed chair, Diane was revelling in the company of a man with considerably more charm and practicality than Benjamin Tite.

'You don't have to stay up, Mrs Mandrake,' he said. 'The others have chosen to have an early night. You could do the same.'

'I wouldn't dream of leaving you alone.'

'After the ordeal of last night, you need your sleep.'

'And I'll get it – all in good time.'

'I wasn't trying to give you orders.'

'I should hope not. This is my home.'

Peter found her company pleasant. She was an intelligent woman with good conversation and a variety of interests. He sought to learn more about the man whose death had brought them together in the first place.

'Tell me about Mr Paige,' he said.

'Which one – Leo or Virgil?'

'You've only met one of them, Mrs Mandrake.'

'I feel that I know Leo's brother as well. Having spent so much time studying his work, I've got an insight into his character. I look forward to meeting him.'

'I'd like to hear more about his brother.'

She took a deep breath. 'Where shall I start?' she wondered. 'I suppose that you'd like to know how we first met, wouldn't you? It was completely by accident. I was trying to get into my curricle when a dog frightened my horse and it bolted. Leo leapt into the street and grabbed its bridle to slow it down. I remember thinking how brave he was. Then he kicked the dog and I thought how cruel he was.'

As she let her memories flow, Peter gained a lot of new information about the murder victim. Though she described him as her lodger, she never for a second hinted at a closer relationship and Peter felt slightly embarrassed that he knew Paige had been her lover for a while. Light was starting to fade now and, as she talked, she lit the candles. She was just settling into her chair again when there was a loud knock on the door. Peter leapt to his feet and pulled out his pistol.

'Go upstairs, Mrs Mandrake,' he ordered. 'Leave this to me.'

She folded her arms. 'I'm staying here.'

Peter went to the door, pulled back the bolts and turned the key in the lock. He then opened it cautiously and saw Jem Huckvale standing on the threshold. Lowering his pistol, he opened the door wide.

'What are you doing here, Jem?'

'I've brought news about Paul.'

The play being performed that night at the Theatre Royal in Covent Garden was *The Duenna* by Richard Brinsley Sheridan. During the interval, Sir Humphrey Coote was part of a swirling crowd in the foyer. When he saw the familiar face of Julian Harvester, he went across to the man.

'I didn't realise that you were here,' he said.

'I was very well aware of *your* presence, Sir Humphrey. As soon as we entered, I saw you and your entourage up in your box.'

'Three or four old friends hardly constitute an entourage.

I like company when I come to the theatre – and at a cricket match, of course. Incidentally, what did you think of the second day's play? It even surpassed the standard set on the first day.'

'Unhappily, I was not there.'

Sir Humphrey was shocked. 'You *missed* an event like that?'

'It was unavoidable.'

'Nothing would have kept me away.'

'Duty called, I fear.' He glanced in the direction of the auditorium. 'Are you enjoying the performance?'

'I'm thoroughly enjoying the music and the singing. It was a stroke of genius by Sheridan to make it into a comic opera. Such a pity that he's not here to bathe in the waves of applause.'

'Yes,' said Harvester, 'he's a great loss. I attended his funeral earlier this month. Such a sad end for such an extraordinary man! The fellow died in penury. They say that his house was stripped of its furnishings because he'd been forced to sell them off. How can we let our great playwrights sink to such depths?'

'Sheridan was a fine playwright, I grant you, but he was less successful as a politician. I know that,' said Sir Humphrey, 'because I had to sit through his speeches. Some were good and well argued but others . . . well, they're best consigned to history. I vow that he'll be remembered much more for his work in the theatre than for his political career. His last appointment was as treasurer of the navy – without Cabinet rank – and he didn't distinguish himself in that post because he wasn't prepared to work hard enough.'

'Nobody works hard enough in Parliament,' teased Harvester. 'You all hold sinecures.'

Sir Humphrey laughed. 'I'm in too good a humour to rise to the bait.'

'Then I'll stop dangling it in front of you.' He stepped in closer. 'What do you think of the angel playing Louisa? Isn't she a perfect darling?'

'Miss Villmont is competent in the role, Julian.'

'Come now – she's much more than that. Look around you, Sir Humphrey. See the covetous smiles on men's faces. She's bewitching. Every time she steps on stage, she sets hearts aflutter.'

'She did nothing whatsoever to mine, alas.'

'Have you no eyes – have you no ears?'

'I have the requisite number of both.'

'Then open them wide, man. This is the performance of the season. I'm astonished that a connoisseur of the fair sex such as you does not appreciate her magnificence. Miss Arabella Villmont is the finest actress in London.'

'That's only because someone else has vacated the stage for a while.'

'Ah,' said Harvester, realising, 'you speak of Miss Granville.'

'I do, indeed,' said Sir Humphrey with a lubricious smile. 'Not to put too fine a point on it, Miss Villmont is base metal to Hannah's pure gold.'

Prison was not a place for those who valued peace and quiet. At all hours of the day and night, it reverberated with noise. Paul Skillen heard shouts, screams, violent arguments and unidentifiable bangs. He tried to block out the sounds by thinking about the last time he'd seen Hannah Granville. It had been in the port of Dover when she embarked for France. After an exchange of promises on the quayside, he'd given her a farewell kiss then stayed until the ship set sail. Paul had assumed that she'd win the hearts of the Parisian public as quickly and easily as she'd done so with their English counterparts.

Paul was realistic. When he fell in love with a beautiful woman, he knew that she'd be the object of continual male attention. Even if she were married, she'd find admirers clustered around the stage door and receive unsolicited gifts from those who sought to win her favours. There was nothing he could do to prevent it. Instead of worrying about it, therefore, he saw it as something of which to be proud. Paul relished the envy of other men. He actually enjoyed what so many of them sought. What did trouble him, however, was the way that old roués like Sir Humphrey Coote looked at her. They didn't see her as the lively, intelligent and gifted woman she was in reality. Hannah Granville was to them simply one more conquest.

He remembered the cartoon that his brother had been given as a present by Diane Mandrake. It depicted Sir Humphrey cavorting with a prostitute while dozens of others waited outside to take their place in his bed. While it had made him laugh, it had also disgusted him and he now squirmed at the memory of sitting beside the man at a cricket match. Sir Humphrey Coote was an amiable monster. There were many others like him. That was why Hannah had turned to someone like Paul. When they were together, she could feel that she had a protective ring of steel around her.

Another aspect of the drawing came to mind and it prompted a grin. It was the sight of Micah Yeomans struggling to keep the queue of harlots in order. It was, in Paul's view, a telling comment on the Runner's abilities. All that he was fitted for was to act as a doorman at a brothel and as a pimp for Sir Humphrey Coote. There was no doubting the latter's generosity. On the table beside the bed was a huge pile of banknotes. Sir Humphrey was ready to pay extravagantly for his pleasures.

What price would he set on the favours of Hannah Granville?

The moment that light started to be sucked out of the sky, Chevy Ruddock was back on patrol in Holborn. Bolstered by his wife's ecstatic reaction to the news of his heroism in the face of the fire, he was eager to be given the opportunity to repeat it in a different emergency. He was striding along with his head held high when Yeomans came up to him.

'Good evening, sir,' he said.

'Remember what I said, Ruddock.'

'Yes, sir.'

'The moment you see anything remotely suspicious, you come and fetch us.'

'Why don't you simply walk up and down with me, Mr Yeomans?'

'Do as you're told, man.'

'I just wondered why you and Mr Hale are lurking around the corner.'

'There's a reason for that.'

He refused to tell Ruddock what it was. Micah Yeomans had been expressly forbidden by Diane Mandrake to loiter outside her shop. To win her approval, he accepted her edict. At the same time, he was determined to be on hand in case another crisis occurred.

'What exactly did he say?' asked Ruddock.

'Who are you talking about?'

'The chief magistrate – you mentioned my name to him.'

'Yes, yes,' said Yeomans, briskly, 'I put in a good word.'

'What was his reply?'

'Does it matter?'

'My wife was so impressed. She loves to hear praise of me.'

'I can't remember it word for word,' said Yeomans, evasively, 'but he said that you were a shining example.'

'Agnes will love that phrase – a shining example.'

'He said the same about me, of course. You shared some of my lustre.'

He was about to give further instruction when he saw the door of the print shop open. Peter Skillen walked across the road towards them. Yeomans was outraged at the thought that his rival was actually inside the house when he was not even allowed to stay outside it.

'I understand that congratulations are in order,' said Peter, pleasantly. 'Mrs Mandrake has told me how grateful she is.'

'I raised the alarm about the fire,' said Ruddock.

'Be quiet,' hissed Yeomans.

'Well, I did, sir.'

'Mrs Mandrake is well aware of that,' said Peter. 'The message she's sent me out to deliver is that she no longer needs you on patrol. I have supplanted you.'

'You mean that you're staying in there all night?' gasped Yeomans.

'I insisted on it.'

'But it's not your place to do so.'

'We go wherever we're needed, Mr Yeomans.'

Ruddock peered at him. 'Are you Mr Peter or Mr Paul Skillen?'

'Haven't you learnt to tell the difference yet?'

'No, sir.'

'This is Paul Skillen,' said Yeomans, authoritatively.

'My brother will not be flattered,' said Peter. 'Actually, I'm Peter Skillen.'

'I had a feeling that you were,' said Ruddock.

'Disappear,' snarled Yeomans. 'Wait at the end of the street.'

'Oh, yes . . . if you say so.'

'You might as well join him,' said Peter as he watched Ruddock walk away. 'There's no work for you here tonight.'

'What if there's another attack?' asked Yeomans, indignantly.

'I'll deal with it.'

'I have half a dozen men within call.'

'Then you can assign them to other duties.'

'Don't presume to tell me my job, Mr Skillen.'

'I'm simply passing on a request from Mrs Mandrake.'

'Has she *told* you what happened during the fire?'

'Yes,' said Peter, 'you and Ruddock have earned her undying gratitude. But she does not wish to glance out of her bedroom window and see either of you on patrol outside. Your presence out here will deter any attack. If the street is empty, however, the person or persons who started that blaze are more likely to return. That will give me the chance to apprehend them.'

'It's our job – not yours!'

'Does it matter which of us does it as long as they're caught?'

'It's of great consequence to me.'

'Then you should stop pretending that only the Runners have powers of arrest. My brother and I are doing what any right-minded citizens should do and that's to take any brutal killers off the streets of London so that people can sleep in relative safety. We've done it before,' Peter reminded him. 'Paul and I have sent a number of villains up the steps to the gallows.'

'I'd like to send the pair of *you* there,' said Yeomans under his breath. Aloud, he became pugnacious. 'I've warned you before. Keep out of our way.'

'We're only trying to uphold the law.'

'The chief magistrate regards the two of you as a menace.'

'That's strange,' said Peter, seizing on the chance to slap him down. 'When I called on the Home Secretary recently, he said how grateful he was for the work that my brother and I do. Please pass that on to the chief magistrate. Good night.'

'Wait,' said Yeomans, before Peter could turn away. 'How do I know that you're repeating Mrs Mandrake's instructions? You could be trying to get rid of us so that you alone are in a position to grab any glory.'

'Is he still there?' yelled Diane, opening the window of her bedroom. 'Don't you understand English, man? Please go away.'

Peter smiled. 'Does that answer your question, Mr Yeomans?'

'Damnation!' exclaimed the Runner.

'I heard that,' said Diane before closing the window.

'Mrs Mandrake abhors that kind of language,' said Peter.

'Then she'd better stay indoors or she'll hear a great deal more of it.'

Suffused with rage, Yeomans strode off down the street.

Sustained applause greeted the end of the performance at the Theatre Royal. The whole cast took several bows but the undisputed cynosure was Arabella Villmont. In the role of Louisa, she'd captivated the entire audience. As the spectators streamed out into the foyer, it was her name on most of their lips. Julian Harvester was no exception. When he saw the opportunity of a word with Sir Humphrey Coote, he elbowed his way through the crowd to get close to him.

'What do you say now, Sir Humphrey?' he asked. 'Isn't she divine?'

'She's divinely pretty, I'll own that.'

'Miss Villmont kept me spellbound.'

'I found her charms too intermittent.'

'Then we must agree to differ.'

They chatted about various aspects of the performance until they came out on to the pavement. A long line of coaches and carriages was waiting to spirit people back to their homes. Harvester was reminded of something.

'I gather that you loaned Penhallurick your coach,' he said.

'It was the least I could do. Guy had more need of it than I did.'

'Did he say why?'

'If he did, then I've forgotten what his answer was. It matters not. The one thing I can tell you, Julian, is that he didn't make use of it to go to St John's Wood. Cricket has no appeal for him.'

'I found that out during the first day's play.'

'What do you make of him?'

'Guy is a brilliant physician and a thoroughly engaging fellow.'

'How will he fare as a politician, do you think?'

'He'll shine at whatever he does.'

'Of course, he'll have to win the election first.'

'Oh, there's no whisper of a doubt there,' said Harvester, grandiloquently. 'I've offered my support – financial and literal. I've no wish to be a Member of Parliament myself but I like to have a modicum of control in the House. He'll be the latest addition to my little coterie. What's your opinion of Guy Penhallurick?'

'He'll adorn Westminster,' replied Sir Humphrey, lowering his voice before he continued. 'The reason I was happy to give him free use of my coach is that he did me a special favour.'

'What was that?'

'He concocted an aphrodisiac of quite unprecented power. You should ask him for some of it, Julian.'

'My aphrodisiac was up there onstage this evening – Arabella Villmont.'

'Contrive to be alone with her and all you have to do is to slip some of the powder into her drink. Guy's concoction is foolproof. It would turn a Mother Superior into the Whore of Babylon.'

Harvester laughed. 'I'll take your word for it.'

'When I give some of it to Hannah Granville,' said the other, face aglow, 'she'll surrender at last and throw herself into my arms.' As two carriages rolled away, he saw his coach being driven forward. 'I'm going to my club for a drink or two,' he went on. 'Why not join me for a nightcap?'

'It's a kind invitation,' said Harvester, 'but it's one I must decline. The truth is that I have a very important appointment. Good night, Sir Humphrey. I wish you and your aphrodisiac well . . .'

There was no need to wait this time. When he got to the designated place, the coach was already waiting. Abel Fearon ran the last dozen yards and opened the door to climb in. The man used his stick to bang on the roof of the vehicle and it set off.

'What are our orders, sir?' asked Fearon.

'The first thing you must do is to close your mouth and listen.'

'Yes, sir.'

'Your instructions are simple.'

He spoke slowly and distinctly, repeating certain details in order to stress their importance. Fearon took it all in, nodding obediently throughout. When he'd committed everything to memory, he asked a final question.

'So we have to kill this man in the King's Bench,' he said. 'Does that mean we forget all about Mrs Mandrake?'

'Oh, no – her turn will come next.'

CHAPTER SEVENTEEN

It was a pointless gesture. They soon came to accept that. When they rode through the darkness to Southwark and reined in their horses outside the prison, they found that they were in the middle of a gushing stream of beggars, prostitutes, homeless men and drunken revellers. Caught up in the mass of people, it was impossible to see their faces properly or to discern their purpose in being there. Nobody was let into the King's Bench and nobody emerged from it. The gate remained defiantly closed. An hour scudded by.

'We're wasting our time, Jem.'

'They may turn up,' said Huckvale.

'How will we recognise them in this crowd?'

'Think of that sketch we have of Fearon.'

'That's no help at all in the dark.'

'If they come, they'll try to gain entry. We simply watch the gate.'

'But they may already have been allowed inside.'

'Then why don't we ask to be let in ourselves?'

Ackford laughed. 'You've a good heart,' he said, 'but you have a lame brain at times. If we rouse the gatekeeper and tell him that we're worried about the safety of a friend, he's going to ask what Paul Skillen is doing in there when his name is not listed among the prisoners.'

'Ah, yes . . . perhaps that would be foolish.'

'He'll also wonder why Virgil Paige is no longer there. In other words, you'll be giving both him and Paul away.'

'It was a stupid idea,' conceded Huckvale.

'Let's go back to the gallery.'

'Can't we stay another hour?'

'No, we can't.'

'Can we come again at first light, then?'

'Is there any need to do so?'

'I think there is.'

'Well, I think you should have more faith in Paul. He does, after all, have the advantage of surprise,' Ackford pointed out. 'He's expecting an attack. If it comes, it will involve someone who has no idea that he's lying in wait for them.'

'But there could be two of them, Gully.'

'At a pinch, he could handle four or five.'

Huckvale agreed reluctantly to go back and they were soon picking their way through the traffic on the bridge. Arriving at the gallery, they stabled their horses and let themselves into the building.

'Time for bed,' suggested Ackford.

'I'll be too worried about Paul to sleep.'

'Fatigue will wipe away your worries, Jem. Close your eyes

and think about Meg Rooke. She'll give you sweet dreams.'

They were about to go to their respective rooms when they heard the sounds of gunfire above their heads. Dashing into the office, Ackford grabbed a pistol, loaded it and gave it to Huckvale. He then found a weapon for himself. Holding a lantern to guide the way, he crept upstairs with Huckvale right behind him. The gunfire was coming from the shooting gallery. When they got there, they could see light from inside the room spilling under the door.

Ackford grasped the handle and flung the door open, levelling his pistol at the same time. Huckvale come rushing into the room behind him. They stopped dead.

Virgil Paige stood there with a hand clasped to his heart.

'You frightened the life out of me,' he complained.

'What are you doing?' asked Huckvale.

'I'm trying to rub off a little of the rust, lad. It's a long time since I've borne arms. I never thought I'd have need of a weapon again but, obviously, I do. Since you both went out, I thought I'd get in some practice.'

'You needed it,' said Ackford, examining the target. 'Every shot hit the rim.'

'Leave it to Paul,' advised Huckvale. 'He can hit the bull's eye time and again with either hand. He always says that the first shot must be accurate because it may be the only one you get to fire.'

'That's horribly true.'

'My weapon of choice was a Brown Bess musket,' said Paige. 'I can't get the hang of this pistol.' He put the weapon resignedly on the table. 'I hate to admit it but my soldiering days are definitely behind me.'

'I thought that when I was discharged,' said Ackford with a wry smile, 'then I opened this gallery and have had a weapon in my hand every single day since then.' He looked at Paige's shirt, waistcoat and breeches. 'How do you feel in my clothes?'

'I feel hopelessly inadequate.'

'Why?'

'Instead of sneaking out of prison, I should have stayed to fight.'

'You *do* fight – but it's with a pen instead of a gun.'

'Because of me, Mr Skillen is in danger.'

'That's his natural habitat.'

'I'd never forgive myself if anything bad happens to him,' said Paige with an anguished expression. 'And neither will his brother.'

'Don't worry about Peter,' said Huckvale. 'He told me that you'd done the right thing. If those men do go to the prison, they'll be searching for someone who is roughly the same age as your brother. They won't give Paul a second look.'

Paul Skillen employed the same code as his predecessor. He'd wedged the chair against the door so that it couldn't be opened from outside. When he heard the distinctive knock that morning, he knew that Snapper was outside. Moving the chair, he let the boy into the room.

'Ya still 'ere, then,' observed Snapper.

'I'm still here and still alive.'

'Nobody came – I watched all night.'

'Thank you, Snapper.'

'Gor any breckf'st?'

'There's some bread in the cupboard and a few other things. Help yourself.'

The boy rushed over to the cupboard and plundered it. Sitting cross-legged on the mattress, he munched away happily. He looked more waif-like than ever.

'Won't your family miss you?'

'Nah – they'll be glad to get rid o' me, sir.'

'How many of you are there?'

'Too many,' said Snapper through a mouthful of bread.

'Will you ever get out?'

'One day, I 'opes. Mr Paige said 'e'd pay orff our debts bur my farver wood'n ler 'im. Dad says we pays our own debts.'

'Isn't that a case of looking a gift horse in the mouth?'

'Mr Paige never said 'e'd give us an 'orse.'

'It's an old saying, Snapper. It means that, if something good is offered to you, then you ought to take it.'

'Iss thar why Mr Paige ain't in 'ere no more?'

'Yes,' said Paul, laughing, 'you're quite right. I made him a tempting offer and he accepted it.'

'I misses 'im.'

'He'll be back one day.'

'When?'

'When I catch the people trying to kill him.'

The boy's eyes were whirlpools of dread. 'Wor if they kills ya first?'

'That will never happen,' said Paul. 'I've got this wonderful lookout.'

Snapper giggled so much that he began to choke.

* * *

The night had passed without incident at the print shop. Peter had made a couple of forays out into the darkness to check that the Runners had indeed dispersed and to see if there was any suspicious activity. Convinced that they were completely safe, he'd even managed an hour or two of sleep. Though her own slumbers had been curtailed by fear of attack, Diane was now in a cheerful frame of mind. Over breakfast with Peter and Tite, she became expansive.

'We've scared them off,' she decided. 'They've realised that they've met their match in me and crawled away with their tails between their legs. I usually see off my enemies in the end. It's true, isn't it, Ben?'

'Yes, Mrs Mandrake,' said Tite, dutifully.

'Nobody picks an argument with me twice.'

'I can appreciate why,' said Peter, tactfully.

'The glazier is coming this morning to put in the new window.'

Tite was vexed. 'Is that altogether wise, Mrs Mandrake?'

'We can't have a shop without a shop window, Ben.'

'But we have no stock to put in it.'

'We'll bring it back soon.'

'I feel safer with the boarding up,' he admitted. 'When we have another window, anybody will be able to look inside at us.'

'We can pull the curtain across.'

'What if someone gallops past and throws another stone?'

'They won't try the same trick twice, Mr Tite,' said Peter. 'Besides, that's too mild a warning now. Since they've already made one attempt on your lives, they won't draw back from making another.'

Tite blanched. 'Please, please stay with us, Mr Skillen. We need you.'

'We may do so at night,' agreed Diane, 'but I sense that we're out of danger during the day. In any case, Peter can't build his life around us. He has family commitments. He'll want to see his wife at some point.'

'If I don't go home,' said Peter, 'Charlotte will probably come here.'

'There's no reason why we should make her do that.'

'You could always stay at *our* house, Mrs Mandrake.'

'Someone has to stand over the glazier to make sure that he does the job properly. I have a gift for handling tradesmen. They know that I'll not accept shoddy workmanship.'

'I will slip away later this morning, then,' said Peter.

'There may be more news about your brother.'

'If that were the case, Jem would have already delivered it to me.'

'How close are you and Paul?'

'We work together so we spend a lot of time in each other's company. Where leisure is concerned, however, we live in different worlds. My wife and I enjoy things that Paul would consider far too tame and conventional.'

'I read somewhere that twins have a special means of communication.'

'Oh, no, we speak to each other in English, just like everyone else.'

'What I mean is that . . . well, you can sense things about each other when you're apart. Is there any truth in that?'

'Yes, there is,' replied Peter. 'Each of us seems to know if the

310

other one is in serious danger. That's what happened in my case anyway. I was too unwary on one occasion when I walked down an alleyway and I was felled by a cudgel. I had enough strength to get up and fight but there were two of them and I couldn't have held out indefinitely. All of a sudden, Paul came riding to my rescue,' he continued. 'He swung his horse round so that the animal's flank knocked one man flying then he leapt from the saddle to grapple with the other. I can't tell you how pleased I was to see him or how glad I was that I'd told him exactly where I was going.'

'How did he know that you were in trouble?'

'He told me that he sensed it somehow.'

'It sounds to me as if you're very much indebted to him, Peter,' said Diane, hand on his arm. 'That was taking brotherly love to an extreme. I hope that you get a chance to repay him for his timely intervention.'

Knowing that he was a stickler for punctuality, Yeomans and Hale were waiting for him at precisely the minute he arrived at court. Kirkwood dispensed with greetings.

'What's happened?' he demanded. 'Did they strike again last night?'

'No, sir,' replied Yeomans.

'They might have done,' said Hale. 'We weren't there.'

'Why not?' asked Kirkwood, looking accusingly from one to the other. 'I understood that you were going to maintain the patrol.'

'That was the intention,' said Yeomans.

'Yet you didn't actually go there.'

'We went there, Mr Kirkwood but . . . our services were not required.'

'What he means,' explained Hale, 'is that Mrs Mandrake sent us on our way.'

'But you were there to protect her.'

'So was Paul Skillen.'

'In point of fact,' corrected Yeomans, 'it was Peter Skillen.'

'There's nothing to choose between them, Micah.'

Kirkwood became angry. 'I hope you're not telling me that you ceded the duty of mounting a patrol to one of the Skillen brothers. In my codex, that would be viewed as a case of dereliction of duty.'

'Skillen did not patrol the street, sir.'

'Then what *did* the fellow do?'

'At Mrs Mandrake's invitation, he stayed the night inside the shop.'

'But you saved the woman's life and her property. Didn't she think that you were worthy of thanks?'

'They both were,' said Hale. 'Mr Yeomans and Ruddock were heroes.'

'Who's Ruddock?'

'He's the member of the foot patrol who first saw the place was on fire.'

'Why wasn't I told about this?'

'I did mention his name to you,' claimed Yeomans, shooting a poisonous glance at Hale. 'He's a promising young man.'

'Then he should have been brought to my attention.'

'I thought he had been, sir.'

'I'd remember a name like Ruddock,' said the chief

magistrate, pointedly. 'Have you returned to the print shop this morning?'

'No, sir, I wanted to report to you first.'

'But you have nothing worth reporting. There was I last evening, telling Brunt that you were making steady progress and it's not true. The next time I see him at my club, I'll have to admit to Brunt that you are struggling.'

'Is that Mr Gerard Brunt, the Member of Parliament?'

'Yes, it is, Yeomans. For some reason he's taken an inordinate interest in this case. It will be embarrassing to inform him that you failed miserably.'

'That's unfair, sir.'

'We did our best,' argued Hale. 'Chevy Ruddock patrolled the street itself while the rest of us stayed within easy reach. When Mr Yeomans went to speak to Ruddock, out came Peter Skillen with a message from Mrs Mandrake that they were to stand down for the night.'

Kirkwood was almost apoplectic. 'Since when has the owner of a print shop been in control of the deployment of the Bow Street Runners?'

'The lady seems to have some animosity towards us.'

'Be quiet,' whispered Yeomans.

'Let's be honest about it. She has no respect for who we are and what we do. Mrs Mandrake was grateful that Mr Yeomans and Ruddock fought the blaze but she remained unfriendly towards them. To be frank, Micah,' he went on, turning to his companion, 'I don't think she liked the look of you after your eyebrows got singed.'

'This is preposterous,' howled Kirkwood. 'For all we know,

the woman could be lying in a pool of blood because you were not there to keep the killers at bay last night. Why did you let her send you packing? Does Mrs Mandrake own the whole street? How did she acquire a legal right to control access to and from Holborn?'

'She has no such right, sir,' said Yeomans.

'Then why did you bow to her wishes?'

'Mrs Mandrake is a rather forthright lady, sir.'

'Then she needed to be put firmly in her place.'

'That's a rather problematical task, Mr Kirkwood.'

'Nevertheless, it should not have been shirked. The simple fact is that you allowed one of the Skillen brothers to take priority over you. That's unacceptable. Get back to that shop, Yeomans, and assert your authority.'

'Yes, sir.'

'I will not have you treated as shabbily as this.'

'No, sir.'

'Find out what actually happened there last night,' concluded Kirkwood, 'and, above all else, evict Skillen from that print shop. Mrs Mandrake is all *yours*.'

Fired by the prospect, Yeomans emitted a maniacal laugh.

They were both allowed into the coach this time. Higlett was struck by its plush interior and by its relative comfort. He was also struck by the peremptory manner of their paymaster. He repeated the orders he'd earlier given to Fearon.

'I'll brook no mistakes this time,' he said, menacingly.

'There won't be any, sir,' said Fearon.

'Are you both armed?'

'We both have daggers and I have my special weapon.' Fearon pulled a coil of rope from inside his coat. 'This is what I used to garrotte Paige. It will serve to strangle the life out of his brother as well.'

'If it doesn't,' said Higlett, sniggering, 'I'll stab him through the heart.'

'It must be done as quickly and quietly as possible.'

'If he has a room of his own, it will be easy.'

'Fearon told me that burning down the shop would be easy,' said the other, rancorously. 'That proved to be a hollow boast. If you fail again, you know what to expect. I'll have the pair of you skinned like rabbits.' Fearon and Higlett quailed. The man produced a letter from his pocket. 'This is a pass to get you into the King's Bench. All you have to do is to find him and murder him.'

'Where will you be, sir?' asked Fearon.

'I'll be waiting outside the prison. When you come out, raise a hand to show me that Virgo is dead.'

'He will be – dead as a doornail.'

'That's all I ask.'

Higlett smirked. 'What about our reward?'

'You get that when you kill Mrs Mandrake as well.'

The glazier and his apprentice arrived on site early. Having taken down the boarding, they assessed the damage. The large stone hurled with force through the window had broken many of the glazing bars and shattered most of the small windows. Repair would be lengthy and laborious. Diane Mandrake stood over them, issuing commands and urging them to be as quick as possible. Her attention was then diverted by the sight of two men walking towards the shop. In any other part of the capital, Micah Yeomans and Alfred Hale sauntered down a street as if they owned it. Their gait was more tentative now. It was almost as if they were trespassing.

'Good morning, Mrs Mandrake,' said Yeomans, lifting his hat.

She was inhospitable. 'What are you doing here?'

'We've brought a message from the chief magistrate.'

'Then deliver it and be on your way.'

'We represent law and order in the city,' said Hale. 'Mr Kirkwood wanted us to impress that upon you.'

'In other words,' added Yeomans, 'you have no right to clear us away from your property. If we believe that a crime is imminent, we're entitled to go wherever we wish. This is not meant as a criticism of you,' he went on, trying to pacify her with a gruesome smile. 'We admire your courage in the face of a possible threat, but we insist on being able to patrol this area without interference.'

'Is that all?' she demanded.

'Yes, Mrs Mandrake.'

'Then here's my reply to the chief magistrate. When London is awash with crime, why does he permit the Bow Street Runners to spread themselves so thinly? The men on duty here last night would have been better used in districts of the city that are crawling with burglars and infested with harlots. I already had someone protecting me,' she said, 'and his presence was far more reassuring than that of you and your cohorts.'

Yeomans cringed. Wanting to be more forceful, he was held back by his adoration of the woman. When, as now, she was roused, there was a tension in her body and a fire in her eye that made her even more attractive to him. He wanted to reach out and embrace her but the only way he might be allowed that privilege was to catch those who'd tried to burn her alive. Glancing at the house, he was shaken afresh by the realisation that Peter Skillen had actually spent the night there. The pangs of envy made him gasp for a moment.

'I need to speak to Mr Skillen,' he said, recovering his composure.

'I will pass on any message to him, Mr Yeomans.'

'We need to see him in person,' said Hale, speaking with more authority than Yeomans was prepared to do. 'Mr Skillen and his brother have a nasty habit of ignoring any messages passed on to them. We must confront him face to face.'

'Then you will need to find him.'

'Is he not still here?'

'Mr Skillen left a while ago.'

'Where has he gone?' asked Yeomans.

'He's gone to do what you and your men should be doing,' she said, sharply. 'Mr Skillen is hunting the killers.'

Paul Skillen had a definite advantage in daylight. The window of his room looked down on the main courtyard. Since he commanded a good view of the gate, he'd stationed Snapper there as his lookout. The boy was gregarious and very popular among the other denizens. During the years he'd been in the King's Bench, he'd got to know all of the turnkeys. When he lingered near the gate, therefore, he was able to chat idly to his friend, the keeper, while taking note of everyone who entered the prison. The two men who now presented a letter to the gatekeeper awakened his suspicion at once. One of them – a stocky individual with a square jaw and eyes unusually far apart – appeared to fit the brief description that Paul had given the boy. When he overheard the man asking where Virgil Paige could be found, Snapper walked swiftly away and gave his signal. Paul had been warned.

Fearon and Higlett followed the directions they'd been given. Higlett was uneasy.

'I hate being behind prison walls again,' he muttered.

'There's a difference this time, Sim. We can just walk out.'

'What if he's not here?'

'He's bound to be here. Paige is not allowed to leave.'

'Who is that man in the coach, Abel?'

'He's the person who's going to make us rich.'

'How does he have the power to decide who goes in and out of prison?'

'Just be grateful that we were the ones who got released.'

'I don't trust him,' said Higlett. 'He looks down his nose at us.'

'Who cares? He filled our purses last time. There'll be even more money when we get rid of Paige and that woman.' They'd reached a door and halted. 'His room is on the third floor. Let's go up.'

'Have you got the rope ready?'

'Yes – keep a hand on your dagger.'

Paul heard them coming up the stairs. He stood outside his room, lounging against a wall with graffiti scratched into the brickwork. Concealed under his coat was a dagger but he hoped that it would not be needed because he was set on taking them alive. He'd arranged a distraction for his visitors. Everything he could lay his hands on had been piled on to the mattress and covered with a blanket so that it looked as if someone was still there. The footsteps were heavy and urgent. Two figures eventually came into view. The first was unmistakably Abel Fearon. He halted when he saw Paul.

'We're looking for Virgil Paige,' he said.

Paul used his thumb to indicate. 'He's in there, fast asleep.'

'Disappear.'

'Why?'

Fearon glared at him. 'Do as I say.'

'I'm going, I'm going,' said Paul, retreating.

But he only went down the first flight of stairs. When he heard the door of the room open, he ran swiftly back up the steps on his toes. The two assassins, meanwhile, were grinning as they stood over the body of what they thought was their intended victim. Rope at the ready, Fearon flung back the blanket and bent forward. 'There's nobody here!' he yelled.

'We've been tricked.'

As Higlett turned to face him, Paul snatched up the chair and brought it crashing down on his head, opening up a gash and making him reel. After hitting him again with the chair, Paul tossed it away then kicked him hard in the stomach. Higlett collapsed to the floor in agony.

Fearon was agog. 'Who, in hell's name, are *you*?'

By way of an answer, Paul leapt on him and got in a relay of telling punches before Fearon could retaliate. They grappled fiercely in what soon became a trial of strength, moving to and fro and trying to squeeze the resistance out of each other. Though Paul had to endure being spat in the face, he managed to avoid being bitten or headbutted. Fearon was a veteran of many pub brawls but he'd never met anyone as powerful and slippery before. He was slowly losing the fight.

'Get up, Sim!' he yelled. 'I need help.'

'He split my head open,' moaned Higlett.

The next moment, Paul got a firm grip on Fearon, caught him off balance and threw him on top of his friend. As he tried to get up, Higlett was knocked to the floor again. Fearon was enraged. Hauling himself up, he pulled out his dagger and lunged at Paul who evaded the weapon with ease, grabbed Fearon's wrist and swung him so hard against the wall that the dagger was knocked from his grasp. Paul retrieved it quickly and threatened Fearon with it. Higlett, however, recovered enough to join in the fight. He seized Paul's ankle and tried to drag him down to the floor. After kicking him viciously away, Paul used the handle of the dagger as a club, smashing it down on his blood-covered head until Higlett lapsed into unconsciousness.

Fearon lost his nerve. Making a dash for the door, he pushed Paul aside and ran out, descending the steps in a series of panic-stricken leaps. Determined to catch him, Paul went off in pursuit but the chase was short-lived. As soon as Fearon opened the door at the bottom of the staircase, he found his way blocked by a man holding a rapier. When he saw the face smiling at him, he reacted as if he'd seen a ghost.

'I just left you upstairs.'

'You must be mistaken,' said Peter Skillen. His brother came charging into view. 'This fellow had the temerity to accuse me of being *you*, Paul.' He let the point of the rapier draw blood from his captive's neck. Fearon gave a yelp, 'But there's no mistaking who *you* are, is there? Dear God, you're even uglier than I thought.'

'Where on earth did you spring from?' asked Paul.

'I sensed that you might need some help.'

'The other one is flat out upstairs. I'd have caught Fearon as well.'

'I saved you the trouble, Paul, and I didn't miss out on the action. Thanks to you, he came running straight into my arms.' He grinned at Fearon. 'I'm sorry if I hurt your neck, Mr Fearon. Don't worry – the blood will have dried by the time the hangman puts a noose around it.'

He waited in the coach with increasing dread. Something had evidently gone wrong. A task which should have taken no more than a few minutes had stretched out to well over half an hour. They were not coming back. It was futile to wait for a signal that they'd never deliver. Somehow, he realised, Fearon and Higlett had been caught. That put his life in jeopardy. Grabbing his cane, he used it to bang furiously on the roof of the coach. It was imperative to get away as fast as possible.

'Then what happened?' asked Charlotte.

'We took them before a magistrate,' said Paul, 'and they're now in custody.'

'So the danger is over?'

'Fearon and Higlett pose no threat whatsoever now.'

'That's cheering news,' said Paige, pumping his hand in congratulations. 'Well done, Paul! You and Peter have taken a huge load off my mind.'

'We all feel a sense of profound relief,' said Charlotte.

Ackford was puzzled. 'What I can't understand is how Peter *knew* that you were in need of some help.'

'It's just something that happens,' said Paul. 'We're brothers.'

'Leo was my brother,' Paige put in, 'but I didn't realise the peril *he* was in.'

'It's different with twins.'

They were in the office at the gallery, listening to an account of the arrests made at the King's Bench. The mood was joyous. A shadow then fell on Paige's delight. He suddenly looked hunted.

'What sort of punishment will I get?' he asked.

'You shouldn't get any at all,' said Paul.

'But I broke the rules by absconding from prison. When that sort of thing happens, the marshal can be very strict.'

'Don't have any qualms about him.'

'Why not?'

'Peter will sort everything out. He's gone to see the Home Secretary. If you wish to be pedantic,' said Paul with a chuckle, 'then *I'm* the real offender. I aided and abetted your escape, I was a counterfeit prisoner and I instigated a violent brawl. Oh, and you can add on a charge of suborning a child to act as an accessory, because that's what Snapper was. In all fairness, I should be locked up with you.'

'Oh, it's wonderful to be able to breathe freely again,' said Charlotte. 'That nagging fear has finally gone away.'

'Not necessarily,' her brother-in-law argued. 'There's still someone else to apprehend and that's the man who employed those two killers.'

'Who is he?' asked Paige.

'We don't know.'

'Fearon and Higlett must know, surely,' said Ackford. 'Didn't you interrogate them?'

'We did everything but stretch them on the rack, Gully, but they haven't a clue as to his identity. He took immense care to conceal it from them.'

'You can't let him get away.'

'He won't, I promise you. Peter will see to that.'

'I think we already know his name,' said Charlotte, confidently. 'It's Gerard Brunt. He's the suspect that Peter picked out, anyway.'

'My mind is turning towards Julian Harvester,' said Paul, thoughtfully. 'Our prisoners told us that he had a sumptuous coach and seemed to be made of money. That description fits Harvester like a glove.'

'I don't care who he is as long as he's caught.'

'That might be tricky, Charlotte,' said Ackford. 'In his position, I'd make myself scarce. His plots to kill Mrs Mandrake and Mr Paige have both failed, and his hired assassins are in chains. Peter and Paul will soon be on his tail. That will put the fear of God into him. He'll make a run for it.'

'We'll catch him wherever he goes,' promised Paul. 'Meanwhile, we can spread the good news about the arrests.'

'Jem is already on his way to Holborn to do so.'

'I wish I could be there when Mrs Mandrake hears it.'

* * *

Even though the horse jiggled him around, Huckvale didn't mind. He was happy to endure the headache he was given in the interest of being the bringer of glad tidings. When he got to the print shop, the glaziers were hard at work with Diane Mandrake standing over them with Benjamin Tite at her side. Seeing the horse cantering towards them, Tite was terrified that another missile was going to be thrown at the window and he hid behind the ample frame of his employer.

'Don't be silly, Ben,' she chided. 'It's Jem Huckvale from the gallery.'

'Oh,' said Tite, overwhelmed with relief. 'Thank God!'

Huckvale reined in his mount and leapt to the ground.

'They've done it!' he announced.

'Who has done what?' asked Diane.

'Peter and Paul have caught those two men. They're in custody.'

'That's marvellous,' she cried, embracing him so tightly that his face almost disappeared between her breasts. She stood him away from her. 'Tell me all, Jem. Are we truly free of any danger?'

'Yes, Mrs Mandrake.'

'I can't believe it,' said Tite, eyes streaming with tears. 'It's over at last. We can open the shop again.'

'We'll need to reclaim our stock first,' Diane reminded him. 'But let's hear the details from Jem. When and how did it happen?'

Huckvale was very proud to be chosen as the messenger. Still nervous in Diane's presence, he nevertheless gave a report that was articulate and laced with moderate excitement. He freely embellished the details of the actual arrest, knowing the kind of skill and bravado that Peter and Paul always showed in a fight. At the end of his recitation, he was given a kiss on both cheeks by Diane and a pat on the back by Tite. In effect, he'd just torn up their respective death warrants.

'Oh,' cried Diane, 'if only *he* were with us to hear this news.'

'Who do you mean?' asked Huckvale.

'I mean that detestable man with the singed eyebrows.'

'Credit where it's due,' said Tite. 'Mr Yeomans did manage to put out the fire and save the shop. I could never detest a man for doing that.'

'Nor should I,' she said, apologetically. 'It's just that he's going to go bright green with jealousy when he realises that Peter and Paul have done his job for him better than he himself could. What will the chief magistrate say to that?'

They had never seen Eldon Kirkwood in such a state of quivering fury before. As the Runners stood abjectly before him in his office, the chief magistrate subjected them to withering scorn. Yeomans and Hale hardly heard a word of his vituperation. They were trying to take in the news that Peter and Paul Skillen had arrested the two men responsible for the murder of Leonidas Paige and for attempted arson at the print shop. When he finally reached the end of his harangue, Kirkwood eyed them darkly.

'Well,' he said, 'what have you to say for yourselves?'

'We're very sorry, sir,' ventured Hale.

'Is that all?'

'The Skillen brothers always have good luck.'

'Solving a murder is not a matter of luck, Hale. It requires hard work and an insight into the criminal mentality. Bravery, too, is involved. Paul Skillen, I'm led to believe, took on two armed men.'

'Where was this, sir?'

'I don't know all the details. What I do know is that those brothers stand to collect a large reward while you are mired in failure once again.'

'That's unjust,' said Yeomans. 'Don't forget about the fire.'

'I haven't done so,' returned Kirkwood. 'Only this morning, I wrote a letter of thanks to Ruddock for raising the alarm that night. Had he not done so in time, the print shop would have been razed to the ground.'

'I played *my* part, sir.'

'That's true, Yeomans, and it deserves commendation. But the good work you did in fighting that fire has been eclipsed by the pusillanimous way in which you let Mrs Mandrake expel you from Holborn like so many naughty children, and by the fact that you let someone else catch the villains in your place.'

'We didn't "let" them, sir.'

'Then how do you explain their success?'

'They use different methods to us.'

'Yes,' said Hale, 'and they don't share the evidence they find. If they'd told us what they'd found out, *we* could have put those men behind bars.'

'I beg leave to doubt that,' said Kirkwood, curling his lip. 'The only person who's emerged from this farce unsullied is Ruddock. You have both blotted your escutcheons badly. It's high time you redeemed yourselves.'

Yeomans winced at the praise bestowed on Ruddock. He

was desperate to repair his damaged reputation without quite knowing how. Hale provided the answer.

'I've been wondering, sir,' he said, tapping the side of his nose. 'There's somebody else, isn't there? Why should those two men kill someone who helped to make caricatures, then try to burn down the shop that sold them? It doesn't make any sense. They were suborned by someone else.'

'Now you're beginning to think like a Runner.'

'Yes,' said Yeomans, pouncing on the idea as if it had just emerged full-grown from his brain, 'they must have been controlled by someone who took offence at the cartoons sold by Mrs Mandrake. The Skillen brothers may have caught two people but it's a third one who instigated the crimes.'

'Find him,' said Kirkwood. 'That's the way for you to redeem yourselves. Find this man quickly and earn back my respect.'

Having ordered his valet to pack his trunk, he had it carried downstairs. As it was loaded on to the coach, he announced that he had no idea when he'd return to the house. A minute later, he was being driven away.

CHAPTER EIGHTEEN

Peter Skillen had always been saddened by the wide disparity
between inmates in the city's debtors' prisons. The majority of
those incarcerated were doomed to lives of misery, packed into
filthy, stinking cells that were breeding grounds for disease
and forced to rub shoulders with seasoned criminals. Peter
had heard of cases where prisoners had parted with clothing
and shoes in exchange for sustenance. In stark contrast,
there were those in the King's Bench with money enough to
purchase healthier and more comfortable accommodation.
They dressed well, moved freely around the place, ate heartily
and might even bring a cook into the prison to prepare their
food. Virgil Paige had occupied a position between the two
extremes, able to pay for a limited number of privileges but
still having to provide his own bedding and endure the many
shortcomings of the prison community. By inclination, he
sided with the real paupers, like Snapper and his family, who
suffered severe deprivation.

Having been inside the King's Bench during the arrest of the two men, Peter had seen the yawning gap between poverty and plenty with his own eyes. He'd been amazed by the number of elegant bucks promenading in the courtyard while ragged children hunted for scraps of food or huddled in corners. It was something he took up with Geoffrey Lanning, the marshal.

'Do you have no pity for the scarecrows in your keep, sir?' he asked.

'I am merely enforcing the law.'

'Yet you do so from *outside* the prison.'

'I have a care for the air I breathe, Mr Skillen. Some of the scarecrows you refer to are no more than disease-ridden, lice-ridden wretches.'

'Can you not cure their diseases and get rid of their lice?'

'Had I the money to do so,' said Lanning, impassively, 'I could hire a team of doctors for that purpose. Since you show such an interest in their welfare, sir, perhaps you'd like to make a donation to that end.'

Peter said nothing because he believed that any money he donated would get no further than the marshal. He was sitting in the commodious office in the well-appointed apartments occupied by the man, a thin, sleek individual in his fifties with a powdered wig and immaculate attire. The marshal's face was carved from granite.

'State your business, sir,' said Lanning. 'I am a busy man.'

'I am here with regard to Mr Virgil Paige,' said Peter. 'Two men were hired to kill him and were admitted to this prison by means of a letter signed by you.'

329

The marshal flicked the charge contemptuously away. 'I deny the allegation.'

'Somebody obtained that document from you, Mr Lanning.'

'I have no memory whatsoever of that.'

'You deny obliging a gentleman who called on you here yesterday?'

'My job is to run this prison efficiently,' said the other, coldly. 'It is not to oblige anyone by writing a letter on his or her behalf.'

'Then perhaps you can explain this,' challenged Peter, extracting the missive from his pocket and handing it over. 'Your gatekeeper was kind enough to give it to me. That *is* your signature, is it not? Or is it a clever forgery?'

The marshal glanced at the paper then put it hastily aside. While his features remained immobile, his eyes smouldered with anger.

'Why have you come here, Mr Skillen?'

'I want the name of the man who called on you to have Mr Paige's freedom rudely curtailed. Or is your memory unequal to *that* task as well?'

'Sarcasm ill becomes you.'

'What is your answer?'

Lanning rose to his feet. 'My answer is that I'd like you to leave immediately. You have no right to be here and no warrant to make distasteful insinuations. Good day to you, Mr Skillen.'

'Before I leave,' said Peter, remaining in his seat, 'I have another letter to show you. This one comes from Viscount Sidmouth. Rightly anticipating a lack of cooperation from you, I took the precaution of visiting him before I came here. When I explained the situation to him, he was kind enough to offer his assistance.' He took a second letter from his pocket and passed it to Lanning. 'That signature, I can assure you, is *not* a forgery.'

The marshal unfolded the letter and read its contents. To his dismay, it was highly complimentary about his visitor. He looked up.

'How did you come to have the ear of the Home Secretary?'

'I had the privilege of rendering him service during and after the war, sir.'

'He considers you to be a hero.'

Peter smiled modestly. 'I make no such claim,' he said. His voice hardened. 'I simply wish to know the name of the man who asked a favour of you.'

'That's out of the question.'

'Why?'

Lanning shook his head. 'I couldn't possibly break a confidence.'

'You'd be helping in a murder investigation.'

'That makes no difference, Mr Skillen. A promise is a promise.'

'Not when it's made to a man who ordered an assassination.'

'I gave him my word.'

'And what did he give *you* in return?'

'How dare you!' yelled the other, stamping his foot.

'He's a rich man. He could well afford a hefty bribe.'

Lanning was about to explode when his eye fell on the Home Secretary's letter. It enjoined to him to give whatever information Peter Skillen requested. Mastering his fury, he adopted a dignified pose.

'I accept bribes from nobody, sir.'

'Then what emolument *did* you receive?'

'I received overwhelming evidence that one of the prisoners in my charge had repeatedly flouted his freedom. I would be slack in my discipline if I'd allowed that to continue. That's why the fellow was denied the right to leave the premises.'

'And who provided this so-called evidence?' asked Peter. There was a long pause. He brought his ultimate sanction into play. 'Would you rather tell me or wait until the Home Secretary drags the name out of you by threat of dismissal?'

Head lowered, the marshal sank back into his seat with an air of defeat. He could see that his visitor would not be thwarted. Yet if he surrendered the name, he might have to face retribution from the man who'd demanded that Virgil Paige be penned without explanation inside the prison. Lanning did not see the sizeable amount of money that he'd been given as a bribe at all. In his view, it was simply a payment for services rendered, so his conscience was untroubled.

'Since you can't remember the name,' said Peter, tired of waiting, 'then let me supply it for you. I put it to you that your visitor was Mr Gerard Brunt.'

Lanning was surprised. 'Mr Brunt – the Member of Parliament?'

'Am I right?'

'Most certainly not.'

'Then who was it?'

'His name was Dr Penhallurick.'

After his brawl with the two men in the prison, Paul Skillen had collected a number of scratches and bruises. Yet he felt no pain whatsoever. The successful arrest of Fearon and Higlett was a soothing balm to his wounds. Charlotte couldn't believe that he was not aching and smarting all over.

'You have a nasty graze over your eye,' she said with sympathy.

'It will heal.'

'Would you like me to bathe that lump on your temple?'

'No, thank you. It will go down of its own accord.'

'You should have waited until Peter came to help.'

'Fearon and Higlett denied me that option,' said Paul, smiling, 'and I was happy to take on the two of them. I've not had such a bracing fight for some while. I'm just glad that I was wearing Mr Paige's clothes at the time and not my own. They have a lot of bloodstains on them.'

'Mr Paige didn't mind in the least,' said Charlotte. 'He's so relieved by what you and Peter achieved today. As for *your* apparel, he didn't enjoy wearing it at all.'

'It served its purpose.'

'He thought it looked a trifle garish.'

'It's the height of fashion,' insisted Paul with a hint of vanity. 'I couldn't wait to put it back on again.'

They were alone in the office at the gallery. After the excitement of capturing the two men, Paul was able to relax and let his mind wander away from the murder investigation.

Charlotte saw the dreamy look in his eyes and the sad smile on his lips.

'You're thinking about Hannah, aren't you?'

He nodded. 'How did you guess?'

'I know you too well.'

'You're right as usual. Now that I'm no longer so preoccupied, I'm going through the wording of her last letter.'

'I still think you're mistaken about that, Paul.'

'Well, I don't. Something is definitely amiss.'

'Yes – she's parted from the man she loves. That's what's amiss. It can be very painful. I suffered agonies every time Peter went to France during the war. I was never sure if he'd come back alive. Bear in mind that you don't have that problem to contend with. Hannah is well and her commitments in Paris finish before long.'

'There's something else, Charlotte, something undisclosed.'

'Then why didn't she tell you about it?'

'I don't know. It's just . . . very unsettling.'

'She's due back in England by the end of the month.'

'I'm not sure that I can wait that long.'

'But there is still unfinished business here,' she said. 'Those two men may be in custody but their paymaster is still at liberty.'

'True.'

'He must be brought to justice.'

'Peter can do that perfectly well without me.'

'What if he needs help?'

'Gully or Jem can provide it.'

'They have too much work to do here, Paul. Don't desert your brother.'

'I'll explain the situation to him. Peter will understand.'

'Don't bank on that.'

'Hannah *needs* me,' he stressed. 'I must go to Paris.'

Tracking down Penhallurick took some time. Peter had to be patient. Having discovered the doctor's address, he went to the house at once, only to be told that its owner was visiting a patient before going on to his consulting rooms in Piccadilly. Since there was no sign of him at the latter venue, Peter waited near the door so that he could intercept him on arrival. When a carriage eventually rolled to a halt nearby, he watched a man alight and decided that he had to be Guy Penallurick because he looked so much like the figure in the various cartoons.

Stepping forward, Peter stood in the man's path and tipped his hat.

'Good day to you, Dr Penhallurick.'

'Good day to you, sir,' replied the other.

'I'd value a word with you.'

'That's not possible, I fear, because I have a patient waiting for me.'

'Allow me to correct you,' said Peter, smoothly. 'My information is that your patient is not due until this afternoon. By that time, you may not be in a position to see him unless he wishes to join you at the magistrate's court.'

Penhallurick started. 'What the devil do you mean, sir?'

Peter indicated the door. 'You might care to have this discussion inside rather than out here in the street.'

'Well, I don't – say what you have to say and be off.'

'My name is Peter Skillen and I am searching for the person who hired men to kill Leonidas Paige.'

'Don't ask me to mourn for Paige,' said Penhallurick, bitterly. 'The man did untold damage to the reputations of blameless individuals.'

'Would you include yourself in that category?'

'Indeed, I would.'

'Conniving at murder is therefore a blameless activity, is it?'

'I don't have to listen to this nonsense,' said Penhallurick, trying to walk past but Peter obstructed him. 'Get out of my way, man.'

'Mr Lanning has named you, sir.'

'Who on earth is Mr Lanning?'

'He's the marshal of the King's Bench Prison and you procured a favour from him yesterday.'

'I did nothing of the kind, Mr Skillen.'

'I have his word.'

'Then you've been cruelly misled,' said Penhallurick with mounting irritation. 'I've never heard of a Mr Lanning and I certainly didn't ask a favour of him. What exactly is going on?'

As Peter explained, the other man's irritation became, by turns, curiosity, surprise, bafflement, realisation, then something bordering on frenzy. Eyes flashing, his arms gesticulated wildly.

'I see what has happened here,' he said, vengefully. 'Someone has used my name in order to conceal his own. You told me that you were aware that I had the loan of a coach from a friend of mine. That much is true, Mr Skillen, though how you came by the intelligence is a mystery to me. I had arranged to take someone for a drive in the country and decided that my open carriage was unsuitable. A coach provides some insurance against inclement weather and guarantees privacy. Need I go on, sir?'

Peter shook his head and sighed with disappointment. Guy Penhallurick was not his man, after all. Patently, he'd borrowed the coach to further a dalliance with a lady who'd either be more impressed by a coach than a carriage or who preferred to remain unseen with her beau. Peter apologised for the mistake.

'For my part,' said Penhallurick, 'I'm grateful that you brought this deception to my attention. I will take it up with the man who dared to steal my name.'

'I have an idea who that might be.'

'I can tell you for certain. It was unquestionably Sir Humphrey Coote.'

When the coach came to a halt at the inn, someone opened the door for him.

'Would you care to step inside while the horses are changed, sir?'

'I'll stay here.'

'Shall I bring some refreshment out to you?'

'No,' said Sir Humphrey, impatiently, 'I simply want to be on my way as soon as possible. How far is it to Dover?'

Even though he had good news to impart, Jem Huckvale had not been looking forward to the meeting with Diane

Mandrake. As a rule he was not fearful, but somehow she frightened him at a deep level. In the event, she was extremely pleasant to him and the visit yielded an unexpected bonus. Deciding that the glaziers no longer needed her, she announced that she would reclaim her stock from Peter's house and asked Huckvale if he would ride ahead and warn the household. He was back in the saddle at once. The chance of a few moments with Meg Rooke was too enticing to miss. He set off at a good pace.

When he reached the house, it was Meg who answered the door.

'Oh, Mr Huckvale!' she cried. 'What a lovely surprise!'

'There's no need to be so formal. You know my name.'

'Yes, I do, Jem. And you know mine.'

'I know it very well.' They shared a laugh.

'Why are you here? Not that you need a reason,' she went on, quickly. 'You're always welcome. That's to say, it's always a pleasure to see you.'

'I'm here on an errand,' he explained. 'First, however, you must know that Mr Skillen and his brother have arrested the killers and they are now in custody.'

'That's wonderful news.'

'As danger has now passed, Mrs Mandrake is going to collect all the stock that was left here in case there was another fire at the print shop. I thought that you should be warned she's on her way.'

'That's very kind of you!'

'I can lend a hand loading it.'

'We can do it together.'

They grinned at each other until they heard the sound of a horse and curricle approaching at speed. Diane had come to collect her possessions. They didn't mind the interruption in the least. The bond had already been formed.

Sir Humphrey Coote's town house was in a tree-lined avenue in Mayfair. It was large without verging on the palatial and had a pleasing symmetry. Marble statuary stood either side on the portico. Since the nude females from antiquity were life-size, they were appropriate companions for the owner. Having tethered his horse, Peter rang the bell and waited for the front door to be opened by the butler.

'May I help you, sir?' asked the man, appraising him.

'I'd like to speak with Sir Humphrey, please.'

'The master is not at home.'

'Can you tell me when he's likely to return?'

'I'm afraid that I can't, sir. However, if you'd like to leave a message, I'll make sure that he gets it.'

'I need to see him in person,' said Peter, forcefully.

'That won't be possible for some time.'

'Why is that?'

'Sir Humphrey has gone away for an indefinite period.'

'Has he returned to his home in the country?' The butler shook his head. 'Then where *has* he gone?'

'I'm not at liberty to tell you, sir.'

Tall, stout and aloof, the butler tried to close the door in his face. Peter was quick to put a foot in the way. He gave the man a challenging stare.

'A choice confronts you,' he said, icily. 'I am involved in a murder enquiry that has the approval of the Home Secretary, so you can understand its importance. You can either tell me where your master is or, when you've been arrested – by force, if necessary – we can continue this discussion in front of a magistrate.' He spread his arms interrogatively. 'Which is it to be?'

Alfred Hale let him quaff half a pint of ale before daring to speak. They were at the Peacock Inn and Micah Yeomans was still trying to absorb the shock of being told that the Skillen brothers had made two significant arrests.

'The worst of it is,' he complained, 'that Ruddock will get a letter of thanks from Kirkwood simply because he smelt smoke.'

'He did so before anyone else,' Hale reminded him.

'I'd have raised the alarm myself seconds later.'

'A delay of a few seconds could have been fatal, Micah.'

'*I* put that fire out yet Ruddock gets the credit.'

'That's not quite true. Mr Kirkwood congratulated you on the bravery and competence you showed. He just happened to think that Chevy Ruddock deserved some sort of acknowledgement.'

'Why did you have to mention his blessed name to Kirkwood?'

'You obviously forgot to do so, that's why.'

'I didn't forget. He wasn't really worthy of a mention.'

'I disagree – and so did Mr Kirkwood. However,' said Hale, moving on swiftly, 'that's irrelevant now. The fact is that the Skillen brothers caught the villains before we even had the slightest idea who they were. They won the first round but the contest is not yet over. If we win the second round, the real victory is ours.'

'Well remembered, Alfred,' said Yeomans, sitting upright. 'The killers merely obeyed orders. Who *gave* them?'

'It was someone who wanted Paige dead.'

'Why?'

'Because he'd either made fun of them in that newspaper of his or in that series called the *Parliament of Foibles*. You saw those prints in Mrs Mandrake's window.'

'I did,' murmured the other.

'Some of them were spiteful and malicious. Look at the one in which *you* appeared.'

Yeomans tensed. 'That was not me, I tell you.'

'No, no, you're right,' said Hale with a smile of appeasement. 'There's no resemblance, especially since you had your eyebrows singed. It's uncanny. You look like a new man, Micah.'

'Forget me and concentrate. Who were Paige's main targets?'

Hale ran a hand across his chin. 'Let me think . . .'

'Mr Harvester popped up in quite a few of those prints. Everyone knows that he uses his money to influence decisions in Parliament. He has to be a suspect. And so does Gerard Brunt. He's always sniffing around for favours from Cabinet members. Brunt and Harvester would be my choices.'

'What do we do?'

'We go and interview them right away.'

'Supposing that neither of them is involved?'

'Then we work our way through other likely names,' said Yeomans, stirred into action and ignoring the rest of his ale. 'We've got no time to sit in here, Alfred. The most important

person in this whole affair has yet to be identified and arrested.'
He led the way to the door. 'We have to get to him before those
infernal twins do.'

Gully Ackford found a moment between his appointments at
the gallery to have a chat with Paul Skillen. He was astounded
by the latter's decision.

'Paris!' he exclaimed.

'That's right.'

'Why ever do you want to go to Paris?'

'Someone very dear to me is there, Gully.'

'But the investigation is not over yet.'

'It is for me,' said Paul.

'Don't you want to be here when the man behind the murder
is unmasked?'

'I'd love to be but I'm needed in France.'

'What's happened?'

'Nothing has actually happened,' confessed the other, 'I just
have this feeling that I've been sent for. I can't refuse to go.'

'Did Miss Granville actually beseech you?'

'Well, no . . .'

'Is she in some sort of jeopardy?'

'Not that I'm aware of . . .'

'Then why are you leaving us in the lurch and going to Paris?'

'I've told you,' said Paul. 'I have this feeling.'

'I don't know Miss Granville very well,' said Ackford, levelly,
'but she strikes me as the kind of lady who speaks in plain terms.
If you were needed, she'd have called for you loud and clear. Yet
that isn't the case at all.'

'Stop trying to talk me out of it, Gully.'

'I'm simply asking you to see sense.'

'In my position, you'd do exactly the same.'

'That's open to debate, I'm afraid. Unlike you, I've never been very lucky in love so I've no real experience of this sort of entanglement.'

Paul jumped up. 'It's not an entanglement. It's a commitment.'

'The one leads to another.'

'Will you please stop being so pig-headed?'

Ackford confronted him. 'I will – if *you* will.'

There was a moment of tension that quickly disappeared. Realising that it was foolish of friends to bicker, they laughed. Peter Skillen entered the room in time to see them taking it in turns to apologise.

'What's going on?' he asked.

'I've just talked your brother out of going to France,' said Ackford.

'No, you haven't,' asserted Paul.

'Well, I was getting very close to that point.'

'My mind is made up, Gully, and nobody can change it.' He looked at Peter. 'I need to go to Paris and it's not only because I'm missing Hannah. I feel as if I've been summoned. I'm sorry to leave you like this, Peter, but I'm confident that you can make the final arrest on your own.'

'I'm sure that I can,' said Peter.

'What did the marshal say?'

'Under duress, he admitted that someone did call at the prison yesterday to insist that Virgil Paige's liberty be curtailed. The man in question, he told me, was Dr Penhallurick.'

343

'I never thought that *he* was behind this,' said Ackford.

'Neither did I, Gully. I had favoured Mr Brunt. As it turned out, it was neither him nor the doctor.'

'But you just told us that Penhallurick made sure that Virgil was kept inside the King's Bench so that he could be easily got at.'

'I was misled,' explained Peter, 'and so was the marshal. He was given a false name by the man who really devised the plot – Sir Humphrey Coote.'

'So it was that old lecher all along,' said Paul, grinning. 'He'll be hanged alongside the others. I'm just sorry I won't be there when you arrest him.'

'But you may well be at my side.'

'I've just told you, Peter. I have to go to Paris.'

'So have I. It took me some time to extract the information out of his butler but I succeeded in the end. Sir Humphrey left for France this very morning. Having caught wind of the arrest of Fearon and Higlett, he's obviously decided to put the English Channel between himself and justice. His hope, I daresay,' added Peter, 'is that the danger will eventually blow over and he can return to England to watch cricket and indulge in his other favourite hobby.'

Paul was stunned. 'Sir Humphrey is going to *Paris*?'

'According to his butler, he has friends there.'

'You must both go after him,' urged Ackford. 'Your wish is granted Paul. Chance has contrived better than you could yourself. You now have a second good reason to go to France.'

Paul was deaf to his comment. The words that he heard were spoken by Sir Humphrey about the woman he'd lusted after for a long time. Hannah Granville was in danger. The most degenerate man in London was on his way to Paris and Paul was not there to protect her from his overtures.

'Let's go, Peter,' he declared. 'Let's go after that disgusting rake at once.'

Sir Humphrey Coote was in luck. When he reached the port of Dover, he was just in time to board a small vessel about to set sail for France. The packet offered little in the way of comfort but he was not concerned about that. Since weather conditions were favourable, it would get him to Calais in five hours or so. Having shaken the dust of England from his feet, he'd escaped from any pursuit by those responsible for the arrest of his hired killers. He was safe. There was another reason why he was going to relish the voyage. On its journey from Calais to Dover, one of the passengers on the ship had bought a French newspaper and left it on board. Sir Humphrey pounced on it to see what was happening in Paris. One of the first things that caught his eye was a glowing review of a production of Shakespeare's *Macbeth*. A member of the cast was singled out for extravagant praise.

Hannah Granville.

It was a gift from the gods.

Alfred Hale was still wary about approaching the print shop but Micah Yeomans led the way with a confident step. He had a legitimate reason to call there and a chance to meet Diane Mandrake again. That being the case, he was prepared to put up with any tart remarks from her. They arrived shortly after she and Benjamin Tite had finished unloading the boxes of cartoons from the curricle. Diane was pleased to see them for once because she could pour scorn on them.

'You come, as usual, too late,' she began. 'The killers are already in custody.'

Yeomans winced. 'We crave a word with you, Mrs Mandrake.'

'Let it be a short one. As you see, I have tradesmen to supervise and stock to put on display once the window is restored.'

'It's about your stock that we wish to speak.'

'Two men may be caught,' said Hale, 'but there's a third still at liberty and he's the biggest villain of the three. We were about to confront the most likely suspects when we thought there might be a quicker way to identify the person we're after. It's highly likely that his name can be found somewhere among your caricatures.'

Diane laughed. 'You've realised that at last, have you?'

'What do you mean?'

'It was one of the first things that Peter Skillen suggested.'

'Let's keep him out of this,' suggested Yeomans.

'But he's been at the very heart of the investigation.'

'He had no authority to be involved, Mrs Mandrake.'

'Oh yes, he did. He also had common sense and iron determination, two qualities that you so palpably lack. Between them, Peter and his brother have done far more than you and all your patrols to cleanse the city of crime.'

Yeomans was stung. 'Who saved the shop from being burnt down?'

'You did, sir, and I've expressed my thanks more than once. I'll not easily forget your precipitate action on that dreadful night – though I still hold that the greater share of gratitude should go to the man who first raised the alarm. His name has slipped my mind.'

'It's Chevy Ruddock,' said Hale.

'No need to bring him into this,' complained Yeomans.

'Give him his due, Micah.'

'It was your behaviour *after* the fire that distressed me,' said Diane. 'I didn't ask you to perambulate outside my shop all night, especially when I already had adequate protection inside the building in the shape of Peter Skillen. His is a soothing presence, Mr Yeomans, while yours is abrasive.'

He was hurt. 'That's not by design, dear lady, I do assure you.'

'You can be prickly at times,' said Hale, before being nudged into silence.

'The fault,' said Yeomans, gently, 'lies in the necessities of our profession. Since we deal with deep-dyed villains every day, we have perforce to develop a hardness that's foreign to our true characters. Kind words and soft smiles are wasted on the rascals we encounter. Pain is the only language they understand.'

'If that's all you have to say to me,' declared Diane, 'I bid you farewell.'

'But we need your help, Mrs Mandrake.'

'Are you well versed in glazing?'

'No, I'm not . . .'

'Have you ever organised a window display?'

'That, too, would be a novel undertaking.'

'Then you are no use to me, I fear. I need a window to be repaired and my stock to be exhibited in it. People need to see that it's a case of business as usual.'

'Which cartoons arouse most interest?' asked Hale.

'Our best sales come from the *Parliament of Foibles*.'

'I *told* you that should be our starting point, Micah.'

'A politician instigating a murder?' said Yeomans, dubiously. 'No, it's far too unlikely.'

'You are wondrously ignorant of the ways of the world, sir,' said Diane, crisply. 'Politicians commit murder every time they draft legislation. They kill off our liberties, they smother us with taxes and they bore us to death with their empty rhetoric. That's why I can always sell Virgo's caricatures,' she went on. 'They prick self-important politicians until they explode like so many balloons.'

'May we take a close look at your stock, please?'

'No, Mr Yeomans – not unless you intend to buy some of it, that is.'

'I couldn't be caught in possession of anything satirical,' he said, piously. 'It would reflect badly on someone in my position.'

'And yet you once *tried* to purchase a caricature from me.'

'Did you, Micah?' asked Hale. 'You never told me that.'

'It was actually featured Mr Yeomans.'

'Oh, yes, I remember that one.' He suffered a dig in the ribs this time. 'But I didn't recognise Mr Yeomans,' he lied. 'It was nothing at all like him. He'd never be seen herding harlots outside a brothel.'

'Mrs Mandrake,' said Yeomans, almost pleading, 'it's in your interests to help us. The man we want is the one who ordered the destruction of your property and, by extension, the death of your good self. Until he has been caught and convicted, you will never enjoy complete safety. All that we ask is a brief glance at your stock.' He looked at the glaziers. 'It would be folly to pay for new windows if someone is bent on burning your shop down. I would hate to lose you or your premises. Help us, dear lady, I implore you.'

Diane was moved by the sincerity of his plea and by his simple logic. There was still a notional danger to her. The Runners might be a hindrance but there was no harm in letting them look through her prints.

'Very well,' she decided. 'You may look your fill – and then depart.'

Their preparations took time. They had to secure passports, pack their luggage, saddle their horses, give instructions to their respective servants and take their leave of everyone at the shooting gallery. Peter was sad to leave his wife in order to go to France again but it was unavoidable. Having identified the man behind murder, arson and attempted homicide, he wanted to be the person to arrest him. Paul was hoping to reserve that luxury for himself. As they cantered along the Dover Road, he stated his case.

'Sir Humphrey is *mine*, Peter,' he claimed. 'I was the one who put up with his antics at the cricket match and who was forced to listen to his revolting suggestions with regard to Hannah.'

'Yet I was the one who tore off his mask.'

'You only see him as a despicable criminal.'

'Don't you?'

'I view him as a threat to the woman I love.'

'Someone as beautiful and self-possessed as Hannah is expert at keeping undesirable suitors at arm's length.'

'Sir Humphrey is no ordinary suitor,' argued Paul. 'What he can't get by persuasion, he'll take by other means. I heard him boasting about it.'

'I still think that I should be the one to call him to account.'

'You don't even need to come to Paris.'

'Oh, yes, I do,' said Peter, laughing. 'You have many talents, Paul, but you lack a real command of the French language and that's going to be a necessity. You need an interpreter and a guide to the city of Paris. I'm the ideal choice in both roles.'

Paul was grudging. 'I accept that. Your time spent abroad as an agent gave you insights that I lack. But I still claim the right of arresting Sir Humphrey,' he said.

'It's a question of which one of us gets to him first.'

'So be it – we'll make a competition out of it.'

'Yes,' agreed Peter. 'When I catch him, you admit that I'm the better man.'

'There'll be nothing to admit,' said Paul, laughing. 'I have more incentive to track him and more skill to corner him. I *know* the sort of man he is. That will give me an immediate advantage.'

'Try saying that in French,' suggested his brother. 'By the time you've managed to do that, I'll have Sir Humphrey well and truly under arrest.'

Virgil Paige was glad to be back in King's Bench Prison. Though his would-be assassins had been caught and his freedom of movement restored, he was still too cautious to venture outside. Having settled back into his room, he used Snapper to run errands for food or anything else he needed. Paige was reclining on his mattress when he heard the footsteps coming up the uncarpeted stairs and realised that two people were approaching. He got to his feet at once. There was a tap on the door. Snapper's head appeared.

'Ya gor a vis'ter,' he announced.

'Who is it?'

The door swung open and Diane Mandrake sailed into the room.

'Hello, Virgil,' she said, beaming. 'I thought that it was high time we met.'

CHAPTER NINETEEN

The decisive Battle of Waterloo had brought France to its knees. The country was weakened, rudderless, demoralised and bereft of the dreams of glory that had inspired it to overthrow its monarchy and adopt a policy of military expansion. When the British army marched to Paris in the immediate aftermath of hostilities, they camped in the Bois de Boulogne. Once a beautiful and extensive garden, it became a wild, overgrown, pathless wood that resembled nothing so much as a swamp in places. The Prussians, who bivouacked nearby, added outright vandalism to neglect, cutting down the finest trees indiscriminately then burning groves to the ground. The city itself bore the scars of a long war and the crushing burden of defeat.

Within a year, profound changes had taken place. Though unwelcome to many, the restoration of the Bourbon dynasty helped to rebuild and reinvigorate the nation's capital. It began to recapture its reputation as the centre of European fashion and gaiety. Theatres flourished, restaurants abounded and visitors flocked in from other countries. Money, the essential lifeblood, was flowing freely once again.

What had greeted Hannah Granville on her arrival there was a scene of sophisticated pleasure. Paris was once more pulsating with life. Like all major cities, it had its slums and its dark underbelly but its palaces, its civic buildings, its plethora of churches, its famous river and its long, wide, accommodating avenues were a sight to behold. Not having been there since she was a child, Hannah had been entranced. There was an unexpected delight. Her old governess, now in her eighties, was still alive. Though she could barely walk, Marie Boisseau had written to her former pupil to welcome her to the city and to offer her services should Hannah have any difficulty with the language. Well taught from a young age by a true Parisian, the actress felt more than able to portray Lady Macbeth in a French translation. What she did ask from her quondam governess was the pleasure of calling on her from time to time so that – liberated from the strain of rehearsals – she could reminisce about her childhood in a calmer atmosphere.

Old friends were the best kind in Hannah's opinion. It was one of the main reasons that she'd retained Jenny Pye as her dresser over the years. A short, plump woman in her forties with a fierce loyalty and a capacity for adapting quickly to any situation, Jenny was much more than the person who helped her to change in and out of her costumes. She was a friend, helpmeet, hairdresser, counsellor and, on occasion, even acted as a kind of bodyguard. What Hannah liked about her was her defiant Englishness. Though they were in the French capital,

Jenny had categorically refused to learn a single word of the language.

'The house is full yet again, Miss Granville,' she said.

'That's very gratifying.'

'It's a tribute to your talent. Paris is at your feet.'

'Yes,' said Hannah, 'it's strange, isn't it? I portray a villainous woman who urges her husband to kill a king and the audiences applaud me for it. There must be a deeply engrained hatred of royalty in the French public. On the other hand,' she went on, thoughtfully, 'Macbeth wants to kill Duncan in order to replace him, so Scotland won't actually get rid of a king. They'll simply have a new one on the throne.'

'You know how to enslave an audience,' said Jenny, combing Hannah's hair. 'It's the same with whatever part you play.'

'Lady Macbeth is a monster.'

'Yes, but you make her a lovable monster.'

They were in the dressing room two hours before the performance. Hannah was a tall, slim, lithe young woman with a natural grace and an arresting beauty. She liked to get to the theatre early so that she had plenty of time to rehearse her major speeches before going onstage to deliver them. Audiences had been kind to her and critics had been, for the most part, extremely complimentary but her stay in Paris was not entirely without its problems.

'Will he be in the audience again tonight?' she asked.

'He'll follow you wherever you go, Miss Granville.'

'You make him sound like a dog, not a gentleman of distinction.'

'A gentleman wouldn't badger you the way that he does.'

'He doesn't exactly badger me, Jenny. He just wishes to worship from afar and turn this place into a perfumed garden for me.' She indicated the baskets of flowers that surrounded her. 'I don't feel threatened by him in any way. Unlike so many of the others, he's very benign. However, while admiration is always pleasing, a superfluity of it can get very tiresome.'

'You could easily get him forbidden entry to the theatre.'

'That would be cruel.'

'It would save you the trouble of worrying about him.'

'I don't really worry,' said Hannah. 'I'm just very much aware of his presence, that's all. In his letter, he told me that he sees himself as my guardian angel.'

Jenny rolled her eyes but held her peace. In her opinion, amorous Frenchmen were all the same. They needed to be watched carefully and kept firmly at bay.

'We won't be here much longer, Miss Granville.'

'That's what I keep telling myself.'

'You'll soon be playing Lady Macbeth in London,' said Jenny, adding a last deft touch with the comb. 'And it won't be in this heathen language.'

Hannah laughed. 'The magic of France has clearly failed to work on you.'

'I want to be back in my own country.'

'And so do I, Jenny – though it's not only for the pleasure of portraying Lady Macbeth in the words that Shakespeare actually wrote for her. I have a much greater need to return to London.' She sat back with a sigh. 'Somebody very dear and wonderful is awaiting me.'

* * *

They picked up his trail at once. When they stopped at the inn to change horses, they learnt that a coach had called there earlier in the day and that its occupant had been so eager to get to Dover that he didn't even alight for refreshment. Peter and Paul Skillen rode on with fresh mounts. Having seen it when it arrived at the cricket match, Paul was able to describe Sir Humphrey's coach in detail. Every time they broke their journey, they found someone who had noticed the vehicle and who could give them an idea of the precise time when it had been there.

'He's hours ahead of us, Peter,' complained his brother.

'He may well be at sea by now.'

'I was hoping to catch him before he embarked.'

'There's no chance of doing that. Besides,' said Peter with a grin, 'do you really want to miss the opportunity of going to Paris?'

'No, I don't. Whatever happens, I must see Hannah.'

'His butler told me that Sir Humphrey had friends in the city. He'll seek sanctuary there so it may be difficult to find him.'

'We don't *need* to find him, Peter.'

'Why not?'

'Hannah will do that for us,' explained Paul. 'When Sir Humphrey reaches the city, he'll think that he's perfectly safe. It won't cross his evil mind that we're on his heels. He'll want to revel in the joys of Paris and – amongst other things – that means going to the theatre. Which play do you think he'll choose first?'

'It will be the one in which Miss Hannah Granville is appearing.'

'That's right. Unbeknownst to her, Lady Macbeth is our bait. It's only a matter of time before Sir Humphrey arrives to gloat over her. That's when we strike.'

. .

Virgil Paige had been astonished when his unexpected visitor had popped up and he was not altogether pleased at first. He felt that his privacy had been invaded. Diane Mandrake's warmth and amiability soon dispelled his reservations and he began to enjoy her company. Since he was now able to go outside the King's Bench again, they adjourned to a tavern and got to know each other better over some refreshment.

'I still can't believe it,' she said. 'In all the years I knew Leo, he never once mentioned that he had a brother.'

'That was on my instruction. I liked to be anonymous.'

'Why?'

'After a lifetime of service in the army, I sought peace and isolation.'

Her eyes twinkled. 'You don't look like a man with monkish inclinations.'

'I'm not,' he agreed with a chuckle. 'I've always found the devil a more appealing deity. Drawing cartoons as Virgo gave me the chance to take on the role of a demon and cause mischief.'

'There was a lot of demon in Leo as well.'

'We worked well together. When it came to politicians, my brother and I thought and felt alike. Those who abuse their power should be exposed and flayed in public. The *Parliament of Foibles* was Leo's creation.'

'It was a brilliant concept that cost him his life.'

'I came close to paying the same price, Mrs Mandrake.'

Sipping her drink, she sat back to scrutinise him. Physically, he looked very different to his brother but his voice and demeanour were the same. He also shared his brother's passion and she liked him for that.

'Do you really want to spend your life in a debtor's prison?' she asked.

'It has its compensations.'

'I didn't notice any of them.'

'Oh, they are there, believe me.'

'Will you be able to continue your work there?'

'There's no point,' he said, sadly. 'Apart from anything else, my materials were stolen. I'm unable to draw or engrave. Virgo no longer exists.'

'He could do.'

'No, Mrs Mandrake. Without Leo, I'm useless. He supplied the clever ideas and the wicked words. They're beyond me.'

'I can't believe that.'

'I'm a self-taught artist who knows his limitations.'

'Will you let Virgo's work perish when he has such a following?'

'I have no choice.'

'What's happened to the demon you enjoyed being?' she taunted.

'He's lost his inspiration.'

'I've an idea how it can be revived.'

'Not without Leo – he supplied the fuel over which we could roast the political ogres who exploit us. When I drew a cartoon, I loved the smell of burning flesh that drifted into my nostrils.'

'You could inhale that aroma again, Mr Paige.'

'I think not.'

'Hear me out,' she said, leaning forward. 'I have an idea to put to you and it may just help to change your mind . . .'

They had not stayed long at the print shop. Allowed to look through the entire stock, the Runners quickly identified the main targets of Virgo's mordant satire. By the time they left, they'd settled on the same quartet chosen by Peter and Paul Skillen.

'It *has* to be one of them,' decided Yeomans.

'Yes,' said Hale, 'but which one is it, Micah?'

'I fancy that it has to be Gerard Brunt.'

'Julian Harvester seems the more likely man to me.'

'Let's visit each in turn. We'll start with Mr Brunt.'

'Do you know his address?'

'I know how to find it.'

Hale fell in beside him and they set off at a demanding pace.

'Is it true what Mrs Mandrake said?' asked Hale. 'Did you really try to buy one of the caricatures from her?'

'Of course not,' growled Yeomans. 'Why would I possibly want one?'

'She seemed very certain about it.'

'Diane – Mrs Mandrake to you – was confusing me with someone else. Let's think about Gerard Brunt, shall we? In some of those cartoons we saw, he was turned into a laughing stock. How did he react to that . . . ?'

He was there as usual. Seated in the same box, he rose to his feet and clapped his hands as Hannah came out onstage to acknowledge the ovation. English voices joined with those of the French to acclaim her performance. The audience was even rowdier than the one she usually faced in London but the man who'd elected himself as her guardian angel didn't join in the raucous shouting. Short, compact, spruce and well into his sixties, he cut a dignified figure. When Hannah turned to look at him, he gave her a paternal smile.

It was not the last she saw of him. Leaving a theatre often posed a problem for a leading lady, especially for one as gorgeous and blessed with histrionic talent as Hannah. There was usually a large cluster of men at the stage door, ready to press their suits by offering her all manner of blandishments. Since Paul Skillen had come into her life, the problem had been more or less eliminated because he was always there to shepherd her past the waiting mob. Having no such protection now, she had to rely on her dresser and left the theatre on Jenny's arm. Ardent admirers pushed forward to get a look at her or even to brush against her body. They buzzed around her like so many bees and Hannah found it distressing. Aid, however, was at hand.

'*Silence, messieurs!*' yelled a voice. '*Silence, s'il vous plaît!*'

Quelled by the rasping authority in the command, the noise died instantly and the crowd parted to let Hannah and her dresser through. She was able to see her saviour and recognised him as the dapper Frenchman with an aristocratic bearing who'd attended every performance of the play. He was using his silver-topped cane to hold back her admirers so that the women could reach the carriage waiting for them.

'*Bravo, mademoiselle!*' he said, doffing his hat as she went past.

'*Merci,*' she replied. '*Merci, mon ange.*'

Arriving at last at Dover, they discovered just how far ahead of them their quarry was. Paul Skillen was disappointed.

'His ship left hours ago,' he said. 'He's probably halfway to France by now. That's maddening.'

'It's an irritation,' said Peter, 'but no more than that. After a hectic rush to the coast and a voyage across the Channel, he'll be fatigued. Sir Humphrey will have need of a rest. If we can sail soon, we'll make up ground on him.'

'The next packet won't be ready for some time.'

'Then we take our ease here.'

'I won't be able to relax until I see Hannah again.'

Standing on the quayside, they felt the wind freshening enough to pluck at their clothes and threaten to lift off their hats. The gallop to Dover had given the brothers little time for conversation. Peter was glad that they had time for reflection.

'I've always wanted to take Charlotte to Paris,' he said.

'Why haven't you done so?'

'We've always been too busy. London has first claim on my attention and it's the capital city of crime. That's not a complaint, by the way. I'm proud of the work we do and grateful that it brings in handsome rewards.'

'How much will we get for the capture of Sir Humphrey Coote?'

'Don't count our chickens, Paul . . .'

'There's no way he can escape us.'

'I can think of lots of ways. To start with, he may have

powerful friends in France who'll help him to resist extradition. Then again, he may have a small army on whom he can call. There are only the two of us.'

'We'll take him back to England somehow.'

'I will, anyway,' said Peter. 'You might wish to linger in France to improve your knowledge of Shakespeare's Macbeth.'

Paul was derogatory. 'Not if the whole thing is in French.'

'You'll get a stirring drama and an education rolled into one. And don't look down on our erstwhile enemies. France has a culture that can rival any in the civilised world. Granted, they may not have a Shakespeare but they've produced notable playwrights, authors, artists and composers galore.'

'I'll take your word for it, Peter.' He turned to his brother. 'Are you looking forward to going back there after all this time?'

'Very much – it will be a change to walk through the streets of Paris without having to dodge patrols. The countryside around the city is beautiful, as you'll see for yourself.'

'I won't be looking. All I'm interested in is seeing Hannah and arresting the man who plotted the murder of Mr Paige and his brother. He needs to be dragged back to England for an appointment with the hangman.'

'They use the guillotine in France. It's far quicker.'

'Hanging is better. It draws out the suffering, and those men – Fearon and Higlett – deserve to suffer. So does Sir Humphrey.'

'There's no need to be so vindictive, Paul. I pity anyone who mounts the gallows in front of a howling mob. It's a cruel way to die. As for France,' continued Peter, 'I predict that you'll change your opinion of it when you've supped its splendours. You might even consider living there one day.'

'That will *never* happen.'

'How can you be so adamant?'

'The French have one fatal defect, Peter – they don't play cricket.'

It was very late when he finally climbed into bed but Micah Yeomans felt that his labours had been productive. Thanks to the names he'd gleaned from looking at caricatures in the print shop, he'd worked his way towards an important discovery. Meanwhile, he could luxuriate in dreams of Diane Mandrake. Early next morning, he went to court in order to deliver his report to the chief magistrate. Before he did so, he had to listen to some reports himself.

'I was accosted at my club by Gerard Brunt,' said Kirkwood, 'and he didn't mince his words. He complained that you called on him and more or less accused him of hiring men to kill Leonidas Paige.'

'That's not quite true, sir—'

'I also had the same protest from Mr Harvester, who blamed me for sending two thugs – his actual description of you and Hale – to harass him in his own home. And there was a third outrage,' he went on, waving a letter. 'According to this, not content with enraging both Brunt and Harvester, you descended on Dr Penhallurick and challenged him to admit that he was part of a murder plot.' He smacked the letter down on to the desk. 'What, in the name of all that's holy, have you been doing?'

'Hale and I were making enquiries, sir.'

'It sounds as if you were deliberately trying to stain the reputation of the Bow Street Runners. Three persons of substantial influence have had cause to complain at your disrespectful treatment of them. Never – *never*, I say – make such allegations unless you have incontrovertible evidence to back them up.'

'In the end,' argued Yeomans, 'our persistence yielded a dividend.'

'Why – who else did you upset?'

'The last person we called on was Sir Humphrey Coote.'

'Dear God!' cried the other. 'I'll have *him* on my back now.'

'He's gone to France.'

'Did you frighten him that much?'

'Please listen, sir. You'll then understand.'

Yeomans explained that he and Hale had called in turn at the homes of three suspects they'd singled out. Each man was clearly innocent of any charge but the fourth was not. The circumstances of his departure suggested flight from arrest. Yeomans had bullied the truth out of the butler. His master had gone abroad.

'It was Dr Penhallurick who confirmed it,' said Yeomans. 'He was furious that Sir Humphrey had asked a favour of the marshal of the King's Bench while using the doctor's name. His flight is a confession of guilt. In short, when Sir Humphrey is arrested, the whole investigation is over.' He shuffled his feet. 'There is, however, one problem,' he admitted, sheepishly.

'What's that?'

'Peter Skillen got to Sir Humphrey's house before we did.'

'Did he winkle the same information out of the butler?'

'It seems that he did, sir.'

'Then he'll undoubtedly have gone in pursuit of Sir Humphrey.'

'That was the sad conclusion we reached.'

'So why did you waste a whole night before telling me all this?'

'I was here the second you appeared, sir.'

'You should have banged on my door and roused me from my bed,' said Kirkwood, hotly. 'When there's a chance of catching Sir Humphrey, you must seize it with both hands. Instead of leaving it to someone else, you should have been galloping through the night to Dover.'

Yeomans was shaken. 'Well, yes . . . I suppose that I should have, sir.'

'Didn't you hear me, man? Go to France now by the swiftest means possible. And make sure you get to Sir Humphrey Coote first! Don't just stand there with your mouth open – away with you!'

As soon as he'd set foot on French soil, he felt safe. Nobody would find him there. Sir Humphrey was therefore able to move at a more leisurely pace, taking the time to enjoy the scenic magnificence or making a detour for some other reason. He estimated that it would take him the best part of a day to reach Paris. Once there, he would be able to sample its multifarious delights. Chief among them, he reminded himself, was Miss Hannah Granville.

The flight from England had been necessary because he feared that a hue and cry would be set up. Now that he was out of danger, he could take a more considered look at the situation. Nobody could link his name to those of Fearon and Higlett and they'd been kept ignorant of it themselves. He'd passed himself off as Dr Penhallurick at the King's Bench but the marshal need never know his true identity. Sir Humphrey had such a low opinion of the Runners that he refused to believe that they could identify him as being party to a murder and come in pursuit.

He therefore stopped seeing himself as a fugitive and began to behave as a foreign visitor. Paris was his ultimate destination and Hannah his destined prize.

When the two women arrived at the theatre that evening, he was waiting for them at the stage door. Jenny was all for hustling her into the building but Hannah felt obliged to stop and talk to the man. Since the conversation was in French, the dresser couldn't understand a word of it but M. Pernelle, the actress's self-appointed guardian, was so expressive with his gestures that Jenny picked up the essence of the exchange. Hannah first thanked him for coming to her rescue on the previous evening. Pernelle raised his cane upright against his chest as if presenting a sword and offering his service. He then gave a low bow, indicated the door and watched until they both went through it. After exchanging a greeting with the stage doorkeeper, the women went through to their dressing room. Two more large baskets of flowers had arrived. Hannah sniffed at some of the blooms.

'M. Pernelle sent these,' she said.

'Why?'

'It's because he's just a charming old gentleman.'

'He looked to me as if he'd been a soldier at one time.'

'Yes, he was, but it was many years ago.'

'Why does he keep bothering you?'

Hannah smiled. 'You obviously didn't realise what he said. M. Pernelle was offering to protect me from people who *did* bother me. That's what he did last night, Jenny. All he wants in return is my gratitude.'

The dresser was cynical. 'What form is that gratitude supposed to take?'

'Don't be so suspicious. All men aren't the same.'

'All *Frenchmen* are.'

They'd lost track of him. Somewhere along the way, he'd gone off the main road. Peter and Paul had assumed that he'd travel post-haste in a fast, light carriage but Sir Humphrey seemed to have chosen another means of transport. When they'd arrived that night in Paris, it was far too late to search for him and the performance of Macbeth was long over. All that the brothers could do was to find accommodation and bide their time. After so long in the saddle, they found the beds in their tavern supremely comfortable. They talked by the light of a candle.

'Where can I take Hannah?' asked Paul.

'You won't have time to take her anywhere,' replied his brother. 'We're here to arrest someone and he takes priority. Besides, Hannah will not be available of an evening. She'll be onstage, plotting to seize the Scottish crown for her husband.'

'We'll find a moment to dine together.'

'You'll need more than a moment. French cuisine can't be rushed. It must be eaten slowly and savoured. As for restaurants, the most celebrated when I was here was that of Beauvilliers in the rue de Richelieu. It's like being in a gilded palace and the food is delicious. Another place of note is the Rocher de Cancale in the rue de Bandar. It's run by M. Borel who used to be chef to no less a person than Napoleon.'

Paul was amazed. 'Did you eat at these places when you were here?'

'Heavens, no – I survived on meagre fare. If I'd dined at either of the places I mentioned, I'd have drawn attention to myself. My task was to stay largely invisible. As a result, I had to make sacrifices.'

There was a long pause. Paul rolled over in bed and Peter thought that he'd dropped off to sleep. A few minutes later, however, Paul spoke again.

'Where do you think Sir Humphrey will be?'

'The sort of friends he has would live in the more salubrious quarters.'

'Do you think he knows we're stalking him?'

'I think he feared it when he took to his heels,' said Peter. 'He just wanted to get out of the country fast. Now that he's here, the panic is over. He'll regard himself as just another English sightseer.'

'Yes,' said Paul, bitterly, 'and we know one of the sights he's keen to see.'

'Lady Macbeth.'

'What was she like?'

'Superb – there's no other word for it.'

'Yet she's acting the part in French.'

'She did so like a native Parisian. I couldn't fault her.'

'Where is she staying?'

'Miss Granville is living at the home of the theatre manager.'

'A hotel would be more suitable for my purpose.'

'Half of the young bloods in the city have tried to entice her into one but she's turned them all down. You have competition, Sir Humphrey.'

'That's never troubled me in the past.'

When he'd arrived after dark in the French capital, Sir Humphrey knew that he'd be given a cordial welcome by his old friend and drinking companion, Lancelot Usborne. True to form, Usborne was carousing with an attaché from the British Embassy when his visitor suddenly appeared on the doorstep. Sir Humphrey was whisked inside, given a warm embrace and introduced to the other man. All three of them drank deeply until they heard the chimes of midnight. When the attaché had withdrawn, Sir Humphrey was able to ask about the woman who'd occupied his mind from the moment he'd landed in Calais. Usborne, an obese, red-faced, middle-aged man whose spreading contours had hampered his career as a voluptuary, had seen Hannah Granville give a dazzling performance. With wine dribbling down his chin, he listed her many virtues as an actress.

'Enough of her ability onstage,' said Sir Humphrey, irritably. 'How would she perform in the bedchamber?'

'She'd be an absolute joy,' said Usborne, smirking. 'The problem you'll have is getting her there in the first place.'

'That problem is not insurmountable. Oh, the very thought of her excites me, Lancelot. I haven't had a woman for days. I'm positively *bursting* with lust for Hannah Granville,' he said with an obscene gesture. 'I simply must have her.'

Gully Ackford had just unlocked the gallery when the first visitor of the day arrived. It was Virgil Paige and he looked subtly different. They went into the office and sat down. Ackford noticed that the other man had taken rather more care with his appearance than usual and was reminded of the time when he'd turned up in Paul Skillen's clothing after his unauthorised exit from the prison. The reason for the close shave and the well-brushed hair soon became clear.

'I had a long talk with Mrs Mandrake,' volunteered Paige.

'That's an achievement in itself,' said Ackford. 'Whenever I tried to have a conversation with her, she did all the talking and I merely did the listening.'

'I think she's a remarkable lady.'

'Oh, I'd agree on that.'

'She did something that I'd never have believed possible. Diane, as I was invited to call her, shook me out of my torpor. When my brother died,' said Paige, soulfully, 'Virgo died with him. I had neither the urge nor the talent to go on without Leo. At least, that's what I thought.'

'Has Mrs Mandrake changed your mind?'

'She's very close to doing so. My brother was an inveterate scribbler. He was always noting down something disparaging about politicians, either in the form of articles or in verse. It was a compulsion. I'd assumed that he kept all his papers at his lodging but that wasn't true at all.'

'Where else did he keep them?'

'Whole sheaves were left at the print shop when he moved out of there. Diane said that they were a treasure trove. When she moved her stock to Peter's house for safety, my brother's papers went with her.'

'That was very sensible.'

'We've arranged to meet this morning so that I can see what she has of Leo's.'

'Are you hoping that it will inspire you to carry on?'

'To some extent,' confided Paige, 'Diane has already done that. She made me see that it's what my brother would have wanted.'

'So Virgo may rise from the dead.'

'We can't let corrupt politicians off the hook – that's what she says.'

'While you're here,' said Ackford, 'there's something I've been meaning to ask you.' He indicated the framed cartoon on the wall. 'Mrs Mandrake gave it to Peter as a present and he thought that this was the best place to hang it because it ridicules our old foe, Micah Yeomans. It's only a sketch but it's obviously him. How could you draw him so accurately?'

'I've seen him more than once.'

'Really?'

'If you inhabit the King's Bench, you'll catch sight of Runners from time to time. They're always coming in search of someone or other. Yeomans was pointed out to me years ago and once you've seen him,' said Paige with a grin, 'you never forget him. Those bushy, black eyebrows of his are a sort of trademark.'

What remained of the eyebrows had come together to form an angry chevron. As they bumped and rattled their way along the

Dover Road in a light carriage, Yeomans and Hale were bounced up and down. The driver seemed unable to avoid potholes.

'This is a nightmare,' complained Yeomans.

'There may be worse to come,' said Hale. 'If the sea is choppy, we'll have a terrible crossing. I hate sailing.'

'In the cause of justice, we'll have to endure it.'

'What's the point, Micah? The Skillen brothers may already be in Paris.'

'Yes, but they won't know where to find Sir Humphrey, will they? He'll go to ground somewhere and we'll be the ones to sniff him out. I'll put up with any amount of discomfort for the thrill of hauling him back to England to meet his fate.' The carriage hit another pothole and they were thrown inches into the air. 'Be more careful, man!' he yelled at the driver. 'We'd like to get there without any broken bones.'

While he had no idea where their quarry might be, Paul Skillen knew exactly where to find Hannah Granville because her letters had contained her address. She and her dresser were staying with the theatre manager and his wife in their house. It was in one of the more desirable quarters of the city and he was impressed by the size and charm of the edifice. When Paul rang the doorbell, a manservant opened the door. Having been taught a little French for the occasion by his brother, Paul tried to get his tongue around the words but could not make himself understood. The sound of his voice, however, gained him entry. Hearing it through the open door of the dining room, Hannah came running on tiptoe into the hall and threw herself into his arms.

'*Quelle bonne surprise!*' she exclaimed.

'Do you mind talking in English?'

'Oh, I'm sorry. It's force of habit.' Standing back, she looked him up and down. 'Whatever are you doing here?'

'I was anxious to see you, Hannah. Your last letter worried me. Without actually saying so, you seemed to be troubled about something.'

'It must have been written during rehearsals,' she said, 'when I was having doubts about my performance. That usually happens at some point. I sent a letter explaining that. Evidently, you haven't received it yet.'

'No matter, darling. I'm here now and I can see how well you look.'

'It's so kind of you to come all this way.'

'I'd go to the ends of the earth for you, Hannah,' he said, squeezing her hands. 'Though, if I'm honest, there's a secondary reason to be in Paris.'

'Is there?'

'Peter and I have come in pursuit of a fugitive. He needs to be taken back to England to face trial. While I have the supreme pleasure of a reunion with you, my brother is trying to find him.'

The search began at the British Embassy. When Peter got there, he was shown into an office occupied by two attachés. The senior of them offered the visitor a seat then took details of his request. Having come in expectation of help, Peter was baulked. The attaché, a gaunt, beak-nosed man of indeterminate age was brusque.

'Do you have a warrant for the arrest?'

'Well. Not exactly . . .'

'Do you have any authority for being in Paris?'

'Sir Humphrey incited a murder,' affirmed Peter. '*That's* our authority.'

'His guilt or otherwise can only be established in a court of law, Mr Skillen, and you have no legal right to take him there. This is a foreign country. It has its own legal system and we have to respect that.'

'Are you suggesting that a criminal should be allowed to go free?'

'Firstly,' said the man, 'I'm not convinced of his criminality. Secondly, you are a British citizen and, as such, not qualified to do what you set out so recklessly to do. And thirdly, I don't have a clue where Sir Humphrey Coote might be. What I can tell you is that he's a Member of Parliament and enjoys certain immunities.'

'He's party to murder and arson, man!'

'There's no need to shout at me, sir. I'm simply reminding you that there's such a thing as parliamentary privilege.'

Peter rose to his feet. 'Even politicians don't have the right to kill people without being punished,' he said, bitterly. 'Good day to you, sir.'

He stalked out and left the two attachés to trade a glance. The man who'd interviewed Peter then turned to some documents. He was too preoccupied to notice that his colleague was writing a hasty letter to a close friend.

They were enjoying a late breakfast when the letter arrived. After reading it, Usborne passed it to his guest with a mixture of dismay and disbelief.

'There's no truth in this, surely?'

'Damnation!' cried Sir Humphrey as he read it.

'Those allegations are preposterous.'

'Of course they are, Lancelot. There's not a scintilla of evidence to support them. And who is this fellow, Peter Skillen? I know a *Paul* Skillen. We watched a cricket match together and he was splendid company.'

'This is a timely warning,' said Usborne. 'That's the value of drinking with someone from the Embassy. When you met Wragby last night, I'll wager you didn't think he'd come in so useful.'

'No, I didn't,' said the other with relief. 'It was a pleasing coincidence that I made his acquaintance. I must find a way to thank Mr Wragby.'

'The saving grace is that this man, Skillen, has absolutely no idea where you are. Paris is like a rabbit warren. It would take him months to search every last burrow. Even if he did run you to earth, he has no authority to arrest you on such absurd charges. Nevertheless,' said Usborne, 'my suggestion is that you stay here until he gets tired of looking.'

Sir Humphrey was deeply upset, though he took care to hide his fears from his friend. The complacency that had set in when he reached France had suddenly been shattered. He had been followed, after all, and he was in danger. But for the accidental encounter with an attaché at the British Embassy, he might have paraded around Paris without a care and been spotted by someone who'd come after him. His apprehension was tempered by his urge to see and possess Hannah Granville. It had reached the level of desperation. He refused to be thwarted.

* * *

While he had come to Paris for the prime purpose of seeking his beloved, Paul Skillen was mindful of the demands of her profession. He knew how tense she became before a performance and how she needed plenty of time alone to prepare for it. Having spent much of the day with her, therefore, he let her go off to the theatre with Jenny and went in search of his brother. Peter was waiting in the tavern where they'd spent the night. Over a drink, he recounted the experience he'd had at the British Embassy.

'That's truly dreadful,' said Paul. 'Is Paris to become a safe haven for any fugitive from England? A criminal should be liable to arrest in any country.'

'I agree,' said Peter. 'We ignore the advice from the Embassy and go our own sweet way. Sir Humphrey is here – I feel it. We'll take him back somehow.'

'Then we need Shakespeare to help us.'

'Are you certain that he'll attend a performance?'

'Having spoken to Hannah, I'm utterly convinced. When I mentioned Sir Humphrey's name, she shivered with disgust. He's been harassing her for months in various ways.'

'Why didn't she report it to you earlier?'

'Hannah felt, quite rightly, that I wouldn't be content merely to warn him off. I'd have challenged the scoundrel to a duel,' said Paul. 'It was the repercussions that frightened Hannah. She feared that I'd be put under arrest for murder. Sir Humphrey has influential friends who might well have ganged up on me.'

'You can get your revenge now, Paul. If we see him at the theatre, you can have the pleasure of calling him to account.'

'It will have to be after the play is over,' said the other, smiling. 'Hannah would never forgive me if I interrupted her performance. Were I to commit that act of sacrilege, she'd be encouraging Macbeth to stab *me* with the dagger instead.'

Word of mouth and a good critical reception filled every seat at the theatre that evening. There was an anticipatory buzz of excitement. What Peter and Paul observed as they watched the crowd stream in was how many English spectators there were. Shakespeare was not universally popular in Paris. French audiences, reared on Racine and Corneille, were less enthralled for the most part by a translation of a famous tragedy from the country which had humbled Napoleon. Among the many Parisians who did attend, however, was M. Pernelle, as neat and trim as ever. The box in which he sat with friends gave him a perfect view of the stage.

Peter Skillen also chose a seat with an excellent view but it was not the stage that interested him so much. Seated at the rear of the stalls, he was able to keep an eye on everyone in front of him and guard the exit at the same time. Paul had selected a seat in the dress circle which enabled him to see everyone else in that part of the theatre. If their target did turn up, one of them would see him because Sir Humphrey would be bound to be in one of the more expensive seats or boxes. As it was, there was no sign of him and neither of the brothers sensed that he was there. Deciding that their vigilance would go unrewarded, they settled back to watch the play.

In fact, Sir Humphrey Coote was in the audience. Cleverly disguised, he sat in a box at the side of the stage with Lancelot Usborne and two of his friend's burly servants. By wearing

377

a wig, a false beard and nondescript attire, he managed to disappear as the flamboyant character he was. No chances had been taken. In case someone did try to arrest him, Sir Humphrey was armed and the loaded pistol was there for another purpose as well.

When the play began, he was perched on the edge of his seat, waiting for Hannah Granville to appear and ignoring the rest of the cast. Every time she stepped onstage, there was a concerted gasp of amazement. Her appearance, deportment and use of gesture set her apart from everyone else but it was her voice that endeared her most. Speaking the language with fluency, she had an extraordinary range, welcoming her husband with soft, seductive words then, later on, exhorting him, in a voice of animal intensity, to commit regicide.

That was the woman he wanted – wild, passionate and indomitable. He could see the full breasts rising and falling beneath her nightgown. When she strode across the stage, he caught a glimpse of her bare legs. Sir Humphrey was enraptured.

The ovation went on longer than ever. Peter and Paul Skillen clapped until their palms hurt. Up in his box, M. Pernelle was beaming like a proud father. Lady Macbeth had surpassed herself and she deserved to bask in the acclaim. When the applause finally died down and the spectators began to disperse, the two brothers joined in the general exodus and made their way around to the stage door.

Unknown to them, however, another drama was taking place. With the two servants at his shoulders, Sir Humphrey had climbed on to the stage, stepped behind the scenery, walked to the dressing rooms, found the one that had Hannah's name emblazoned upon it then, without even knocking, opened the door and stepped inside.

Jenny was in the act of helping Hannah to remove her costume.

'Get out!' she demanded. 'I'll call the manager.'

'*Sortez!*' cried Hannah, thinking that the intruder was French. '*Sortez!*'

'I told you I'd come for you one day,' he said, ogling her.

'Who are you?'

'I'm the luckiest man in Paris.'

He pulled out his pistol and pointed it at her. Hannah was too scared to utter a word but Jenny emitted a scream of horror. It earned her a violent push that sent her sprawling on the floor. Sir Humphrey grabbed a cloak from its hook and put it around Hannah's naked shoulders.

'Come with me,' he ordered. 'Come with me to paradise.'

Peter and Paul were approaching the stage door when they heard Jenny's scream. Pushing their way through the group of admirers waiting for a sight of Hannah, they rushed to the door as the two brawny servants were coming out of it. When they tried to enter the building, the brothers were held back by force. Another piercing screech was heard. Recognising Hannah's voice, Paul went berserk but he was firmly held and unable to break free. Peter, meanwhile, was getting the better of his assailant, grappling and punching to weaken the man's hold. The door was then flung open and Sir Humphrey came out, one arm around a terrified Hannah while the other brandished the pistol. In the interests of safety, everyone scattered immediately.

Walking slowly backwards towards a waiting coach, Sir Humphrey dragged Hannah with him and waved his weapon menacingly.

'Stay back!' he shouted with a manic laugh. 'She's all mine!'

It was too much for Paul. Even at the risk of being shot, he had to rescue her. With a surge of energy, he shoved his adversary against the wall, banged the man's head repeatedly against the brickwork then lifted him bodily and flung him to the ground. Defying the pistol, he ran straight towards Hannah.

Sir Humphrey cocked his weapon and aimed it at Paul but it was never fired. Before he could pull the trigger, the blade of a sword was thrust into his back and through his heart with practised force. It came out through his chest. Shaking with terror, Hannah hurled herself into Paul's arms. Everybody watched aghast as the lifeless body of Sir Humphrey Coote shuddered, sagged then fell forward on to the ground.

M. Pernelle stepped in close to extract his sword from its victim with a sudden pull. Though it was dripping with blood, he inserted the weapon back into the cane from which he'd taken it. After giving a polite bow to Hannah, her guardian angel turned on his heel and left.

Yeomans and Hale were inexperienced horsemen. Having ridden all the way to Paris on hired mounts, they were tired, woebegone and in considerable pain. The first place they went was the British Embassy. To their utter vexation, they saw Peter and Paul Skillen emerging blithely from the building.

'Welcome to Paris!' said Peter, raising his hat to them. 'I hope that you enjoy your stay here.'

'We'll not be staying,' said Hale. 'We've come to make an arrest.'

'Yes,' added Yeomans, 'we're here to speak to Sir Humphrey Coote.'

'You may find that rather difficult,' warned Paul.

'Why is that?'

'He's no longer in a mood for conversation.'

Gully Ackford and Virgil Paige were part of a huge crowd that gathered outside Newgate prison for the executions. As a rule, neither man would have attended such an event. They found it too barbaric and hated the savage baying of the mob. Whole families had gathered to watch Abel Fearon and Sim Higlett being hanged. It was a gruesome affair. The noise was deafening, the taunting was obscene and the execution itself was crude in the extreme. When the first of them was squirming wildly at the end of a rope, the cry of delight that went up was blood-curdling. It was a long time before the friends could make themselves heard.

'Leo can rest in peace now,' said Paige. 'I'm only sorry that they didn't string up Sir Humphrey Coote as well.'

'He met a grisly enough end in Paris,' said Ackford.

'I still can't believe that you'd all go to such lengths on our behalf.'

'Leo was a friend of mine, remember.'

'Yes, but the Skillen brothers didn't know him. Even so, they took enormous risks to catch the rogues who killed him.'

'Peter and Paul thrive on risks.'

'They went all the way to Paris for our sakes.'

'They had their rewards,' said Ackford. 'Peter went back to a city that held fond memories for him and Paul was reunited with the woman he loves. Both of them witnessed the death of Sir Humphrey Coote. There'll be financial reward as well, of course,' he went on, 'but that won't bring them the greatest satisfaction.'

'What will do that, do you think?'

'It's the knowledge that they beat their rivals yet again. That's what drives them on. The Bow Street Runners used to rule the roost but Peter and Paul Skillen are the cocks of the walk now.'

To discover more great books and to
place an order visit our website at
allisonandbusby.com

Don't forget to sign up to our free newsletter at
allisonandbusby.com/newsletter
for latest releases, events and exclusive offers

f Allison & Busby Books
@AllisonandBusby

You can also call us on
020 7580 1080
for orders, queries
and reading recommendations